# PRAISE FOR *THE TENT*

"In another spellbinding adventure tale, a worthy sequel to his *Celestine* masterpiece, James Redfield packs thrills, suspense, and spiritual wisdom into a book you cannot put down. You must read THE TENTH INSIGHT!"

—Brian Weiss, M.D., author of *Only Love Is Real*
and *Many Lives, Many Masters*

"Everybody's reading THE TENTH INSIGHT, James Redfield's sequel to *The Celestine Prophecy*. Run, don't walk, to your nearest bookstore."

—Los Angeles Features Syndicate

"THE TENTH INSIGHT captures not only the adventures of this life but the true spiritual essence of what we are trying to achieve."

—Dannion Brinkley, author of *Saved by the Light*
and *At Peace in the Light*

"Will move us further along toward spiritual enlightenment as we near the millennium. . . . With INSIGHT, Redfield has tried to stress that *everyone's* life, like his, is a 'spiritual adventure.' "

—*Detroit News*

"James Redfield has achieved what the greatest storytellers across time and culture aspire to. He has woven a parable accessible to all . . . an extraordinary map for the evolutionary journey begun in *The Celestine Prophecy*."

—Michael Murphy, chairman, Esalen Institute,
and author of *Golf in the Kingdom,*
*The Kingdom of Shivas Irons,*
and *The Future of the Body*

*more . . .*

"In THE TENTH INSIGHT, Redfield continues the *Celestine* message of living a life that will help others."

—*Rocky Mountain News*

"James Redfield has distilled the spiritual teachings of the ages into a thrilling, fast-paced adventure . . . to help humanity."

—Joan Borysenko, Ph.D., author of *Fire in the Soul*

"Enlightening. . . . Profound teachings interwoven within a gripping story of good versus evil, of life and death, that both delights the senses and stretches the mind."

—*Tulsa World*

"Not to be missed."

—*New Age Journal*

"Will take readers to unimagined plateaus of spirituality . . . may change forever the way we look at life, death, and our purpose here on Earth."

—*Arizona Networking News*

"Inspiring . . . unique and joyful . . . Redfield has again captured our deepest intuitions as he illuminates the worlds outside us and within us . . . a must-read for everyone!"

—*Commonwealth Journal*

"A profoundly moving continuation of *The Celestine Prophecy*. . . . The plot has many clues and visions and moves with the speed of a first-class thriller."

—*Abilene Reporter-News*

"The strength of this book comes from Redfield's message that the future will be dramatically better than the present. The story in this book goes well beyond its predecessor, especially in the range of ideas it covers."

—*Body Mind Spirit* magazine

"As you read THE TENTH INSIGHT, you might see parts of yourself and others that you've never seen before. You might also see the need for change. . . . The Tenth Insight must be experienced personally. In the first nine insights, for example, intuition is experienced as gut feeling, but in The Tenth Insight you actually live it out."

—*Sunday Record* (NJ)

"A colorful, imaginative pilgrimage. . . . Some of the visionary moments in the story remind me of the kind of imagination operating in classic stories like the Hindu *Ramayan* or the Chinese *Journey to the West*. It is a way of thinking that gives palpability to obscure areas of psychological and spiritual experience, so that impulses toward what is traditionally viewed as other-worldly are given a level of earthiness."

—*Bookscapes*

ALSO BY JAMES REDFIELD

*The Celestine Prophecy*
*The Tenth Insight: Holding the Vision*

BY JAMES REDFIELD AND CAROL ADRIENNE

*The Celestine Prophecy: An Experiential Guide*
*The Tenth Insight: Holding the Vision: An Experiential Guide*

James Redfield's Web site:
www.celestinevision.com

# THE TENTH INSIGHT

*Holding the Vision*

Further Adventures of *The Celestine Prophecy*

---

# JAMES REDFIELD

**WARNER BOOKS**

A Time Warner Company

Copyright © 1996 by James Redfield
All rights reserved.
Warner Books, Inc., 1271 Avenue of the Americas, New York, NY 10020

Visit our Web site at
http://warnerbooks.com

 A Time Warner Company

Printed in the United States of America

First Trade Printing: December 1998

10   9   8   7   6   5   4   3   2

The Library of Congress has cataloged the hardcover edition as follows:

Library of Congress Cataloging-in-Publication Data

Redfield, James.
The tenth insight : holding the vision / James Redfield.
p.   cm.
ISBN 0-446-51908-1
1. Redfield, James—Journeys—Peru—Fiction.   2. Spiritual Life—Fiction.
3. Millennialism—Fiction.   4. Manuscripts—Collectors and collecting—Peru—Fiction.
5. Peru—Fiction.   6. Adventure stories.   7. Parables.   I. Title.
PS3568.E3448T46   1996
813'.54—dc20          96-60026
CIP
ISBN: 0-446-67457-5 (pbk.)

*Cover design by James Redfield*
*Cover illustration by Kimko Y. Craft*
*Book design by Stanley S. Drate / Folio Graphics Co., Inc.*

*For my wife and inspiration*
*Salle Merrill Redfield*

# ACKNOWLEDGMENTS

My heartfelt thanks to everyone who had a part in this book, particularly Joann Davis at Warner Books for her ongoing guidance and Albert Gaulden for his sage counsel. And certainly, my friends in the Blue Ridge Mountains, who keep the fires of a safe haven burning.

# AUTHOR'S NOTE

Like *The Celestine Prophecy,* this sequel is an adventure parable, an attempt to illustrate the ongoing spiritual transformation that is occurring in our time. My hope with both books has been to communicate what I would call a *consensus picture,* a lived portrait, of the new perceptions, feelings, and phenomena that are coming to define life as we enter the third millennium.

Our greatest mistake, in my opinion, is to think that human spirituality is somehow already understood and established. If history tells us anything, it is that human culture and knowledge are constantly evolving. Only individual opinions are fixed and dogmatic. Truth is more dynamic than that, and the great joy of life is in letting go, in finding our own special truth that is ours to tell, and then watching the synchronistic way this truth evolves and takes a clearer form, just when it's needed to impact someone's life.

Together we are going somewhere, each generation building upon the accomplishments of the previous one, destined for an end we can only dimly remember. We're all in the process of awakening and opening up to who we really are, and what we came here to do, which is often a very difficult task. Yet I firmly believe that if we always integrate the best of the traditions we find before us and keep the process in mind, each challenge along the way, each interpersonal irritation can be overcome with a sense of destiny and miracle.

I don't mean to minimize the formidable problems still facing humanity, only to suggest that each of us in our own way is involved in the solution. If we stay aware and acknowledge the great mystery that is this life, we will see that we have been perfectly placed, in exactly the right position . . . to make all the difference in the world.

JR
Spring, 1996

. . . I looked, and behold,
a door was opened in heaven:
and the first voice which I heard was as . . . a trumpet
talking with me; which said, Come up hither, and I will show you
things which must be hereafter. And immediately
I was in the spirit: and, behold, a throne was set in heaven. . . .
and there was a rainbow round about the throne,
in sight like unto an emerald. And round about the throne
were four and twenty seats: and upon the seats I saw four
and twenty elders sitting, clothed in white raiment. . . .
And I saw a new heaven and a new earth: for the first
heaven and the first earth were passed away. . . .

REVELATION

# CONTENTS

# IMAGING
# THE
# PATH

I walked out to the edge of the granite overhang and looked northward at the scene below. Stretching across my view was a large Appalachian valley of striking beauty, perhaps six or seven miles long and five miles wide. Along the length of the valley ran a winding stream that coursed through stretches of open meadowland and thick, colorful forests—old forests, with trees standing hundreds of feet high.

I glanced down at the crude map in my hand. Everything in the valley coincided with the drawing exactly: the steep ridge on which I was standing, the road leading down, the description of the landscape and the stream, the rolling foothills beyond. This had to be the place Charlene had sketched on the note found in her office. Why had she done that? And why had she disappeared?

Over a month had now passed since Charlene had last contacted her associates at the research firm where she worked, and by the time Frank Sims, her officemate, had thought to call *me,* he had become clearly alarmed.

"She often goes off on her own tangents," he had said. "But she's never disappeared for this long before, and never when she had meetings already set with long-term clients. Something's not right."

"How did you know to call me?" I asked.

He responded by describing part of a letter, found in Charlene's office, that I had written to her months earlier chronicling my experiences in Peru. With it, he told me, was a scribbled note that contained my name and telephone number.

"I'm calling everyone I know who is associated with her," he added. "So far, no one seems to know a thing. Judging from the letter, you're a friend of Charlene's. I was hoping you had heard from her."

"Sorry," I told him. "I haven't talked to her in four months."

Even as I had said the words, I couldn't believe it had been that long. Soon after receiving my letter, Charlene had telephoned and left a long message on my answering machine, voicing her excitement about the Insights and commenting on the speed with which knowledge of them seemed to be spreading. I remembered listening to Charlene's message several times, but I had put off calling her back—telling myself that I would call later, maybe tomorrow or the day after, when I felt ready to talk. I knew at the time that speaking with her would put me in the position of having to recall and explain the details of the Manuscript, and I told myself I needed more time to think, to digest what had occurred.

The truth, of course, was that parts of the prophecy still eluded me. Certainly I had retained the ability to connect with a spiritual energy within, a great comfort to me considering that everything had fallen through with Marjorie, and I was now spending large amounts of time alone. And I was more aware than ever of intuitive thoughts and dreams and the luminosity of a room or landscape. Yet, at the same time, the sporadic nature of the coincidences had become a problem.

I would fill up with energy, for instance, discerning the question foremost in my life, and would usually perceive a clear hunch about what to do or where to go to pursue the answer— yet, after acting accordingly, too often nothing of importance would occur. I would find no message, no coincidence.

This was especially true when the intuition was to seek out someone I already knew to some extent, an old acquaintance perhaps, or someone with whom I worked routinely Occasionally this person and I would find some new point of interest, but just as frequently, my initiative, in spite of my best efforts to send energy, would be completely rebuked, or worse, would begin with excitement only to warp out of control and finally die in a flurry of unexpected irritations and emotions.

Such failure had not soured me on the process, but I had realized something was missing when it came to living the Insights long-term. In Peru, I had been proceeding on momentum, often acting spontaneously with a kind of faith born out of desperation. When I arrived back home, though, dealing again with my normal environment, often surrounded by outright skeptics, I seemed to lose the keen expectation, or firm belief, that my hunches were really going to lead somewhere. Apparently there was some vital part of the knowledge I had forgotten . . . or perhaps not yet discovered.

"I'm just not sure what to do next," Charlene's associate had pressed. "She has a sister, I think, somewhere in New York. You don't know how to contact her, do you? Or anyone else who might know where she is?"

"I'm sorry," I said, "I don't. Charlene and I are actually rekindling an old friendship. I don't remember any relatives and I don't know who her friends are now."

"Well, I think I'm going to file a police report, unless you have a better idea."

"No, I think that would be wise. Are there any other leads?"

"Only a drawing of some kind; could be the description of a place. It's hard to tell."

Later he had faxed me the entire note he had found in Charlene's office, including the crude sketch of intersecting lines and numbers with vague marks in the margins. And as I had sat in my study, comparing the drawing to the road numbers in an *Atlas of the South,* I had found what I suspected to be the actual location. Afterward I had experienced a vivid image of Charlene in my mind, the same image I had perceived in Peru when told of the existence of a Tenth Insight. Was her disappearance somehow connected to the Manuscript?

A wisp of wind touched my face and I again studied the view below. Far to the left, at the western edge of the valley, I could make out a row of rooftops. *That* had to be the town Charlene had indicated on the map. Stuffing the paper into my vest pocket, I made my way back to the road and climbed into the Pathfinder.

The town itself was small—population two thousand, according to the sign beside the first and only stoplight. Most of the commercial buildings lined just one street running along the edge of the stream. I drove through the light, spotted a motel near the entrance to the National Forest, and pulled into a parking space facing an adjacent restaurant and pub. Several people were entering the restaurant, including a tall man with a dark complexion and jet-black hair, carrying a large pack. He glanced back at me and we momentarily made eye contact.

I got out and locked the car, then decided, on a hunch, to walk through the restaurant before checking into the motel. Inside, the tables were near empty—just a few hikers at the bar and some of the people who had entered ahead of me. Most were oblivious to my gaze, but as I continued to survey the room, I again met eyes with the tall man I had seen before; he was walking toward the rear of the room. He smiled faintly, held the eye contact another second, then walked out a back exit.

I followed him through the exit. He was standing twenty feet away, bending over his pack. He was dressed in jeans, a western shirt and boots, and appeared to be about fifty years old. Behind him, the late afternoon sun cast long shadows among the tall trees and grass, and, fifty yards away, the stream flowed by, beginning its journey into the valley.

He smiled halfheartedly and looked up at me. "Another pilgrim?" he asked.

"I'm looking for a friend," I said. "I had a hunch that you could help me."

He nodded, studying the outlines of my body very carefully. Walking closer, he introduced himself as David Lone Eagle, explaining, as though it was something I might need to know, that he was a direct descendant of the Native Americans who originally inhabited this valley. I noticed for the first time a thin scar on his face that ran from the edge of his left eyebrow all the way to his chin, just missing his eye.

"You want some coffee?" he asked. "They're good at Perrier

in the saloon there, but lousy at coffee." He nodded toward an area near the stream where a small tent stood among three large poplars. Dozens of people were walking in the area, some of them along a path that crossed a bridge and led into the National Forest. Everything appeared safe.

"Sure," I replied. "That would be good."

At the campsite he lit a small butane camp stove, then filled a boiler with water and set it on the burner.

"What's your friend's name?" he finally asked.

"Charlene Billings."

He paused and looked at me, and as we gazed at each other, I saw a clear image in my mind's eye of him in another time. He was younger and dressed in buckskins, sitting in front of a large fire. Streaks of war paint adorned his face. Around him was a circle of people, mostly Native Americans, but including two whites, a woman and a very large man. The discussion was heated. Some in the group wanted war; others desired reconciliation. He broke in, ridiculing the ones considering peace. How could they be so naive, he told them, after so much treachery?

The white woman seemed to understand but pleaded with him to hear her out. War could be avoided, she maintained, and the valley protected fairly, if the spiritual medicine was great enough. He rebuked her argument totally, then, chiding the group, he mounted his horse and rode away. Most of the others followed.

"Your instincts are good," David said, snapping me from my vision. He was spreading a homespun blanket between us, offering me a seat. "I know of her." He looked at me questioningly.

"I'm concerned," I said. "No one has heard from her and I just want to make sure she's okay. And we need to talk."

"About the Tenth Insight?" he asked, smiling.

"How did you know that?"

"Just a guess. Many of the people coming to this valley aren't just here because of the beauty of the National Forest. They're here to talk about the Insights. They think the Tenth is somewhere out there. A few even claim to know what it says."

He turned away and put a tea ball filled with coffee into the steaming water. Something about his tone of voice made me think he was testing me, trying to check out whether I was who I claimed.

"Where is Charlene?" I asked.

He pointed a finger toward the east. "In the Forest. I've never met your friend, but I overheard her being introduced in the restaurant one night, and I've seen her a few times since. Several days ago I saw her again; she was hiking into the valley alone, and judging from the way she was packed, I'd say she's probably still out there."

I looked in that direction. From this perspective, the valley looked enormous, stretching forever into the distance.

"Where do you think she was going?" I asked.

He stared at me for a moment. "Probably toward the Sipsey Canyon. That's where one of the *openings* is found." He was studying my reaction.

"The openings?"

He smiled cryptically. "That's right, the dimensional openings."

I leaned over toward him, remembering my experience at the Celestine Ruins. "Who knows about all this?"

"Very few people. So far it's all rumor, bits and pieces of information, intuition. Not a soul has seen a manuscript. Most of the people who come here looking for the Tenth feel they're being synchronistically led, and they're genuinely trying to live the

Nine Insights, even though they complain that the coincidences guide them along for a while and then just *stop*." He chuckled lightly. "But that's where we all are, right? The Tenth Insight is about understanding this whole awareness—the perception of mysterious coincidences, the growing spiritual consciousness on Earth, the Ninth Insight disappearances—all from the higher perspective of the other dimension, so that we can understand why this transformation is happening and participate more fully."

"How do you know that?" I asked.

He looked at me with piercing eyes, suddenly angry. "I know!"

For another moment his face remained serious, then his expression warmed again. He reached over and poured the coffee into two cups and handed one to me.

"My ancestors have lived near this valley for thousands of years," he continued. "They believed this forest was a sacred site midway between the upper world and the middle world here on Earth. My people would fast and enter the valley on their vision quests, looking for their specific gifts, their medicine, the path they should walk in this life.

"My grandfather told me about a shaman who came from a faraway tribe and taught our people to search for what he called a state of purification. The shaman taught them to leave from this very spot, bearing only a knife, and to walk until the animals provided a sign, and then to follow until they reached what they called the sacred opening into the upper world. If they were worthy, if they had cleared the lower emotions, he told them, they might even be allowed to enter the opening, and to meet directly with the ancestors, where they could remember not just their own vision but the vision of the whole world.

"Of course, all that ended when the white man came. My

grandfather couldn't remember how to do it, and neither can I. We're having to figure it out, like everyone else."

"You're here looking for the Tenth, aren't you?" I asked.

"Of course . . . of course! But all I seem to be doing is this penance of forgiveness." His voice became sharp again, and he suddenly seemed to be talking more to himself than to me. "Every time I try to move forward, a part of me can't get past the resentment, the rage, at what happened to my people. And it's not getting any better. How could it happen that our land was stolen, our way of life overrun, destroyed? Why would that be allowed?"

"I wish it hadn't happened," I said.

He looked at the ground and chuckled lowly again. "I believe that. But still, there is a rage that comes when I think of this valley being misused.

"You see this scar," he added, pointing to his face. "I could have avoided the fight where this happened. Texas cowboys with too much to drink. I could have walked away but for this anger burning within me."

"Isn't most of this valley now protected in the National Forest?" I asked.

"Only about half of it, north of the stream, but the politicians always threaten to sell it or allow development."

"What about the other half? Who owns that?"

"For a long time, this area was owned mostly by individuals, but now there's a foreign-registered corporation trying to buy it up. We don't know who is behind it, but some of the owners have been offered huge amounts to sell."

He looked away momentarily, then said, "My problem is that I want the past three centuries to have happened differently. I resent the fact that Europeans began to settle on this continent with no regard for the people who were already here. It was criminal. I want it to have happened differently, as though I could somehow change the past. Our way of life was important. We were learning the value of *remembering*. This was the great message the Europeans could have received from my people if they had stopped to listen."

As he talked, my mind drifted into another daydream. Two people—another Native American and the same white woman—were talking on the banks of a small stream. Behind them was a thick forest. After a while, other Native Americans crowded around to hear their conversation.

"We can heal this!" the woman was saying.

"I'm afraid we don't know enough yet," the Native American replied, his face expressing great regard for the woman. "Most of the other chiefs have already left."

"Why not? Think of the discussions we've had. You yourself said if there was enough faith, we could heal this."

"Yes," he replied. "But faith is a certainty that comes from knowing how things should be. The ancestors know, but not enough of us here have reached that knowing."

"But maybe we can reach this knowledge now," the woman pleaded. "We have to try!"

My thoughts were interrupted by the sight of several young Forest Service officers, who were approaching an older man on the bridge. He had neatly cut gray hair and wore dress slacks and a starched shirt. As he moved, he seemed to limp slightly.

"Do you see the man with the officers?" David asked.

"Yeah," I replied. "What about him?"

"I've seen him around here for the past two weeks. His first name is Feyman, I think. I don't know his last name." David leaned toward me, sounding for the first time as if he trusted me completely. "Listen, something very strange is going on. For several weeks the Forest Service seems to have been counting the hikers who go into the forest. They've never done that before, and yesterday someone told me they have completely closed off the far eastern end of the wilderness. There are places in that area that are ten miles from the nearest highway. Do you know how few people ever venture out that far? Some of us have begun to hear strange noises in that direction."

"What kind of noises?"

"A dissonance of some kind. Most people can't hear it."

Suddenly he was up on his feet, quickly taking down his tent.

"What are you doing?" I asked.

"I can't stay here," he replied. "I've got to get into the valley."

After a moment he interrupted his work and looked at me again. "Listen," he said. "There's something you have to know. That man Feyman. I saw your friend with him several times."

"What were they doing?"

"Just talking, but I'm telling you there's something wrong here." He began packing again.

I watched him in silence for a moment. I had no idea what to think about this situation, but I sensed that he was right about Charlene being somewhere out in the valley. "Let me get my equipment," I said. "I'd like to go with you."

"No," he said quickly. "Each person must experience the valley alone. I can't help you now. It's my own vision I must find." His face looked pained.

"Can you tell me exactly where this canyon is?"

"Just follow the stream for about two miles. You'll come to another small creek that enters the stream from the north. Follow this creek for another mile. It will lead you right through the mouth of the Sipsey Canyon."

I nodded and turned to walk away, but he grabbed my arm.

"Look," he said. "You can find your friend if you raise your energy to another level. There are specific locations in the valley that can help you."

"The dimensional openings?" I asked.

"Yes. There you can discover the perspective of the Tenth Insight, but to find these places you must understand the true nature of your intuitions, and how to *maintain* these mental images. Also watch the animals and you'll begin to remember what you are doing here in this valley . . . why we're all here together. But be very careful. Don't let them see you enter the forest." He thought for a moment. "There's someone else out there, a friend of mine, Curtis Webber. If you see Curtis, tell him that you've talked to me and that I will find him."

He smiled faintly and returned to folding his tent.

I wanted to ask what he meant about intuition and watching the animals, but he avoided eye contact and stayed focused on his work.

"Thanks," I said.

He waved slightly with one hand.


I quietly shut the motel door and eased out into the moonlight. The cool air and the tension sent a shiver through my body. Why, I thought, was I doing this? There was no proof that Charlene was still out in this valley or that David's suspicions were correct. Yet my gut told me that indeed something was wrong. For several hours I had mulled over calling the local sheriff. But what would I have said? That my friend was missing and she had been seen entering the forest of her own free will, but was perhaps in trouble, all based on a vague note found hundreds of miles away?

Searching this wilderness would take hundreds of people, and I knew they would never mount such an effort without something more substantial.

I paused and looked at the three-quarters moon rising above the trees. My plan was to cross the stream well east of the rangers' station and then to proceed along the main path into the valley. I was counting on the moon to light my way, but not to be this bright. Visibility was at least a hundred yards.

I made my way past the edge of the pub to the area where David had camped. The site was completely clean. He had even spread leaves and pine straw to remove any sign of his presence. To cross where I had planned, I would have to walk about forty yards in plain sight of the rangers' station, which I could now see clearly. Through the station's side window, two officers were busy in conversation. One rose from his seat and picked up a telephone.

Crouching low, I pulled my pack up on my shoulders and walked out onto the sandy flood wash that bordered the stream, and finally into the water itself, sloshing through mounds of smooth river stone and stepping over several decayed logs. A symphony of tree frogs and crickets erupted around me. I glanced at the rangers again: both were still talking, oblivious to my stealth. At its deepest point, the moderately swift water reached my upper thigh, but in seconds I had moved across the thirty feet of current and into a stand of small pines.

I carefully moved forward until I found the hiking path leading into the valley. Toward the east, the path disappeared into the darkness, and as I stared in that direction, more doubts entered my mind. What was this mysterious noise that so worried David? What might I stumble upon in the darkness out there?

I shook off the fear. I knew I had to go on, but as a compromise, I walked only a half mile into the forest before making my way well off the path into a heavily wooded area to raise the tent and spend the rest of the night, glad to take off my wet boots and let them dry. It would be smarter to proceed in the daylight.

The next morning I awoke at dawn thinking about David's cryptic remark about *maintaining* my intuitions, and as I lay in my sleeping bag, I reviewed my own understanding of the Seventh Insight, particularly the awareness that the experience of synchronicity follows a certain structure. According to this Insight, each of us, once we work to clear our past dramas, can identify certain questions that define our particular life situation, questions related to our careers, relationships, where we should live, how we should proceed on our path. Then, if we remain aware, gut feelings, hunches, and intuitions will provide impressions of where to go, what to do, with whom we should speak, in order to pursue an answer.

After that, of course, a coincidence was supposed to occur, revealing the reason we were urged to follow such a course and providing new information that pertained in some way to our question, leading us forward in our lives. How would maintaining the intuition help?

Easing out of my sleeping bag, I pulled the tent flaps apart and checked outside. Sensing nothing unusual, I climbed out into the crisp fall air and walked back to the stream, where I washed my face in the cool water. Afterward I packed up and headed east again, nibbling on a granola bar and keeping myself hidden as much as possible in the tall trees that bordered the stream. After traveling perhaps three miles, a perceptible wave of fear and nervousness passed through my body and I immediately felt fatigued, so I sat down and leaned against a tree, attempting to focus on my surroundings and gain inner energy. The sky was cloudless and the morning sun danced through the trees and along the ground around me. I noticed a small green plant with yellow blossoms about ten feet away and focused on its beauty. Already draped in full sunlight, it seemed brighter suddenly, its leaves a richer green. A rush of fragrance reached my awareness, along with the musty smell of leaves and black soil.

Simultaneously, from the trees far toward the north, I heard the call of several crows. The richness of the sound amazed me, but surprisingly I couldn't distinguish their exact location. As I concentrated on listening, I became fully aware of dozens of individual sounds that made up the morning chorus: songbirds in the trees above me, a bumblebee among the wild daisies at the edge of the stream, the water gurgling around the rocks and fallen branches . . . and then something else, barely perceptible, a low, dissonant *hum*. I stood up and looked around. What was this noise?

I picked up my pack and proceeded east. Because of the crunching sound created by my footsteps on the fallen leaves, I had to stop and listen very intensely to still hear the hum. But it was there. Ahead the woods ended, and I entered a large meadow, colorful with wildflowers and thick, two-foot-tall sage grass that seemed to go on for half a mile. The breeze brushed the tops of the sage in currents. When I had almost reached the edge of the meadow, I noticed a patch of blackberry brambles growing beside a fallen tree. The bushes struck me as exceedingly beautiful, and I walked over to look at them more closely, imagining that they were full of berries.

As I did this, I experienced an acute feeling of déjà vu. The surroundings suddenly seemed very familiar, as though I had been here in this valley before, eaten berries before. How was that possible? I sat down on the trunk of the fallen tree. Presently, in the back of my mind rose a picture of a crystal-clear pool of water and several tiers of waterfalls in the background, a location that, as I imaged it, seemed equally familiar. Again I felt anxious.

Without warning, an animal of some kind ran noisily from the berry patch, startling me, and headed north for about twenty feet and then abruptly stopped. The creature was hidden in the tall sage, and I had no idea what it was, but I could follow its wake in the grass. After a few minutes it darted back a few feet to the south, remained motionless again for several seconds, then darted ten or twenty feet back again toward the north, only to stop again. I guessed it was a rabbit, although its movements seemed especially peculiar.

For five or six minutes I watched the area where the animal had last moved, then slowly walked that way. As I closed to about five feet, it suddenly sped away again toward the north. At one point, before it disappeared into the distance, I glimpsed the white tail and hind legs of a large rabbit.

I smiled and proceeded east again along the trail, coming finally to the end of the meadow, where I entered an area of thick woods. There I spotted a small creek, perhaps four feet wide, that entered the stream from the left. I knew this must be the landmark David had mentioned. I was to turn northward. Unfortunately there was no trail in that direction, and worse, the woods along the creek were a snarl of thick saplings and prickly briers. I couldn't get through; I would have to backtrack into the meadow behind me until I could find a way around.

I made my way back into the grass and walked along the edge of the woods looking for a break in the dense undergrowth. To my surprise, I ran into the trail the rabbit had made in the sage and followed its path until I caught sight of the small creek again. Here the dense undergrowth receded partially, allowing me to push my way through into an area of larger, old-growth trees, where I could follow the creek due north.

After proceeding for what I judged to be about another mile, I could see a range of foothills rising in the distance on both sides of the creek. Walking farther, I realized that these hills were forming steep canyon walls and that up ahead was what looked to be the only entrance.

When I arrived, I sat down beside a large hickory and surveyed the scene. A hundred yards on both sides of the creek, the hills butted off in fifty-foot-high limestone bluffs, then bent outward into the distance, forming a huge bowl-like canyon perhaps two miles wide and at least four long. The first half mile was thinly wooded and covered with more sage. I thought about the hum and listened carefully for five or ten minutes, but it seemed to have ceased.

Finally I reached into my pack and pulled out a small butane stove and lit the burner, then filled a small pan with water from my canteen, emptied the contents of a package of freeze-dried vegetable stew into the water, and set the pan on the flame. For a few moments I watched as strands of steam twisted upward and disappeared into the breeze. In my reverie I again saw the pool and the waterfall in my mind's eye, only this time I seemed to be there, walking up, as if to greet someone. I shook the picture from my head. What was happening? These images were growing more vivid. First David in another time; now these falls.

Movement in the canyon caught my eye. I glanced at the creek and then beyond to a lone tree two hundred yards away which had already lost most of its leaves. It was now covered with what looked like large crows; several flew down to the ground. It came to me that these were the same crows I had heard earlier. As I watched, they suddenly all flew and dramatically circled above the tree. At the same moment, I could hear their cawing again, although, as before, the loudness of their cries didn't match the distance; they sounded much closer.

Splashing water and hissing steam pulled my attention back to the camp stove. Boiling stew was overflowing onto the flame. I grabbed the pan with a towel, turning off the gas with the other hand. When the boiling subsided, I returned the pan to the burner and looked back at the tree in the distance. The crows were gone.

I hurriedly ate the stew, cleaned up, and packed the gear, then headed into the canyon. As soon as I passed the bluffs, I noticed the colors had amplified. The sage seemed amazingly golden, and I noticed, for the first time, that it was peppered with hundreds of wildflowers—white and yellow and orange. From the cliffs to the east, the breeze carried the scent of cedar and pine.

Although I continued to follow the creek running north, I kept my eye on the tall tree to my left where the crows had circled. When it was directly west of me, I noticed the creek was suddenly widening. I made my way through some willows and cattails and realized I had come to a small pool that fed not only the creek I was following but a second creek angling off farther to the southeast. At first I thought this pool was the one I had seen in my mind, but there were no waterfalls.

Ahead was another surprise: to the north of the pool, the creek had completely disappeared. Where was the water coming from? Then it dawned on me that the pool and the creek I had been following were all fed from an enormous underground spring surfacing at this location.

To my left, fifty feet away, I noticed a mild rise on which grew three sycamore trees, each more than two feet in diameter—a perfect place to think for a moment. I walked over and snuggled in among them, sitting down and leaning against the trunk of one of the trees. From this perspective, the two remaining trees were six or seven feet to my front, and I could look both to the left to see the crow tree and to the right to observe the spring. The question now was where to go from here. I could wander for days without seeing any sign of Charlene. And what about these images?

I closed my eyes and attempted to bring back the earlier picture of the pool and waterfalls, but as much as I struggled, I couldn't remember the exact details. Finally I gave up and gazed out again at the grass and wildflowers and then at the two sycamores right in front of me. Their trunks were a scaly collage of dark gray and white bark, streaked with brushstrokes of tan and multiple shades of amber. As I focused on the beauty of the scene, these colors seemed to intensify and grow more iridescent. I took another deep breath and looked out again at the meadow and flowers. The crow tree seemed particularly illuminated.

I picked up my pack and walked toward the tree. Immediately the image of the pool and waterfalls flashed across my mind. This time I tried to remember the entire picture. The pool I saw was large, almost an acre, and the water flowing into it came in from the rear, cascading down a series of steep terraces. Two smaller falls dropped only about fifteen feet, but the last dropped over a long, thirty-foot bluff into the water below. Again, in the image that came to mind, I seemed to be walking up to the scene, meeting someone.

The sound of a vehicle to my left stopped me firmly in my tracks. I kneeled down behind several small bushes. From the forest on the left a gray Jeep moved across the meadow heading southeast. I knew that Forest Service policy prohibited private vehicles this far into the wilderness, so I expected to see a Forest Service insignia on the Jeep's door. To my surprise it was unmarked. When it was directly in front of me, fifty yards away, the vehicle stopped. Through the foliage I could make out a lone figure inside; he was surveying the area with field glasses, so I lay flat and hid myself completely. Who was he?

The vehicle started up again and quickly vanished out of sight in the trees. I turned and sat down, listening again for the hum. Still nothing. I thought about returning to town, of finding another way to search for Charlene. But deep inside I knew there was no alternative. I shut my eyes, and thought again of David's instruction to maintain my intuitions, and finally retrieved the full image of the pool and falls in my mind's eye. As I got to my feet and headed again toward the crow tree, I tried to keep the details of the scene in the back of my mind.

Suddenly I heard the shrill cry of another bird, this time a hawk. To my left, far past the tree, I could barely make out her shape; she was streaking hard toward the north. I increased my pace, trying to keep the bird in sight for as long as possible.

The bird's appearance seemed to increase my energy, and even after she had disappeared over the horizon, I kept moving in the direction she had been flying, walking for another mile and a half over a series of rocky foothills. At the top of the third hill, I froze again, hearing another sound in the distance, a sound much like water running. No, it was water *falling*.

Carefully I walked down the slope and through a deep gorge that evoked another experience of déjà vu. I climbed the next hill and there, beyond the crest, were the pool and falls, exactly as I had pictured them—except that the area was much larger and more beautiful than I had pictured. The pool itself was almost two acres, nestled in a cradle of enormous boulders and outcroppings, its crystal-clear water a sparkling blue under the afternoon sky. To the left and right of the pool were several large oak trees, themselves surrounded by a multicolored array of smaller maples and sweet gums and willows.

The far edge of the pool was an explosion of white spray and mist, the foam accentuated by the churning action of the two smaller falls higher up the ridge. I realized there was no runoff from the pool. The water went underground from here, traveling silently to emerge as the source of the large spring near the crow tree.

As I surveyed the beauty of this sight, the sense of déjà vu increased. The sounds, the colors, the scene from the hill—it all looked extremely familiar. I had been at this location too. But when?

I moved down to the pool and then walked around the entire area, to the edge to taste the water, up the cascades to feel the spray from each of the falls, over atop the large boulders, where I could touch the trees. I wanted to immerse myself in the place. Finally I stretched out on one of the flatter rocks twenty feet above the pool and looked toward the afternoon sun with my eyes closed, feeling its rays against my face. In that moment another familiar sensation swept across my body—a particular warmth and regard I hadn't sensed in months. In fact, until this instant, I had forgotten its exact feeling and character, although it was perfectly recognizable now. I opened my eyes and turned around quickly, certain of whom I was about to see.

# REVIEWING
# THE
# JOURNEY

On a rock above my head, half obscured by an overhanging ledge, stood Wil, his hands on his hips, smiling broadly. He appeared slightly out of focus, so I blinked hard and concentrated, and his face cleared somewhat.

"I knew you would be here," he said, nimbly climbing off the ledge and jumping to the rock beside me. "I've been waiting."

I looked at him in awe, and he pulled me into an embrace; his face and hands looked slightly luminescent but otherwise seemed normal.

"I can't believe you're here," I stammered. "What happened when you disappeared in Peru? Where have you been?"

He gestured for me to sit facing him on a nearby shelf.

"I'll tell you everything," he said, "but first I have to know about you. What circumstances brought you to this valley?"

In detail I told him about Charlene's disappearance, the map of the valley, and meeting David. Wil wanted to know more of what David had said, so I told him everything I could remember about the conversation.

Wil leaned toward me. "He told you the Tenth was about understanding the spiritual renaissance on Earth in light of the other dimension? And learning the true nature of your intuitions?"

"Yes," I said. "Is that right?"

He seemed to think for a moment, then asked, "What has been your experience since entering the valley?"

"I immediately started to see images," I said. "Some were of other historical times, but then I began to see repeated visions of this pool. I saw everything: the rocks, the falls, even that someone was waiting here, although I didn't know it was you."

"Where were you in the scene?"

"It was as if I was walking up and seeing it."

"So it was a scene of a *potential future* for you."

I squinted at him. "I'm not sure I follow."

"The first part of the Tenth, as David said, is about understanding our intuitions more fully. In the first nine Insights, one experiences intuitions as fleeting gut feelings or vague hunches. But as we gain familiarity with this phenomenon, we can now grasp the nature of these intuitions more clearly. Think back to Peru. Didn't intuitions come to you as pictures of what was going to happen, images of yourself and others at a specific location, doing certain things, leading you to go there? Wasn't that how you knew when to go to the Celestine Ruins?

"Here in the valley the same thing has been happening. You received a mental image of a potential event—finding the falls and meeting someone—and you were able to live it out, bringing on the coincidence of actually discovering the location and encountering me. If you had shrugged off the image, or lost faith in looking for the falls, you would have missed the synchronicity, and your life would have stayed flat. But you took the image seriously; you *kept* it in your mind."

"David said something about learning to 'maintain' the intuition," I said.

Wil nodded.

"What about the other images," I asked, "the scenes of an earlier time? And what about these animals? Does the Tenth Insight talk about all this? Have you seen the Manuscript?"

With a gesture of his hand, Wil waved off my questions. "First, let me tell you about my experience in the other dimension, what I call the *Afterlife* dimension. When I was able to maintain my energy level in Peru, even when the rest of you grew fearful and lost your vibration, I found myself in an incredible world of beauty and clear form. I was right there in the same place, but everything was different. The world was luminous and awing in a way I still can't describe. For a long time I just walked around in this incredible world, vibrating even higher, and then I discovered something quite amazing. I could will myself anywhere on the planet, just by imaging a destination in my mind. I traveled everywhere I could think of, looking for you and Julia and the others, but I couldn't find any of you.

"Finally I began to detect another ability. By imaging just a blank field in my mind, I could travel off the planet, into a place of pure ideas. There I could create anything I wanted just by imaging it. I made oceans and mountains and scenic vistas, images of people who behaved just as I wanted, all kinds of things. And every bit of it seemed just as real as anything on Earth.

"Yet in the end, I realized that such a constructed world was not a fulfilling place. Just creating arbitrarily gave me no inner satisfaction. After a while, I went home and thought about what I wanted to do. At that time I could still become dense enough so that I could talk with most people of a higher awareness. I could eat and sleep, although I didn't have to. Finally I realized that I had forgotten about the thrill of evolving and experiencing coincidences. Because I was already so buoyant, I had mistakenly thought that I was maintaining my inner connection, but in fact, I had become too controlling and had lost my path. It is very easy to lose one's way at this level of vibration, because it is so easy and instantaneous to create with one's will."

"What happened then?" I asked.

"I focused within, looking for a higher connection with divine energy, just the way we've always done it. That's all it took; my vibration rose even higher and I began to receive intuitions again. I saw an image of you."

"What was I doing?"

"I couldn't tell; the image was hazy. But when I thought about the intuition and maintained it in my mind, I began to move into a new area of the Afterlife where I could actually see other souls, groups of souls really, and while I couldn't exactly speak to them, I could vaguely pick up on their thoughts and knowledge."

"Were they able to show you the Tenth Insight?" I asked.

He swallowed hard and looked at me as though he was about to land a bombshell. "No, the Tenth Insight has never been written down."

"What? It's not part of the original Manuscript?"

"No."

"Does it even exist?"

"Oh yes, it exists. But not in the Earthly dimension. This Insight hasn't made it to the physical plane yet. This knowledge exists only in the Afterlife. Only when enough people on Earth sense this information, intuitively, can it become real enough in everyone's consciousness for someone to write it down. That's what happened with the first nine Insights. In fact, that's what has happened with all spiritual texts, even our most sacred scriptures. Always it is information that first exists in the Afterlife, and is finally picked up clearly enough in the physical dimension to be manifested by someone who is supposed to write it down. That's why these writings are called divinely inspired."

"So why has it taken so long for someone to grasp the Tenth?"

Wil looked perplexed. "I don't know. The soul group I was communicating with seemed to know, but I couldn't quite understand. My energy level was not high enough. It has something to do with the Fear that arises in a culture that is moving from a material reality to a transformed, spiritual worldview."

"Then you think the Tenth is ready to come in?"

"Yes, the soul groups saw the Tenth coming in now, bit by bit, all over the world, as we gain a higher perspective that comes from a knowledge of the Afterlife. But it has to be grasped in sufficient numbers, just as with the first nine, in order to overcome the Fear."

"Do you know what the rest of the Tenth is about?"

"Yes, apparently just knowing the first nine isn't enough. We have to understand how we will implement this destiny. Such knowledge comes from grasping the special relationship between the physical dimension and the Afterlife. We have to understand the birth process, where we come from, the larger picture of what human history is trying to accomplish."

A thought suddenly came to me. "Wait a minute. Weren't you able to see a copy of the *Ninth* Insight? What did it say about the Tenth?"

Wil leaned toward me. "It said that the first nine Insights

have described the reality of spiritual evolution, both personally and collectively, but actually implementing these Insights, living them, and fulfilling this destiny requires a fuller understanding of the process, a Tenth Insight. This Insight would show us the reality of Earth's spiritual transformation not just from the perspective of the Earthly dimension but from the perspective of the Afterlife dimension as well. It said we would understand more fully why we were uniting the dimensions, why humans must fulfill this historical purpose, and it would be this understanding, once integrated into culture, that would ensure this eventual outcome. It also mentioned the Fear, saying that at the same time a new spiritual awareness was emerging, a reactive polarization would also rise up in fearful opposition, seeking to willfully control the future with various new technologies—technologies even more dangerous than the nuclear menace—that are already being discovered. The Tenth Insight resolves this polarization."

He stopped abruptly and nodded toward the east. "Do you hear that?"

I listened but could hear only the falls.

"What?" I asked.

"That hum."

"I heard it earlier. What is it?"

"I'm not sure, exactly. But it can be heard in the other dimension as well. The souls I saw seemed very disturbed about it."

As Wil spoke, I clearly saw Charlene's face in the back of my mind.

"Do you think the hum is related to this new technology?" I asked, partially distracted.

Wil didn't answer. I noticed he had an absent look on his face.

"The friend that you're looking for," he asked, "does she have blond hair? And large eyes . . . very inquisitive-looking?"

"Yes."

"I just saw an image of her face."

I stared at him. "So did I."

He turned and looked at the falls for a moment, and I followed his gaze. The white foam and spray formed a majestic background to our conversation. I could feel the energy increasing in my body.

"You don't have enough energy yet," he said. "But because this place is so powerful, I think that if I help, and we both focus on your friend's face, we can move fully into the spiritual dimension and maybe find out where she is and what's happening in this valley."

"Are you sure I can do that?" I said. "Maybe you can go and I can wait here for you." His face was fading out of focus.

Wil touched my lower back, giving me energy, smiling again. "Don't you see how purposeful it is that we are here? Human culture is beginning to understand the Afterlife and grasp the Tenth. I think we have the opportunity to explore the other dimension together. You know this feels destined."

At that moment I noticed the noise of the hum in the background, even over the sound of the falls. In fact, I could feel it in my solar plexus.

"The hum's getting louder," Wil said. "We have to go now. Charlene could be in trouble!"

"What do we do?" I asked.

Wil moved slightly closer, still touching my back. "We have to re-create the image we received of your friend."

"Maintain it?"

"Yes. As I said, we are learning to recognize and believe in our intuitions at a higher level. We all want the coincidences to come more consistently, but for most of us, this awareness is new and we're surrounded by a culture that still operates too much in the old skepticism, so we lose the expectation, the faith. Yet what we're beginning to realize is that when we fully pay attention, inspecting the details of the potential future we're shown, purposely keeping the image in the back of our minds, intentionally believing—when we do this—then whatever we are imaging tends to happen more readily."

"Then we 'will' it to happen?"

"No. Remember my experience in the Afterlife. There you can make anything happen just by wishing it so, but such creation isn't fulfilling. The same is true of this dimension, only everything moves at a slower rate. On Earth, we can will and create almost anything we wish, but real fulfillment comes only when we first tune into our inner direction and divine guidance. Only then do we use our will to move toward the potential futures we received. In this sense, we become cocreators with the divine source. Do you see how this knowledge begins the Tenth Insight? We are learning to use our visualization in the same way it is used in the Afterlife, and when we do, we fall into alignment with that dimension, and that helps unite Heaven and Earth."

I nodded, understanding completely. After taking several deep breaths, Wil exerted more pressure on my back and instructed me to re-create the details of Charlene's face. For a moment nothing happened, and then suddenly I felt a rush of energy, twisting me forward and pushing me into a wild acceleration.

I was streaking at fantastic speeds though a multicolored tunnel of some kind. Fully conscious, I wondered why I had no fear, for what I really felt was a sense of recognition and contentment and peace, as though I had been here before. When the movement stopped, I found myself in an environment of warm, white light. I looked for Wil and realized he was standing to my left and slightly behind me.

"There you are," he said, smiling. His lips weren't moving, but I could clearly hear his voice. I then noticed the appearance of his body. He looked exactly the same, except he seemed to be completely illuminated from within.

I reached over to touch his hand and noticed that my body appeared the same way. When I touched him, what I felt was a field several inches outside the arm I could see. Pushing harder, I realized I couldn't penetrate this energy; I only moved his body away from me.

Wil was near bursting with mirth. In fact, his expression was so humorous that I laughed myself.

"Amazing, isn't it?" he asked.

"This is a higher vibration than at the Celestine Ruins," I replied. "Do you know where we are?"

Wil was silent, gazing out at our surroundings. We seemed to be in an environment that was spatial, and we had a sense of up and down, but we were suspended motionless in midair and there were no horizons. The white light was a constant hue in all directions.

Finally Wil said, "This is an observation point; I came here briefly, when I first imaged your face. More souls were here."

"What were they doing?"

"Observing the people who had come over after death."

"What? You mean this is where people come right after they have died?"

"Yes."

"Why are we here? Has something happened to Charlene?"

He turned more directly toward me. "No, I don't think so. Remember what happened to me when I began to image you. I moved to many locations before we finally met at the falls. There's probably something we need to see here before we can find Charlene. Let's wait and see what happens with these souls." He nodded to our left, where several humanlike entities were materializing directly in front of us, at a distance of what appeared to be about thirty feet.

My first reaction was to be cautious. "Wil, how do we know their intentions are friendly? What if they try to possess us or something?"

He gave me a serious expression. "How do you know if someone on Earth is trying to control you?"

"I would pick up on it. I could tell that the person was being manipulative."

"What else?"

"I guess they would be taking energy away from me. I would feel a decrease in my sense of wisdom, self-direction."

"Exactly. They wouldn't be following the Insights. All these principles work the same way in both dimensions."

As the entities formed completely, I remained cautious. But eventually I felt a loving and supportive energy emanating from their bodies, which seemed to be comprised of a whitish-amber light that danced and shimmered in and out of focus. Their faces had human characteristics but could not be looked at directly. I couldn't even tell how many souls were there. At one moment, three or four seemed to be facing us, then I would blink and there would be six, then three again, all dancing in and out of view. Overall, they looked like a flickering, animated cloud of amber, against the background color of white.

After several minutes, another form began to materialize beside the others, only this figure was more clearly in focus and appeared in a luminous body similar to Wil and myself. We could see that it was a middle-aged man; he looked around wildly, then saw the group of souls and began to relax.

To my surprise, when I focused closely on him, I could pick up on what he was feeling and thinking. I glanced at Wil, who nodded that he was also sensing the person's reaction.

I focused again and observed that, in spite of a certain detachment and sense of love and support, he was in a state of shock at having discovered he had died. Only minutes before, he had been routinely jogging, and while attempting to run up a long hill, had suffered a massive heart attack. The pain had lasted only a few seconds, and then he was hovering outside his body, watching a stream of bystanders rush up to help him. Soon a team of paramedics arrived and worked feverishly to bring him back.

As he sat beside his body in the ambulance, he had listened in horror as the team leader had pronounced him dead. Frantically he had attempted to communicate, but no one could hear. At the hospital a doctor confirmed to the crew that his heart had literally exploded; that no one could have done anything to save his life.

Part of him tried to accept the fact; another resisted. How could he be dead? He had called out for help and had instantly found himself in a tunnel of colors that had brought him to where he now stood. As we watched, he seemed to become more aware of the souls and moved toward them, shifting out of focus to us, appearing more like them.

Then abruptly he pulled back toward us and was quickly surrounded by an office of some kind, filled with computers and wall charts and people working. Everything looked perfectly real, except the walls were semitransparent, so that we could see what was happening inside, and the sky above the office was not blue, but a strange olive color.

"He's deluding himself," Wil said. "He's re-creating the office where he worked on Earth, trying to pretend he hasn't died."

The souls moved closer and others came until there were dozens of them, all flickering in and out of focus in the amber light. They seemed to be sending the man love and some kind of information I couldn't understand. Gradually the constructed office began to fade and eventually disappeared completely.

The man was left with an expression of resignation on his face, and he again moved into focus with the souls.

"Let's go with them," I heard Wil say. At the same moment, I felt his arm, or rather, the energy of his arm, pushing against my back.

As soon as I inwardly agreed, there was the slight sensation of movement, and the souls and the man all came into clearer focus. The souls now had glowing faces much as Wil and I did, but their hands and feet, instead of being clearly formed, were mere radiations of light. I could now focus on the entities for as long as four or five seconds before losing them and having to blink to find them again.

I became aware that the group of souls, as well as the deceased individual, was watching an intense point of bright light moving toward us. It eventually swelled into a massive beam that covered everything. Unable to look directly at the light, I turned so I could just see the silhouette of the man, who was staring fully at the beam without apparent difficulty.

Again I could pick up on his thoughts and emotions. The light was filling him with an unimaginable sense of love and calm perspective. As this sensation swept over him, his viewpoint and knowledge expanded until he could clearly see the life he had just lived from a broad and amazingly detailed perspective.

Immediately he could see the circumstances of his birth and early family life. He was born John Donald Williams to a father who was slow intellectually and to a mother who was extremely detached and absent because of her involvement in various social events. He himself had grown up angry and defiant, an interrogator eager to prove to the world that he was a brilliant achiever who could master science and mathematics. He earned a doctorate in physics at MIT at age twenty-three and taught at four prestigious universities before moving on to the Defense Department and then later to a private energy corporation.

Clearly he had thrown himself into this latter position with total abandon and disregard for his health. After years of fast food and no exercise he was diagnosed with a chronic heart condition. An exercise routine pursued too aggressively had proved fatal. He had died in his prime at age fifty-eight.

At this point Williams' awareness shifted and he began to have profound regrets and severe emotional pain concerning the way he had led his life. He realized that his childhood and early family had been set up perfectly to expose what was already his soul's tendency to use defiance and elitism to feel more important. His main tool had been ridicule, putting down others by criticizing their abilities and work ethic and personality. Yet now he could see that all the teachers had been in place to help him overcome this insecurity. All of them had arrived at just the right time to show him another way, but he had ignored them completely.

Instead he had just pursued his tunnel vision to the end. All the signs had been there to choose his work more carefully, to slow down. There were a multitude of implications and dangers inherent in his research of new technologies that he had failed to consider. He had allowed his employers to feed him new theories, and even unfamiliar physical principles, without even questioning their origin. These procedures worked, and that was all he cared about, because they led to success, gratitude, recognition. He had succumbed to his need for *recognition* . . . again. My God, he thought, I've failed just as I did before.

His mind abruptly shifted to a new scene, an earlier existence. He was in the southern Appalachians, nineteenth century, a military outpost. In a large tent several men leaned over a map. Lanterns flickered their light against the walls. A consensus had been reached among all the field officers present: there was no hope for peace now. War was inevitable, and sound military principles dictated an attack, quickly.

As one of the commanding general's top two aides, Williams had been forced to concur with the others. No other choice existed, he had concluded; disagreement would have ended his career. Besides, he couldn't have dissuaded the others even if he had wanted to. The offensive would have to be carried out, likely the last major battle in the eastern war against the Natives.

A sentry interrupted with a communication for the general. A settler wanted to see the commander immediately. Looking through the open tent flap, Williams had seen the frail white woman, perhaps thirty, desperation in her eyes. He found out later that she was the daughter of a missionary, bringing word of a possible new Native American initiative for peace, an appeal that she personally had negotiated at great risk.

But the general had refused to see her, remaining in the tent as she shouted at him, finally ordering her from his camp at gunpoint, not knowing the content of her message, not wanting to know. Again Williams kept quiet. He knew his commander was under great pressure, having already promised that the region would be opened up for economic expansion. A war was necessary if the vision of the power brokers and their political allies was to be actualized. It was not enough to let the settlers and the Indians create their own frontier culture. No, in their view, the future had to be shaped and manipulated and controlled for the best interests of those who made the world secure and abundant. It would be far too frightening and altogether irresponsible to let the little people decide.

Williams knew that a war would greatly please the railroad and coal tycoons and the newly emerging oil interests, and would, of course, ensure his own future as well. All he had to do was keep his mouth shut and play along. And he would, under silent protest—unlike the general's other primary aide. He remembered looking across the room at his colleague, a small man who limped slightly. No one knew why he limped. Nothing was wrong with his leg. Here was the ultimate yes-man. He knew what the secret cartels were up to and he loved it, admired it, wanted to become a part of it. And there was something more.

This man, like the general and the other controllers, feared the Native Americans and wanted them removed not just because of the Natives' alienation from the expanding industrial economy that was poised to overrun their lands. They feared these people because of something deeper, some terrifying and transformative idea, known in its entirety only by a few of the elders, but which bubbled up throughout their culture and called out for the controllers to change, to remember another vision of the future.

Williams had found out that the missionary's daughter had arranged for the great medicine chiefs to come together in one last attempt to agree on this knowledge, to find the words to share it—one last bid to explain themselves, to establish their value to a world quickly turning against them. Williams had known, deep within, that the woman should have been heard, but in the end he had remained silent, and with one quick nod the general had pushed away the possibility of reconciliation and had ordered the battle to begin.

As we watched, Williams' recollection shifted to a gorge in the deep woods, site of the coming battle. Cavalry poured over a ridge in a surprise offensive. The Native Americans rose to the defense, attacking the cavalry from the bluffs on either side. A short distance away, a large man and a woman huddled among the rocks. The man was a young academic, a congressional aide, there only to observe, terrified he was this close to the battle. It was wrong, all wrong. His interest was economics; he knew nothing of violence. He had come there convinced that the white man and the Indian need not be in conflict, that the growing economic surge through the region might be adapted, evolved, integrated to include both cultures.

Beside him in the rocks was the young woman seen at the military tent earlier. At this moment she felt abandoned, betrayed. Her effort could have worked, she knew, if those with the power had listened to what was possible. But she would not give up, she had told herself, not until the violence stopped. She kept saying, "It can be healed! It can be healed."

Suddenly on the downslope behind them, two cavalrymen rode hard toward a single Native. I strained to see who it was, finally recognizing the man as the angry chief I had seen in my mind when talking to David, the chief who had been so vocal against the white woman's ideas. As I watched, he turned quickly and shot an arrow into the chest of one of his pursuers. The other soldier leaped from his horse and fell upon the Native American. Both struggled furiously, the soldier's knife finally plunging deep into the throat of the darker man. Blood gushed across the torn ground.

Watching the events, the panicked economist pleaded with the woman to flee with him, but she motioned for him to stay, to be calm. For the first time Williams could see an old medicine man beside a tree next to them, his form flickering in and out of focus. At that instant another troop of cavalry crested the rise and was on top of them, firing indiscriminately. Bullets tore through both the man and the woman. With a smile the Indian defiantly stood and was likewise destroyed.

At this point Williams' focus drifted to a hill that overlooked the entire scene. Another individual was looking down on the battle. He was dressed in buckskins and led a pack mule, a mountain man. He turned from the battle and walked down the hill in the opposite direction, past the pool and falls, and then out of sight. I was astounded: the battle had taken place right here in the valley, just south of the falls.

When my attention returned to Williams, he was reliving the horror of the bloodshed and the hatred. He knew his failure to act during the Native American wars had set up the conditions and hopes of his most recent life, but just as before, he had failed to awaken. He had been together again with the congressional aide who had been killed with the woman, and still he had failed to remember their mission. Williams intended to meet the younger man on a hilltop, among a circle of large trees, and there his friend was supposed to awaken and go on to find six others in the valley, forming a group of seven. Together the group was to help resolve the Fear.

The idea seemed to thrust him into a deeper recollection. Fear had been the great enemy throughout humanity's long and tortuous history, and he seemed to know that present human culture was polarizing, giving the controllers in this historical time one last opportunity to seize power, to exploit the new technologies for their own purpose.

He seemed to cringe in agony. He knew that it was tremendously important for the group of seven to come together. History was poised for such groups, and only if enough of them formed, and only if enough of them *understood* the Fear, could the polarization be dispelled and the experiments in the valley ended.

Very slowly I became aware that I was again in the place of soft, white light. Williams' visions had ended, and both he and the other entities had quickly vanished. Afterward I had experienced a quick movement backward that had left me dizzy and distracted.

I noticed Wil beside me to the right.

"What happened?" I asked. "Where did he go?"

"I'm not sure," he replied.

"What was happening to him?"

"He was experiencing a *Life Review.*"

I nodded.

"Are you aware of what that is?" he asked.

"Yeah," I said. "I know that people who have had near-death experiences often report that their whole lives flash before them. Is that what you mean?"

Wil looked thoughtful. "Yes, but the increased awareness of this review process is having great impact on human culture. It's another part of the higher perspective provided by a knowledge of the Afterlife. Thousands of people have had near-death experiences, and as their stories are shared and talked about, the reality of the Life Review is becoming part of our everyday understanding. We know that after death, we have to look at our lives again; and we're going to agonize over every missed opportunity, over every case in which we failed to act. This knowledge is contributing to our determination to pursue every intuitive image that comes to mind, and keep it firmly in awareness. We're living life in a more deliberate way. We don't want to miss a single important event. We don't want the pain of looking back later and realizing that we blew it, that we failed to make the right decisions."

Suddenly Wil paused, cocking his head as though hearing something. Immediately I felt another jolt in my solar plexus and heard the dissonant hum again. Moments later the sound faded.

Wil was looking around. The solid white environment was shimmering with intermittent streaks of dull gray.

"Whatever is going on is affecting this dimension too!" he said. "I don't know if we can maintain our vibration."

As we waited, the dull streaks gradually diminished and the solid white background returned.

"Remember the warning about new technology in the Ninth Insight," Wil added, "and Williams' comment about those in Fear trying to control this technology."

"What about this *group of seven* coming back?" I asked. "And those visions that Williams was having of this valley in the nineteenth century? Wil, I've seen them too. What do you think the visions mean?"

Wil's expression grew more serious. "I think all this is what we're supposed to be seeing. And I think *you* are part of this group."

Suddenly the hum began to increase again.

"Williams said we first had to understand this Fear," Wil

stressed, "in order to help resolve it. That's what we have to do next; we have to find a way to understand this Fear."

Wil had barely finished his thought when an ear-shattering sound tore through my body, pushing me backward. Wil reached out for me, his face distorted and out of focus. I tried to grab his arm, but he was suddenly gone, and I was falling downward, out of control, amid a panorama of colors.

# OVERCOMING
# THE
# FEAR

Shaking off the vertigo, I became aware that I was back at the falls. Across from me, under a rocky overhang, was my pack, lying exactly where I had placed it earlier. I looked around: no sign of Wil. What had happened? Where did he go?

According to my watch, less than an hour had passed since Wil and I had entered the other dimension, and as I thought about the experience, I was struck with how much love and calm I had felt, and how little anxiety—until now. Now everything around me seemed dull and muted.

Wearily I walked over and picked up my pack, fear welling up in my stomach. Sensing too much exposure in the openness of the rocks, I decided to walk back into the hills to the south until I could decide what to do. When I had crested the first hill and started down the slope, I spotted a small man, perhaps fifty years old, walking up to my left. He had red hair and a thin goatee and wore hiking clothes. Before I could hide, he spotted me and headed straight my way.

When he reached me, he smiled cautiously and said, "I'm afraid I'm turned around a bit. Could you direct me back to town?"

I gave him directions south to the spring and then on to the main stream, which he could follow west to the rangers' station.

He appeared relieved. "I ran into someone east of here, earlier, who told me how to get back, but I must have made a wrong turn. Are you also heading toward town?"

Looking closely at the expression on his face, I seemed to pick up a sadness and anger in his personality.

"I don't think so," I said. "I'm looking for a friend who is out here somewhere. What did the person you met look like?"

"It was a woman with blond hair and bright eyes," he replied. "She talked rapidly. I didn't catch her name. Who are you looking for?"

"Charlene Billings. Is there anything else about the woman you saw that you can remember?"

"She said something about the National Forest that made me think she might be one of those *searcher* types that hang out around here. But I couldn't tell. She warned me to leave the valley. She told me she had to get her gear and then she was leaving also. She seemed to think something was wrong out here, that everyone was in danger. She was actually very secretive. Frankly I didn't know what she was talking about." His tone suggested he was accustomed to speaking with directness.

As friendly as possible I said, "It sounds as if the person you met could have been my friend. Where did you see her exactly?"

He pointed toward the south, and told me he had run into her about half a mile back. She had been walking alone and had headed southeast from there.

"I'll walk with you as far as the spring," I said.

I picked up my pack, and as we walked down the hill, he asked, "If that was your friend, where do you think she was going?"

"I don't know."

"Into some mystical space, perhaps? Looking for utopia." He was smiling cynically.

I realized he was baiting me. "Maybe," I said. "Don't you believe in the possibility of utopia?"

"No, of course not. It's neolithic thinking. Naive."

I glanced at him, fatigue beginning to overwhelm me, trying to end the conversation. "Just a difference of opinion, I guess."

He laughed. "No, it's fact. There's no utopia coming. Everything is getting worse out there, not better. Economically things are swinging out of control, and eventually it will explode."

"Why do you say that?"

"It's simple demographics. For most of this century there has been a large middle class in the Western countries, a class who have promoted order and reason and carried a general faith that the economic system could work for everyone.

"But this faith is beginning to collapse now. You can see it everywhere. Fewer people every day now believe in the system, or play by the rules. And it's all because the middle class is shrinking. Technological development is making labor valueless and splitting human culture into two groups: the haves and the have-nots, those who have investments and ownership in the world economy and those who are restricted to menial, service jobs. Couple this with the failure of education and you can see the scope of the problem."

"That sounds awfully cynical," I said.

"It's realistic. It's the truth. For most people it takes more and more effort just to survive out there. Have you seen the surveys on stress? Tension is off the scale. Nobody feels secure, and the worst hasn't even begun yet. Population is exploding, and as technology expands even more, the distance will grow between the educated and the uneducated, and the haves will control more and more of the global economy, while drugs and crime will continue to soar with the have-nots.

"And what do you think," he continued, "will happen in the underdeveloped countries? Already much of the Middle East and Africa is in the hands of religious fundamentalists whose aim is to destroy organized civilization, which they think is a satanic empire, and replace it with some kind of perverted theocracy, where religious leaders are in charge of everything and they have the sanctioned power to condemn to death those they consider heretics, anywhere in the world

"What kind of people would agree with this kind of butchery in the name of spirituality? Yet they are increasing every day. China still practices female infanticide, for example. Do you believe that?

"I'm telling you: law and order and respect for human life are on their way out. The world is degenerating into a mob mentality, ruled by envy and revenge and led by shrewd charlatans, and it's probably too late to stop it. But do you know what? Nobody really cares. Nobody! The politicians won't do anything. All they care about is their personal fiefdoms, and how to retain them. The world is changing too fast. No one can catch up, and that makes us just look out for number one and get whatever we can as fast as we can, before it's too late. This sentiment permeates the whole of civilization and every occupational group."

He took a breath and looked at me. I had stopped on the crest of one of the hills to view the impending sunset, and our eyes met. He seemed to realize he had gotten carried away with his tirade, and in that moment he began to look deeply familiar to me. I told him my name and he responded with his, Joel Lipscomb. We looked at each other for another long moment, but he offered no indication that he knew me. Why had we met in this valley?

As soon as I had formulated that last question in my mind, I knew the answer. He was voicing the vision of Fear that Williams had mentioned. A chill ran through me. This was supposed to happen.

I looked at him with a new seriousness. "Do you really think things are that bad?"

"Yes, absolutely," he replied. "I'm a journalist, and you can see this attitude playing out in our profession. In the past we at least attempted to do our job with certain standards of integrity. But no longer. It's all hype and sensationalism. No one's looking for the truth anymore or trying to present it in the most accurate way. Journalists are looking for the scoop, the most outrageous perspective—every bit of dirt they can dig up.

"Even if particular accusations have a logical explanation, they are reported anyway, for their impact on ratings and circulation. In a world where the people are numbed and distracted, the only thing that sells is the unbelievable. And the pity is that this kind of journalism is self-perpetuating. A young journalist looks at this situation and thinks that to survive in the business he has to play the game. If he doesn't, he thinks he'll be left behind, ruined, which is what leads to so-called investigative reports being intentionally faked. It happens all the time."

We had proceeded south and were making our way down the rocky terrain.

"Other occupational groups suffer from the same condition," Joel went on. "God, look at attorneys. Perhaps there was a time when being an officer of the court meant something, when the participants in the process shared a common respect for the truth, for justice. But no longer. Think about the recent celebrity trials covered by television. Lawyers now do everything they can to subvert justice, intentionally, trying to convince jurors to believe the hypothetical when there is no evidence—hypotheticals that the attorneys know are lies—just to get someone off. And other attorneys comment on the proceedings as though these tactics are common practice and absolutely justified under our system of law, which is not true.

"Under our system, everyone is entitled to a fair trial. But the lawyers are beholden to ensure fairness and correctness, not to distort the truth and undermine justice simply to get their client off at all costs. Because of television, at least we've been able to see these corrupt practices for what they represent: simple expediency on the part of trial lawyers to enhance their reputations in order to command higher fees. The reason they're so blatant is that they think no one cares, and obviously no one does. Everyone else is doing the same thing.

"We're cutting corners, maximizing short-term profits instead of planning long-term, because inside, consciously or unconsciously, we don't think our success can last. And we're doing this even if we have to break the spirit of trust we have with others and advance our own interests at the expense of someone else.

"Pretty soon all the subtle assumptions and agreements that hold civilization together will be totally subverted. Think what will happen once unemployment gets to a certain level in the inner cities. Crime is out of control now. Police officers aren't going to keep risking their lives for a public that doesn't notice anyway. Why find yourself on the stand twice a week getting grilled by some attorney who's not interested in the truth anyway, or worse, writhing in pain while your lifeblood runs out on the ground in some dark alley somewhere, when no one cares? Better to look the other way and do your twenty years as quietly as possible, maybe even take a few bribes on the side. And it goes on and on. What's going to stop it?"

He paused and I glanced back at him as we walked.

"I guess you think some spiritual renaissance is going to change all this?" he asked.

"I sure hope so."

He struggled over a fallen tree to catch up with me. "Listen," he continued, "I bought into this spirituality stuff for a while, this idea of purpose and destiny and Insights. I could even see some interesting coincidences happening in my own life. But I decided it was all crazy. The human mind can imagine all sorts of silly things; we don't even realize we're doing it. When you get right down to it, all this talk of spirituality is just weird rhetoric."

I started to counter his argument but changed my mind. My intuition was to hear him out first.

"Yeah," I said. "I guess it sometimes sounds that way."

"Take for instance the talk I've heard about this valley," he went on. "That's the kind of nonsense I used to listen to. This is just a valley full of trees and bushes like a thousand others." He put his hand on a large tree as we passed. "You think this National Forest is going to survive? Forget it. With the way humans are polluting the oceans, and saturating the ecosystem with man-made carcinogenics, and consuming paper and other wood products, this place will become a garbage bin, like everywhere else. In fact, no one cares about trees now. How do you think the government gets away with building roads in here at taxpayer expense and then selling the timber at below-market value? Or

swapping the best, most beautiful areas for ruined land somewhere else, just to make the developers happy?

"You probably think something mystical is happening here in
this valley. And why not? Everyone would love for there to be
something mystical going on, especially considering the diminishing quality of life. But the fact is, there's nothing esoteric happening. We're just animals, creatures smart enough and unlucky
enough to have figured out we're alive, and we're going to die
without ever knowing any purpose. We can pretend all we want
and we can wish all we want, but that basic existential fact remains—we can't know."

I looked back at him again. "Don't you believe in any kind of
spirituality?"

He laughed. "If a God exists, he must be an exceedingly cruel
monster of a God. There couldn't be a spiritual reality operating
here! How could there be? Look at the world. What kind of God
would design such a devastating place where children die horri-
bly by earthquakes and senseless crimes and *starvation,* when res-
taurants toss out tons of food every day?

"Although," he added, "perhaps that's the way it's supposed
to be. Perhaps that's God's plan. Maybe the 'end times' scholars
are correct. They think life and history are all just a test of faith
to see who will win salvation and who won't, a divine plan to
destroy civilization in order to separate the believers from the
wicked." He attempted a smile, but it quickly faded as he drifted
into his own thoughts.

Finally he quickened his pace to walk up even with me. We
were entering the sage meadow again, and I could see the crow
tree a quarter of a mile away.

"Do you know what these end-times people really believe is

happening?" he asked. "I did a study of them several years ago; they're fascinating."

"Not really," I said, nodding for him to go on.

"They study the prophecies hidden in the Bible, especially in the book of Revelation. They believe that we live in what they call the *last days,* the time when all the prophecies will come true. Essentially what they think is this: History is now set up for the return of the Christ and the creation of the heavenly kingdom on Earth. But before this can occur the Earth has to suffer a series of wars, natural disasters, and other apocalyptic events predicted in the Scriptures. And they know every one of these predictions, so they spend their time watching world events very closely, waiting for the next event on the timetable."

"What's the next event?" I asked.

"A peace treaty in the Middle East that will allow the rebuilding of the Temple in Jerusalem. Sometime after that, according to them, a massive rapture will begin among true believers, whoever they are, and they will be snatched off the face of the Earth and lifted into Heaven."

I stopped and looked at him. "They think these people will begin to disappear?"

"Yeah, that's in the Bible. Then comes the tribulation, which is a seven-year period when all hell breaks loose for whoever is left on Earth. Apparently everything is expected to fall apart: giant earthquakes destroy the economy; ocean levels destroy many cities; plus rioting and crime and the rest of it. And then a politician emerges, probably in Europe, who offers a plan to pull things back together, if, of course, he's set up with supreme power. This includes a centralized electronic economy which co-ordinates commerce in most parts of the world. To participate in this economy, however, and take advantage of the automation, one has to swear allegiance to this leader and have a chip implanted in one's hand, through which all economic interactions are documented.

"This Antichrist at first protects Israel and facilitates a peace treaty, then attacks later, starting a world war that ultimately involves the Islamic nations, Russia, and finally China. According to the prophecies, just as Israel is about to fall, the angels of God swoop down and win the war, installing a spiritual utopia that lasts a thousand years."

He cleared his throat and looked at me. "Walk through a religious bookstore sometime and look around; there are commentaries and novels about these prophecies everywhere, and more coming out all the time."

"Do you think these end-times scholars are correct?"

He shook his head "I don't think so. The only prophecy that's being played out in this world is man's greed and corruption. Some dictator might rise up and take over, but it will be because he saw a way to take advantage of the chaos."

"Do you think this will happen?"

"I don't know, but I'll tell you one thing. If the collapse of the middle class continues, and the poor get poorer and the inner cities get more crime-infested and spread into the suburbs, and then on top of that we experience, say, a series of big natural disasters and the whole economy crashes for a while, we'll have bands of hungry marauders preying on the masses and total panic everywhere. In the face of this kind of violence, if someone comes along and proposes a way to save us, to straighten things out, asking only that we surrender some civil liberties, I have no doubt that we'll do it."

We stopped and drank some water from my canteen. Fifty yards ahead was the crow tree.

I perked up; far in the background I could detect the faint dissonance of the hum.

Joel's eyes squinted in concentration, watching me closely. "What are you hearing?"

I turned around and faced him. "It's a strange noise, a hum we've been perceiving. I think it may be some kind of experiment going on in the valley."

"What kind of experiment? Who's conducting it? Why can't I hear it?"

I was about to tell him more when we were interrupted by another sound. We listened carefully.

"That's a vehicle," I said.

Two more gray Jeeps were approaching from the west and heading toward us. We ran behind a patch of tall briers and hid, and they passed within a hundred yards without stopping, heading southeast along the same path the earlier Jeep had followed.

"I don't like this," Joel said. "Who was that?"

"Well, it's not the Forest Service, and no one else is supposed to be driving in here. I think it must be the people involved with the experiment."

He looked horrified.

"If you want," I said, "you can take a more direct route back to town. Just head southwest toward that ridge in the distance. You'll run into the stream after about three-quarters of a mile and you can follow it west into town from there. I think you can arrive before it gets too dark."

"You're not coming?"

"Not now. I'm going directly south to the stream and wait awhile for my friend."

He tensed his forehead. "These people couldn't be conducting an experiment without someone in the Forest Service know-ing about it."

"I know."

"You don't think you can do anything about this, do you? This is something big."

I didn't respond; a pang of anxiety rushed through me.

He listened for a moment and then moved past me into the valley, walking quickly. He looked back once and shook his head.

I watched him until he crossed the meadow and disappeared into the forest on the other side, then I hurriedly walked toward the south, thinking again of Charlene. What had she been doing out here? Where was she going? I had no answers.

Pushing hard, I reached the stream in about thirty minutes. The sun was now completely hidden by the band of clouds at the western horizon, and the twilight cast the woods in ominous gray tones. I was tired and dirty, and I knew that listening to Joel and seeing the Jeeps had affected my mood severely. Perhaps I had enough evidence now to go to the authorities; perhaps that was the way I could help Charlene most. Several options danced through my head, all rationalizing my return to town.

Because the woods on both sides of the stream were thin, I decided to wade across and make my way into the thicker forest on the other side, although I knew that area was private property.

Once across, I stopped abruptly, hearing another Jeep, then broke into a run. Fifty feet ahead the land rose quickly into a knob of boulders and outcroppings, twenty feet high. Climbing quickly, I reached the top and accelerated my pace, then leaped upon a pile of large rocks, intending to jump them quickly to the other side. When my foot hit the topmost rock, the huge stone rolled forward, throwing my feet out from under me and starting the whole pile moving. I bounced once on my hip and landed in a small gully, the pile still tumbling my way. Several of the rocks, each two or three feet in diameter, were careening down, coming squarely for my chest. I had time to roll onto my left side and raise my arms, but I knew I couldn't get out of the way.

Then, out of the corner of my eye, I saw a wispy white form moving in front of my body. Simultaneously an unusual knowing came over me that the huge rocks would somehow miss. I closed my eyes and heard them crash on both sides. Slowly I opened my eyes and peered out through the dust, wiping the dirt and rock chips from my face. The rocks were lying neatly beside me. How had that happened? What was that white form?

For a moment I looked around the scene, and then behind one of the rocks I saw a slight movement. A small bobcat cub eased around and looked directly into my eyes. I knew it was big enough to have run away, but it was lingering, looking at me.

The rising sound of the approaching vehicle finally sent the bobcat scampering into the woods. I jumped to my feet and ran several more steps before landing awkwardly on another rock. A bolt of throbbing pain raced through my whole leg as my left foot gave way. I fell to the ground and crawled the last two yards into the trees. I rolled around behind a huge oak as the vehicle pulled up to the stream, slowed for a few minutes, then raced away, again toward the southeast.

My heart pounding, I sat up and pulled off my boot to inspect the ankle. It was already beginning to swell. Why this? I thought. As I slid around to stretch out my leg, I observed a woman staring at me from about thirty feet away. I froze as she walked toward me.

"Are you all right?" she asked, her voice concerned but wary. She was a tall black woman, perhaps forty, dressed in loose-fitting sweat clothes and tennis shoes. Strands of dark hair had pulled out of her ponytail and dangled in the breeze above her temples. In her hand was a small green knapsack.

"I was sitting over there and saw you fall," she said. "I'm a doctor. Do you want me to take a look?"

"I'd appreciate that," I said dizzily, not believing the coincidence.

She knelt down beside me and moved the foot gently, at the same time surveying the area toward the creek. "Are you out here alone?"

I told her briefly about looking for Charlene, but left out everything else. She said she had seen no one of that description. As she talked, finally introducing herself as Maya Ponder, I became convinced that she was completely trustworthy. I told her my name and where I lived.

When I finished, she said, "I'm from Asheville, although I have a health center, with a partner, a few miles south of here. It's new. We also own forty acres of the valley right here that joins the National Forest." She pointed to the area where we were sitting. "And another forty acres up the ridge to the south."

I unzipped a pocket on my hiking pack and pulled out my canteen.

"Would you like some water?" I asked.

"No thanks, I have some." She reached inside her own pack, retrieved a canteen, and opened the top. But instead of drinking, she soaked a small towel and wrapped my foot, an action that made me grimace in pain.

Turning and looking into my eyes, she said, "You've definitely sprained this ankle."

"How badly?" I asked.

She hesitated. "What do you think?"

"I don't know. Let me try to walk on it."

I attempted to stand, but she stopped me. "Wait a minute," she said. "Before you try to walk, analyze your attitude. How badly do you think you're hurt?"

"What do you mean?"

"I mean that very often your recuperation time depends on what *you* think, not me."

I looked down at the ankle. "I think it could be pretty bad. If it is, I'll have to get back to town somehow."

"What then?"

"I don't know. If I can't walk, I may have to go find someone else to look for Charlene."

"Do you have any idea why this accident happened now?"

"Not really. Why does that matter?"

"Because, again, very often your attitude about why an accident or illness has happened has an effect on your recuperation."

I looked at her closely, well aware that I was resisting. Part of me felt as though I didn't have time for this discussion right now. It seemed too self-involved for the situation. Although the hum had ceased, I had to assume that the experiment was continuing. Everything felt too dangerous and it was almost dark . . . and Charlene could be in terrible trouble for all I knew.

I was also aware of a deep sense of guilt toward Maya. Why would I feel guilty? I tried to shake off the emotion.

"What kind of doctor are you?" I asked, sipping some water.

She smiled, and for the first time I saw her energy lift. She had decided to trust me too.

"Permit me to tell you about the kind of medicine I practice," she said. "Medicine is changing, and changing rapidly. We don't think of the body as a machine anymore, with parts that eventually wear out and have to be fixed or replaced. We're beginning to understand that the health of the body is determined to a great degree by our mental processes: what we think of life and especially of ourselves, at both the conscious and the unconscious levels.

"This represents a fundamental shift. Under the old method the doctor was the expert and healer, and the patient the passive recipient, hoping the doctor would have all the answers. But we know now that the inner attitude of the patient is crucial. A key factor is fear and stress and the way we handle it. Sometimes the fear is conscious, but very often we repress it entirely.

"This is the brave, macho attitude: deny the problem, push it away, conjure up our heroic agenda. If we take this attitude, then the fear continues to eat at us unconsciously. Adopting a positive outlook is very important in staying healthy, but we have to engage in this attitude in full awareness, using love, not macho, for this attitude to be completely effective. What I believe is that our unspoken fears create blocks or crimps in the body's energy flow, and it's these blocks that ultimately result in problems. The fears keep manifesting in ever-greater degrees until we deal with them. Physical problems are the last step. Ideally these blocks would be dealt with early, in a preventive way, before illness develops."

"So you think all illness can ultimately be prevented or cured?"

"Yes, I'm sure we will have longer or shorter life spans; that's probably up to the Creator, but we don't have to be sick, and we don't have to be the victim of so many accidents."

"So you think this applies to an accident, like my sprain, as well as to illnesses?"

She smiled. "Yes, in many cases."

I was confused. "Look, I don't have time for this right now. I'm really worried about my friend. I've got to do something!"

"I know, but I have a hunch this conversation won't take

long. If you rush by and disregard what I'm saying, you may miss the meaning of what is obviously quite a coincidence here." She looked at me to see whether I had picked up on her reference to the Manuscript.

"You're aware of the Insights?" I asked.

She nodded.

"What exactly do you suggest I do?"

"Well, the technique I've had great success with is this: first, we try to remember the nature of your thoughts just prior to the health problem—in your case, the sprain. What were you thinking? What is the fear this problem is revealing to you?"

I thought for a moment, then said, "I felt afraid, ambivalent. The situation here in this valley seemed much more sinister than I thought. I didn't feel as though I could handle it. On the other hand, I knew Charlene might need help. I was confused and torn over what to do."

"So you sprained your ankle?"

I leaned toward her. "Are you saying that I sabotaged myself so I wouldn't have to take action? Isn't that too simple?"

"That's for you to say, not me. But very often it is simple. Besides, the most important thing is not to spend time defending or proving. Just play with it. Try to remember everything you can about where the health problem came from. Explore for yourself."

"How do I do that?"

"You have to calm your mind and receive this information."

"Intuitively?"

"Intuitively, prayerfully, however you conceive the process."

I resisted again, not sure whether I could relax and clear my mind. Finally I closed my eyes, and for a moment my thoughts ceased, but then a succession of memories of Wil and the day's events intruded. I let them go by and cleared my mind again. Immediately I saw a scene of myself at age ten, limping away from a touch football game, well aware that I was faking the injury. That's right! I thought. I used to fake sprains to avoid having to perform under pressure. I had forgotten all about this! I realized that later I began to actually hurt the ankle frequently, in all kinds of situations. As I pondered the memory, another flash of recollection entered my mind, a cloudy scene of myself in another time, feeling cocky, confident, impulsive, then as I worked in a dark, candlelit room, the door crashed in and I was dragged away in terror.

I opened my eyes and looked at Maya "Maybe I have something."

I shared the content of my childhood memory, but the other vision felt too vague to be described, so I didn't mention it.

Afterward, Maya asked, "What do you think?"

"I don't know; the sprain seemed the result of pure chance. It's hard to imagine that the accident came from this need to avoid the situation. Besides, I've been in worse situations than this many times and I didn't sprain an ankle. Why did it happen now?"

She looked thoughtful. "Who knows? Perhaps now is the time to see through the habit. Accidents, illness, healing, they're all more mysterious than any of us ever imagined. I believe that we have an undiscovered ability to influence what happens to us in the future, including whether we are healthy—although, again, the power has to remain with the individual patient.

"There was a reason that I didn't offer an opinion concerning how badly you were hurt. We in the medical establishment have learned that medical opinions have to be offered very carefully. Over the years the public has developed almost a worship of doctors, and when a physician says something, patients have tended to take these opinions totally to heart. The country doctors of a hundred years ago knew this, and would use this principle to actually paint an overly optimistic picture of any health situation. If the doctor said that the patient would get better, very often the patient would internalize this idea in his or her mind and actually defy all odds to recover. In later years, however, ethical considerations have prevented such distortions, and the establishment has felt that the patient is entitled to a cold scientific assessment of his or her situation.

"Unfortunately when this was given, sometimes patients dropped dead right before our eyes, just because they were told their condition was terminal. We know now that we have to be very careful with these assessments, because of the power of our minds. We want to focus this power in a positive direction. The body is capable of miraculous regeneration. Body parts thought of in the past as solid forms are actually energy systems that can transform overnight. Have you read the latest research on prayer? The simple fact that this kind of spiritual visualization is being scientifically proven to work totally undermines our old physical model of healing. We're having to work out a new model."

She paused and poured more water on the towel around my ankle, then continued, "I believe the first step in the process is to identify the fear with which the medical problem seems to be connected; this opens up the energy block in your body to conscious healing. The next step is to pull in as much energy as possible and focus it at the exact location of the block."

I was about to ask how this was done, but she stopped me. "Go ahead and raise your energy level as much as you can."

Accepting her guidance, I began to observe the beauty around me and to concentrate on a spiritual connection within, evoking a heightened sensation of love. Gradually the colors became more vivid and everything in my awareness increased in presence. I could tell that she was raising her own energy at the same time.

When I felt as though my vibration had increased as much as possible, I looked at her.

She smiled back at me. "Okay, now you can focus the energy on the block."

"How do I do that?" I asked.

"You use the pain. That's why it's there, to help you focus."

"What? Isn't the idea to get rid of pain?"

"Unfortunately that's what we've always thought, but pain is really a beacon."

"A beacon?"

"Yes," she said, pressing several locations on my foot. "How badly does it hurt right now?"

"It's a throbbing ache, but not too bad."

She unwrapped the towel. "Focus your attention on the pain and try to feel it as much as possible. Determine its exact location."

"I know where it is. It's in the ankle."

"Yes, but the ankle is a large area. Where exactly?"

I studied the throbbing. She was correct. I had been generalizing the pain to the whole ankle. But as my leg was stretched out with the toes of my foot pointed upward, the pain was more precisely centered in the top left portion of this joint and about an inch inward.

"Okay," I said. "I've got that."

"Now place all your attention on that specific area. Be there with all of your being."

For a few minutes I said nothing. With total concentration I felt this location in my ankle completely. I noticed that all the other perceptions of my body—breathing, the location of my hands and arms, sticky sweat on the back of my neck—faded far into the background.

"Feel the pain totally," she reminded.

"Okay," I said. "I'm there."

"What's happening with the pain?" she asked.

"I still feel it, but it has changed in character or something. It's becoming warmer, less bothersome, more like a tingling." As I talked, the pain began to take on its normal sensation again.

"What happened?" I asked.

"I believe that pain serves another function beyond just telling us that something is wrong. Perhaps it also points out exactly where the difficulty is, so that we can follow it into our bodies like a beacon and place our attention and energy in exactly the right spot. It's almost as if both the pain and our concentrated attention can't occupy the same space. Of course, in cases of severe pain, where concentration is impossible, we can use anesthetics to ease the intensity, although I think it's best to leave some pain so that the beacon effect can be utilized."

She paused and looked at me.

"What's next?" I asked.

"Next," she replied, "is to consciously send higher divine energy into the exact spot identified by the pain, intending that the love will transform the cells there into a state of perfect functioning."

I just stared.

"Go ahead," she said. "Get completely connected again. I'll guide you through it."

I nodded when I was ready.

"Feel the pain with all your being," she began, "and now

image your love energy going right into the heart of the pain, lifting that exact point of your body, the atoms themselves, into a higher vibration. See the particles take a quantum jump into the pure energy pattern that is their optimum state. Literally feel a tingling sensation in that spot as the vibration accelerates."

After pausing for a full minute, she continued. "Now, without changing your focus on the point of the pain, begin to feel your energy, the tingle, moving up both legs . . . through your hips . . . into your abdomen and chest . . . and finally into your neck and head. Feel your whole body tingling with the higher vibration. See every organ operating at optimal efficiency."

I followed her instructions exactly, and after a few moments my whole body felt lighter, more energized. I held that state for about ten minutes, then opened my eyes and looked at Maya.

Using a flashlight in the darkness, Maya was putting up my tent on a flat area between two pines. Glancing over at me, she said, "Feel better?"

I nodded.

"Do you understand the process so far?"

"I think so. I sent energy into the pain."

"Yes, but what we did earlier was just as important. You begin by looking at the meaning of the injury or illness, what its occurrence is pointing out about some fear in your life that is holding you back, manifesting in your body. This is what opens the fear block so that the visualization can penetrate.

"After the block is open, then you can use pain as a beacon, raising the vibration in that area and then in your entire body. But finding the origin of the fear is vitally important. When the origin of the illness or accident is very deep, it often requires hypnosis or intensive counseling."

I told her about the medieval image I had seen of the door being kicked in and of myself being dragged away.

She looked thoughtful. "Sometimes the root of the block goes back a very long way. But as you explore it further, and begin to work through the fear that is holding you back, you will usually discover a fuller understanding of who you are, of what your current life on Earth is all about. And this sets the stage for the last—and, I firmly believe, the most important—step in the healing process. Most important of all is to look deeply enough to *remember* what you want to do with your life. Real healing takes place when we can envision a new kind of future for ourselves that excites us. *Inspiration* is what keeps us well. People aren't healed to watch more TV."

I looked at her for a moment, then said, "You mentioned that prayer works. How is the best way to pray for someone who is not well?"

"We're still trying to figure that out. It has something to do with the Eighth Insight process of sending the energy and love that flow through us from the divine source to the person, and at the same time visualizing that the individual will remember what they really want to do with their life. Of course, sometimes what the person remembers is that it's time to make a transition into the other dimension. When that's the case, we have to accept it."

Maya was finishing with the tent and added, "Also keep in mind that the procedures I've recommended should be done in conjunction with the very best in traditional medicine. If we were near my clinic, I would take you in for a full examination, but in this case, unless you disagree, I suggest you stay here tonight. It's better if you don't move much."

As I watched, she set up my stove, turned it on, and placed a boiler containing freeze-dried soup on the flame. "I'm going back into town. I need to get a splint for your ankle and some other supplies, just in case we need them, then I'll hike back out and check on you. I'll bring a radio too, in case we have to send for help."

I nodded.

She poured her canteen's water into mine and looked over at me. Behind her, the last streak of light was vanishing toward the west.

"Did you say your clinic was near here?" I asked.

"Actually it's only about four miles to the south," she said, "over the ridge, but there's no way to come into the valley from that direction. The only pass is the main road that comes in south of town."

"How did you happen to be here?"

She smiled and looked slightly embarrassed. "It's funny. I had a dream last night about hiking into the valley again, and this morning I decided I would do just that. I've been working hard and I guess I needed some time to reflect on what I'm doing at the clinic. My partner and I have a great deal of experience with alternative approaches, Chinese medicine, herbs, yet at the same time, we have the resources of the world's best in traditional medicine at our fingertips through computer. I'd dreamed about this kind of clinic for years."

She paused for a moment, then said, "Before you showed up I was sitting right over there, and my energy just shot through the roof. It seemed as though I could see the whole story of my life, every experience I've had, from my early childhood all the way up until this moment, stretched out before me in plain view. It was the clearest Sixth Insight experience I've ever had.

"All those events were a preparation," she continued. "I grew up in a family where my mother struggled with chronic disease all her life, but would never participate in her own healing. At the time, the doctors knew no better, but throughout my childhood, her refusal to explore her own fears irritated me, and I noticed every bit of new information about diet, vitamins, stress levels, meditation, and their role in health, trying to convince her to become involved. During my adolescence I was torn between joining the clergy and becoming a doctor. I don't know; it was as if I was driven to figure out how we use insight, faith, to change the future, to heal.

"And my father," she continued. "He was something else. He worked in the biological sciences, but he never would explain any of his results except in his academic papers. 'Pure research,' he called it. His associates treated him like a god. He was unapproachable, the ultimate authority. I was grown, and he had died of cancer, before I understood his real interest—the immune system, and specifically how commitment and excitement with life enhance the immune system.

"He was the first one to see this relationship, and that's what all the current research shows now. Yet I never got to talk with him about it. At first I wondered why I would be born to a father who behaved like that. But I finally accepted the fact that my parents had the exact combination of traits and interests to inspire my own evolution. That's why I wanted to be with them in my early life. Looking at my mother, I knew that each of us must take responsibility for our own healing. We can't just turn it over to others. Healing in its essence is about breaking through the fears associated with life—fears that we don't want to face—and finding our own special inspiration, a vision of the future, that we know we're here to help create.

"From my father, I saw clearly that medicine must be more

responsive, must acknowledge the intuition and vision of the people we treat. We have to come down from our ivory tower. The combination of the two set me up to look for a new paradigm in medicine: one based on the patient's ability to take control of his or her life and to get back on the right path. That's my message, I guess, the idea that inwardly we know how to participate in our own healing, physically and emotionally. We can become inspired to shape a higher, more ideal future, and when we do, *miracles happen*."

Standing up, she glanced at my ankle, then at me. "I'm leaving now," she said. "Try not to put any weight on your foot. What you need is complete rest. I'll be back in the morning."

I think I must have looked anxious, because she knelt down again and put both hands on the ankle. "Don't worry," she said. "With enough energy there's nothing that can't be healed—hatred . . . war. It's just a matter of coming together with the right vision." She patted my foot gently. "We can heal this! We can heal this!"

She smiled once, then turned and walked away.

I suddenly wanted to call out and tell her everything I had experienced in the other dimension and what I knew about the Fear and about the group coming back, but instead I remained quiet, fatigue overwhelming me, content to watch her disappear into the trees. Tomorrow would be soon enough, I thought . . . because I knew exactly who she was.

# REMEMBERING

The next morning I jerked awake, the shrill cry of a hawk, high overhead, pulling me into awareness. For a few moments I listened carefully, imagining her lofty rolls. She cried one more time then stopped. I sat up quickly and looked through the tent flap; the day was cloudy but warm, and a light breeze swayed the treetops.

Taking an Ace bandage from my pack, I carefully wrapped the ankle, working the joint carefully and feeling very little pain, then crawled out of the tent and stood up. After a few moments I put weight on my foot and took a tentative step. The ankle felt weak, but if I limped slightly, it seemed to support me. I wondered: had Maya's procedure helped, or had the ankle not been hurt that badly? There was no way to know.

Digging into my pack again, I retrieved a change of clothes, then grabbed the dirty dishes from the night before. Cautiously, alert for any odd sound or movement, I made my way back to the stream. When I located a place where I was shielded from view, I slipped off my clothes and entered the water, finding it cold and refreshing. I lay there without thinking, trying to forget the anxiety rising in my gut, gazing out at the colors of the leaves above my head.

Suddenly I began to recall a dream from the night before. I was sitting on a rock . . . something was happening . . . Wil was there . . . and others. I vaguely remembered a field of blue and amber. I struggled a moment longer but could recall nothing more.

As I opened a bottle of soap, I noticed that the trees and bushes around me were amplified in appearance. Somehow the act of remembering my dream had increased my energy. Feeling lighter, I hastily bathed and washed off the dishes, noticing as I finished that a large rock to my right looked very similar to the one on which I was sitting in my dream. I stopped and inspected the boulder more closely. Flat and about ten feet in diameter, its shape and color matched exactly.

In a few minutes I had taken down the tent, packed, and hidden my gear under some fallen limbs. Then, returning to the rock, I sat down and tried to recall the blue field and the exact position Wil had occupied in the dream. He had been to my left and slightly behind me. At that moment a clear image of his face came to my mind, as in a close-up photo. Struggling to maintain the exact detail, I re-created his image and surrounded it with the blue field.

Seconds later I felt a pulling sensation in my solar plexus, and then I was again streaking through the colors. When I stopped, the environment was pale blue and luminous, and Wil was beside me.

"Thank God you're back!" he said, moving in closer. "You became so dense I couldn't find you."

"What happened before?" I asked. "Why did the hum get so loud?"

"I don't know."

"Where are we now?"

"It's a particular level where dreams seem to take place."

I looked out into the blue. Nothing was moving. "You've been here?"

"Yes, I came here before I found you at the falls, although at the time I didn't know why."

For a moment we both surveyed the environment again, then Wil asked, "What happened to you when you went back?"

With excitement I began to describe everything that had occurred, focusing first on Joel's forecast of environmental and civil collapse. Wil listened intently, digesting every aspect of Joel's outlook.

"He was voicing the Fear," Wil commented.

I nodded. "That's what I think. Do you suppose all of what he said is really occurring?" I asked.

"I think the danger is that a lot of people are beginning to believe it's happening. Remember what the Ninth Insight said: as the spiritual renaissance progresses, it must overcome a polarization of Fear."

I caught Wil's eye. "I met someone else, a woman."

Wil listened as I described my experience with Maya, particularly the injury to my ankle and her healing procedures.

When I finished, he gazed into the distance, thinking.

"I think Maya is the woman in Williams' vision," I added. "The woman who was trying to stop the war with the Native Americans."

"Perhaps her idea of healing holds the key to dealing with the Fear," Wil replied.

I nodded for him to continue.

"This all makes sense," he said. "Look at what has already occurred. You came here searching for Charlene and met David, who said the Tenth was a greater understanding of the spiritual renaissance happening on this planet, an understanding attained by grasping our relationship to the Afterlife dimension. He said the Insight has something to do with clarifying the nature of intuitions, of maintaining them in our minds, of seeing our synchronistic path in a fuller way.

"Later, you figured out how to maintain your intuitions in this way and found me at the falls, and I confirmed that maintaining the intuitions, the mental images of ourselves, was the operative mode in the Afterlife as well, and that humans are moving into alignment with this other dimension. Soon after, we found ourselves watching Williams' Life Review, watching him agonize over not remembering something he had wanted to do, which was to come together with a group of people to help deal with this Fear that threatens our spiritual awakening.

"He says we have to understand this Fear in order to do something about it, and then we get separated and you run into a journalist, Joel, who takes a long time to enunciate what? A fearful vision of the future. In fact, a fear of the complete destruction of civilization.

"Then, of course, you next run into a woman whose life is all about healing, and the way she facilitates healing is to help people work through fear blocks by prodding their memory, helping them to discern why they're on the planet. This *remembering* has to be the key."

A sudden movement drew our attention. Another group of souls seemed to be forming about a hundred feet away.

"They are probably here to help someone with their dreaming," Wil said.

I looked hard at him. "They help us dream?"

"Yes, in a way. Some other souls were here when you dreamed last night."

"How did you know about my dream?"

"When you were jolted back into the physical, I tried to find you but I couldn't. Then, when I waited, I began to see your face, and moved here. The last time I came to this place, I couldn't quite grasp what was occurring, but now I think I understand what happens when we dream."

I shook my head, not comprehending.

He gestured out toward the souls. "It apparently all happens synchronistically. These beings you see probably found themselves here just as I did earlier, by coincidence, and now they're probably waiting to see who comes by in their dream body."

The background hum grew louder and I couldn't respond. I felt confused, dizzy. Wil came closer to me, touching my back again. "Stay with me!" he said. "There's some reason we need to see this."

I struggled to clear my head, then noticed another form manifesting in the space beside the souls. At first I thought other souls were appearing, but then I realized the formation was much larger than anything I'd seen before: a whole scene was being projected in front of us, like a hologram, complete with characters, setting, and dialogue. A single individual seemed to be at the center of the action, a man vaguely familiar. After a moment of concentration I realized that the person before us was Joel.

As we watched, the scene began to unfold, like the plot of a movie. I strained to follow along, but my head was still foggy; I couldn't quite understand what was happening. As the episode progressed and the dialogue became more intense, both the souls and the journalist moved closer together. After several minutes the drama seemed to end, and everyone disappeared.

"What was happening?" I asked.

"The individual in the center of the scene was dreaming," Wil said.

"That was Joel, the man I told you about," I replied.

Wil turned to me in astonishment. "Are you sure?"

"Yes."

"Did you understand the dream he just had?"

"No, I couldn't quite get it. What happened?"

"The dream was about a war of some kind. He was fleeing a bomb-ravaged city with shells exploding all around him, running for his life, thinking of nothing but safety and survival. When he successfully evaded the horror and climbed a mountain to look back at the city, he remembered that his orders had been to meet another group of soldiers and supply a secret part to a new device that would make the enemy weapons inactive. To his horror he now realized that because he had failed to show up, the soldiers and the city were being systematically destroyed before his eyes."

"A nightmare," I commented.

"Yes, but it has meaning. When we dream, we unconsciously travel back to this sleep level, and other souls come and help us. Don't forget what dreams do: they clarify how to handle current situations in our lives. The Seventh Insight says to interpret dreams by superimposing the plot of the dream against the real situation facing us in life."

I turned and looked at Wil. "But what role do the souls play?"

As soon as I had asked that question, we began to move again. Wil kept his hand against my back. When we stopped, the light was shifting to a rich green, but I could observe beautiful waves of amber circulating around us. When I focused intently, the amber streaks became individual souls.

I glanced at Wil, who was smiling broadly. This location seemed to carry an increased mood of celebration and joy. As I watched the souls, several moved directly in front of us and closed together into a group. Their faces were broad and smiling, although still hard to focus on for any length of time.

"They're so full of love," I said.

"See if you can pick up on their knowledge," Wil advised.

When I focused on them with this intent, I realized that these souls were associated with Maya. In fact, they were ecstatic about her recent self-revelations, especially her understanding of the life preparation her mother and father had provided. They seemed to know that Maya had experienced a full Sixth Insight review and was on the verge of remembering why she had been born.

I turned to face Wil, who acknowledged that he, too, was seeing the images.

At this moment I could hear the hum again; my stomach tensed. Wil held my shoulders and back tightly. When the sound had ceased, my vibration fell dramatically, and I looked out at the group of souls, attempting to open up and connect with their energy in an attempt to boost my own. To my amazement they suddenly shifted out of focus and moved away from me to a new position twice as far away.

"What happened?" I asked.

"You tried to connect with them to increase your energy," Wil replied, "instead of going within and connecting directly to God's energy inside. I did this myself once. These souls won't allow you to mistake them for the divine source. They know such an identification would not help your growth."

I concentrated within and my energy returned. "How do we get them back?" I asked.

As soon as I spoke, they returned to their original position.

Wil and I glanced at each other, then he began to stare intensely at the group, a look of surprise on his face.

"What are you seeing?" I asked.

He nodded toward them without breaking his gaze, and I focused on the soul group as well, trying to pick up on their knowledge again. After several moments I began to see Maya. She was immersed in the green environment. Her features seemed slightly different and were glowing brightly, but I was absolutely certain it was her. As I focused on her face, a holographic image appeared in front of us—an image of Maya again in the time of the nineteenth-century war, standing in a log cabin with several other people, excited about stopping the conflict.

She seemed to sense that accomplishing such a feat was just a matter of remembering how to attain the energy. It could be done only if the right people came together with a common intention, she thought. Most attentive was a young man who was richly dressed. I recognized him to be the large man who was later killed with her. Racing forward, the vision moved to her failed attempt to speak with the army leaders and then to the wilderness, where she and the young man were killed.

As we watched, she awakened after her death in the Afterlife and reviewed her lifetime, appalled at how single-mindedly, even naively, she had pursued her goal of stopping the war. She knew many of the others had been correct: the time wasn't right. We had not remembered enough of the Afterlife knowledge to accomplish such a feat. Not yet.

After the review, we saw her move into the green environment, surrounded by the same group of souls that was in front of us now. Amazingly there seemed to be a common core expression in the faces throughout the group. At a certain level, beneath their features, the souls all resembled Maya.

I glanced questioningly at Wil.

"This is Maya's *soul group*," he said.

"What do you mean?" I asked.

"It's a group of souls with whom she resonates closely," he said with excitement. "This makes perfect sense. One of the journeys I took, before I found you, was to another group who, in a way, looked like *you*. I think it was *your* soul group."

Before I could say anything, there was movement in the soul group in front of us. Again, an image of Maya was emerging. Still surrounded by her group in the green environment, she seemed to be standing quietly in front of an intense white light, similar to the one we had seen at Williams' Life Review. She was aware that something very profound was happening. Her ability to move around in the Afterlife had diminished, and her attention was shifting toward Earth again. She could see her prospective mother, newly married, sitting on a porch, wondering if her health would hold up well enough to have a child.

Maya was beginning to realize the great progress that could be achieved if she were to be born to this mother. The woman had deep fears about her own health and so would generate an awareness of health issues very quickly in the mind of a child. It would be the perfect place to develop an interest in medicine and healing, and it wouldn't be a knowledge contemplated on merely intellectual terms, where the ego comes up with some fancy theory and never tests it against the challenges of real life, not if she was growing up with the psychology of this woman. Maya knew that she herself had the tendency to be unrealistic and fanciful, and she had already paid dearly for such brashness. That wouldn't happen again, not with the unconscious memory of what had occurred in the nineteenth century reminding her to be very cautious. No, she would go slow, be more isolated, and the environment established by this woman would be perfect.

Wil caught my eye. "We're seeing what occurred when she began to contemplate her current life," he said.

Maya now envisioned how her relationship with her mother could unfold. She would grow up exposed to her mother's negativity, her fears, her tendency to blame the doctors, which would inspire her interest in the mind/body connection and the patient's responsibility in healing, and she would bring this information back to her mother, who could then become involved in her own recovery. Her mother would become her first patient, and then a key supporter, a prime example of the benefits of the new medicine.

Maya's focus moved to the prospective father, sitting next to the woman on the swing. Occasionally the woman would ask a question and he would utter a one-line answer. Mainly he wanted just to sit and contemplate, not to talk. His mind was virtually exploding with research possibilities and exotic biological questions he knew had never been posed before—most particularly the relationship between inspiration and the immune system. Maya saw the advantages of this aloofness. With him, she would be able to work through her own tendency to delude herself; she would have to think for herself and become realistic, right from the beginning. Eventually she and her father would be able to communicate on a scientific basis, and he would open up and provide her with a rich technical background with which to ground her new methods.

She saw clearly that her birth to these parents could be equally advantageous for them. At the same time her parents were stimulating an early interest in healing, she would be stretching them in a destined direction as well: the mother toward an acceptance of her personal role in avoiding illness, the father toward overcoming his tendency to hide from others and to live only in his head.

As we watched, her vision proceeded past her anticipated birth and into what might happen in childhood. She saw a multitude of specific people arriving in her life at just the right moment to stimulate learning and experience. In medical school, just the right patients and doctors would cross her path to stimulate an alternative orientation in her practice.

Her vision moved to the meeting of her clinic partner and the establishment of a new model of healing. And then her vision revealed something else: she would be involved in a more global awakening. Before us, we saw her discovery of the Insights and then her reunion with a particular group, one of many independent groups that would begin to gravitate together all over the world. These groups would remember who they were at a higher level and be instrumental in overcoming the polarization of Fear.

She suddenly saw herself engaged in important conversations with one particular man. He was large, athletic, capable, and dressed in army fatigues. To my amazement I realized that she knew he was the man with whom she had been killed during the nineteenth century. I focused on him intently and received another shock. This was the same man I had seen in Williams' Life Review, the work colleague he had failed to help awaken.

With this, her vision seemed to amplify to a level beyond my ability to comprehend, her body uniting with the blinding light behind it. All I could receive was that her personal vision of what she might accomplish with this birth was being enveloped within a larger vision that encompassed the whole history and future of humankind. She seemed to see her possible lifetime in ultimate perspective, situated clearly within the full expanse of where humanity had been and where it was going. I could sense all this but could not quite see the images themselves.

Finally Maya's vision seemed to be over, and we could see her again in the green environment, still surrounded by her group. Now they were watching a scene on Earth. Apparently her prospective parents had indeed decided to conceive a child and were coming together in the very act of love that would ensure her conception.

Maya's soul group had intensified in energy and now appeared as a large whitish swirl of moving amber, drawing its intensity from the bright light in the background. I could sense the energy myself as a deeply felt, almost orgasmic level of love and vibration. Down below, the couple embraced, and at the moment of orgasm, a whitish-green energy seemed to flow from the light, passing through Maya and her soul group, and enter into the couple. With an orgasmic rush, the energy came through their bodies toward each other, pushing the sperm and egg toward their fated union.

As we watched, we could see the moment of conception and the miraculous joining of the two cells into one. Slowly at first, and then more rapidly, the cells began to divide and differentiate, finally forming the shape of a human being. When I looked at Maya, I realized that with every cell division, she became more hazy and out of focus. Finally, as the fetus matured, she disappeared from view completely. Her soul group remained.

More knowledge seemed to be available on what we had just witnessed, but I lost concentration and missed it. Then suddenly the soul group itself was gone and Wil and I were left staring at each other. He seemed terribly excited.

"What were we watching?" I asked.

"It was the whole process of Maya's birth into her current lifetime," Wil replied, "held in the memory of her soul group. We got to see it all: her awareness of prospective parents, what she felt might be accomplished, and then the actual way she was drawn into the physical dimension at conception."

I nodded for Wil to continue.

"The act of lovemaking itself opens up a portal from the Afterlife into the Earthly dimension. The soul groups seem to exist in a state of extreme love even beyond what you and I can experience, extreme to the point that it feels orgasmic in nature. Sexual culmination creates an opening into the Afterlife, and what we experience as orgasm is just a glimpse of the Afterlife level of love and vibration as the portal is opened and the energy rushes through, potentially bringing in a new soul. We watched that happen. Sexual union is a holy moment in which a part of Heaven flows into the Earth."

I nodded, thinking about the implications of what we had seen, then said, "Maya seemed to know how her life could turn out if she was born to these particular parents."

"Yes, apparently, before we are born, each of us experiences a vision of what our life can be, complete with reflections on our parents and on our tendencies to engage in particular control dramas, even how we might work through these dramas with these parents and go on to be prepared for what we want to accomplish."

"I saw most of that," I said, "but it seemed strange. Based on what she told me about her real life, her pre-life vision was more ideal than what really happened—for instance, her relationship to her family. It didn't exactly turn out the way she wanted. Her mother never understood Maya, or faced her own illness, and her father was so aloof she never knew what he was researching until after his death."

"But that makes sense," Wil said. "The vision apparently is an ideal guide for what our highest self intends to happen in life, the best-case scenario, so to speak, if all of us were following our intuitions perfectly. What actually occurs is an approximation of this vision, the best everyone can do under the actual circumstances. But all this is more Tenth Insight information about the Afterlife that clarifies our spiritual experience on Earth, particularly the perception of coincidences, and how synchronicity really operates.

"When we have an intuition or a dream to pursue a particular course in our lives and we follow this guidance, certain events transpire that feel like magic coincidences. We feel more alive and excited. The events seem *destined,* as though they were supposed to happen.

"What we just saw puts all this into a higher perspective. When we have an intuition, a mental image of a possible future, we're actually getting flashes of memory of our Birth Vision, what we wanted to be doing with our lives at that particular point on our journey. It may not be exact, because people have free will, but when something happens that is close to our original vision, we feel inspired because we recognize that we are on a path of destiny that we intended all along."

"But how does our soul group fit in?"

"We're connected with them. They know us. They share our Birth Visions, follow us through life, and afterward stay with us while we review what happened. They act as a reservoir for our memories, maintaining the knowledge of who we are as we evolve."

He paused momentarily, looking straight into my eyes. "And

apparently, when we're in the Afterlife, and one of them is born into the physical dimension, we act in the same capacity toward them. We become part of the soul group that supports them."

"So while we are on Earth," I commented, "our soul groups give us our intuition and direction?"

"No, not at all. Judging from what I could pick up from the soul groups I've seen, the intuitions and dreams are our own, coming from a higher connection with the divine. The soul groups just send us extra energy and uplift us in a particular manner—a manner that I haven't been able to pinpoint. By up-lifting us in this way, they help us to more readily remember what we already knew."

I was fascinated. "So that explains what was happening with my dream and Joel's."

"Yes. When we dream, we reunite with our soul group, and that jogs our memory of what we really wanted to do in our current life situation. We get glimpses of our original intention. Then when we return to the physical, we retain that memory, although it is sometimes expressed in archetypal symbols. In the case of your dream, because you are more open to spiritual meaning, you could remember the dream information in very literal terms. You recalled that in your original intention, you saw us finding each other again when you imaged my face, and so you dreamed almost exactly that.

"Joel, on the other hand, was less open; his dream came through in a more garbled, symbolic fashion. His memory was fuzzy, and his conscious mind fashioned the message in the sym-bolism of a war, conveying to him only the general message that in his Birth Vision he intended to stay and help with the current problem in the valley, making it clear that if he ran away, he would regret it."

"So the soul groups are always sending us energy," I said, "and hoping we will remember our Birth Visions?"

"That's right."

"And that's why Maya's group was so happy?"

Wil's expression grew more serious. "They were happy because she was remembering why she was born to her particular parents, and how her life experiences had prepared her for a career in healing. But . . . this was only the first part of her Birth Vision. She still has more to remember."

"I saw the part when she was meeting again in this life with the man with whom she was killed in the nineteenth century. But there were other parts that I couldn't understand. How much of that did you get?"

"Not all of it. There was more about the rising Fear. It confirmed that she's part of the group of seven that Williams saw coming back. And she saw the group able to remember some kind of larger vision that's behind our individual intentions, a remembrance that is necessary if we are to dispel the Fear."

Wil and I gazed at each other for a long time, then I felt another vibration in my body from the experiment. In that moment an image of the large man with whom Maya had seen herself reuniting came into my mind. Who was he?

I was about to mention the image to Wil, when my breath left me, forced out by a cramping pain that seized my stomach. Simultaneously, another high-pitched screech rocked me backward. As before, I reached out for Wil and saw his face fading out of focus. I struggled to look one more time, then completely lost my equilibrium, slipping again into free fall.

# OPENING
# TO THE
# KNOWLEDGE

Damn, I thought—lying flat on the rock, the coarse surface of the stone edging into my back—I was back at the stream again. For a long moment I stared up at the gray sky, now threatening rain, listening to the water flow past me. I raised up on one elbow and looked around, noticing immediately that my body felt heavy and fatigued, just as it had the last time I left the other dimension.

Clumsily I got to my feet, a slight pain throbbing in my ankle, and limped back into the forest. I uncovered my pack and prepared some food, moving very slowly without thinking. Even as I ate, my mind remained surprisingly blank, like after a long meditation. Then slowly I began to increase my energy, taking several deep breaths and holding them. Suddenly I could hear the hum again. As I listened, another image came to mind. I was walking east in the direction of the sound, in search of its cause.

The thought terrified me and I felt the old urge to flee. Instantly the hum vanished, and I heard a rustling of leaves to my rear. I jerked around and saw Maya.

"Do you always show up at the right time?" I stammered.

"Show up! Are you crazy? I've been looking for you every-where around here. Where did you come from?"

"I was down by the stream."

"No, you weren't; I've been looking down there." She stared at me for a moment, then glanced at my foot. "How's that ankle?"

I managed a smile. "It's fine. Listen, I've got to talk to you about something."

"I have to speak with you too. There's something very strange happening. One of the Forest Service agents saw me walking into town last night, and I told him about your situation. He seemed to want to keep it quiet, and he insisted on sending a truck to get you this morning. I told him your general location, and he made me promise to ride out here with him this morning. Some-thing about the way he was talking felt so odd, I decided to hike up ahead of him instead, but he'll probably be here any minute."

"Then we need to go," I said, scrambling to pack.

"Wait a minute! Tell me what is happening." She looked pan-icked.

I stopped and faced her. "Someone—I don't know who it is—is doing some kind of experiment or something like that here in the valley. I think my friend Charlene is involved somehow, or may be in danger. Someone in the Forest Service must have se-cretly approved this."

She stared, trying to take it all in.

I picked up my pack and took her hand. "Walk with me for a while. Please. There's more I need to tell you."

She nodded and grabbed her pack, and as we walked east

along the edge of the stream, I told her the whole story, from meeting David and Wil to seeing Williams' Life Review and listening to Joel. When I came to the part about her Birth Vision, I moved over to some rocks and sat down. She leaned against a tree to my right.

"You're involved in this too," I said. "Obviously you already know that your life is supposed to be about introducing alternative techniques of healing, but there's more that you intended to do. You're supposed to be part of this group that Williams saw coming together."

"How do you know all that?"

"Wil and I saw your Birth Vision."

She shook her head and closed her eyes.

"Maya, each of us comes here with a vision of how our lives can be, what we want to do. The intuitions we have, the dreams and coincidences, they're all designed to keep us on the right path, to bring back our memory of how we wanted our lives to unfold."

"And what else did I want to do?"

"I don't know exactly; I couldn't get it. But it had something to do with this collective Fear that is rising in human consciousness. The experiment is a result of this Fear . . . Maya, you intended to use what you've learned about physical healing to help resolve what's happening in this valley. You must remember!"

She stood and looked away. "Oh no, you can't put that kind of responsibility on me! I don't remember any of this. I'm doing exactly what I'm supposed to be doing as a doctor. I hate this kind of intrigue! Understand? I hate it! I finally have the clinic set up just as I want. You can't expect me to get involved in all this. You've got the wrong person!"

I looked at her, trying to think of something else to say. During the silence, I heard the hum again.

"Can you hear that sound, Maya, a dissonance in the air, a hum? That's the experiment. It's happening right now. Try to hear it!"

She listened for a moment, then said, "I don't hear anything."

I grabbed her arm. "Try to raise your energy!"

She pulled away. "I don't hear a hum!"

I took a breath. "Okay, I'm sorry. I don't know, maybe I'm wrong. Maybe it's not supposed to happen this way."

She looked at me for a moment. "I know someone with the Sheriff's Department. I'll try to get in touch with him for you. That's all I can do."

"I don't know if that will help," I said. "Apparently not everyone can hear this sound."

"Do you want me to call him?"

"Yes, but tell him to investigate independently. I'm not sure he can trust everyone in the Forest Service." I picked up my pack again.

"I hope you understand," she said. "I just can't be involved in this. I feel as though something horrible would happen."

"But that's just because of what happened when you tried this before, in the nineteenth century, here in this valley. Can you remember any of that?"

She closed her eyes again, not wanting to listen.

I suddenly saw a clear image of myself in buckskins, running up a hill, pulling a packhorse. It was the same image I had seen before. The mountain man was me! As the vision continued, I made my way to the top of the hill and then paused to glance back to my rear. From there I could see the falls and the gorge on the other side. There was Maya and the Indian and the young congressional aide. As before, the battle was just beginning. Anxiety swept over me, and I pulled at the horse and walked on, unable to help them avoid their fate.

I shook off the images. "It's okay," I said, giving up. "I know how you feel."

Maya walked closer. "Here's some extra water and food I brought. What are you planning to do?"

"I'm going to head toward the east . . . for at least a while. I know Charlene was going in that direction."

She looked at my foot. "Are you sure your ankle will hold up?"

I moved closer and said, "I haven't really thanked you for what you did. My ankle will be fine, I think, just a little sore. I guess I'll never know how bad it might have been."

"When it happens this way, no one ever does."

I nodded, then picked up my pack and headed east, glancing back once at Maya. She looked guilty for an instant, than an expression of relief swept across her face.

I walked toward the sound of the hum, keeping the stream in sight to my left, pausing only to rest my foot. About noon the sound ceased, so I stopped to eat lunch and assess the situation. My ankle was swelling slightly and I rested for an hour and a half before resuming my journey. After covering only another mile, fatigue overwhelmed me, and I rested again. By midafternoon I was looking for a place to camp.

I had been walking through thick woods that grew right to the edge of the stream, but ahead the landscape opened up in a series of gently rolling foothills covered with old-growth forest— three- and four-hundred-year-old trees. Through a break in the limbs, I could see a large ridge rising toward the southeast, perhaps another mile away.

I spotted a small grassy knoll near the top of the first hill, which looked like a perfect place to spend the night. As I approached, movement in the trees caught my eye. I slipped behind a large outcropping and looked. What was that? A deer? A person? I waited for several minutes, then carefully moved away toward the north. As I inched along, I saw a large man a hundred yards to the south of the knoll I had seen before, apparently setting up a camp himself. Staying very low to the ground and moving with skill, he deftly raised a small tent and camouflaged it with branches. For an instant I thought it might be David, but his movements were different, and he was too big. Then I lost sight of him.

After waiting for several more minutes I decided to move farther to the north until I was completely out of sight. I'd been moving no more than five minutes when the man suddenly stepped out in front of me.

"Who are you?" he asked. I told him my name and decided to be open. "I'm trying to find a friend."

"It's dangerous out here," he said. "I would recommend that you go back. This is all private property."

"Why are *you* out here?" I asked.

He was silent, staring.

Then I remembered what David had told me. "Are you Curtis Webber?" I inquired.

He looked at me for a moment longer, then abruptly smiled. "You know David Lone Eagle!"

"I only talked to him briefly, but he told me you were out here, and to tell you he was coming into the valley and that he would find you."

Curtis nodded and looked toward his camp. "It's getting late, and we need to get out of sight. Let's go up to my tent. You can spend the night up there."

I followed him down a slope and up into the deep cover of the larger trees. While I pitched my tent, he fired up his camp stove for coffee and opened a can of tuna. I contributed a package of bread Maya had given me.

"You mentioned that you were looking for someone," Curtis said. "Who?"

Briefly I told him about Charlene's disappearance and that David had seen her hiking into the valley; also that I thought she had been seen coming in this direction. I didn't talk about what had occurred in the other dimension, but I did mention hearing the hum and seeing the vehicles.

"The hum," he responded, "comes from an energy-generating device; someone's experimenting with it here for some reason. I can confirm that much. But I don't know whether the experiment is being conducted by some secret government agency or a private group. Most of the Forest Service agents seem to be unaware that it's happening; but I don't know about the administrators."

"Have you gone to the media," I asked, "or to the local authorities about this?"

"Not yet. The fact that not everyone hears the hum is a real problem." He looked out at the valley. "If I just knew where they were. Counting the private land and the National Forest, there are tens of thousands of acres where they might be. I think they want to conduct the experiment and get out before anyone knows what happened. That is, if they can avoid a tragedy."

"What do you mean?"

"They could totally ruin this place, make it into a twilight zone, another Bermuda Triangle where the laws of physics are in unpredictable flux." He looked directly at me. "The things they know how to do are incredible. Most people have no idea of the complexity of electromagnetic phenomena. In the latest super-string theories, for instance, one has to assume this radiation emanates across nine dimensions just to make the math work. This device has the potential to disrupt these dimensions. It could trigger massive earthquakes or even complete physical disintegration of certain areas."

"How do you know all this?" I asked.

His face fell. "Because in the decade of the eighties I helped develop some of this technology. I was employed with a multinational corporation I thought was named Deltech, although later, after I was fired, I found out that Deltech was a fictitious name. You've heard of Nikola Tesla? Well, we expanded many of his theories and tied some of his discoveries to other technologies that the company supplied. The funny thing is that this technology is composed of several dissimilar parts, but basically it works this way. Imagine that the electromagnetic field of the Earth is a giant battery that can provide plenty of electrical energy if you can tie into it in the correct way. For that you combine a room temperature, superconductive generator system with a very complicated electronic feedback inhibitor, which mathematically enhances certain static output resonances. Then you tie several of these in a series, amplifying and generating the charge, and when you get the calibrations exact, presto, you have virtually free energy right out of the immediate space. You need a small amount of power to start, perhaps a single photocell or a battery, but then it's self-perpetuating. A device the size of a heat pump could power several houses, even a small factory.

"However, there are two problems. First, calibrating these minigenerators is unbelievably complicated. We had access to some of the largest computers in existence and couldn't do it. Second, we discovered that when we tried to increase the total output beyond this relatively small size by enlarging the mass displacement, the space around the generator became very unstable and began to warp. We didn't know it then, but we were tapping into the energy of another dimension, and strange things began to happen. Once, we made the whole generator disappear, exactly like what happened in the Philadelphia Experiment."

"Do you think they really made a ship disappear and show up again in a new location, in 1943?"

"Of course they did! There's a lot of secret technology around, and they're smart. In our case, they were able to shut our team down in less than a month and fire all of us without a breach of security because each team was working on an isolated part of the technology. Not that I wondered much about it then. I mostly bought the idea that the obstacles were just too great to proceed, so I thought it was dead-end research—although I did hear that several of the old employees were hired again by another company."

He looked thoughtful for a moment, then continued. "I knew I wanted to do something else anyway. I'm a consultant now, working with small technology firms, providing advice for improving their research efficiency and use of resources and disposal of wastes, that sort of thing. And the more I work with them, the more I'm convinced the Insights are having an effect on the economy. The way we do business is shifting. But I figured we had to work with traditional power sources for a long time. I hadn't thought about the energy experiments in years until I moved into this area. You can imagine how shocked I was to walk into this valley and hear the same sound—this characteristic hum—that I heard every day for years when we were working on the project.

"Someone has continued the research, and judging from the resonances, they're much further along than we were. Afterward I tried to contact the two people who could verify the sound and maybe go to the EPA or a congressional committee with me, but I found out one had been deceased for ten years and the other, my best friend when I was at the corporation, was also dead. He had a heart attack just yesterday." His voice trailed off.

"Since then," he went on, "I've been out here listening, trying to figure out why they're in this valley. Ordinarily one would expect this kind of experiment to be done in a laboratory somewhere. I mean, why not? Its energy source is space itself, and that's everywhere. But then it dawned on me. They must think they are very close to perfecting the calibrations, which means they're working on the amplification problem. I think they're trying to tie into the energy vortexes in this valley in an attempt to stabilize the process."

A wave of anger crossed his face. "Which is crazy and totally unnecessary. If they really can find the calibrations, then there's no reason not to utilize the technology in small units. In fact, that's the perfect way of using it. What they're trying now is insane. I know enough to see the dangers. I'm telling you, they could totally wreck this valley, or worse. If they focus this thing on the interdimensional pathways, who knows what might happen?"

He stopped suddenly. "Do you know what I'm talking about? Have you heard of the Insights?"

I stared for a moment, then said, "Curtis, I have to tell you what I've been experiencing in this valley. You may find it unbelievable."

He nodded and then listened patiently as I described meeting Wil and exploring parts of the other dimension. When I came to the Life Review, I asked, "This friend of yours who recently died? Was he named Williams?"

"That's right. Dr. Williams. How did you know that?"

"We saw him reach the other dimension after his death. We watched as he experienced a Life Review."

He appeared shaken. "That's hard for me to believe. I know the Insights, at least intellectually, and I believe in the probable existence of other dimensions, but as a scientist, the Ninth Insight stuff is much harder to take literally, the idea of being able to communicate with people after death . . . You're saying that Dr. Williams is still alive in the sense that his personality is intact?"

"Yes, and he was thinking about you."

He looked at me intently as I continued to tell him about Williams' realization that Curtis and he were supposed to be involved in resolving the Fear . . . and stopping this experiment.

"I don't understand," he said. "What did he mean when he talked about a growing *Fear*?"

"I don't know exactly. It has to do with a certain percentage of the population refusing to believe that a new spiritual awareness is emerging. Instead, they think human civilization is degenerating. This is creating a polarization of opinion and belief. Human culture can't continue to evolve until the polarization is ended. I was hoping that you might remember something about it."

He looked at me blankly. "I don't know anything about a polarization, but I *am* going to stop this experiment." His face grew angry again and he looked away.

"Williams seemed to understand the process for stopping it," I said.

"Well, we'll never know now, will we?"

As he said that, I fleetingly saw again the image of Curtis and Williams talking on the grassy hilltop, surrounded by several large trees.

Curtis served our food, still appearing upset, and we finished eating in silence. Later as I stretched out and leaned against a small hickory, I glanced up the hill at the grassy knoll above us. Four or five huge oaks made almost a perfect semicircle on its crest.

"Why didn't you camp up on the hill?" I asked Curtis, pointing.

"I don't know," he said. "The idea came to me, but I guess I thought it was too exposed, or maybe too powerful. It's called Codder's Knoll. Do you want to walk up there?"

I nodded and rose to my feet. A gray twilight was descending across the forest. Commenting on the beauty of the trees and shrubs as we walked, Curtis led the way up the slope. At the top, in spite of the fading light, we could see almost a quarter of a mile toward the north and east. In the latter direction a near full moon was rising above the tree line.

"Better sit down," Curtis advised. "We don't want to be seen."

For a long while we sat in silence, admiring the view and feeling the energy. Curtis took a flashlight out of his pocket and laid it on the ground beside him. I was mesmerized by the colors of the fall foliage.

Presently Curtis looked over at me and asked, "Do you smell something, smoke?"

I immediately looked out at the woods, suspecting a forest fire, and sniffed the air. "No, I don't think so." Something about Curtis' demeanor was shifting the mood, introducing a feeling of sadness or nostalgia. "What kind of smoke do you mean?"

"Cigar smoke."

In the growing moonlight I could tell he was smiling reflectively, thinking about something. Then suddenly I began to smell the smoke.

"What is that?" I asked, looking around again.

He caught my eye. "Dr. Williams smoked cigars that smelled just like that. I can't believe he's gone."

As we talked, the smell subsided and I dismissed the whole experience, content to stare out at the sage and the large oaks beside us. In that moment I realized that this was the very spot where Williams saw himself meeting with Curtis. It was to take place right here!

Seconds later I observed a figure forming just beyond the trees.

"Do you see anything out there?" I quietly asked Curtis, pointing in that direction.

As soon as I spoke, the form disappeared.

Curtis was straining to see. "What? I don't see anything."

I didn't respond. Somehow I had begun to intuitively receive knowledge, exactly as I had received it from the soul groups, except the connection was more distant and garbled. I could sense something about the energy experiment, a confirmation of Curtis' suspicions; the experimenters were indeed attempting to focus in on the dimensional vortexes.

"I just remembered," Curtis said abruptly. "One of the devices Dr. Williams was working on years ago was a remote focus, a dish projection system. I bet that's what they're using to focus on the openings. But how do they know where the openings *are*?"

Immediately I perceived an answer. Someone of a higher awareness pointed them out until they learned the spatial variances as they showed up on the remote focus computer. I had no idea what that meant.

"There's only one way," Curtis said. "They would have to find someone to point them out—someone who could sense these higher energy locations. Then they could map out an energy profile of the site and focus precisely by scanning with a focus beam. Probably the individual wouldn't even know what they were doing." He shook his head. "These people are vicious. There's no doubt about it. How could they do this?"

As if in response, I sensed other knowledge that was too vague to understand completely, but seemed to maintain that there was, in fact, a reason. But we had to first understand the Fear and how to overcome it.

When I looked at Curtis, he seemed to be deep in thought.

Finally he looked at me and said, "I wish I knew why this Fear is coming up now."

"During a transition in culture," I said, "old certainties and views begin to break down and evolve into new traditions, causing anxiety in the short run. At the same time that some people are waking up and sustaining an inner connection of love that sustains them and allows them to evolve more rapidly, others feel as though everything is changing too fast and that we're losing our way. They become more fearful and more controlling to try to raise their energy. This polarization of fear can be very dangerous because fearful people can rationalize extreme measures."

As I was saying all of this, I felt as though I was expanding on what I had earlier heard Wil say, and Williams, but I also had the distinct sensation that it was something I knew all along but didn't realize I knew until this very moment.

"I understand that," Curtis said with certainty. "That's why these people are so willing to waste this valley. They rationalize that civilization will fall apart in the future, and they won't be safe unless they seize more control. Well, I'm not going to allow it to happen. I'll blow the whole thing sky-high."

I looked hard at him. "What do you mean?"

"Just that. I used to be a demolitions expert. I know how."

I must have looked alarmed because he said, "Don't worry, I'll figure out a way to do it where no one gets hurt. I wouldn't want that on my conscience."

A wave of knowledge filled me. "Any kind of violence," I said, "just makes it worse, don't you see?"

"What other way is there?"

Out of the corner of my eye I glimpsed the form again for an instant, and then it disappeared. "I don't know exactly," I said, "But if we fight them with anger, hate, they just see an enemy. It makes them more entrenched. They become more fearful. Somehow this group that Williams was talking about is supposed to do something else. We're supposed to fully remember our Birth Visions . . . and then we can remember something more, a *World Vision.*"

Somehow I knew the term, but I couldn't remember where I had heard it before.

"A World Vision . . ." Curtis pondered, deep in thought again. "I think David Lone Eagle mentioned that."

"Yes," I said. "That's right."

"What do you think a World Vision is?"

I was about to say I didn't know when a thought came to me. "It's an understanding—no, a memory—of how we will fulfill human purpose. It brings in another level of love, an energy, that can bridge the polarization, end this experiment."

"I don't see how that's possible," Curtis said.

"It involves the energy level around people who are in Fear,"

I said, somehow knowing. "They would be touched, awakened from their preoccupation. They would choose to stop."

For several moments we were silent, then Curtis said, "Maybe, but how do we bring in this energy?"

Nothing more came to mind.

"I wish I knew how far they're prepared to go with this experiment," he added.

"What causes the hum?" I asked.

"The hum is a linking dissonance between the small generators. It means that they're still trying to calibrate the device. The more grating and disharmonious it is, the more it's out of phase." He thought for another moment. "I just wonder which energy vortex they're going to focus on."

I suddenly sensed a particular nervousness, not within myself, but outwardly, as if I was around someone else who was anxious. I looked at Curtis, who seemed relatively calm. Beyond the trees I again saw the vague outlines of a form. It moved as if agitated or frightened.

"I would imagine," Curtis said absently, "that if one were close to the target location, one would hear the hum and then feel a kind of static electricity in the air."

We looked at each other, and in the silence I could hear a faint sound, merely a vibration.

"Do you hear that?" Curtis asked, now alarmed.

As I looked at him, I felt the hair rise on the back of my neck and forearms. "What is this?"

For an instant Curtis observed his own arms, then looked at me in horror.

"We've got to get out of here!" he screamed, grabbing his flashlight, leaping to his feet, and half dragging me off the crest of the slope.

Suddenly the same ear-shattering roar I had heard with Wil descended again and carried with it a shock wave that knocked both of us to the ground. Simultaneously the earth beneath us shook violently and a massive fissure opened twenty feet away, creating an explosion of dust and debris.

Behind us one of the towering oaks, undermined by the shifting earth, leaned and then fell to the ground in a thunderous roar, adding to the noise. Seconds later another, larger fissure tore open right beside us and the ground tilted. Curtis, unable to hold on, slid toward the widening abyss. I held onto a small bush and reached out for Curtis' hand. For a moment we held tight, then our grip slipped, and I watched helplessly as he slid over the edge. The fissure moved and widened, spewed another plume of dust and rock, shook once more, and then was still. A limb under the fallen tree cracked loudly, and then the night was again silent.

As the dust cleared, I let go of the bush and crawled toward the edge of the massive hole. When I could see, I realized that Curtis was lying prone at the edge, even though I was sure I had seen him fall in. He rolled toward me and jumped to his feet.

"Let's go!" he yelled. "It could start again!"

Without speaking we ran down the hill toward the campsite, Curtis ahead, me limping behind. When Curtis reached the site, he seized both tents and ripped them from the ground, stakes dangling, and stuffed them into the packs. I pushed in the other gear, and we continued toward the southwest until the ground flattened into thick underbrush. After another half mile, exhaustion and my weakening ankle forced me to stop.

Curtis surveyed the terrain. "Maybe we'll be safe here," he said, "but let's move deeper into the thicket." I followed as he led us fifty feet farther into the dense woods.

"This will do right here," he commented. "Let's put up the tents."

Within a couple of minutes both tents were up and covered with limbs and we were looking at each other breathlessly, sitting on his tent's large entrance flap.

"What do you think happened?" I asked.

Curtis' face looked gaunt as he dug into his pack for water. "They're doing exactly what we thought," he said. "They're trying to focus the generator on a remote space." He took a long drink from his canteen. "They're going to ruin this valley; these people have to be stopped."

"What about the smoke we smelled?"

"I don't know what to think," Curtis said. "It was as though Dr. Williams was there. I could almost hear his inflection, his tone of voice, what he would have said in that situation."

I caught Curtis' eye. "I think he *was* there."

Curtis handed me the canteen. "How is that possible?"

"I don't know," I said. "But I think he came to convey a message, a message to *you*. When we saw him during his Life Review, he was agonizing because he had failed to wake up, to remember why he had been born. He was convinced that you were supposed to be a part of this group he mentioned. Can't you remember anything about that? I think he wanted you to know that violence won't stop these people. We have to do it another way, with this World Vision that David talked about."

He gave me a blank look.

"What about when the earth movement started," I asked, "and that fissure opened? I know I saw you roll in, yet you were lying at the edge when I got there."

He looked totally perplexed. "I'm not sure really. I couldn't hold on and was slipping into the hole. As I dropped down, this incredibly peaceful feeling came over me, and I was cushioned, like falling onto a soft mattress. All I could see was a white blur around me. The next thing I knew I was lying at the side of the fissure again and you were there. Do you think Dr. Williams could have done that?"

"I don't think so," I said. "I had a similar experience yesterday. I was almost crushed by stones and I saw the same white form. Something else is happening."

Curtis stared at me for a moment and then said something else, but I didn't respond. I was drifting into sleep.

"Let's turn in," he said.


Curtis was already up when I climbed out of my tent. The morning was clear, but a ground fog covered the forest floor. Instantly I knew he was angry.

"I can't stop thinking about what they're doing," he said. "And they aren't going to give up." He took a breath. "By now they've figured out what a mess they made on the hill. They'll spend some time recalibrating, but not for long, and then they'll try again. I can stop them but we have to find out where they are."

"Curtis, violence just makes it worse. Didn't you understand the information coming from Dr. Williams? We have to discover how to use the Vision."

"No!" he shouted with deep emotion. "I've tried that before!"

I looked at him. "When?"

His expression changed to confusion. "I don't know."

"Well," I stressed, "I think I do."

He waved me off with his hand. "I don't want to hear it. This is too crazy. Everything that's happening is my fault. If I hadn't worked on this technology, they might not be doing this. I'm going to handle it my way." He walked over and began packing.

I hesitated, then started taking down my own tent, trying to think. After a moment I said, "I've already sent for some help. A woman I met, Maya, thinks she can persuade the Sheriff's Department to investigate this. I want you to promise me you'll give me some time."

He was kneeling beside his backpack, checking a bulging side pocket. "I can't do that. I may have to act when I can."

"You have explosives in your pack?"

He walked toward me. "I told you before I'm not going to hurt anyone."

"I want some time," I repeated. "If I can reach Wil again, I think I can find out about this World Vision."

"Okay," he said. "I'll give you as long as I can, but if they start experimenting again, and I think I'm out of time, I'll have to do something."

As he spoke, I saw Wil's face again in my mind's eye, surrounded by a rich emerald color. "Is there another high-energy location near here?" I asked.

He pointed south. "Somewhere up the big ridge, there's a rock overhang I've heard about. But that's private land that was recently sold. I don't know who owns it now."

"I'm going to look for it. If I can find the right place, then maybe I can locate Wil again."

Curtis finished packing and helped me tie up my own gear and spread leaves and branches where the tents had been. Toward the northwest we could hear the faint sound of vehicles.

"I'm heading east," he said.

I nodded as he walked away, then pulled my pack onto my shoulders and started up the rocky slope to the south. I traveled over several small hills and then tackled the steep incline of the main ridge. About halfway up I began to look through the dense forest for an overhang but found no sign of an opening.

After climbing several hundred more yards I stopped again. Still no outcropping, and I could see none at the crest of the ridge above. I was confused about which way to go and decided to sit down and attempt to raise my energy. After a few minutes I felt better, and was listening to the sounds of birds and tree frogs in the thick limbs over my head, when a large golden eagle fluttered from its nest and flew east along the top of the ridge.

I knew the presence of the bird had meaning, so, as with the hawk before, I decided to follow. Gradually the slope became more rocky. I crossed a small spring flowing from the rocks and refilled my canteen and washed my face. Finally, a half mile farther, I pushed my way through a grove of small fir trees, and there before me lay the majestic overhang. Almost half an acre of the slope was covered with huge terraces of thick limestone, and at the farthermost edge, a twenty-foot-wide shelf jutted out at least forty feet from the ridge, providing a spectacular view of the valley below. For an instant I detected a dark emerald highlight around the lower shelf.

I took off my pack and pushed it out of sight under a pile of leaves and then walked out and sat on the ledge. As I centered myself, the image of Wil came easily to mind. I took one more deep breath and began to move.

# A HISTORY
# OF
# AWAKENING

When I opened my eyes, I was in an area of rich blue light, feeling the now-familiar sense of well-being and peace. I could detect Wil's presence to my left.

As before, he looked enormously relieved and happy that I had returned. He moved closer and whispered, "You are going to love it here."

"Where are we?" I asked.

"Look more closely."

I shook my head. "I have to talk to you first. It's imperative that we find this experiment and stop them. They've destroyed a hilltop. God knows what they're about to do next."

"What will we do if we find them?" Wil inquired.

"I don't know."

"Well, neither do I. Tell me what happened."

I closed my eyes and tried to center, then described the experience of seeing Maya again, particularly her resistance to my suggestion that she was part of the group.

Wil nodded without comment.

I went on to describe meeting Curtis, communicating with Williams, and surviving the effects of the experiment.

"Williams spoke to you?" Wil asked.

"Not really. The communication wasn't mental, as with you and me. He seemed to be influencing the ideas that were coming to us in some way. It felt like information I already knew at some level; yet both of us seemed to be saying what he was trying to communicate. It was odd, but I know he was there."

"What was his message?"

"He confirmed what you and I saw with Maya; he said we could remember beyond our individual birth intentions to a broader knowledge of human purpose and how we could complete this purpose. Apparently, remembering this knowledge brings in an expanded energy that can end the Fear . . . and this experiment. He called it a World Vision."

Wil was silent.

"What do you think?" I asked.

"I think all this is just more of the Tenth Insight knowledge. Please understand: I share your sense of urgency. But the only way we can help is to continue exploring the Afterlife until we find out about this larger Vision that Williams was trying to communicate. There must be an exact process for remembering what it is."

In the distance a movement caught my eye. Eight or ten very distinct beings, only partially out of focus, moved to within fifty feet. Behind them were dozens more, blended together in the usual amber-colored blur. All of them exuded a particular feeling of sentiment and nostalgia that was distinctly familiar.

"Do you know who these souls are?" Wil asked, smiling broadly.

I looked out at the group, sensing kinship. I did know, but I didn't. As I looked upon the soul group, the emotional connection continued to grow more intense, beyond anything I could remember ever experiencing. Yet, at the same time, the closeness was recognizable; I had been *here* before.

The group moved within twenty feet of me, increasing the euphoria and acceptance even more. I gladly let go, turning myself over to the feeling, wishing only to bask in it—content— perhaps for the first time in my life. Waves of acknowledgment and appreciation filled my mind.

"Have you figured it out?" Wil asked again.

I turned and looked at him. "This is my soul group, isn't it?"

With that thought came a flood of memories. Thirteenth- century France, a monastery and courtyard. All around me a group of monks, laughter, closeness, then walking alone on a wooded road. Two ragged men, ascetics, asking for help, something about preserving some secret knowledge.

I shook off the vision and looked at Wil, gripped by a perverse fear. What was I about to see? I attempted to center, and my soul group edged four feet closer.

"What is happening?" Wil asked. "I couldn't quite understand."

I described what I had observed.

"Probe further," Wil suggested.

Immediately I saw the ascetics again, and somehow knew they were members of a secret order of Franciscan "Spirituals" who had recently been excommunicated, after Pope Celestine V had resigned.

Pope Celestine? I glanced at Wil. "Did you get that? I never knew there were popes by that name."

"Celestine V was late thirteenth century," Wil confirmed.

"The ruins in Peru, where the Ninth Insight was ultimately found, were named after him when first discovered in the 1600s."

"Who were the Spirituals?"

"They were a group of monks who believed that a higher awareness could be achieved by extracting themselves from human culture and returning to a contemplative life in nature. Pope Celestine supported this idea and, in fact, lived in a cave himself for a while. He was deposed, of course, and later, most sects of the Spirituals were condemned as Gnostics and excommunicated."

More memories surfaced. The two ascetics had approached me asking for help, and I had reluctantly met with them deep in the forest. I had had no choice, so entrancing were their eyes and the fearlessness of their demeanor. Old documents were in great danger of being lost forever, they told me. Later I had smuggled them back to the abbey and had read them by candlelight in my chambers, the doors closed and locked securely.

These documents were old Latin copies of the Nine Insights, and I had consented to copy them before it was too late, working every moment of my spare time to painstakingly reproduce dozens of the manuscripts. At one point I was so enthralled by the Insights that I sought to persuade the ascetics to make them public.

They adamantly refused, explaining that they had held the documents for many centuries, waiting for the correct understanding to emerge within the church. When I questioned the meaning of this latter phrase, they explained that the Insights would not be accepted until the church reconciled what they referred to as the *Gnostic dilemma*.

The Gnostics, I somehow remembered, were early Christians

who believed that followers of the one God should not merely revere Christ but strive to emulate him in the spirit of Pentecost. They sought to describe this emulation in philosophical terms, as a method of practice. As the early church formulated its canons, the Gnostics were eventually considered willful heretics, opposed to turning their lives over to God as a matter of faith. To become a true believer, the early church leaders concluded, one had to forgo understanding and analysis and be content to live life through divine revelation, adhering to God's will moment by moment, but content to remain ignorant of his overall plan.

Accusing the church hierarchy of tyranny, the Gnostics argued that their understandings and methods were intended to actually facilitate this act of "letting go to God's will" that the church was requiring, rather than giving mere lip service to the idea, as the churchmen were doing.

In the end the Gnostics lost, and were banished from all church functions and texts, their beliefs disappearing underground among the various secret sects and orders. Yet the dilemma was clear. As long as the church held out the vision of a transformative spiritual connection with the divine, yet persecuted anyone who talked openly about the specifics of the experience—how one might actually attain such an awareness, what it felt like—then the "kingdom within" would remain merely an intellectualized concept within church doctrine, and the Insights would be crushed anytime they surfaced.

At the moment, I listened with concern to the ascetics and said nothing, but inwardly I disagreed. I was sure the Benedictine Order of which I was a part would be interested in these writings, especially at the level of the individual monk. Later, without telling the Spirituals, I shared a copy with a friend who was the closest adviser to Cardinal Nicholas in my district. Reaction came swiftly. Word arrived that the cardinal was out of the country, but I was asked to cease any discussion of the subject and to depart at once for Naples to report my findings to the cardinal's superiors. I panicked and immediately dispensed the manuscripts as widely as possible throughout the order, hoping that I might garner support from other interested brothers.

In order to postpone my summons, I faked a severe ankle injury and wrote a series of letters explaining my disability, delaying the trip for months while I copied as many manuscripts as I could in my isolation. Finally, on the night of a new moon, my door was kicked down by soldiers and I was beaten severely and taken blindfolded to the castle of the local noble, where I later languished at the stock for days before being decapitated.

The shock of remembering my death cast me into fear again and created a powerful tingling in my injured ankle. The soul group continued to move several feet closer until I managed to center myself. Still, I was left with a degree of confusion. A nod from Wil told me he had seen the entire story.

"This was the beginning of my ankle problem, wasn't it?" I asked.

"Yes," Wil replied.

I caught his eye. "What about all the other memories? Did you understand the Gnostic dilemma?"

He nodded and squared up to face me directly.

"Why would the church create such a dilemma?" I asked.

"Because the early church was afraid to come out and say that Christ modeled a way of life that each of us could aspire to, although that is what is clearly said in the Scriptures. They feared that this position would give too much power to individuals, so they perpetrated the contradiction. On the one hand the churchmen urged the believer to seek the mystical kingdom of God within, to intuit God's will, and to be filled with the Holy Spirit. But on the other hand they condemned as blasphemous any discussion of how one might go about achieving these states, often resorting to outright murder to protect their power."

"So I was a fool for trying to circulate the Insights."

"I wouldn't say a fool," Wil mused, "more like undiplomatic. You were killed because you tried to force an understanding into culture before its time."

I looked into Wil's eyes for another moment, then drifted back into the knowledge of the group, finding myself at the scene of the nineteenth-century wars again. I was back at the meeting of chiefs in the valley, holding the same packhorse, apparently just before departing. A mountain man and trapper, I was friends with both the Native Americans and the settlers. Almost all the Indians wanted to fight, but Maya had won the hearts of some with her search for peace. Remaining silent, I listened to both sides, then watched as most of the chiefs had left.

At one point Maya walked up to me. "I suppose you're leaving too."

I nodded affirmatively, explaining that if these Native medicine chiefs didn't understand what she was doing, I surely didn't.

She looked at me as though I must be kidding, then, turning, she directed her attention to another person. Charlene! I suddenly recalled that she had been there; she was an Indian woman of great power, but often ignored by the envious male chiefs because of her gender. She seemed to know something important about the role of the ancestors, but her voice was falling on deaf ears.

I saw myself wanting to stay, wanting to support Maya, wanting to reveal my feelings for Charlene, yet in the end I walked away; the unconscious memory of my mistake in the thirteenth century was too close to the surface. I wanted only to run away, avoid any responsibility. My life pattern was set: I trapped for furs, I got along, and I didn't stick my neck out for anyone. Perhaps I would do better next time.

Next time? My mind raced forward, and I saw myself looking outward toward the Earth, contemplating my present incarnation. I was watching my own Birth Vision, seeing the full possibility of resolving my reluctance to act or to take a stand. I envisioned how I might utilize my early family to its greatest potential, learning spiritual sensitivity from my mother, integrity and fun from my father. A grandfather would provide a connection with the wilderness, an uncle and aunt would provide a model for tithing and discipline.

And being placed with such strong individuals would bring my tendency to be aloof quickly into consciousness. Because of their ego and strong expectation, I would at first retreat from their messages, and try to hide, but then I would work through this fear and see the positive preparation they were giving me, clearing this tendency so that I could fully follow my life path.

It would be a perfect preparation, and I would leave that upbringing looking for the details of spirituality I had seen in the Insights centuries before. I would explore the psychological descriptions of the Human Potential Movement, the wisdom of Eastern experience, the mystics of the West, and then eventually I would run into the actual Insights again, just at the time they were surfacing to be brought finally into mass awareness. All this preparation and clearing would then allow me to further explore how these Insights were changing human culture and to be a part of Williams' group.

I pulled back and looked at Wil.

"What's wrong?" he asked.

"It hasn't exactly gone the ideal way for me either. I feel as if I've wasted the preparation. I haven't even cleared myself of the aloofness. There were so many books I didn't read, so many people that could have given me messages that I ignored. When I look back now, it seems as though I missed everything."

Wil almost laughed. "None of us can follow our Birth Visions exactly." He paused and stared. "Do you realize what you're doing at this moment? You just remembered the ideal way you wanted your life to go, the way that would have given you the most satisfaction, and when you look at how you actually lived, you are filled with regrets, just the way Williams felt after he died and saw all the opportunities he had missed. Instead of having to wait until after death, you're experiencing a Life Review *now*."

I couldn't quite understand.

"Don't you see? This has to be a key part of the Tenth. Not only are we discovering that our intuitions and our sense of destiny in our lives are remembrances of our Birth Visions. As we understand the Sixth Insight more fully, we're analyzing where we have been off track or failed to take advantage of opportunities, so that we can immediately get back on a path more in line with why we came. In other words, we're bringing more of the process into consciousness on a day-to-day basis. In the past we had to die to engage in a review of our lives, but now we can wake up earlier and eventually make death obsolete, as the Ninth Insight predicts."

I finally understood. "So this is what humans came to the Earth to do, to systematically remember, to gradually awaken."

"That's right. We're finally becoming aware of a process that has been unconscious since human experience began. From the start, humans have perceived a Birth Vision, and then after birth have gone unconscious, aware of only the vaguest of intuitions.

At first, in the early days of human history, the distance between what we intended and what we actually accomplished was very great, and then, over time, the distance has closed. Now we're on the verge of remembering everything."

At that moment I was drawn back into the knowledge of the soul group. In an instant my awareness seemed to increase another level, and all that Wil had said was confirmed. Now, finally, we could look at history not as the bloody struggle of the human animal, who selfishly learned to dominate nature and to survive in greater style, pulling himself from life in the jungle to create a vast and complex civilization. Rather, we could look at human history as a spiritual process, as the deeper, systematic effort of souls, generation after generation, life after life, struggling through the millennia toward one solitary goal: to remember what we already knew in the Afterlife and to make this knowledge conscious on Earth.

As from a great height, a large holographic image opened up around me and I could somehow see, in one glance, the long saga of human history. Without warning I was drawn into the image, and I felt myself being swept forward into the story, reliving it somehow in fast-forward, as if I had really been there, experiencing it moment by moment.

Suddenly I was witnessing the dawn of consciousness. Before me was a long, windswept plain, somewhere in Africa. Movement caught my eye; a small group of humans, unclothed, was foraging on a field of berries. As I watched, I seemed to pick up on the consciousness of the period. Intimately connected to the rhythms and signals of the natural world, we humans lived and responded instinctively. The routines of daily life were oriented toward the challenges of the search for food and toward membership within our individual band. Levels of power flowed downward from one physically stronger, attuned individual, and within this hierarchy we accepted our place in the same way we accepted the constant tragedies and difficulties of existence: without reflection.

As I watched, thousands of years passed by and countless generations lived and perished. Then, slowly, certain individuals began to grow restless with the routines they saw before them. When a child died in their arms, their consciousness expanded and they began to ask why. And to wonder how it might be avoided in the future. These individuals were beginning to gain *self-awareness*—beginning to realize that they were here, now, alive. They were able to step back from their automatic responses and glimpse the full scope of existence. Life, they knew, endured through the cycles of the sun and moon and seasons, but as the dead around them attested, it also had an end. What was the purpose?

Looking closely at these reflective individuals, I realized I could perceive their Birth Visions; they had come into the Earthly dimension with the specific purpose of initiating humanity's first existential awakening. And, even though I couldn't see its full scope, I knew that in the back of their minds was held the larger inspiration of the World Vision. Before their birth, they were aware that humanity was embarking on a long journey that they could already see. But they also knew that progress along this journey would have to be earned, generation by generation—for as we awakened to pursue a higher destiny, we also lost the calm peace of unconsciousness. Along with the exhilaration and freedom of knowing we were alive came the fear and uncertainty of being alive without knowing why.

I could see that humanity's long history would be moved by these two conflicting urges. On the one hand, we would be moved past our fears by the strength of our intuitions, by our mental images that life was about accomplishing some particular goal, of moving culture forward in a positive direction that only we, as individuals, acting with courage and wisdom, could inspire. From the strength of these feelings we would be reminded that, as insecure as life appeared, we were, in fact, *not* alone, that there was purpose and meaning underlying the mystery of existence.

Yet, on the other hand, we would often fall prey to the opposite urge, the urge to protect ourselves from the Fear, at times losing sight of the purpose, falling into the angst of separation and abandonment. This Fear would lead us into a frightened self-protection, fighting to retain our positions of power, stealing energy from each other, and always resisting change and evolution, regardless of what new, better information might be available.

As the awakening continued, millennia passed, and I watched as humans gradually began to coalesce into ever-larger groups, following a natural drive to identify with more people, to move into more complex social organizations. I could see that this drive came from the vague intuition, known fully in the Afterlife, that human destiny on Earth was to evolve toward unification. Following this intuition, we realized that we could evolve beyond the nomadic life of gathering and hunting and begin to cultivate the Earth's plants and harvest them on a regular basis. Similarly we could domesticate and breed many of the animals around us, ensuring a constant presence of protein and related products. With the images of the World Vision deep within our unconscious, driving us archetypically, we began to envision a shift that would be one of the most dramatic transformations in human history: the leap from nomadic wandering to the establishment of large farming villages.

As these farming communities grew more complex, surpluses of food prompted trade and allowed humanity to divide into the first occupational groups—shepherds and builders and weavers, then merchants and metalworkers and soldiers. Quickly came the invention of writing and tabulation. But the whims of nature and the challenges of life still pierced the awareness of early humanity, and the unspoken question still loomed: why were we alive? As before, I watched the Birth Visions of those individuals who sought to understand spiritual reality at a higher level. They came into the Earth dimension to specifically expand human awareness of the divine source, but their first intuitions of the divine remained dim and incomplete, taking polytheistic form. Humanity began to acknowledge what we supposed was a multitude of cruel and demanding deities, gods that existed outside of ourselves and ruled the weather, the seasons, and the stages of the harvest. In our insecurity we thought that we must appease these gods with rites and rituals and sacrifice.

Over thousands of years the multitude of farming communities coalesced further into large civilizations in Mesopotamia, Egypt, the Indus Valley, Crete, and northern China, each inventing its own version of the nature and animal gods. But such deities could not long forestall the anxiety. I watched generations of souls come into the Earthly dimension intending to bring a message that humanity was destined to progress by sharing and comparing knowledge. Yet, once here, these individuals succumbed to the Fear and distorted this intuition into an unconscious need to conquer and dominate and impose their way of life on others by force.

So began the great era of the empires and tyrants, as one great leader rose up after another, uniting the strength of his people, conquering as much land as possible, convinced that the views of his culture should be adopted by all. Yet, throughout this era, these many tyrants were always, in turn, conquered themselves and pressed under the yoke of a larger, stronger cultural view. For thousands of years different empires bubbled up to the top of humanity's consciousness, disseminating their ideas, rising for a time with a more effective reality, economic plan, and war technology, only to be later deposed by a stronger and more organized vision. Ever so slowly, through this method old, outdated ideas were replaced.

I could see that, as slow and bloody as this process was, key truths were gradually making their way from the Afterlife into the physical dimension. One of the most important of these truths—a new ethic of interaction—began to surface in various places around the globe, but ultimately found clear expression in the philosophy of the ancient Greeks. Instantly I could see the Birth Visions of hundreds of individuals born into the Greek culture, each hoping to remember this timely insight.

For generations they had seen the waste and injustice of mankind's unending violence upon itself, and knew that humans could transcend the habit of fighting and conquering others and implement a new system for the exchange and comparison of ideas, a system that protected the sovereign right of every individual to hold his unique view, regardless of physical strength—a system that was already known and followed in the Afterlife. As I watched, this new way of interaction began to emerge and take form on Earth, finally becoming known as *democracy*.

In this method of exchanging ideas, communication between humans still often degenerated into an insecure power struggle, but at least now, for the first time ever, the process was in place to pursue the evolution of human reality at the verbal rather than the physical level.

At the same time, another watershed idea, one destined to completely transform the human understanding of *spiritual reality,* was surfacing in the written histories of a small tribe in the Middle East. Similarly I could also see the Birth Visions of many of the proponents of this idea as well. These individuals, born into the Judaic culture, knew before birth that while we were correct to intuit a divine source, our description of this source was flawed and distorted. Our concept of many gods was merely a fragmented picture of a larger whole. In truth, they realized, there was only one God, a God, in their view, that was still demanding and threatening and patriarchal—and still existing outside of ourselves—but for the first time, personal and responsive, and the sole creator of all humans.

As I continued to watch, I saw this intuition of one divine source emerging and being clarified in cultures all over the world. In China and India, long the leaders in technology, trade, and social development, Hinduism and Buddhism, along with other Eastern religions, moved the East toward a more contemplative focus.

Those who created these religions intuited that God was more than a personage. God was a force, a consciousness, that could only be completely found by attaining what they described as an enlightenment experience. Rather than just pleasing God by obeying certain laws or rituals, the Eastern religions sought connection with God on the inside, as a shift in awareness, an opening up of one's consciousness to a harmony and security that was constantly available.

Quickly my view shifted to the Sea of Galilee, and I could see that the idea of one God that would ultimately transform Western cultures was evolving from the notion of a deity outside of us, patriarchical and judging, toward the position held in the East, toward the idea of an inner God, a God whose kingdom lay within. I watched as one person came into the Earth dimension remembering almost all of his Birth Vision.

He knew he was here to bring a new energy into the world, a new culture based on love. His message was this: the one God was a holy spirit, a divine energy, whose existence could be felt and proven experientially. Coming into spiritual awareness meant more than rituals and sacrifices and public prayer. It involved a repentance of a deeper kind; a repentance that was an inner psychological shift based on the suspension of the ego's addictions, and a transcendent "letting go," which would ensure the true fruits of the spiritual life.

As this message began to spread, I watched as one of the most influential of all empires, the Roman, embraced the new religion and spread the idea of the one, inner God throughout much of Europe. Later, when the barbarians struck from the north, dismembering the empire, the idea survived in the feudal organization of Christendom that followed.

At this point I saw again the appeals of the Gnostics, urging the church to focus more fully on the inner, transformative experience, using Christ's life as an example of what each of us might achieve. I saw the church lapse into the Fear, its leaders sensing a loss of control, building doctrine around the powerful hierarchy of the churchmen, who made themselves mediators, dispensers of the spirit to the populace. Eventually all texts related to Gnosticism were deemed blasphemous and excluded from the Bible.

Even though many individuals came from the Afterlife dimension intending to broaden and democratize the new religion, it was a time of great fear, and efforts to reach out to other cultures were distorted again into the need to dominate and control.

Here I saw the secret sects of the Franciscans again, who sought to include a reverence for nature and a return to the inner experience of the divine. These individuals had come into the Earth dimension intuiting that the Gnostic contradiction would eventually be resolved, and were determined to preserve the old texts and manuscripts until that time. Again I saw my ill-fated attempt to make the information public too soon, and my untimely departure.

Yet I could see clearly that a new era was unfolding in the West. The power of the church was being challenged by another social unit: the nation-state. As more of the Earth's peoples were becoming conscious of each other, the era of the great empires was coming to a close. New generations arrived able to intuit our destiny of unification, working to promote a consciousness of national origin based on common languages and tied more closely to one sovereign area of land. These states were still dominated by autocratic leaders, often thought of as ruling by divine right, but a new human civilization was unfolding, one with recognized borders and established currencies and trade routes.

Finally, in Europe, as wealth and literacy spread, a wide renaissance began. As I watched, the Birth Visions of many of the participants came into my view. They knew that human destiny was to develop an empowered democracy, and they came hoping to bring it into being. The writings of the Greeks and Romans were discovered, stimulating their memories. The first democratic parliaments were established, and calls were issued for an end to the divine right of kings and the bloody reign of the church over spiritual and social reality. Soon came the Protestant Reformation, which held the promise that individuals could go directly to important Scriptures and conceive a direct connection to the divine.

At the same time, individuals seeking greater empowerment and freedom were exploring the American continent, a landmass symbolically lying between the cultures of the East and the West. As I watched the Birth Visions of the Europeans most inspired to enter this new world, I could see that they came knowing that this land was already inhabited, aware that communication and immigration should be undertaken only by invitation. Deep inside, they knew that the Americans were to be the grounding, the road back, for a Europe quickly losing its sense of sacred intimacy with the natural environment and moving toward a dangerous secularism. The Native American cultures, while not perfect, provided a model from which the European mentality could regain its roots.

Yet, again because of the Fear, these individuals were able to intuit only the drive to move to this land, sensing a new freedom and liberty of spirit, but bringing with them the need to dominate and conquer, and to pursue their own security. The important truths of the Native cultures were lost in the rush to exploit the region's vast natural resources.

Meanwhile, in Europe, the Renaissance continued, and I began to see the full scope of the Second Insight. The power of the church to define reality was diminishing, and Europeans were feeling as though they were awakening to look at life anew. Through the courage of countless individuals, all inspired by their intuitive memories, the scientific method was embraced as a democratic process of exploring and coming to understand the world in which humans found themselves. This method— exploring some aspect of the natural world, drawing conclusions, then offering this view to others—was thought of as the consensus-building process through which we would be able, finally, to understand mankind's real situation on this planet, including our spiritual nature.

But those in the church, entrenched in Fear, sought to squelch this new science. As political forces lined up on both sides, a compromise was reached. Science would be free to explore the outer, material world, but must leave spiritual phenomena to the dictates of the still-influential churchmen. The entire inner world of experience—our higher perceptual states of beauty and love, intuitions, coincidences, interpersonal phenomena, even dreams—all were, at first, off limits to the new science.

Despite these restrictions, science began to map out and describe the operation of the physical world, providing information rich in ways to increase trade and utilize natural resources. Human economic security increased, and slowly we began to lose our sense of mystery and our heartfelt questions about the purpose of life. We decided it was purposeful enough just to survive and build a better, more secure world for ourselves and our children. Gradually we entered the consensus trance that denied the reality of death and created the illusion that the world was explained and ordinary and devoid of mystery.

In spite of our rhetoric, our once-strong intuition of a spiritual source was being pushed farther into the background. In this growing materialism, God could only be viewed as a distant Deist's God, a God who merely pushed the universe into being and then stood back to let it run in a mechanical sense, like a predictable machine, with every effect having a cause, and unconnected events happening only at random, by chance alone.

Yet here I could see the birth intent of many of the individuals of this time period. They came knowing that the development of technology and production was important because it could eventually be made nonpolluting and sustainable and could liberate humankind beyond all imagination. But in the beginning, born into the milieu of the time, all they could remember was the general intuition to build and produce and work, holding tightly to the democratic ideal.

The vision shifted, and I could see that nowhere was this intuition stronger than in the creation of the United States, with its democratic Constitution and its system of checks and balances. As a grand experiment, America was set up for the rapid exchange of ideas that was to characterize the future. Yet below the surface, the messages of the Native Americans, and the Native Africans, and other peoples on whose back the American experiment was initiated, all cried out to be heard, to be integrated into the European mentality.

By the nineteenth century we were on the verge of a second great transformation of human culture, a transformation that would be built on the new energy sources of oil and steam and finally electricity. The human economy had developed into a vast and complicated field of endeavor that supplied more products than ever before through an explosion of new techniques. In great numbers people were moving from rural communities to great urban centers of production, shifting from life on the farm to involvement in the new, specialized *industrial revolution*.

At the time, most believed that a democratically founded capitalism, unfettered by government regulation, was the desired method of human commerce. Yet, again, as I picked up on individual Birth Visions, I could see that most people born into this period had come hoping to evolve capitalism toward a more perfect form. Unfortunately the level of Fear was such that all they managed to intuit was a desire to build individual security, to exploit other workers, and to maximize profits at every turn, often entering into collusive agreements with competitors and with governments. This was the great era of the robber barons and of secret banking and industrial cartels.

However, by the early twentieth century, because of the abuses of this freewheeling capitalism, two other economic systems were set to be offered as alternatives. Earlier, in England, two men had posed an alternative "manifesto" which called for a new system, run by workers, that would eventually create an economic utopia, where the resources of the whole of humanity would be made available to each person according to his needs, without greed or competition.

In the horrible working conditions of the day, the idea attracted many supporters. But I quickly saw that this materialistic workers' "manifesto" had been a corruption of the original intention. When the Birth Visions of the two men came into view, I realized that what they were intuiting was that human destiny was eventually to achieve such a utopia. Unfortunately they failed to remember that this utopia could only be accomplished through democratic participation, born of free will and slowly evolved.

Consequently the initiators of this communist system, from the first revolution in Russia, erroneously thought that this system could be created through force and dictatorship, an approach that failed miserably and cost millions of lives. In their impatience the individuals involved had envisioned a utopia but had created communism and decades of tragedy.

The scene shifted to the other alternative to a democratic capitalism: the evil of fascism. This system was designed to enhance the profits and control of a ruling elite, who thought of themselves as privileged leaders of human society. They believed that only through the abandonment of democracy, and the union of government with the new industrial leadership, could a nation reach its greatest potential and position in the world.

I saw clearly that in creating such a system, the participants were almost totally unconscious of their Birth Visions. They had come here wishing only to promote the idea that civilization was evolving toward perfectibility and that a nation of people, totally unified in purpose and will, striving to attain their fullest potential, could reach great heights of energy and effectiveness. What was created was a fearful, self-serving vision wrongly claiming the superiority of certain races and nations, and the possibility of developing a supernation whose destiny was to rule the world. Again the intuition that all humans were evolving toward perfection was distorted by weak, fearful men into the murderous reign of the Third Reich.

I watched as others—who had likewise envisioned the perfectibility of mankind, but who were in greater touch with the importance of an empowered democracy—intuited that they must stand up against both alternatives to a freely expressed economy. The first stand resulted in a bloody world war against the fascist distortion, won finally at extreme cost. The second resulted in a long and bitter cold war against the communist bloc.

I suddenly found myself focusing on the United States during the early years of this cold war, the decade of the fifties. At this time, America stood successfully at the apex of what had been a four-hundred-year preoccupation with secular materialism. Affluence and security had spread to include a large and growing middle class, and into this material success was born an enormous new generation, a generation whose intuitions would help lead humanity toward a third great transformation.

This generation grew up constantly reminded that they lived

in the greatest country in the world, the land of the free, with liberty and justice for all its citizens. Yet, as they matured, members of this generation found a disturbing disparity between this popular American self-image and actual reality. They found that many people in this land—women and certain racial minorities—were, by law and custom, definitely *not free*. By the sixties the new generation was inspecting closely, and many were finding other disturbing aspects of the United States' self-image—for instance, a blind patriotism that expected young people to go into a foreign land to fight a political war that had no clearly expressed purpose and no prospect of victory.

Just as disturbing was the culture's spiritual practice. The materialism of the previous four hundred years had pushed the mystery of life, and death, far into the background. Many found the churches and synagogues full of pompous and meaningless ritual. Attendance seemed more social than spiritual, and the members too restricted by a sense of how they might be perceived and judged by their onlooking peers.

As the vision progressed, I could tell that the new generation's tendency to analyze and judge arose from a deep-seated intuition that there was more to life than the old material reality took into account. The new generation sensed new spiritual meaning just beyond the horizon, and they began to explore other, lesser known religions and spiritual points of view. For the first time the Eastern religions were understood in great numbers, serving to validate the mass intuition that spiritual perception was an inner experience, a shift in awareness that changed forever one's sense of identity and purpose. Similarly the Jewish Cabalist writings and the Western Christian mystics, such as Meister Eckehart and Teilhard de Chardin, provided other intriguing descriptions of a deeper spirituality.

At the same time, information was surfacing from the human sciences—sociology, psychiatry, psychology, and anthropology—as well as from modern physics, that cast new light on the nature of human consciousness and creativity. This cumulation of thought, together with the perspective provided by the East, gradually began to crystallize into what was later called the *Human Potential Movement,* the emerging belief that human beings were presently actualizing only a small portion of their vast physical, psychological, and spiritual potential.

I watched as, over the course of several decades, this information and the spiritual experience it spawned grew into a *critical mass* of awareness, a leap in consciousness from which we began to formulate a new view of what living a human life was all about, including, ultimately, an actual remembrance of the Nine Insights.

Yet, even as this new view was crystallizing, surging through the human world as a contagion of consciousness, many others in the new generation began to pull back, suddenly alarmed at the growing instability in culture which seemed to correspond to the arrival of the new paradigm. For hundreds of years the solid agreements of the old worldview had maintained a well-defined, even rigid, order for human life. All roles were clearly defined, and everyone knew his place: for instance, men at work, women and children at home, nuclear and genetic families intact, a ubiquitous work ethic. Citizens were expected to discover a place in the economy, to find meaning in family and children, and to know that the purpose of life was to live well and create a more materially secure world for the succeeding generation.

Then came the sixties wave of questioning and analysis and criticism, and the unwavering rules began to crumble. No longer was behavior effectively governed by powerful agreements.

Everyone now seemed empowered, liberated, free to chart his or her own course in life, to reach out for this nebulous idea of potential. In this climate what others thought ceased to be the real determinant of our action and conduct; increasingly our behavior was being determined by how we felt inside, by our own inner ethics.

For those who had truly adopted a more lived, spiritual point of view, characterized by honesty and love toward others, ethical behavior was not a problem. But of concern were those who had lost the outer guidelines for living, without yet forming a strong inner code. They seemed to be falling into a cultural no-man's-land, where now anything seemed to be permissible: crime and drugs and addictive impulses of all kinds, not to mention a loss of the work ethic. To make matters worse, many seemed to be using the new findings of the Human Potential Movement to imply that criminals and deviates weren't really even responsible for their own actions, but were, instead, victims of an oppressive culture that shamelessly allowed the social conditions that shaped this behavior.

As I continued to watch, I understood what I was seeing: a polarization of viewpoint was quickly forming around the planet, as those who were undecided now reacted against a cultural viewpoint they saw leading to runaway chaos and uncertainty, perhaps even to the total disintegration of their way of life. In the United States especially, a growing number of people were becoming convinced they were now facing what amounted to a life-and-death struggle against the permissiveness and liberalism of the past twenty-five years—a culture war, as they called it— with nothing short of the survival of Western civilization at stake. I could see that many of them even considered the cause already near lost, and thus advocated extreme action.

In the face of this backlash, I could see the advocates of Human Potential moving into fear and defensiveness themselves, sensing that many hard-earned victories for individual rights and social compassion were now in danger of being swept away by a tide of conservatism. Many considered this reaction against liberation an attack by the embattled forces of greed and exploitation, who were pushing forth in one last attempt to dominate the weaker members of society.

Here I could clearly see what was intensifying the polarization: each side was thinking the other to be a conspiracy of evil.

The advocates of the old worldview were no longer considering the Human Potentialists as misguided or naive, but were, in fact, considering them to be part of a larger conspiracy of *big government* socialists, holdout adherents of the communist solution, who were seeking to accomplish exactly what was occurring: the erosion of cultural life to the point where an all-powerful government could come in and straighten everything out. In their view this conspiracy was using fear of increasing crime as an excuse to register guns and systematically disarm the public, giving ever-greater control to a centralized bureaucracy that would finally monitor the movement of cash and credit cards through uplinks into the Internet, rationalizing the growing control of the electronic economy as crime prevention, or as a necessity to collect taxes or prevent sabotage. Finally, perhaps under the ploy of an impending natural disaster, *big brother* would step forward and confiscate wealth and declare martial law.

For the advocates of liberation and change, just the opposite scenario seemed more likely. In the face of the conservatives' political gains, all that they had worked for seemed to be crashing before their eyes. They, too, observed the increasing violent crime and the degenerating family structures, only for them the cause was not too much government intervention, but too little, too late.

In every nation capitalism had failed a whole class of people, and the reason was clear: for poor people there existed no opportunity to participate in the system. Effective education wasn't there. The jobs weren't there. And instead of helping, the government seemed ready to back away, throwing out the antipoverty programs with all the other hard-won social gains of the last twenty-five years.

I could see clearly that, in their growing disillusionment, the reformers were beginning to believe the worst: that the rightward swing in human society could only be the result of increased manipulation and control by the moneyed, corporate interests in the world. These interests seemed to be buying governments, buying the media, and ultimately, as in Nazi Germany, they would slowly divide the world into the haves and the have-nots, with the largest, richest corporations running the small entrepreneurs out of business and controlling more and more of the wealth. Sure there would be riots, but that would just play into the hands of the elite as they strengthened their police control.

My awareness suddenly jumped to a higher level and I finally understood the polarization of Fear completely: great numbers of people seemed to be gravitating to one perspective or the other, with both sides raising the stakes to that of war, of good vs. evil, and both visualizing the other as the perpetrators of a grand conspiracy.

And in the background I now understood the growing influence of those people who claimed to be able to explain this emergent evil. These were the *end-times* analysts to whom Joel had referred earlier. In the growing turmoil of the transition, these interpreters were beginning to increase their power. In their view the Bible's prophecies were to be understood literally, and what they saw in the uncertainty of our time was the long-awaited apocalypse preparing to descend. Soon would come the outright holy war in which humans would be divided between the forces of darkness and armies of light. They envisioned this war as a real physical conflict, fast and bloody, and for those who knew it was coming, only one decision was important: be on the correct side when the fighting began.

Yet simultaneously, just as with the other landmark turns in human history, I could see beyond the Fear and retrenchment to the actual Birth Visions of those involved. Clearly everyone on both sides of the polarization had come into the physical dimension intending that this polarization not be so intense. We wanted a smooth transition from the old materialistic worldview to the new spiritual one, and we wanted a transformation in which the best of the older traditions would be recognized and integrated into the new world that was emerging.

I could clearly see that this growing belligerence was an aberration, coming not from intention, but from the Fear. Our original vision was that the ethics of human society would be maintained at the same time that each person could be fully liberated and the environment protected; and that economic creativity would be at once conserved and transformed by introducing an overriding spiritual purpose. And further, that this spiritual purpose could descend fully into the world and initiate a utopia in a way that symbolically fulfilled the end-times Scriptures.

My awareness amplified even further, and just as when I had watched Maya's Birth Vision, I could almost glimpse this higher spiritual understanding, the full picture of where human history was intended to go from here, how we could achieve this reconciliation of views and go on to fulfill our human destiny. Then, as before, my head began to spin, and I lost concentration; I couldn't reach the level of energy needed to grasp it.

The vision began to disappear, and I strained to hold on, seeing the current situation one last time. Clearly, without the mediating influence of the World Vision, the polarization of Fear would continue to accelerate. I could see the two sides hardening, their feelings intensifying, as both began to think the other to be not just wrong, but hideous, venal . . . in league with the devil himself.

After a moment of dizziness and a sense of rapid movement, I looked around and saw Wil beside me. He glanced my way, then gazed out at the dark gray environment, a concerned expression on his face. We had traveled to a new location.

"Were you able to see my vision of history?" I asked.

He looked at me again and nodded. "What we just saw was a new spiritual interpretation of history, somewhat specific to your cultural view, but amazingly revealing. I've never seen anything like that before. This has to be part of the Tenth—a clear view of the human quest as seen in the Afterlife. We're understanding that everyone is born with a positive intention, trying to bring more of the knowledge contained in the Afterlife into the physical. All of us! History has been a long process of awakening. When we are born into the physical, of course, we run into this problem of going unconscious and having to be socialized and trained in the cultural reality of the day. After that, all we can remember are these gut feelings, these intuitions, to do certain things. But we constantly have to fight the Fear. Often the Fear is so great we fail to follow through with what we intended, or we distort it somehow. But everyone, and I mean everyone, comes in with the best of intentions."

"So you think a serial killer, for instance, really came here to do something good?"

"Yes, originally. All killing is a rage and lashing out that is a way of overcoming an inner sense of Fear and helplessness."

"I don't know," I said. "Aren't some people just inherently bad?"

"No, they just go crazy in the Fear and make horrible mistakes. And, ultimately, they must bear the full responsibility of these mistakes. But what has to be understood is that horrible acts are caused, in part, by our very tendency to assume that some people are naturally evil. That's the mistaken view that fuels the polarization. Both sides can't believe humans can act the way they do without being intrinsically no good, and so they increasingly dehumanize and alienate each other, which increases the Fear and brings out the worst in everyone." He seemed distracted again, looking away.

"Each side thinks the other is involved in a conspiracy of the greatest sort," he added, "the embodiment of all that's negative."

I noticed he was looking out toward the distance again, and when I followed his eyes, and also focused on the environment, I began to pick up an ominous sense of darkness and foreboding.

"I think," he continued, "that we can't bring in the World Vision, or resolve the polarization, until we understand the real nature of evil and the actual reality of Hell."

"Why do you say that?" I asked.

He glanced at me one more time, then gazed out again into the dull gray. "Because Hell is exactly where we are."

# AN
# INNER
# HELL

$A$ chill surged through my body as I looked out on the gray environment. The ominous feeling I perceived earlier was turning into a clear sense of alienation and despair.

"Have you been here before?" I asked Wil.

"Only to the edge," he replied. "Never out here in the middle. Do you feel how cold it is?"

I nodded as a movement caught my eye. "What is that?"

Wil shook his head. "I'm not sure."

A swirling mass of energy seemed to be moving in our direction.

"It must be another soul group," I said.

As they came closer, I tried to focus on their thoughts, feeling an even greater sense of alienation, even anger. I tried to shrug it off, open up more.

"Wait," I vaguely heard Wil say. "You're not strong enough." But it was too late. I was suddenly pulled into an intense blackness and then beyond it into a large town of some kind. In terror

I looked around, struggling to keep my wits, and realized that the architecture indicated the nineteenth century. I was standing on a street corner full of people walking by, and in the distance was the raised dome of a capitol building. At first I thought I was actually in the nineteenth century, but several aspects of the reality were wrong: the horizon faded out to a strange gray color, and the sky was olive green, similar to the sky above the office construction that Williams had created when he was avoiding the realization that he had died.

Then I became aware of four men watching me from the opposite street corner. An icy-cold feeling swept my body. All were well dressed and one cocked his head and took a puff from a large cigar. Another checked a watch and returned it to his vest pocket. Their look was sophisticated but menacing.

"Anyone who has raised their ire is a friend of mine," a low voice spoke from behind me.

I turned to see a large, barrel-shaped man, also well dressed and wearing a wide-brimmed felt hat, walking toward me. His face seemed familiar; I had seen him before. But where?

"Don't mind them," he added. "They're not so hard to outsmart."

I stared at his tall, stooped posture and shifting eyes, then remembered who he was. He had been the commander of the federal troops I had seen in the visions of the nineteenth-century war, the one who had refused to see Maya and had ordered the battle against the Native people to begin. This town was a construction, I thought. He must have re-created his later life situation in order to avoid realizing he was dead.

"This is not real," I blurted. "You're . . . uh . . . deceased."

He seemed to ignore my statement. "So what have you done to piss off that bunch of jackals?"

"I haven't done anything."

"Oh yes, you've done something. I know that look they're giving you. They think they run this town, you know. In fact, they think they can run the whole world." He shook his head. "These people never trust fate. They think they're responsible for seeing that the future turns out exactly as they plan. Everything. Economic development, governments, the flow of money, even the relative value of world currencies. All of which is not a bad idea, really. God knows the world is full of peons and idiots, who will ruin everything if left to their own devices. The people have to be herded and controlled as much as possible, and if one can make a little money along the way, why not?

"But these nuts tried to run me. Of course, I'm too smart for them. I've always been too smart for them. So what did you do?"

"Listen," I said. "Try to understand. None of this is real."

"Hey," he replied, "I would suggest that you take me into your confidence. If they're against you, I'm the only friend you have."

I looked away, but I could tell he was still eyeing me suspiciously.

"They're treacherous people," he went on. "They'll never forgive you. Take my situation, for example. All they wanted was to use my military experience to quash the Indians and open up their lands. But I was onto them. I knew they couldn't be trusted, that I would have to look out for myself." He gave me a wry look. "It's harder for them to use you and throw you away if you're a war hero, right? After the war I sold myself to the public. That way, these characters had to play ball with me. But let me tell you: never underestimate these people. They are capable of anything!"

He backed away from me a moment, as if pondering my appearance.

"In fact," he added, "they may have sent you as a spy."

At a loss as to what to do, I started to walk away.

"You bastard!" he yelled. "I was right."

I saw him reach into a pocket and pull a short knife. Petrified, I forced my body to move, running down the street and into an alleyway, his footsteps heavy behind me. On the right was a door, partially open. I ran through it and slid the bolt into the locked position. My next breath drew in the heavy odor of opium. Around me were dozens of people, their faces staring absently up at me. Were they real, I wondered, or part of the constructed illusion? Most quickly turned back to their muted conversation and hookah pipes, so I started to walk through the dirty mattresses and sofas to another door.

"I know you," a woman slurred. She was leaning against the wall by the door, her head hanging forward as if too heavy for her neck. "I went to your school."

I looked at her in confusion for a moment, then remembered the young girl in my high school who had suffered from repeated episodes of depression and drug use. Resisting all intervention, she had finally overdosed and died.

"Sharon, is that you?"

She managed a smile, and I glanced back at the door, concerned that the knife-bearing commander might have found a way inside.

"It's okay," she said. "You can stay here with us. You'll be safe in this room. Nothing can hurt you."

I walked a step closer and as gently as possible said, "I don't want to stay. All this is an illusion."

As I said that, three or four people turned and looked at me angrily.

"Please, Sharon," I whispered. "Just come with me."

Two of the closest stood up and walked over beside Sharon. "Get out of here," one told me. "Leave her alone."

"Don't listen to him," the other said to Sharon. "He's crazy. We need each other."

I stooped slightly so I could look directly into Sharon's eyes. "Sharon, none of this is real. You're dead. We have to find a way out of here."

"Shut up!" another person screamed. Four or five more people walked toward me, hate in their eyes. "Leave us alone."

I began to back toward the door; the crowd moved toward me. Through the bodies I could see Sharon turning back to her hookah hose. I turned and ran through the door, only to realize that I wasn't outside. I was in an office of some kind, surrounded by computers, filing cabinets, a conference table—modern, twentieth-century furniture and equipment.

"Hey, you're not supposed to be in here," someone said. I turned around to see a middle-aged man looking at me over his reading glasses. "Where's my secretary? I don't have time for this. What do you want?"

"Someone's chasing me. I was trying to hide."

"Good God, man! Then don't come in here. I said I don't have time for this. You haven't the slightest idea what I have to do today. Look at these case files. Who do you think will process them if I don't?" I thought I saw a look of terror on his face.

I shook my head and looked for another door. "Don't you know you're dead?" I asked. "This is all imagined."

He paused, the look of terror shifting to anger, then asked, "How did you get in here? Are you a criminal?"

I found a door that led outside and ran out. The streets were now completely empty except for one carriage. It pulled up to the hotel across from me, and a beautiful woman, dressed in evening attire, got out and glanced over toward me, then smiled. There was something warm and caring about her demeanor. I dashed across the street toward her, and she paused to watch me approach, her smile coy and inviting.

"You're alone," she said. "Why don't you join me?"

"Where are you going?" I asked tentatively.

"To a party."

"Who's going to be there?"

"I have no idea."

She opened the door to the hotel and motioned for me to come with her. I followed aimlessly, trying to think of what to do. We walked into the elevator and she pushed the button for the fourth floor. As we rode up, the sensation of warmth and caring increased with each floor. Out of the corner of my eye I saw her staring at my hands. When I looked, she smiled again and pretended to have been caught.

The elevator opened and she led me down the hall to a particular door and knocked twice. After a moment the door was unlocked and a man opened it. His face lit up at the sight of the woman.

"Come in!" he said. "Come in!"

She invited me to enter ahead of her, and as I walked in, a young woman reached over and took my arm. She was dressed in a strapless gown and was barefooted.

"Oh, you're lost," she said. "Poor thing. You'll be safe in here with us."

Past the door I could see a man without a shirt. "Look at those thighs," he commented, staring at me.

"He has perfect hands," another said.

In a state of shock I realized the room was crowded with people in various stages of nudity and lovemaking.

"No, wait," I said. "I can't stay."

The woman on my arm said, "You would go back out there? It takes forever to find a group like this. Feel the energy in here. Not like the fear of being alone, huh?" She moved her hand across my chest.

Suddenly there was the sound of a scuffle on the other side of the room.

"No, leave me alone!" someone shouted. "I don't want to be here."

A young man no older than eighteen pushed several people away and ran out the door. I used the distraction to run out behind him. Not waiting for the elevator, he bounded down the adjacent stairs and I followed. When I reached the street, he was already on the other side.

I was about to shout for him to stop when I saw him freeze in terror. Ahead on the sidewalk was the commander, still holding the knife, but this time facing the group of men who had watched me earlier. They were all talking at the same time, posturing angrily. Abruptly one of the group pulled a gun, and the commander rushed toward him with the knife. Shots rang out, and the commander's hat and knife flew backward as the bullet pierced his forehead. He dropped to the ground with a thud, and as he did, the other men stopped in midmotion and began to fade away until they disappeared completely. Just as quickly the man on the ground also disappeared.

Across from me, the young man sat wearily down on the curb and put his head in his hands. I rushed up to him, my knees shaking.

"It's okay," I said. "They're gone."

"No, they're not," he said in frustration. "Look over there."

I turned and saw the four men who had disappeared standing

across the street in front of the hotel. Unbelievably they were in the exact position they had been in when I had first seen them. One puffed his cigar and the other checked his watch.

My heart skipped a beat as I also spotted the commander, standing across from them again, staring menacingly.

"This keeps happening over and over," the young man said. "I can't stand this anymore. Someone's got to help me."

Before I could say anything, two forms materialized to his right, but remained obscured, out of focus.

The young man stared at the forms for a long time, then, with a look of excitement on his face, said, "Roy, is that you?"

As I watched, the two forms moved toward him until he was completely hidden by their weaving shapes. After several minutes he had completely disappeared, along with the two souls.

I stared at the empty curb where he had been sitting, feeling remnants of a higher vibration. In my mind's eye I saw my soul group again and felt their deep caring and love. Concentrating on the feeling, I was able to shake off the blanketing anxiety and to amplify my energy in increments until finally I began to open up inside. Immediately the environment shifted to lighter shades of gray and the town disappeared. As my energy increased, I was able to image Wil's face, and instantly he was beside me.

"Are you okay?" he asked, turning to embrace me. His expression showed immense relief. "Those illusions were strong, and you willed yourself right into them."

"I know. I couldn't think, couldn't remember what to do."

"You were gone a long time; all we could do was send you energy."

"Who do you mean by we?"

"All these souls." Wil's hand gestured outwardly.

When I looked fully, I could see hundreds of souls stretching as far as I could see. Some were looking directly at us, but most appeared to be focused in another direction. I looked to see where they were staring, following their gaze to several large swirls of energy far in the distance. When I concentrated my focus, I realized that one of the swirls was in fact the town from which I had just escaped.

"What are those places?" I asked Wil.

"Mental constructions," he replied, "set up by souls who in life lived very restrictive control dramas and could not wake up after death. Many thousands of them exist out there."

"Were you able to see what was happening when I was in the construction?"

"Most of it. When I focused on the souls nearby, I could pick up on their view of what was happening to you. This ring of souls is constantly beaming energy into the illusions, hoping someone will respond."

"Did you see the teenage boy? He was able to wake up. But the others didn't seem to pay attention to anything."

Wil turned to face me. "Do you remember what we saw during Williams' Life Review? At first he couldn't accept what was happening, and he began to repress his death to the extent that he created a mental construction of his office."

"Yes, I thought of that when I was down there."

"Well, that's how it works for everyone. If we die and we have been so immersed in our control drama and routine as a way to repress the mystery and insecurity of life, to such a degree that we can't even wake up after death, then we create these illusions or trances so we can continue the same way of feeling safe, even after we enter the Afterlife. If Williams' soul group had not reached him, he would have entered one of the hellish places where you were. It's all a reaction to Fear. The people there would be paralyzed with Fear if they didn't find some way to ward it off, to repress it below consciousness. What they're doing is repeating the same dramas, the same coping devices, they practiced in life, and they can't stop."

"So these illusional realities are just severe control dramas?"

"Yes, they all fall within the general styles of the control dramas, except that they are more intense and nonreflective. For example, the man with the knife, the commander, was no doubt an intimidator in the way he stole energy from others. And he rationalized this behavior by assuming that the world was out to get him, and of course, in his life on Earth these expectations drew just those kinds of people into his life, so his mental vision was fulfilled. Here he just created imaginary people to be after him so he could reproduce the same situation.

"If he were to run out of people to intimidate and his energy were to fall, anxiety would begin to seep into consciousness again. So he has to keep up the intimidator role constantly. He has to keep this particular kind of action going, the action he learned long ago, the only action he knows that will preoccupy his mind sufficiently to kill the Fear. It is the action itself—the compulsive, dramatic, high-adrenaline nature of the action—that pushes the anxiety so far into the background that he can forget about it, repress it, and feel half at ease in his existence, at least for a little while."

"What about the drug users?" I asked.

"In this case, they were taking passivity, the 'poor me,' to the extreme of projecting nothing but despair and cruelty on the entire world, rationalizing a need to escape. Obsessively pursuing drugs still serves the function of preoccupying the mind and repressing anxiety, even in the Afterlife.

"In the physical dimension drugs often produce a euphoria

quite like the euphoria that comes from love. The problem with this false euphoria, however, is that the body resists the chemicals and counteracts them, which means that, as the drug is repeatedly used, it takes an increasingly larger dose to reach the same effect, which eventually destroys the body."

I thought of the commander again. "Something really strange happened down there. The man who was chasing me was killed, and then he seemed to come back to life and start the drama all over again."

"That's how it works in this self-imposed Hell. All these illusions always play out and blow up in the end. If you had been with someone who had repressed the mystery of life by eating great amounts of fat, a heart attack might have ended it. The drug users eventually destroy their own bodies, the commander dies over and over, and so on.

"And it works the same way in the physical dimension: a compulsive control drama always fails, sooner or later. Usually it happens during the trials and challenges of life; routines break down and the anxiety rushes in. It is what's called hitting bottom. This is the time to wake up and handle the Fear in another way; but if a person can't, then he or she goes right back into the trance. And if one doesn't wake up in the physical dimension, one might have difficulty waking up in the other as well.

"These compulsive trances account for all horrible behavior in the physical dimension. This is the psychology of all truly evil acts, the motivation behind the inconceivable behavior of child molesters, sadists, and serial monsters of all kinds. They're simply repeating the only behavior they know that will numb the mind and keep away the anxiety that comes from the lostness they feel."

"So you're saying," I interjected, "that there is no organized, conspiratorial evil in the world, no satanic plot to which we fall prey?"

"None. There is only human fear and the bizarre ways that humans try to ward it off."

"What about the many references in sacred texts and scriptures to Satan?"

"This idea is a metaphor, a symbolic way of warning people to look to the divine for security, not to their sometimes tragic ego urges and habits. Blaming an outside force for everything bad was perhaps important at a certain stage in human development. But now it obscures the truth, because blaming our behavior on forces outside ourselves is a way of avoiding responsibility. And we tend to use the idea of Satan to project that some people are inherently evil so we can dehumanize the ones we disagree with and write them off. It is time now to understand the true nature of human evil in a more sophisticated way and then to deal with it."

"If there is no satanic plot," I said, "then 'possession' doesn't exist."

"That's not so," Wil said emphatically. "Psychological 'possession' does exist. But it is not the result of a conspiracy of evil; it is just energy dynamics. Fearful people want to control others. That's why certain groups try to pull you in and convince you to follow them, and ask you to submit to their authority, or fight you if you try to leave."

"When I was first drawn into that illusory town, I thought I had been possessed by some demonic force."

"No, you were drawn in because you made the same mistake you made earlier: you didn't just open up and listen to those souls; you gave yourself over to them, as if they automatically had all the answers, without checking to see if they were connected and motivated by love. And unlike the souls who are divinely connected, they didn't back away from you. They just pulled you into their world, the same way some crazy group or cult might do in the physical dimension if you don't discriminate."

Wil paused as if in thought, then continued. "All this is more of the Tenth Insight; that's why we're seeing it. As communication between the two dimensions increases, we'll begin to have more encounters with souls in the Afterlife. This part of the Insight is that we must discern between those souls who are awake and connected with the spirit of love and those who are fearful and stuck in an obsessive trance of some kind. But we must do so without invalidating and dehumanizing those caught in such fear dramas by thinking they are demons or devils. They are souls in a growth process, just like us. In fact, in the Earth dimension those who are now caught up in dramas from which they can't escape are often the very souls who were the most optimistic in their Birth Visions."

I shook my head, not following his meaning.

"That is why," he continued, "they chose to be born into such drastic, fearful situations that necessitate such intense, crazy coping devices."

"You're talking about coming into abusive and dysfunctional families, that sort of situation?"

"Yes. Intense control dramas of all kinds, whether they are violent or just perverse and strange addictions, come from environments where life is so abusive and dysfunctional and constrictive, and the level of Fear is so great, that they spawn this same rage and anger or perversion over and over, generation after generation. The individuals who are born into these situations choose to do so on purpose, with clarity."

The idea seemed preposterous to me. "Why would anyone want to be born into a place like that?"

"Because they were sure they had enough strength to break out, to end the cycle, to heal the family system in which they would be born. They were confident that they could awaken and work through the resentment and anger at finding themselves in these deprived circumstances, and see it all as a preparation for a mission—usually one of helping others out of similar situations. Even if they are violent, we have to see them as having the potential to break free of the drama."

"Then the liberal perspective on crime and violence, the idea that everyone can change and be rehabilitated, is the desirable one. The conservative approach is without merit?"

Wil smiled. "Not exactly. The liberals are right to see that people who have grown up in abusive and oppressive situations are a product of their environments, and the conservatives are out of touch to the extent they believe stopping a life of crime or public dole is just a matter of making a conscious choice.

"But the liberal approach is superficial as well, to the degree they believe people can change if offered different circumstances, better financial support, or education, for instance. Usually intervention programs focus only on helping others to better their decision making and economic choices. In the case of violent offenders, rehabilitation attempts have always offered, at best, superficial counseling and, in the worst cases, excuses and leniency, which is precisely the wrong thing to do. Every time someone with a disturbed control drama is slapped on the hand, turned loose with no consequences, it enables the behavior to continue and reinforces the idea that this behavior is not serious, which just sets up the circumstances that guarantee it will occur again."

"Then what can be done?" I asked.

Wil seemed to be vibrating with excitement. "We can learn to intervene spiritually! And that means helping to bring the whole process into consciousness, as these souls here are doing for those caught in the illusions."

Wil was staring at the souls in the ring, then looked at me and shook his head. "I can get all the information I've just relayed to you from these souls, but I still can't see the World Vision clearly. We haven't learned how to build enough energy yet."

I focused on the souls in the ring but could get no information other than what Wil had conveyed. Clearly the soul groups held a greater knowledge and were projecting this knowledge toward the fear constructions, but like Wil, I still couldn't quite understand anything more.

"At least we have another piece of the Tenth Insight," Wil said. "We know that no matter how undesirable the behavior of others is, we have to grasp that they are just souls attempting to wake up, like us."

I was suddenly jolted backward by a blast of dissonant noise, images of whirling colors seizing my mind. Wil lunged forward and caught me at the last moment, pulling me into his energy and again holding me back firmly. For a moment I seemed to shake violently and then the discord passed.

"They've started the experiment again," Wil said.

I shook off the dizziness and looked at him. "That means Curtis will probably try to use force to stop them. He's convinced that's the only way."

As soon as I spoke those words, I saw a clear picture of Feyman in my mind, the man David Lone Eagle thought had something to do with the experiment. He was somewhere overlooking the valley. Glancing at Wil, I realized that he had seen the same image. He nodded in agreement and we instantly began to move.

When we stopped, Wil and I were facing each other. Around us was more gray. Another loud, disharmonious sound shattered the silence, and Wil's face began to lose focus. He continued to hold onto me, and after several moments the sound ended.

"These sound bursts are coming more frequently now," Wil said. "We may not have much time left."

I nodded, fighting the dizziness.

"Let's look around," Wil said.

As soon as we focused on our surroundings, we saw what appeared to be a mass of energy several hundred yards away. Immediately it closed to within forty or fifty feet.

"Be careful," Wil cautioned. "Don't identify completely with them. Just listen and find out who they are."

I focused warily, and immediately saw souls in motion and an image of the town from which I had escaped.

I recoiled in fear, which actually made them come closer to us.

"Stay centered in love," Wil instructed. "They can't pull us in unless we act as though we want them to save us. Try to send them love and energy. It'll either help them or make them run away."

Realizing the souls were more afraid than I was, I found my center and beamed them love energy. Immediately they moved rapidly away from us to their original position.

"Why can't they accept the love and wake up?" I asked Wil.

"Because when they feel the energy and it raises their con-sciousness a degree, their preoccupation lifts somewhat and doesn't fend off the anxiety of their aloneness. Coming into awareness and breaking free of a control drama always feels anxious at first, because the compulsion has to lift before the inward solution to the lostness can be found. That's why a 'dark night of the soul' sometimes precedes increased awareness and spiritual euphoria."

A movement to the right caught our attention. When I focused, I realized that other souls were in the area; they came closer and the others moved away. I strained to pick up on what the group was doing.

"Why do you think this group is here?" I asked Wil.

He shrugged. "They have something to do with this guy Feyman."

In the space around the group I began to see a moving image, a scene of some kind. When I brought it clearly into focus, I realized it was the image of an expansive industrial plant somewhere on Earth, with large metal buildings and rows of what looked like transformers and pipes and miles of interlinking wire. At the center of the complex, atop one of the largest buildings, was a command center of pure glass. Inside I could see rows of computers and gauges of all descriptions. I glanced at Wil.

"I see it," he said.

As we continued to survey the complex, our perspective expanded so that we could now view the plant from above. From here we could see miles of wire leaving the plant in all directions, feeding huge towers containing some sort of laser beams shooting energy out to other local stations.

"Do you know what all this is?" I asked Wil.

He nodded. "It's a centralized energy-generating plant."

Movement at one end of the complex attracted our attention. Emergency vans and fire trucks were arriving at one of the larger buildings. An ominous glow radiated from the third-floor windows. At one point the glow brightened and then the ground under the entire building seemed to crack. In an explosion of dust and debris the building shuddered and then slowly collapsed. To the right another building burst into flames.

The scene moved to the command center, where inside, technicians moved frantically. From the right a door opened and a man entered with an arm full of charts and blueprints. He laid them out on a table and worked with what appeared to be determined confidence. Walking with a limp to one side of the room, he began to adjust switches and dials. Gradually the ground stopped shaking and the fires were brought under control. He continued to work hastily and to instruct the other technicians.

I looked at the individual now in charge more closely and then turned to Wil. "That's Feyman!"

Before Wil could respond, the scene shifted into fast-forward. Before our eyes the plant was saved, then, quickly, workers began to dismantle it, building by building. At the same time, on a site nearby, a new, smaller facility was being constructed that would manufacture more compact generators. Finally most of the complex had been returned to its natural, wooded state, and the new facility was turning out small units that we could see behind each house and business throughout the countryside.

Abruptly our perspective backed away until we could see a single individual in the foreground watching the same scene we were. When we could see his profile, I realized that it was Feyman, before his current birth, contemplating what he could achieve in life.

Wil and I looked at each other. "This is part of his Birth Vision, isn't it?" I asked.

Wil nodded. "This must be his soul group. Let's see how much more we can find out about him."

We both focused on the group, and another image formed in front of us. It was the nineteenth-century war camp; the headquarters tent again. We could see Feyman together with the commander, the man I had seen again in the illusional town. Feyman was the other aide who had been there with Williams. He was the one who limped.

As we watched their interaction, we began to pick up on the story of their association. A bright tactician, Feyman was in charge of strategy and technological developments. In advance of the attack the commander had ordered smallpox-laden blankets covertly traded to the Native Americans, a tactic Feyman adamantly opposed, not so much because of its effect on the indigenous people as because he felt that it was politically indefensible.

Afterward, even as the success of the battle was being hailed in Washington, the press found out about the use of smallpox, and an investigation was launched. The commander and his cronies in Washington set Feyman up as the scapegoat and his career was ruined. Later the commander set forth on a glorious political career and national stature, before he was also treacherously double-crossed by the same Washington insiders.

Feyman, for his part, never recovered; his own political ambitions had been totally destroyed. Over the years he became increasingly more embittered and resentful, trying desperately to marshal public opinion to challenge his commander's account of the battle. For a while several journalists pursued the story, but soon public interest faded completely and Feyman remained in a state of disgrace. Later, toward the end of his life, he languished in the realization that his political goals would never be reached, and, blaming his old commander for his humiliation, he attempted to assassinate the ex-politician at a state dinner and was shot dead by bodyguards.

Because Feyman had cut himself off from his inner security and love, he could not fully awaken after death. For years he believed he had escaped his ill-fated attempt to kill his old commander, and had lived in illusional constructions, holding on to his hate and doomed to the repeated horror of planning and attempting another assassination, only to be shot, over and over.

As I watched, I realized that Feyman could have been trapped in the illusions for a much longer period of time had it not been for the determined efforts of another man who had been at the military encampment with Feyman. I could see an image of his face, and I recognized his expression.

"That's Joel again, the journalist I met," I said to Wil without losing my focus on the image.

Wil nodded in response.

After death, Joel had become a member of the outer soul ring and became totally dedicated to waking up Feyman. His intention during the lifetime with Feyman had been to expose any cruelty or treachery on the part of the military toward the Native Americans, but even though he had known about the smallpox contamination, he had been persuaded to keep quiet by a combination of bribes and threats. After death he had been devastated by his Life Review, but had remained conscious, and had vowed to help Feyman, who he felt had been ruined because of his failure to intervene.

After a long period of time, Feyman finally responded and underwent a long and painful Life Review himself. He had originally intended in the nineteenth-century life to become a civil engineer, involved in the peaceful development of technology. But he had been beguiled by the prospect of becoming a war hero, like the commander, and of developing new war strategies and devices.

In the years between lives, he had been involved in helping others on Earth with the proper use of technology, when he slowly began to receive a vision of another life approaching. Slowly at first and then with great conviction, he realized that soon mass-energy devices would be discovered that had the potential of liberating humankind, but these devices would be extremely dangerous.

As he felt himself being born, he knew that he would come to work with this technology, and he was well aware that in order to succeed, he would have to again face his tendency to crave power and recognition and status. Yet he saw that he would have help; there would be six other people. He visualized the valley, working together somewhere in the dark, the falls in the background, utilizing a process to bring in the World Vision.

As he began to fade from view, I could make out aspects of the process he was seeing. First the group of seven would begin to remember past experiences with each other and to work through the residual feelings. Then the group would consciously amplify its energy, using the Eighth Insight techniques, and each would express his or her particular Birth Vision, and finally the vibration would accelerate, unifying the soul groups of the seven individuals. Out of the knowledge gained would come the full memory of our intended future, the World Vision, the view of where we're going and what we have to do to reach our destiny.

Suddenly the whole scene disappeared, along with Feyman's group. Wil and I were left there alone.

Wil's eyes were animated. "Do you see what was happening?" he asked. "This means that Feyman's original intention was actually to perfect and decentralize the technology he's working on. If he realizes this fact, he will stop the experiment."

"We've got to find him," I said.

"No," Wil replied, pausing to think. "That won't help, not yet. We've got to find the rest of this group of seven; it must take the pooled energy of a group to bring in the memory of the World Vision, a group that can work through the process of re-membering and energize themselves."

"I don't understand this part about clearing residual feelings."

Wil moved closer. "Remember the other mental images you've been having? The memories of other places, other times?"

"Yes."

"The group that is forming to deal with this experiment has been together before. There will be residual feelings that *must* be worked through! Everyone will have to deal with them."

Wil looked away for a moment, then said, "This is more of the Tenth Insight. Not just one group is coming in; there are many others. We'll all have to learn to clear these resentments."

As he spoke, I thought about the many group situations I'd experienced, where some members of the group liked each other immediately, while others seemed to fall into instant discord, for no apparent reason. I wondered: was human culture now ready to perceive the distant source of these unconscious reactions?

Then, without warning, another shrill sound reverberated through my body. Wil grabbed me and pulled me closer, our faces almost touching. "If you fall again, I don't know if you can get back while the experiment is operating at this level," he shouted. "You'll have to find the others!"

A second blast ripped us apart, and I felt myself release into the familiar swirling colors, knowing that I was heading back, as before, into the Earth dimension. Yet this time, instead of tumbling quickly into the physical, I seemed to linger momentarily; something was pulling at my solar plexus, moving me laterally. As I strained to focus, the surging environment calmed, and I began to sense the presence of another person, without actually seeing the individual's form. I could almost remember the character of the feeling. Who makes me feel this way?

At last I began to discern a blurry figure thirty or forty feet away, which moved closer, gradually, until I recognized who it was. Charlene! As she closed to within ten feet, I sensed a shift in my body, as though I was suddenly relaxing more completely. Simultaneously I noticed a pinkish-red energy field that encircled Charlene. Seconds later, to my amazement, I noticed an identical field around myself. When we were about five feet from each other, the relaxation in my body grew into an increased sensualness and finally into a wave of orgasmic love. I suddenly couldn't think. What was happening?

Just as our fields were about to touch, the shrill dissonance returned and I was jolted backward again, twisting out of control.

# FORGIVING

As my head cleared, I gradually became aware of something cold and wet against my right cheek. Slowly I opened my eyes, the rest of my body frozen in place. For a moment the half-grown wolf looked at me and sniffed hard, his tail bristling, then he dashed into the woods as I jerked back and sat up.

In a tired stupor I retrieved my pack in the fading light and walked into the thick trees and raised my tent, afterward virtually collapsing into the sleeping bag. I struggled to stay awake, intrigued by my strange meeting with Charlene. Why had she been in the other dimension? What had drawn us together?

The next morning I awoke early and made oatmeal, wolfing it down, and then made my way carefully back to the small creek I had passed on my way up the ridge to wash my face and fill my canteen. I still felt tired, but I was also anxious to find Curtis.

Suddenly I was jolted to my feet by the sound of an explosion toward the east. That had to be Curtis, I thought, as I ran to the tent. A wave of fear passed through me as I quickly packed and headed toward the sound of the blast.

After about a half mile the woods ended abruptly at what appeared to be an abandoned pasture. Several strands of rusty barbed wire hung loosely between the trees in my path. I surveyed the open field and the line of trees and dense bush a hundred yards beyond. At that moment the bushes parted and Curtis burst through and headed in a dead run straight toward me. I waved, and he immediately recognized who I was and slowed to a fast walk. When he reached me, he carefully climbed through the barbed wire and collapsed against a tree, breathing rapidly.

"What happened?" I asked. "What did you blow up?"

He shook his head. "I couldn't do much. They're running the experiment underground. I didn't have enough explosives, and I . . . I didn't want to hurt the people inside. All I could do was blow up an outside dish antenna, which hopefully will delay them."

"How did you get close enough to do that?"

"I set the charges last night after dark. They must not expect anyone to be up here, because they have very few guards outside."

He paused for a moment as we heard the sound of trucks in the distance. "We'll have to get out of this valley," he continued, "and find some help. We don't have any choice now. They'll be coming."

"Wait a minute," I said. "I think we have a chance to stop them, but we've got to find Maya and Charlene."

His eyes widened. "Are you talking about Charlene Billings?"

"That's right."

"I know her. She used to do some contract research for the

corporation. I hadn't seen her for years, but I saw her last night going into the underground bunker. She was walking with several men, all of them heavily armed."

"Were they holding her against her will?"

"I couldn't tell," Curtis said distractedly, his ears tuned to the trucks, which now seemed to be heading in our direction. "We've got to get out of here. I know a place where we can hide until dark, but we'll have to hurry." He looked back toward the east. "I set a false trail, but it won't sidetrack them for long."

"I've got to tell you what happened," I said. "I found Wil again."

"Right, tell me on the way," he said, walking quickly. "We've got to move."

I looked out of the mouth of the cave and across the deep gorge to the opposite hillside. No movement. I listened carefully but could hear nothing. We had walked in a northeasterly direction for about a mile, and as quickly as I could, I had told Curtis what I had experienced in the other dimension, stressing my belief that Williams had been correct. We could stop this experiment if we could find the rest of the group and remember the larger Vision.

I could tell that Curtis was resisting. He had listened for a while, but then began rambling about his past association with Charlene. I was frustrated that he knew nothing that might explain what she had to do with this experiment. He also told me how he had come to know David. They had become friends, he explained, after a chance meeting had revealed many common experiences in the military.

I told him it was significant that he and I both had an association with David and that we knew Charlene.

"I don't know what it means," he had said distractedly, and I had dropped it, but I knew it was further proof that we had all come to this valley for a reason. Afterward we had walked in silence as Curtis searched for the cave. When we had found it, he backtracked and erased our tracks with dead pine branches and then had lingered outside until he was convinced we hadn't been seen.

"This soup is ready," Curtis said from behind me. I had used my camp stove and water to cook the last of my freeze-dried food. Walking over, I made us both a bowl and then sat down again at the mouth of the cave, looking out.

"So how do you think this group can build enough energy to have an effect on these people?" he asked.

"I'm not sure exactly," I replied. "We'll have to figure it out."

He shook his head. "I don't think anything like that is possible. Probably all I did with my little bit of explosives was to irritate them and put them more on guard. They'll bring more people in, but I don't think they will stop. They would have had a replacement antenna close by. Maybe I should have taken out the door. God knows I could have. But I just couldn't bring myself to do that. Charlene was inside and who knows how many others. I would have had to shorten the timer, so they would have gotten me . . . but maybe it would have been worth it."

"No, I don't think so," I said. "We're going to find the other way."

"How?"

"It'll come to us."

We heard the faint sound of the vehicles again, and simultaneously I noticed a movement on the downslope below us.

"Someone's out there," I said.

We crouched down and looked closely. The figure moved again, partially obscured by the underbrush.

"That's Maya," I said, disbelieving.

Curtis and I stared at each other for a long moment, then I moved to get up. "I'll go get her," I said.

He grabbed my arm. "Stay low, and if the vehicles close in, leave her and come back here. Don't risk being seen."

I nodded and ran carefully down the hill. When I was close enough, I stopped and listened. The trucks were still moving closer. I called out to her in a low voice. She froze for an instant, then recognized me and climbed up a rocky slope to where I stood.

"I can't believe I found you!" she said, hugging my neck.

I led the way back to the cave and helped her through the opening in the rock. She appeared exhausted and her arms were covered with scratches, some of them still bleeding.

"What happened?" she asked. "I heard an explosion, and then those trucks were everywhere."

"Did anyone see you come this way?" Curtis asked with irritation. He was up and looking outside.

"I don't think so," she said. "I was able to hide."

I quickly introduced them. Curtis nodded and said, "I think I'll take a look." He slipped out through the opening and disappeared.

I opened my pack and took out a first-aid kit. "Were you able to find your friend with the Sheriff's Department?"

"No, I couldn't even get back to town. There were Forest Service agents along all the paths back. I saw a woman I knew and gave her a note to take to him. That's all I could do."

I applied some antiseptic to a long gash across Maya's knee.

"So why didn't you leave with the woman you saw? Why did you change your mind and come back out here?"

She took the antiseptic and silently began applying it herself. Finally she spoke: "I don't know why I came back. Maybe because I kept having these memories." She looked up at me. "I want to understand what's happening here."

I sat down facing her and gave her a sketchy summary of everything that had happened since we parted, particularly the information Wil and I had received about the group process of moving past the resentment to find the World Vision.

She looked overwhelmed but seemed to accept her role. "I noticed your ankle no longer seems to be bothering you."

"Yeah, I guess it cleared up when I remembered where the problem came from."

She stared at me for a moment, then said, "There are only three of us. You said Williams and Feyman had both seen seven."

"I don't know," I replied, "I'm just glad you're here. You're the one who knows about faith and visualization."

A look of terror crossed her face.

A few moments later Curtis came back through the opening and told us he had seen nothing out of the ordinary, then sat down away from us to finish his meal. I reached over and served another plate and gave it to Maya.

Curtis leaned back and handed her a canteen. "You know," he said, "you took a hell of a risk walking around in the open like that. You could have led them right to us."

Maya glanced at me and then said defensively, "I was trying to get away! I didn't know you were up here. I wouldn't even have come this way if the birds hadn't—"

"Well, you've got to understand how much trouble we're in!" Curtis interrupted. "We still haven't stopped this experiment."

He got up and stepped outside again and sat behind a large rock near the opening.

"Why is he so mad at me?" Maya asked.

"You said you were having memories, Maya. What kind?"

"I don't know . . . of another time, I guess, of trying to stop some other violence. That's why all this is so eerie to me."

"Does Curtis seem familiar to you?"

She struggled to think. "Maybe. I don't know. Why?"

"Do you remember when I told you about seeing a vision of all of us in the past, during the Native American wars? Well, you were killed, and someone else was with you who seemed to be following your lead, and he was killed too. I think it was Curtis."

"He blames me? Oh God, no wonder he's so mad."

"Maya, can you remember anything about what you two were doing?"

She closed her eyes and tried to think.

Suddenly she looked at me. "Was a Native American also there? A shaman?"

"Yes," I said. "He was killed too."

"We were thinking about something . . ." She looked me in the eye. "No, we were visualizing. We thought we could stop the war . . . That's all I can get."

"You've got to talk to Curtis and help him work through his anger. It's part of the process of remembering."

"Are you kidding? With him this angry?"

"I'll go speak with him first," I said, standing up.

She nodded slightly and looked away. I moved to the cave's opening, crawled out, and sat down beside Curtis.

"What do you think?" I asked.

He looked at me, slightly embarrassed. "I think there's something about your friend that makes me mad."

"What are you feeling, exactly?"

"I don't know. I felt angry as soon as I saw her out there. I got the sense she might pull some blunder and expose us, or get us captured."

"Maybe killed?"

"Yeah, maybe killed!" The force in his voice surprised both of us, and he took a breath and shrugged.

"Remember when I told you about the visions I saw, of a time during the nineteenth-century Native American wars?"

"Vaguely," he muttered.

"Well, I didn't tell you then, but I think I saw you and Maya together. Curtis, you were both killed by soldiers."

He looked at the ceiling of the cave. "And you think that's why I'm angry at her?"

I smiled.

At that moment a light dissonance filled the air and we both heard the hum.

"Damn," he said. "They're firing it up again."

I grabbed his arm. "Curtis, we've got to figure out what you and Maya were trying to do back then, why you failed, and what you intended to happen differently this time."

He shook his head. "I don't know how much of all this I even believe; I wouldn't know where to begin."

"I think if you just talk with her, something will come up."

He just looked at me.

"Will you try?"

Finally he nodded and we crawled back into the cave. Maya smiled awkwardly.

"I'm sorry I've been so angry," Curtis offered. "It seems maybe I'm mad about something that occurred a long time ago."

"Forget it," she said. "I just wish we could remember what we were trying to do."

Curtis looked hard at Maya. "I seem to remember you're into healing of some kind." He glanced at me. "Did you tell me that?"

"I don't think so," I replied, "but it's true."

"I'm a physician," Maya said. "I use positive imaging and faith in my work."

"Faith? You mean you treat people from a religious perspective?"

"Well, only in a general sense. When I said faith, I meant the energy force that comes from human expectation. I work at a clinic where we're trying to understand faith as an actual mental process, as the way we help create the future."

"And how long have you been into all this?" Curtis asked.

"My whole life has prepared me to explore healing." She went on to tell Curtis the same story of her life that she had told me earlier, including her mother's tendency to worry that she would get cancer. As Maya discussed all that had happened to her, both Curtis and I asked questions. As we listened and gave her energy, the fatigue that had shown on her face began to ease, her eyes brightened, and she began to sit up straight.

Curtis asked, "You believe your mother's worry and negative vision of her future affected her health?"

"Yes. Humans seem to help draw into their lives two particular kinds of events: what we have faith in and what we fear. But we're doing it unconsciously. As a physician, I believe much can be gained by pulling the process fully into consciousness."

Curtis nodded. "But how is that done?"

Maya didn't answer. She stood up and stared straight ahead, a panicked look on her face.

"What's wrong?" I asked.

"I was just . . . I . . . see what happened during the wars."

"What was it?" Curtis asked.

She looked at him. "I remember we were there in the woods. I can see it all: the soldiers, smoke from the gunpowder."

Curtis seemed to be pulled into deep thought, obviously picking up on the memory. "I was there," he mumbled. "Why was I there?" He looked at Maya. "You brought me to that place! I knew nothing; I was just a congressional observer. You told me we could stop the fighting!"

She turned away, obviously struggling to understand. "I thought we could . . . There's a way . . . Wait a minute, we weren't alone." She turned and stared at me, an angry expression appearing on her face. "You were there, too, but you abandoned us. Why did you leave us?"

Her statement stirred the memory I had brought back earlier and told them both what I had seen, describing the others who were also there: the elders of several tribes, myself, Charlene. I explained that one elder voiced strong support of Maya's efforts, but believed the time was not right, arguing that the tribes had not yet found their correct vision. I told them another chief had exploded with rage at the atrocities perpetrated by the white soldiers.

"I couldn't stay," I told them, describing my memory of the experience with the Franciscans. "I couldn't shake the need to run. I had to save myself. I'm sorry."

Maya seemed lost in thought, so I touched her arm and said, "The elders knew it couldn't work; and Charlene confirmed that we hadn't yet remembered the ancestors' wisdom."

"Then why did one of the chiefs stay with us?" she asked.

"Because he didn't want the two of you to die alone."

"I didn't want to die at all!" Curtis snapped, looking at Maya. "You misled me."

"I'm sorry," she said. "I can't remember what went wrong."

"I know what went wrong," he said. "You thought you could stop a war just because you *wanted* to."

She gazed at him for a long moment, then looked at me. "He's right. We were visualizing that the soldiers must stop their aggression, but we had no clear picture of how that could happen. It didn't work because we didn't have all the information. Everyone was visualizing from fear, not faith. It works just like the process of healing our bodies. When we remember what we're really supposed to do in life, it can restore our health. When we're able to remember what all of humanity is supposed to do, starting right now, from this moment, we can heal the world."

"Apparently," I said, "our Birth Vision contains not only what we individually intended to do in the physical dimension but also a larger vision of what humans have been trying to do throughout history, and the details of where we are going from here and how to get there. We just have to amplify our energy and share our birth intentions, and then we can remember."

Before she could respond, Curtis jumped to his feet and moved to the cave's opening. "I heard something," he said. "Someone's out there."

Maya and I crouched beside him, straining to see. Nothing moved; then I thought I detected the rustling sound of someone walking.

"I'm going to check this out," Curtis said, moving through the opening.

I glanced at Maya. "I had better go with him."

"I'm coming too," she said.

We followed Curtis down the slope to an outcropping where we could look straight down at the gorge between the two hills. A man and a woman, partially obscured by the underbrush, were crossing the rocks below us, heading toward the west.

"That woman's in trouble!" Maya said.

"How do you know that?" I asked.

"I just know. She looks familiar."

The woman turned once and the man pushed her menacingly, exposing a pistol held in his right hand.

Maya leaned forward, looking at both of us. "Did you see that? We've got to do something."

I looked closely. The woman had light hair and was dressed in a sweatshirt and green fatigues with leg pockets. As I watched, she turned and said something to her captor, then glanced toward us, giving me a clear look at her face.

"That's Charlene," I said. "Where do you think he's taking her?"

"Who knows?" Curtis replied. "Look, I think I can help her but I have to go alone. I need both of you to stay here."

I protested but Curtis would have it no other way. We watched him as he walked back to the left and down the slope through a section of woods. From there, he crept quietly to another outcropping of rock just ten feet above the bottom of the gorge.

"They'll have to pass right by him," I told Maya.

We observed anxiously as they moved closer to the rocks. At the precise moment they had passed, Curtis bounded down the hill and leaped upon the man, knocking him to the ground and holding his throat in a peculiar fashion until he stopped moving. Charlene jumped back in alarm and gathered herself to run.

"Charlene, wait!" Curtis called. She stopped and took a cautious step forward. "It's Curtis Webber. We worked together at Deltech, remember? I'm here to help you."

She obviously recognized him and moved closer. Maya and I made our way carefully down the hill. When Charlene saw me, she froze and then ran toward my embrace. Curtis rushed up and pushed us to the ground.

"Keep down," he said. "We could be seen here."

I helped Curtis tie up Charlene's guard with a roll of tape we found in his pocket and pulled him up the slope into the forest.

"What did you do to him?" Charlene asked.

Curtis was checking his pockets. "I just knocked him out. He'll be okay."

Maya bent down to check his pulse.

Charlene turned her attention to me, reaching out for my hand. "How did you get here?" she asked.

Taking a breath, I told her about the call from her office informing me of her disappearance and about finding the sketch and coming to the valley to look for her.

She smiled. "I made that sketch intending to call you, but I left so suddenly I didn't have time . . ." Her voice trailed off as she looked deeply into my eyes. "I think I saw you yesterday, in the other dimension."

I pulled her to the side, away from the others. "I saw you too, but I couldn't communicate."

As we stared at each other, I felt my body grow lighter, a wave of orgasmic love sweeping across me, centered not in my pelvic region, but somehow around the outside of my skin. Simultaneously I seemed to be falling into Charlene's eyes. Her smile grew and I realized she must be feeling much the same way.

A movement from Curtis broke the spell, and I realized both he and Maya were staring at us.

I looked back at Charlene. "I want to tell you what's been happening," I said, then described seeing Wil again, learning about the polarization of Fear, and the group coming back, and the World Vision. "Charlene, how did you get into the Afterlife dimension?"

Her face fell. "All this is my fault. I didn't know the danger until yesterday. I'm the one who told Feyman about the Insights. Shortly after receiving your letter, I found out about another group that knew of the nine Insights, and I studied with them intensely. I had many of the same experiences you talked about. Later I came with a friend to this valley because we had heard that the sacred locations here were connected somehow with the Tenth Insight. My friend didn't experience much, but I did, so I stayed to explore. That's when I met Feyman, who employed me to teach him what I knew. From that moment forward he was with me every minute. He insisted I not call my office, for security reasons, so I wrote letters rescheduling all my appointments, only, as it turned out, I guess he was intercepting my letters. That's why everyone thought I was missing.

"With Feyman I explored most of the vortexes, especially the ones at Codder's Knoll and The Falls. He couldn't sense the energy personally, but I found out later that he was tracking us electronically and getting some sort of energy profile on me as we tuned into the locations. After that he could hone in on the area and find the exact location of the vortex electronically."

I glanced at Curtis and he nodded knowingly.

Tears filled Charlene's eyes. "He had me completely fooled. He said that he was working on a very inexpensive source of energy that will liberate everyone. He sent me to remote areas of the forest during much of the experimentation. Only later, after I confronted him, did he admit the dangers of what he was doing."

Curtis turned to face Charlene. "Feyman Carter was a chief engineer at Deltech. Do you remember?"

"No," she said, "but he's totally in control of this project. Another corporation is now involved; and they have these armed men. Feyman calls them operatives. I finally told him I was leaving, and that's when he put me under guard. When I told him he would never get away with this, he just laughed. He bragged about having someone in the Forest Service working with him."

"Where was he sending you?" Curtis asked.

Charlene shook her head. "I have no idea."

"I don't think he intended to let you live," Curtis said. "Not after telling you all that."

An anxious silence fell over the group.

"What I can't understand," Charlene said, "is why he's here in this forest in the first place. What does he want with these energy locations?"

Curtis and I met eyes again, then he said, "He's experimenting with a way of centralizing this energy source he's found by focusing on the dimensional pathways in this valley. That's why it's so dangerous."

I became aware that Charlene was staring at Maya and smiling. Maya returned the gaze with a warm expression.

"When I was at the falls," Charlene said, "I moved through into the other dimension, and all these memories rushed in." She looked at me. "After that, I was able to go back several times, even when I was under guard, yesterday." She looked at me again. "That's where I saw *you* . . . ."

Charlene paused and looked back at the group. "I saw that we're all here to stop this experiment, if we can remember everything."

Maya was watching her closely. "You understood what we

wanted to do during the battle with the soldiers, and supported us," she said. "Even though you knew it couldn't work."

Charlene's smile told me she had remembered.

"We've remembered most of what happened," I said. "But so far we haven't been able to recall how we planned to do it differently this time. Can you remember?"

Charlene shook her head. "Only parts of it. I know we have to identify our unconscious feelings toward one another before we can go on." She looked into my eyes and paused. "This is all part of the Tenth Insight . . . only it hasn't been written down anywhere yet. It's coming in intuitively."

I nodded. "We know."

"Part of the Tenth is an extension of the Eighth. Only a group that's operating fully in the Eighth Insight can accomplish this kind of higher clearing."

"I'm not following you," Curtis said.

"The Eighth is about knowing how to uplift others," she continued, "knowing how to send energy by focusing on another's beauty and higher-self wisdom. This process can raise the energy level and creativity of the group exponentially. Unfortunately, many groups have trouble uplifting each other in this manner, even though the individuals involved are able to do it at other times. This is especially true if the group is work-oriented, a group of employees, for instance, or people coming together to create a unique project of some kind, because so often these people have been together before, and old, past-life emotions come up and get in the way.

"We are thrown together with someone we have to work with, and we automatically dislike them, without really knowing why. Or perhaps we experience it the other way around: the person doesn't like us, again for reasons we don't understand. The emotions that come up might be jealousy, irritation, envy, resentment, bitterness, blame—any of these. What I intuited very clearly was that no group could reach its highest potential unless the participants seek to understand and work through these emotions."

Maya leaned forward. "That's exactly what we've been doing: working through the emotions that have come up, the resentments from when we were together before."

"Were you shown your Birth Vision?" I asked.

"Yes," Charlene replied. "But I couldn't get any further. I didn't have enough energy. All I saw was that groups were forming and that I was supposed to be here in this valley, in a group of seven."

Presently the sound of another vehicle far to the north attracted our attention.

"We can't stay here," Curtis said. "We're too exposed. Let's go back to the cave."

Charlene finished the last of the food and handed me the plate. Having no extra water, I placed it in my pack dirty and sat down again. Curtis slipped through the mouth of the cave and sat down across from me beside Maya, who smiled faintly at him. Charlene sat to my left. The operative had been left outside the cave, still bound and gagged.

"Is everything okay outside?" Charlene asked Curtis.

Curtis looked nervous. "I think so, but I heard some more sounds to the north. I think we need to stay in here until dark."

For a moment we all just looked at each other, each of us obviously trying to raise our energy.

I looked at the others and told them about the process of

reaching the World Vision I had seen with Feyman's soul group. When I had concluded, I looked at Charlene and asked, "What else did you receive about this clearing process?"

"All I got," Charlene replied, "was that the process couldn't begin until we come totally back to love."

"That's easy to say," Curtis said. "The problem is doing it."

We all looked at each other again, then simultaneously realized the energy was moving to Maya.

"The key is to acknowledge the emotion, to become fully conscious of the feeling, and then to share it honestly, no matter how awkward our attempts. This brings the emotion fully into present awareness and ultimately allows it to be relegated to the past, where it belongs. That's why going through the sometimes long process of saying it, discussing it, putting it on the table, clears us, so that we're able to return to a state of love, which is the highest emotion."

"Wait a minute," I said. "What about Charlene? There may be residual emotions toward her." I looked at Maya. "I know you felt something."

"Yes," Maya replied. "But only positive feelings, a sense of gratitude. She stayed and tried to help . . ." Maya paused, studying Charlene's face. "You tried to tell us something, something about the ancestors. But we didn't listen."

I leaned toward Charlene. "Were you killed too?"

Maya answered for her. "No, she wasn't killed. She had gone to try to appeal to the soldiers one more time."

"That's right," Charlene said. "But they were gone."

Maya asked, "Who else feels something toward Charlene?"

"I don't feel anything," Curtis said.

"What about you, Charlene?" I asked. "What do you feel toward us?"

Her gaze swept across each member of the group. "There don't seem to be any residual feelings toward Curtis," she said. "And everything is positive toward Maya." Her eyes settled on mine. "Toward you I think I feel a bit of resentment."

"Why?" I asked.

"Because you were so practical and detached. You were this independent man who wasn't about to get involved if the timing wasn't perfect."

"Charlene," I said, "I'd already sacrificed myself for these Insights as a monk. I felt it would have been useless."

My protests seemed to irritate her and she looked away.

Maya reached over and touched me. "Your comment was defensive. When you respond that way, the other person doesn't feel heard. The emotion she harbors then lingers in her mind because she continues to think of ways to make you understand, to convince you. Or it goes unconscious and then there's ill feeling that dulls the energy between you two. Either way the emotion remains a problem, getting in the way. I suggest you acknowledge how she could be feeling that."

I looked at Charlene. "Oh, I do. I wish that I had helped. Maybe I could have done something, if I had had the courage."

Charlene nodded and smiled.

"How about you?" Maya asked, looking at me. "What do you feel toward Charlene?"

"I guess I feel some guilt," I said. "Not so much guilt about the war, but about now, this situation. I had been withdrawn for several months. I think if I had talked to you immediately after returning from Peru, maybe we could have stopped the experiment earlier and none of this would be happening."

No one replied.

"Are there any other feelings?" Maya asked.

We only looked at each other.

At this point, under Maya's direction, each of us focused on connecting inside, with building as much energy as we could. As I focused on the beauty around me, a wave of love swept through my body. The muted color of the cave walls and floor began to brighten and glow. Each person's face began to appear more energized. A chill ran up my spine.

"Now," Maya said, "we're ready to figure out what we intended to do this time." She again appeared to be in deep thought. "I . . . I knew this was going to happen," she said finally. "This was part of my Birth Vision. I was to lead the amplification process. We didn't know how to do this when we tried to stop the war on the Native Americans."

As she spoke, I noticed a movement behind her against the cave wall. At first I thought it was a reflection of light, but then I detected a deep shade of green exactly like the one I witnessed earlier, when observing Maya's soul group. As I struggled to focus on the foot-square blob of light, it swelled into a full holographic scene, receding into the wall itself, full of fuzzy, humanlike forms. I glanced at the others; no one seemed to see the image except me.

This, I knew, was Maya's soul group, and as soon as I had this realization, I began to receive an inflow of intuitive information. I could see her Birth Vision again, her higher intention of being born to her particular family, her mother's illness, the resulting interest in medicine, particularly the mind/body connection, and now this gathering. I clearly heard that "no group can reach its full creative power until it consciously clears and then amplifies its energy."

"Once free of the emotions," Maya was now saying, "a group can more easily move past power struggles and dramas and find its full creativity. But we have to do it consciously by finding a higher-self expression in every face."

Curtis' blank look provoked more explanation. "As the Eighth Insight reveals," Maya continued, "if we look closely at another person's face, we can cut through any facades, or ego defenses, that may be present, and find the individual's authentic expression, his or her *real* self. Ordinarily most people don't know what to focus on when talking to another. Should it be the eyes? It's hard to focus on both. So which one? Or should it be on the feature that most stands out, such as the nose or mouth?

"In truth, we are called upon to focus on the whole of the face, which with its uniqueness of light and shadow and alignment of features is much like an inkblot. But within this collection of features, one can find an authentic expression, the soul shining forth. When we focus in love, love energy is sent to this higher-self aspect of the person, and the person will seem to change before our eyes as his or her greater capabilities shift into place.

"All great teachers have always sent this kind of energy toward their students. That's why they were great teachers. But the effect is even greater with groups who interact this way with every member, because as each person sends the others energy, all of the members rise to a new level of wisdom which has more energy at its disposal, and this greater energy is then sent back to everyone else in what becomes an amplification effect."

I watched Maya, attempting to find her higher expression. No longer did she appear tired, or reluctant in any way. Instead, her features revealed a certainty and genius she had not expressed before. I glanced toward the others and saw that they were similarly focused on Maya. When I looked at her again, I noticed that she seemed to be taking on the green hue of her soul group. She was not only picking up on their knowledge; she seemed to be moving into a kind of harmony with them.

Maya had stopped speaking and was taking a deep breath. I could feel the energy shifting away from her.

"I've always known that groups could acquire a higher level of functioning," Curtis said, "especially in work settings. But I haven't been able to experience this until now . . . I know I came into this dimension to be involved in transforming business, and shifting our view of business creativity, so that we can ultimately utilize the new energy sources in the correct way and implement the Ninth Insight automation of production."

He paused in thought, then said, "I mean, business is too often labeled as the greedy villain, out of control, with no conscience. And I guess it's been exactly that in the past. But I've felt as though business, too, was moving into a spiritual awareness, and that we needed a new kind of business ethic."

At that moment I saw another movement of light, directly behind Curtis. I watched for a few seconds, then realized I was seeing the formation of his soul group as well. As with Maya's group, when I focused on the emerging image, I was again able to pick up on their collective knowledge. Curtis was born in the peak of the industrial revolution occurring just after World War II. Nuclear power had been the final triumph and shocking horror of the materialist worldview, and he had entered with a vision that technological advancement could now be made conscious and moved, in full awareness, toward its destined purpose.

"Only now," Curtis said, "are we ready to understand how to evolve business and the resulting new technology in a conscious manner; all the measures are now in place. It's not an accident that one of the most important statistical categories in economics is the productivity index: the record of how many goods and services are produced by each individual in our society. Productivity has steadily increased because of technological discoveries and the more expansive use of natural resources and energy. Through the years the individual has found ever-greater ways to create."

As he spoke, a thought came to me. At first I decided to keep it to myself, but then everyone looked my way. "Doesn't the environmental damage that economic growth is causing form a natural limit to business? We can't go on like we have, because if we do, the environment will literally fall apart. Many of the fish in the ocean are already so polluted we can't eat them. Cancer rates are increasing exponentially. Even the AMA says that pregnant women and children should not eat commercial vegetables because of the pesticide residue. If this keeps up, can you imagine what kind of world we'll be leaving our children?"

As soon as I had said this, I recalled what Joel had said earlier about the collapse of the environment. I could feel my energy falling as I felt the same Fear.

Suddenly I was hit with a burst of energy, as each of the others stared in an effort to find my authentic expression again. I quickly reestablished my inner connection.

"You're right," Curtis said, "but our response to this problem is already occurring. We've been advancing technology with a kind of unconscious tunnel vision, forgetting that we're here on an organic planet, an energy planet. But one of the most creative areas of business is the field of pollution control.

"Our problem has been trying to depend on government to police the polluters. Polluting has been against the law for a long time, but there will never be enough government regulation to prevent the illegal dumping of waste chemicals or the midnight venting of smokestacks. This polluting of the biosphere won't completely stop until an alarmed citizenry pulls out their video recorders and takes it upon themselves to catch these people in the act. In a sense, business and the employees of business must regulate themselves."

Maya leaned forward. "I see another problem with the way the economy is evolving. What about all the displaced workers who are losing their jobs as more of the economy is automated? How can they survive? We used to have a large middle class and now it is diminishing rapidly."

Curtis smiled and his eyes brightened. The image of his soul group swelled behind him. "These displaced people will survive by learning to live intuitively and synchronistically," he said. "We all have to understand: there's no going back. We're already living in the information age. Everyone will have to educate themselves the best they can, become an expert in some niche, so that they can be in the right place to advise someone else or perform some other service. The more technical the automation becomes, and the more quickly the world changes, the more we need information from just the right person arriving in our lives at just the right time. You don't need a formal education to do that; just a niche you've created for yourself through self-education.

"Yet, for this flow to be optimally established, across the economy, the stated purposes of business must shift into higher awareness. Our guiding intuitions become most clear when we approach business from an evolutionary perspective. Our questions must change. Instead of asking what product or service I can develop to make the most money, we're beginning to ask, 'What can I produce that liberates and informs and makes the world a better place, yet also preserves a delicate environmental balance?'

"A new code of ethics is being added to the equation of free enterprise. We have to come awake wherever we are and ask, 'What are we creating and does it consciously serve the overall purpose for which technology was invented in the first place: to make everyday subsistence easier, so that the prevailing orientation of life can shift from mere survival and comfort to the interchange of pure spiritual information?' Each of us has to see that we have a part in the evolution toward lower and lower subsistence costs, until finally the basic means of survival is virtually free.

"We can move toward a truly enlightened capitalism if, instead of charging as much as the market will bear, we follow a new business ethic based on lowering our prices a specified percentage as a conscious statement of where we want the economy to go. This would be the business equivalent of engaging in the Ninth Insight force of tithing."

Charlene turned to face him, her face luminous. "I understand what you're saying. You mean, if all businesses reduce prices ten percent, then everyone's cost of living, including the raw materials and supplies to the businesses themselves, will also go down."

"That's right, although some prices might go up temporarily as everyone takes into account the true cost of waste disposal and other environmental effects. Overall, though, prices will systematically decline."

"Doesn't this process already happen at times," I asked, "as a result of market forces?"

"Of course," he replied, "but it can be accelerated if we do it consciously—although as the Ninth Insight predicts, this process will be greatly enhanced by the discovery of a very inexpensive energy source. It appears as if Feyman has done that. But the energy has to be made available in the most inexpensive way possible if it is to have its most liberating impact."

As he spoke, he seemed to grow more inspired. Turning, he looked straight into my eyes. "This is the economic idea I came here wanting to contribute," he said. "I've never seen it so clearly. That's why I wanted to have the life experiences I've had; I wanted to be prepared for delivering this message."

"Do you really think enough people will reduce prices to make a difference?" Maya asked. "Especially if it takes money out of their own pockets? That seems to fly in the face of human nature."

Curtis didn't answer. Instead he looked at me, along with the others, as if I had the answer. For a moment I was silent, feeling the energy shift.

"Curtis is right," I said finally. "We'll do it anyway, even though we may give up some personal profit in the short run. None of this makes any sense at all until we grasp the Ninth and Tenth Insights. If one believes that life is just a matter of personal survival in an essentially meaningless and unfriendly world, then it makes perfect sense to focus all one's wits on living as comfortably as possible and seeing to it that one's children have the same opportunities. But if one grasps the first nine Insights and sees life as a spiritual evolution, with spiritual responsibilities, then our view completely changes.

"And once we begin to understand the Tenth, then we see the birth process from the perspective of the Afterlife, and we realize that we're all here to bring the Earth dimension into alignment with the Heavenly sphere. Besides, opportunity and success are very mysterious processes, and if we operate our economic life in the flow of the overall plan, we synchronistically meet all the other people who are doing the same thing, and suddenly prosperity opens up for us.

"We'll do it," I continued, "because individually that's where the intuition and coincidences will take us. We'll remember more about our Birth Visions and it will become clear that we intended to make a certain contribution to the world. And most important, we'll know that if we don't follow this intuition, not only will the magic coincidences and the sense of inspiration and aliveness stop, but eventually we may have to look at our actions in an Afterlife Review. We'll have to face our failure."

I stopped abruptly, noticing that Charlene and Maya were both staring wide-eyed at the space behind me. Reflexively I turned around; there was the hazy outline of my own soul group, dozens of individuals fading into the distance, again as though the walls of the cave weren't there.

"What are all of you looking at?" Curtis asked.

"It's his soul group," Charlene said. "I saw these groups when I was at the falls."

"I've seen a group behind both Maya and Curtis," I said.

Maya twisted around and looked at the space behind her. The group there flickered once, then came fully into focus.

"I don't see anything," Curtis said. "Where are they?"

Maya continued to stare, obviously seeing all of the groups. "They're helping us, aren't they? They can give us the vision we're looking for."

As soon as she made that comment, all of the groups moved away from us dramatically and became less clear.

"What happened?" Maya asked.

"It's your expectation," I said. "If you look to them for your energy, as a replacement for your own inner connection to divine energy, they leave. They won't allow a dependence. The same thing happened to me."

Charlene gave me a nod of agreement. "It happened to me too. They're like family. We're connected to them in thought, but we have to sustain our own connection with the divine source beyond them before we can link to them and pick up on what they know, which is really your own higher memory."

"They hold the memory for us?" Maya asked.

"Yes," Charlene replied, looking directly at me. She started to say something else, then stopped herself, appearing to drift off in thought. Then she said, "I'm beginning to understand what I saw in the other dimension. In the Afterlife each of us comes from a particular soul group, and these groups each have a particular angle or truth to offer the rest of humanity." She glanced at me. "For instance, you come from a group of facilitators. Do you know that? Souls that help evolve our philosophical understanding of what life is about. Everyone who belongs to this particular soul group is always trying to find the best and most comprehensive way of describing spiritual reality. You struggle with complex information, and because you're so dense, you keep pushing and exploring until you find a way to express it clearly."

I looked at her askance, which made her burst out laughing.

"It's a gift you have," she said reassuringly.

Turning to Maya, she said, "And you, Maya, your soul group is oriented toward health and well-being. They think of themselves as solidifiers of the physical dimension, keeping our cells operating optimally and full of energy, tracing and removing emotional blocks before they manifest in disease.

"Curtis' group is about transforming the use of technology, as well as our overall understanding of commerce. Throughout human history this group has been working to spiritualize our concepts of money and capitalism, to find the ideal conceptualization."

She paused, and I could already see an image of light flickering behind her.

"What about you, Charlene?" I asked. "What is your group doing?"

"We're journalists, researchers," she replied, "working to help people appreciate and learn from each other. What journalism is really all about is looking deeply at the life and beliefs of the people and organizations we cover, at their true substance and higher expression, just the way we're looking at each other now."

I again remembered my conversation with Joel, specifically his jaded cynicism. "It's hard to see journalists doing that," I said.

"We're not," she replied. "Not yet. But this is the ideal toward which the profession is evolving. This is our true destiny, once we become more secure and break free from the old worldview in which we need to 'win' and bring energy and status our way.

"It makes perfect sense why I wanted to be born to my family. They were all so inquisitive. I picked up on their excitement, their need for information. That's why I was a reporter for so long, and then joined the research firm. I wanted to help work out the ethics of reporting and then come together with all of . . ." She drifted away again, staring at the floor of the cave, then her eyes widened and she said, "I know how we're bringing in the World Vision. As we remember our Birth Visions and integrate them together as a group, we *merge* the power of our relative soul groups in the other dimension, which helps us remember even more, so we finally get to the overall vision of the world."

We all stared at her, puzzled.

"Look at the whole picture," she explained. "Each person on Earth belongs to a soul group, and these soul groups represent the various occupational groups that exist on the planet: medical people, lawyers, accountants, computer workers, farmers, every field of human endeavor. Once people find their right work, the job that really fits them, then they are working with other members of their soul group.

"As each of us wakes up and begins to remember our Birth Vision—why we're here—the occupational groups to which we belong come more into alignment with the members of our groups in the other dimension. As this happens, each occupational group on Earth moves toward its true soul purpose, its role of service in human society."

We all continued to be spellbound.

"It's like with us journalists," she continued. "Throughout history we have been the individuals most inquisitive about what others in the culture were doing. And then a few centuries ago, we became conscious enough of ourselves to form a defined occupation. Since then we've been busy broadening our use of the media, reaching more and more people with our newscasts, that sort of thing. But like everyone else, we suffered from insecurity. We felt that to get attention and energy from the rest of humanity we had to create increasingly more sensational stories, thinking that only negativity and violence sell.

"But that's not our true role. Our spiritual role is to deepen and spiritualize our perception of other people. We see and then communicate what the various soul groups, and individuals within these groups, are doing, and what they stand for, making it easier for everyone to learn the truth others provide.

"It's the same for every occupational group; we're all awakening to our true message and purpose. And as this happens all over the planet, we're then able to go further. We can form close spiritual associations with people outside of our particular soul group, just the way we're doing here. We all shared our Birth Visions and raised our vibration together, and that transforms not only human society but the culture in the Afterlife as well.

"First, each of our soul groups comes closer into vibration with us on Earth and we with them, the two dimensions opening into each other. Because of this closure, we can begin to have communication between the dimensions. We are able to see souls in the Afterlife and pick up on their knowledge and memory more readily. That's happening with increasing frequency on the Earth."

As Charlene was speaking, I noticed the soul groups behind each of us widening and spreading out until each touched the others, forming a continuous circle around us. The convergence seemed to jolt me into an even higher awareness.

Charlene seemed to feel it too. She took a breath and then with emphasis continued. "The other thing that happens in the Afterlife is that the groups themselves come closer into resonance with each other. That's why the Earth is the primary focus of the souls in Heaven. They can't unite on their own. Over there, many soul groups remain fragmented and out of resonance with each other because they live in an imaginary world of ideas that manifests instantly and disappears just as quickly, so reality is always arbitrary. There is no natural world, no atomic structure, as we have here, that serves as a stable platform, a background stage, that is common to all of us. We affect what happens on this stage, but ideas manifest much more slowly and we must reach some agreement on what we want to happen in the future. It's this agreement, this consensus, this unity of vision on the Earth, that also pulls the soul groups together in the Afterlife dimension. That's why the Earth dimension is deemed so important. The physical dimension is where the true unification of souls is taking place!

"And it's this unification that's behind the long historical journey that humans have been taking. The soul groups in the Afterlife understand the World Vision, the vision of how the physical world can evolve and the dimensions can close, but this can only be accomplished by individuals who are born into the physical, one at a time, hoping to move the consensus Earth reality in that direction. The physical arena is the theater upon which evolution has been playing out for both dimensions, and now we're bringing it all into culmination as we remember consciously what's going on."

She pointed to us with a sweeping motion of her finger. "This is the awareness that we're remembering together, right now— and it's the awareness that other groups, just like us, are remembering all over the planet. We all have a piece of the complete Vision, and when we share what we know, and unify our soul groups, then we're ready to bring the whole picture into consciousness."

Suddenly Charlene was interrupted by a slight tremor that ran through the earth under the cave. Specks of dust fell from the ceiling. Simultaneously we heard the hum again, but this time the dissonance had disappeared; it sounded almost harmonious.

"Oh God," Curtis said. "They almost have the calibrations right. We have to go back to the bunker." He made a movement to get up, as the energy level of the group plummeted.

"Wait," I said. "What are we going to do there? We agreed that we would wait here until dark; there's still hours of daylight out there. I say we stay here. We achieved a high level of energy, but we haven't moved through the rest of the process yet. We seem to have cleared our residual emotions and amplified our energy and shared our Birth Visions, but we haven't seen the World Vision yet. I think we can do more if we remain where it's safe, and try to go further." Even as I spoke, I saw an image of all of us back in the valley again, together in the darkness.

"It's too late for that," Curtis said. "They're ready to complete the experiment. If anything can be done, we've got to go there and do it now."

I looked hard at him. "You said they were probably going to kill Charlene. If we're caught, they'll do the same to us."

Maya held her head in her hands and Curtis looked away, trying to shake off the panic.

"Well, I'm going," Curtis said.

Charlene leaned forward. "I think we should stay together."

For an instant I saw her in Native American clothing, again in the virgin woods of the nineteenth century. The image quickly faded.

Maya stood up. "Charlene is right," she said. "We have to stay together, and it might help if we can see what they're doing."

I looked out through the cave's entrance, a long, deep-seated reluctance rising in my gut. "What are we going to do with this . . . operative . . . outside?"

"We'll drag him into the cave and leave him here," Curtis said. "We'll send someone for him in the morning, if we can."

I met eyes with Charlene, then nodded agreement.

# REMEMBERING
# THE
# FUTURE

We knelt at the top of the hill and looked carefully down at the base of a larger ridge. I could see nothing out of the ordinary in the fading light; no movement, no guards. The hum, which had persisted for most of the forty-minute walk, had now completely disappeared.

"Are you sure we're at the right place?" I asked Curtis.

"Yes," he said. "Do you see the four large boulders about fifty feet up the slope? The doorway is right beneath them, hidden in the bushes. To the right, you can just make out the top of the projection dish. It looks functional again."

"I see it," Maya said.

"Where are the guards?" I asked Curtis. "Maybe they've abandoned the site."

We observed the doorway for almost an hour, waiting for signs of activity, hesitant to move or talk much until darkness had fallen across the valley. Suddenly we heard movement behind us. Flashlights clicked on, flooding us in light, and four armed men rushed in, demanding that we raise our hands. After spending ten minutes going through our gear, they searched each of us, then moved the group down the hill and up to the bunker's entrance.

The door of the bunker swung open and Feyman charged out, loud and angry. "Are these the ones we've been looking for?" he shouted. "Where did you find them?"

One of the guards explained what had happened as Feyman shook his head and stared at us through the beams of light. He walked closer and demanded, "What are you doing here?"

"You've got to stop what you're doing!" Curtis retorted.

Feyman was struggling to recognize him. "Who are you?" The guards' flashlights settled, illuminating Curtis' face.

"Curtis Webber . . . I'll be damned," Feyman said. "You blew up our dish, didn't you?"

"Listen to me," Curtis said. "You know this generator is too dangerous to operate at these levels. You could ruin this entire valley!"

"You were always an alarmist, Webber. That's why we let you go at Deltech. I've been working on this project for too long to give up at this point. It's going to *work*—exactly as I planned."

"But why are you taking the chance? Concentrate on the smaller, house-size units. Why are you trying to increase the output so much?"

"That's none of your business. You need to keep quiet."

Curtis edged toward him. "You want to centralize the generating process so you can control it. That's not right."

Feyman smiled. "A new energy system has to be phased in. Do you think we can go overnight from energy being a substantial part of household and business costs to practically nothing? The sudden disposable income throughout the world would cause hyperinflation and then probably a massive reaction that would cast us into a depression."

"You know that's not true," Curtis replied. "Reduced energy costs would increase the efficiency of production tremendously, supplying more goods at lower costs. No inflation would occur. You're doing this for yourself. You want to centralize the production so you can control its availability and price, despite the dangers."

He stared angrily at Curtis. "You're so naive. Do you think the interests that act to control energy prices now would allow a sudden, massive shift to an inexpensive source? Of course not! It has to be centralized and packaged to work at all. And I'm going to be known for having done this! It's what I was born to do!"

"That's not true!" I blurted. "You were born to do something else, to help us."

Feyman swung around to face me. "Shut up! Do you hear me? All of you!" His eyes found Charlene. "What happened to the man I sent with you?"

Charlene looked away without responding.

"I don't have time for this!" Feyman was shouting again. "I'd suggest you worry about your personal safety right now." He paused to look us over, then shook his head and walked to one of the armed men. "Keep them here in a group until this is over. All we need is another hour. If they try to escape, shoot them."

The operative spoke briefly to the other three and they formed a perimeter encircling us at a distance of about thirty feet. "Sit down," one of them said.

We sat facing each other in the darkness. Our energy was almost totally deflated. There had been no sign of the soul groups since we left the cave.

"What do you think we should do?" I asked Charlene.

"Nothing's changed," she whispered. "We've got to build our energy again."

The darkness was now almost total, broken only by the operatives' lights sweeping back and forth across the group. I could barely make out the outlines of the others' faces, even though we were sitting in a tight circle, eight feet apart.

"We have to try to escape," Curtis whispered. "I think they will kill us."

Then I remembered the image I'd seen in Feyman's Birth Vision. He envisioned being with us in the woods, in the dark. I knew there was also another landmark in the scene, but I couldn't remember what it was.

"No," I said. "I think we need to try again here."

At that moment the air was filled with a high-pitched sound, a sound similar to the hum but, again, more in harmony, almost pleasing to the ear. Again a perceptible shimmer swept through the ground under our bodies.

"We have to increase our energy *now*!" Maya whispered.

"I don't know if I can do it here," Curtis responded.

"You have to!" I said.

"Focus on each other the way we did before," Maya added.

I tried to screen out the ominous scene around us and return to an inner state of love. Ignoring the shadows and the flickering beams of light, I focused on the beauty of the faces in the circle. As I struggled to locate the others' higher-self expression, I began to notice a shift in the light pattern around us. Gradually I could see every face and expression very clearly, as though I was looking through an infrared viewer.

"What do we visualize?" Curtis asked in desperation.

"We have to get back to our Birth Visions," Maya said. "Remember why we came."

Suddenly the ground shook violently and the sound from the experiment again took on a dissonant, grating quality.

We moved closer together and our collective thought seemed to project the image of fighting back. We knew that somehow we could marshal our forces and push back the negative and destructive attempts of the experiment. I even picked up a picture of Feyman being pushed backward, his equipment blowing up and burning, his men fleeing in terror.

Another surge in the noise disrupted my focus; the experiment was continuing. Fifty feet away, a huge pine tree snapped in half and thundered to the ground. With a ripping sound and a cloud of dust, a fissure, five feet wide, opened up between us and the guard on the right. He reeled back in horror, the beam of his flashlight swinging wild in the night.

"This isn't working!" Maya screamed.

Another tree crashed to the ground on our left as the earth slid four or five feet, knocking us flat.

Maya looked horrified and jumped to her feet. "I've got to get away from here!" she yelled, then began to run north into the darkness. The guard on that side, lying where he had been thrown by the earth's movement, rolled to his knees and caught her form in the beam of his flashlight, then raised his gun.

"No! Wait!" I screamed.

As she ran, Maya looked back, spotting the guard who was now aiming directly at her, preparing to fire. The scene seemed to shift into slow motion, and as the gun discharged, every line in her face revealed an awareness that she was about to die. But instead of the bullets ripping into her side and back, a wisp of white light darted in front of her and the bullets bore no effect. She hesitated momentarily, then disappeared into the darkness.

At the same time, sensing the opportunity, Charlene leaped

up from her position to my right and ran to the northeast, into the dust, her movement unnoticed by the guards.

I started to run but the guard who had fired at Maya turned his weapon toward me. Quickly Curtis reached out and grabbed my legs, dragging me to the ground.

Behind us, the bunker door swung open and Feyman ran to the dish antenna and furiously adjusted the keyboard. Gradually the noise began to diminish and the earth movements slowed to mere tremors.

"For God sakes!" Curtis yelled toward him. "You've got to stop this!"

Feyman's face was covered with dust. "There's nothing wrong that we can't fix," he said with eerie calm. The guards were on their feet, dusting themselves off and walking toward us. Feyman noticed that Maya and Charlene were missing, but before he could say anything, the noise returned with ear-shattering volume and the earth under us seemed to leap upward several feet, rolling everyone to the ground once more. The splintering limbs from a falling tree sent the guards scurrying toward the bunker.

"Now!" Curtis said. "Let's go!"

I was frozen. He jerked me to my feet. "We've got to move!" he yelled in my ear.

Finally my legs worked and we ran northeast in the same direction that Maya had fled.

Several more tremors reverberated under our feet and then the movements and sounds ceased. After making our way through the dark woods for several miles, our path lighted only by the rays of the moon filtering through the foliage, we stopped and huddled in a grove of small pines.

"Do you think they'll follow us?" I asked Curtis.

"Yes," he said. "They can't allow any of us to get back to

town. I would guess that they still have people stationed along the paths back."

While he was talking, a clear picture of the falls entered my mind. It was still pristine, undisturbed. The falling water, I realized, was the landmark in Feyman's vision that I had been trying to remember.

"We have to go northwest to the falls," I said.

Curtis nodded toward the north, and as silently as possible we headed in that direction, crossing the stream and carefully making our way toward the canyon. Periodically Curtis would stop and cover our tracks. During a rest, we could hear the low rumbling of vehicles from the southeast.

After another mile we began to see the moonlit canyon walls rising up into the distance. As we approached the rocky mouth, Curtis led the way across the creek. Suddenly he jumped backward in fright as someone walked around a tree from the left. The person screamed and recoiled, almost losing balance, teetering at the edge of the creek bank.

"Maya!" I yelled, realizing who it was.

Curtis recovered and lunged forward and pulled her back as rocks and gravel slid into the water.

She hugged him intensely and then reached out to me. "I don't know why I ran like that. I just panicked. I could only think to head toward the falls you told me about. I just prayed that some of you would get away too."

Leaning back against a larger tree, she took a deep breath, then asked, "What happened when the guard fired back there? How did those bullets miss me? I saw this strange streak of light."

Curtis and I looked at each other.

"I don't know," I said.

"It seemed to calm me," Maya continued, ". . . in a way I've never experienced before."

We looked at each other; no one spoke. Then, in silence, I heard the distinct sound of someone walking up ahead.

"Wait," I said to the others. "Someone's up there." We crouched down and waited. Ten minutes went by. Then, from the trees ahead, Charlene walked up and dropped to her knees.

"Thank God I found you," she said. "How did you get away?"

"We were able to run when a tree fell," I said.

Charlene looked deep into my eyes. "I thought you might head toward the falls so I walked in this direction, although I don't know if I could have found them in the dark."

Maya motioned for us, and we all moved out to a clearing where the creek went through the mouth of the canyon. Here the full light of the moon illuminated the grass and the rocks to each side.

"Maybe we're going to have another chance," she said, urging us with her hands to sit down and face each other.

"What are we going to do?" Curtis said. "We can't stay here long. They'll be coming."

I looked at Maya, thinking we should go on to the falls, but she seemed so energized that, instead, I asked, "What do you think went wrong before?"

"I don't know; maybe there are too few of us. You said there were supposed to be seven. Or perhaps there's too much Fear."

Charlene leaned toward the group. "I think we have to remember the energy we achieved when we were in the cave. We have to connect at that level again."

For several long minutes we all worked on our inner connection. Finally Maya said, "We have to give each other energy, find the higher-self expression."

I took several deep breaths and watched the faces of the others again. Gradually they became more beautiful and luminescent, and I caught sight of their authentic soul expression. Around us, the surrounding plants and rocks lit up even more, as though the moon's rays had suddenly doubled. A familiar wave of love and euphoria swept through my body and I turned to see the shimmering figures of my soul group behind me.

As soon as I saw them, my awareness seemed to expand even more and I realized that the soul groups of the others were in similar positions, although they had not yet merged.

Maya caught my eye. She was looking at me in a state of complete openness and honesty, and as I watched her, it seemed as though I could see her Birth Vision as a subtle expression on her face. She knew who she was and it beamed outward for everyone to observe. Her mission was clear; her background had prepared her perfectly.

"Feel as if the atoms in your body are vibrating at a higher level," she said.

I glanced at Charlene; on her face was the same clarity. She represented the information bearers, identifying and communicating the vital truths expressed by each person or group.

"Do you see what's happening?" Charlene asked. "We're seeing each other as we really are, at our highest level, without the emotional projections of old fears."

"I can see that," Curtis said, his face again full of energy and certainty.

No one spoke for several minutes. I closed my eyes as the energy continued to build.

"Look at that!" Charlene suddenly said, pointing at the soul groups all around us.

Each soul group was beginning to blend with the others, just as they had done at the cave. I glanced at Charlene and then at Curtis and Maya. I could now see on their faces an even fuller expression of who they were as participants in the long movement of human civilization.

"This is it!" I said. "We're reaching the next step; we're seeing a more complete vision of human history."

Before us, in a huge hologram, appeared an image of history that seemed to stretch out from the very beginning to what appeared to be a distant end. As I strained to focus, I realized that this was an image very similar to the one I had observed earlier while with my soul group—except that in this instance the story was beginning much earlier, with the birth of the universe itself.

We watched as the first matter exploded into being and gravitated into stars that lived and died and spewed forth the great diversity of elements that ultimately formed the Earth. These elements, in turn, combined in the early terrestrial environment into ever-more-complex substances until they finally leaped into organic life—life that then also moved forward, into greater organization and awareness, as if guided by an overall plan. Multicelled organisms became fishes, and fishes progressed into amphibians, and amphibians evolved into reptiles and birds and ultimately into mammals.

As we watched, a clear picture of the Afterlife dimension opened up in front of us, and I understood that an aspect of each of the souls there—in fact, a part of all of humanity—had lived through this long, slow process of evolution. We had swum as fishes, boldly crawled upon the land as amphibians, and struggled to survive as reptiles, birds, and mammals, fighting every step of the way to finally move into human form—all with intention.

We knew that through wave after wave of successive generations, we would be born into the physical plane, and no matter how long it took, we would strive to wake up, and unify, and evolve, and eventually implement on Earth the same spiritual culture that exists in the Afterlife. Certainly the journey would be difficult, even torturous. With the first intuition to awaken, we would sense the Fear of aloneness and separation. Yet we would not go back to sleep; we would fight through the Fear, relying on the dim intuition that we weren't alone, that we were spiritual beings with a spiritual purpose on the planet.

And, following the urge of evolution, we would gravitate together into larger, more complex social groupings, differentiating into more diverse occupations, overcoming a need to defeat and conquer each other, and eventually implement a democratic process through which new ideas could be shared and synthesized and evolved into ever-better truths. Gradually our security would come from inside us, as we progressed from an expression of the divine in terms of nature gods to the divine as one father God outside ourselves to a final expression as the Holy Spirit within.

Sacred texts would be intuited and written, offering heartfelt symbolic expression of our relationship and future with this one deity. Visionaries from both East and West would clarify that this Holy Spirit was always there, always accessible, waiting only for our ability to repent, to open, to clear the blocks that prevent a full communion.

Over time, we knew, our urge to unify and share would expand until we sensed a special community, a deeper association with others who shared a particular geographical location on the planet, and the human world would began to solidify into political nation-states, each holding a unique viewpoint. Soon after would come an explosion of trade and commerce. The scientific method would be instituted, and the resulting discoveries would initiate a period of economic preoccupation and the great secular expansion known as the Industrial Revolution.

And once we developed a web of economic relationships around the globe, we would begin to further awaken and to remember our full spiritual nature. The Insights would gradually permeate human consciousness and we would evolve our economy into a form compatible with the Earth, and, finally, begin to move beyond the last fearful polarization of forces toward a new spiritual worldview on the planet.

Here I momentarily glanced at the others. Their faces told me that they had shared this vision of Earth's history. In one brief revelation we had grasped how human consciousness had progressed from the beginning of time right to the present moment.

Suddenly the hologram focused on the polarization in great detail. All humans on the Earth were migrating into two conflicting positions: one pushing toward a vague but ever-clearer image of transformation, and the other resisting, sensing that important values contained in the old view were being lost forever.

We could see that in the Afterlife dimension, it was known that this conflict would be our greatest challenge to the spiritualization of the physical dimension—particularly if the polarization grew extreme. In this case, both sides would entrench into an irrational projection of evil onto the other, or worse, might believe the literal interpreters of the end-times prophecies and begin to think the coming future was beyond their influence and therefore give up completely.

To find the World Vision and resolve the polarization, we could see that our Afterlife intention was to discern the deeper truths of these prophecies. As with all the Scriptures, the visions in Daniel and Revelation were divine intuitions coming from the

Afterlife into the physical plane, and so must be understood as draped in the symbolism of the seer's mind, much like a dream. We would focus on the symbolic meaning. The prophecies envisioned an eventual end to the human story on Earth; but an "end" that, for *believers*, would be quite different from the one experienced by nonbelievers.

Those in the latter group were seen to experience an end of history that would begin with great catastrophes and environmental disasters and collapsing economies. Then, at the height of the fear and chaos, a strong leader would emerge, the Antichrist, who would offer to restore order, but only if individuals would agree to give up their liberties and carry the "mark of the beast" upon their bodies in order to participate in the automated economy. Eventually this strong leader would declare himself a god and take by force any country that resisted his rule, at first making war on the forces of Islam, then on the Jews and Christians, ultimately casting the whole world into a fiery Armageddon.

For believers, on the other hand, the scriptural prophets predicted a much more pleasant end to history. Remaining true to the spirit, these believers would be given spiritual bodies and be raptured into another dimension called the New Jerusalem, but would be able to go back and forth into the physical. Eventually, at a certain point in the war, God would fully return to end the fighting, restore the Earth, and implement a thousand years of peace where there would be no sickness or death, and everything would be transformed, even the animals of the world, who would no longer eat meat. Instead, "The wolf shall dwell with the lamb . . . and the lion shall eat straw like the ox."

Maya and Curtis caught my eye, and then Charlene looked up; we all seemed to sense, at once, the core meaning of the prophecies. What the end-times seers were receiving was an intuition that in our time, two distinctive futures would be opening before us. We could choose either to languish in the Fear, believing that the world is moving into a Big Brother style of automation and social decay and ultimate destruction . . . or we could follow the other path and consider ourselves the believers who can overcome this nihilism and open to the higher vibrations of love, where we are spared the apocalypse and can enter a new dimension in which we invite the spirit, through us, to create just the utopia the scriptural prophets envisioned.

Now we could see why those in the Afterlife felt that our interpretation of these prophecies was key to resolving the polarization. If we decide that these Scriptures mean that the destruction of the world is inevitable, written unalterably into God's plan, the effect of such a belief would be to create this very outcome.

Clearly we had to choose the path of love and believing. As I had seen earlier, the polarization was not intended to be so severe. It was known in the Afterlife that each side represented a part of the truth that could be integrated and synthesized into the new, spiritual worldview. Further, I saw that this synthesis would be a natural outgrowth of the Insights themselves, especially the Tenth Insight, and of the special groups that would begin to form all over the world.

Suddenly the hologram raced forward and I felt another expansion of consciousness. I knew that we were now moving into the next step of the process: the actual remembrance of how we intended to become believers and accomplish this prophesied utopian future. We were finally remembering the *World Vision*!

As we watched, we first saw the Tenth Insight groups forming all over the planet, reaching a critical mass of energy, and then learning to project this energy in such a way that the entrenched sides of the polarization immediately began to lighten and ease, overcoming the Fear. Especially affected would be the technological controllers, who would remember themselves and give up their last efforts to manipulate the economy and seize power.

The result of the projected energy would be an unprecedented wave of awakening and remembrance and cooperation and personal involvement, and a virtual explosion of newly inspired individuals, all of whom would begin to fully recall their Birth Visions and follow their synchronistic path into exactly the right positions within their culture.

The scene shifted to images of decaying inner cities and forgotten rural families. Here we could see a new consensus forming on how to intervene in the cycle of poverty. No longer would intervention be conceived in terms of government programs or merely in terms of education and jobs; the new approach would be deeply spiritual, for the structures of education were already in place; what was missing was the ability to break free from the Fear and to overcome the hellish diversions set up to ward off the anxiety of poverty.

In this regard I saw a sudden surge of private outreach surrounding each family and each child in need. Waves of individuals began to form personal relationships, beginning with those who saw the family every day—merchants, teachers, police officers on the beat, ministers. This contact was then expanded by other volunteers working as "big brothers," "big sisters," and tutors—all guided by their inner intuitions to help, remembering their intention to make a difference with one family, one child. And all carrying the contagion of the Insights and the crucial message that no matter how tough the situation, or how entrenched the self-defeating habits, each of us can wake up to a memory of mission and purpose.

As this contagion continued, incidents of violent crime began mysteriously to decrease across human culture; for, as we saw clearly, the roots of violence are always frustration and passion and fear scripts that dehumanize the victim, and a growing interaction with those carrying a higher awareness was now beginning to disrupt this mind-set.

We saw a new consensus emerging toward crime that drew from both traditional and human-potential ideas. In the short run, there would be a need for new prisons and detention facilities, as the traditional truth was recognized that returning offenders to the community too soon, or leniently letting perpetrators go in order to give them another chance, reinforced the behavior. Yet, at the same time, we saw an integration of the Insights into the actual operation of these facilities, introducing a wave of private involvement with those incarcerated, shifting the crime culture and initiating the only rehabilitation that works: the contagion of remembering.

Simultaneously, as increasingly more people awakened, I saw millions of individuals taking the time to intervene in conflict at every level of human culture—for we all were reaching a new understanding of what was at stake. In every situation where a husband or wife grew angry and lashed out at the other, or where addictive compulsions or a desperate need for approval led a youthful gang member to kill, or where people felt so restricted in their lives that they embezzled or defrauded or manipulated others for gain; in all these situations, there was someone perfectly placed to have prevented the violence but who had *failed* to act.

Surrounding this potential hero were perhaps dozens of other friends and acquaintances who had likewise failed, because they didn't convey the information and ideas that would have created the wider support system for the intervention to have taken place. In the past perhaps, this failure could have been rationalized, but no longer. Now the Tenth Insight was emerging and we knew that the people in our lives were probably souls with whom we had had long relationships over many lifetimes, and who were now counting on our help. So we are compelled to act, compelled to be courageous. None of us wants to have failure on our conscience, or have to bear a torturous Life Review in which we must watch the tragic consequences of our timidity.

As the scenes rushed past, we saw this burgeoning awareness motivating activity toward other social problems as well. We could see an image of the world's rivers and oceans, and again I observed a synthesis of the old and new which, while admitting the often capricious behavior of government bureaucracy, also raised to a new level of priority the human desire to safeguard the environment, initiating a surge of private intervention.

The wisdom was emerging that, as with the problem of poverty and violence, the crime of pollution always has compliant bystanders. People who would never consciously pollute the environment themselves worked with or knew about others whose projects or business practices damaged the planet's biosphere.

These were the people who in the past had said nothing, perhaps because of job insecurity or because they felt alone in their opinion. Yet now, as they awakened and realized they were in exactly the right position to take action, we watched them rally public opinion against the polluters—whether it was the dumping of industrial wastes into the ocean in the dead of night, venting excess oil from a tanker far at sea, secretly using banned insecticides on commercial vegetable plots, leaving the scrubbers off at an industrial plant between inspections, or faking the research on the dangers of a new chemical. No matter what the crime, now there would be *inspired* witnesses who would feel the support of grassroots organizations offering rewards for such information, and who would take their camcorders and expose the crime themselves.

Similarly we observed the environmental practices of governments themselves being exposed, especially regarding policies toward public lands. For years, it would be discovered, governmental agencies had sold mining and logging rights on some of the most sacred places on Earth, at below-market rates, as political favors and paybacks. Majestic, cathedral forests, belonging to the public, had been unbelievably pillaged and clear-cut in the name of proper forest management—as though planting rows of pine trees would replace the diversity of life, and energies, inherent in a hardwood forest that had matured for centuries.

Yet it would be the emerging spiritual awareness that would finally force an end to such disgrace. We watched a new coalition forming, made up of old-view hunters and nostalgic history buffs and those who perceived the natural sites as sacred portals. This coalition would finally sound the alarm that would save the few remaining virgin forests in Europe and North America, and begin to protect on a larger scale the essential rain forests in the tropical regions of the world. It would be commonly understood that every remaining site of beauty must be saved for the benefit of future generations. Cultivated plant fibers would replace the use of trees for lumber and paper, and the remaining public land would all be protected from exploitation and used to supply the exploding demand to visit such unspoiled and energizing areas of nature. At the same time, as intuition and awareness and remembering expanded, the developed cultures would finally turn to the native peoples of the world with a new respect and appreciation, eager to integrate a mystical redefinition of the natural world.

The holographic scene moved forward again, and I could see the wave of spiritual contagion permeating every aspect of culture. Just as Charlene had foreseen earlier, every occupational group was beginning consciously to shift its customary practice toward a more intuitive and ideal level of functioning, finding its spiritual role, its vision of true service.

Medicine, led by individual practitioners who focused on the spiritual/psychological genesis of disease, was moving from the mechanical treatment of symptoms toward prevention. We could see the legal profession moving from the self-serving methods of creating conflict, and obscuring truth in order to win, into its true role of resolving conflict in the most "win-win" manner possible. And just as Curtis had seen, everyone involved in business, industry by industry, was shifting into an enlightened capitalism, a capitalism oriented not just to profits, but to filling the evolving needs of spiritual beings, and making these products available at the lowest possible prices. This new business ethic would produce a grassroots deflation, initiating a systematic evolution toward an eventual full automation—and ultimately the free availability—of the basic necessities of life, liberating humans to engage in the spiritual "tithe" economy envisioned in the Ninth Insight.

As we continued to watch, the scenes accelerated forward, and we could see individuals remembering their spiritual missions at increasingly younger ages. Here we could see the precise understanding that would soon embody the new spiritual worldview. Individuals would come of age and remember themselves as souls born from one dimension of existence into another. Although memory loss during the transition would be expected, recapturing pre-life memory would become an important early goal of education.

As youths, our teachers would first guide us through the early experience of synchronicity; urge us to identify our intuitions to study certain subjects, to visit particular places, always looking for higher answers as to why we were pursuing these particular paths. As the full memory of the Insights emerged, we would find ourselves involved with certain groups, working on particular projects, bringing in our full vision of what we had wanted to do. And finally we would recover the underlying intention behind our lives. We would know that we came here to raise the vibratory level of this planet, to discover and protect the beauty and energy of its natural sites, and to ensure that all humans had access to these special locations, so that we could continue to increase our energy, ultimately instituting the Afterlife culture here in the physical.

Such a worldview would especially shift the way we looked at other people. No longer would we see human beings merely in the racial dress or national origin of one particular lifetime. Instead, we would see others as brother or sister souls, engaged, like us, in a process of coming awake and of spiritualizing the planet. It would become known that the settling of certain souls into various geographical locations on the planet had occurred with great meaning. Each nation was, in fact, an enclave of specific spiritual information, shared and modeled by its citizens, information waiting to be learned and integrated.

As I watched the future unfold, I could see that a world political unity, envisioned by so many, was finally being achieved— not by forcing all nations into subservience to one political body, but rather through a grassroots acknowledgment of our spiritual similarities while treasuring our local autonomy and cultural differences. As with individuals interacting in a group, each member of the family of nations was being recognized for this culture truth represented to the world at large. Before us, we saw Earth's political struggles, so often violent, shifting into a war of words. As the tide of remembrance continued to sweep the planet, all humans began to understand that our destiny was to discuss and compare the perspectives of our relative religions and, while honoring the best of their individual doctrines at the personal level, ultimately to see that each religion supplemented the others and to integrate them into a synthesized global spirituality.

We could see clearly that these dialogues would result in the rebuilding of a grand temple in Jerusalem, jointly occupied by all the major religions—Jewish, Christian, Islamic, Eastern, even the de facto religion of secular idealism, represented by those economic enclaves in China and Europe who thought primarily in terms of a pantheistic economic utopia. Here, ultimate spiritual perspective would be debated and discussed. And in this war of words and energy, at first the Islamic and the Jewish perspectives would hold center stage, then the Christian perspective would be compared and integrated, along with the inner vision of the Eastern religions.

We saw the awareness of humanity entering another level, with the collective human culture progressing from primarily the sharing of economic information to the synchronistic exchange of spiritual truths. As this occurred, certain individuals and groups would begin to reach levels approaching that of the Afterlife dimension and would disappear to the larger majority remaining on Earth. These select groups would walk intentionally into the other dimension, yet would learn to go back and forth— just as the Ninth Insight predicts and the scriptural prophets saw. Yet, after this Rapture began, those left on Earth would understand what was occurring and accept their role in remaining in the physical, knowing that they would soon follow.

Now it was time for the secular idealists to proclaim their truths on the temple steps. At first their energetic thrust into Jerusalem would come from Europe with its primarily secular vision, with one strong leader proclaiming the spiritual importance of secular matters. This perspective would be met strongly by the determined "otherworldly" spiritualism of the Muslims and the Christians. But then this conflict of energy would be mediated and later synthesized into one by the inner spiritual emphasis of the Eastern perspective. By then, the last attempts of the controllers, who had once conspired to create a tyrannical society of chips and robots and forced compliance, would have been won over by the contagion of awakening. And this last synthesis would open everyone to the final infusion of the Holy Spirit. We saw clearly that through this Middle Eastern dialogue of energy integration, history had fulfilled the scriptural prophecies in a *symbolic and verbal* manner, avoiding the physical apocalypse expected by the literalists.

Suddenly our focus shifted to the Afterlife dimension, and here we could see with great clarity that our intention all along was not merely to create a New Earth, but a New Heaven as well. We watched as the effect of the World Vision remembrance transformed not only the physical dimension but also the Afterlife. During the raptures on Earth, the soul groups would also have been rapturing toward the physical, completing the transfer of energy into the expanded physical dimension.

Here the full reality of what was happening in the historical process became apparent. From the beginning of time, as our memory opened, energy and knowledge had systematically moved from the Afterlife dimension into the physical. At first, the soul groups in the Afterlife had borne full responsibility for maintaining the intention and envisioning the future, helping us to recall what we wanted to do, giving us energy.

Then, as consciousness on Earth progressed and the population increased, the balance of energy and responsibility had slowly shifted toward the physical dimension, until, at this point in history, when enough energy had shifted and the World Vision was being remembered, the full power and responsibility for believing and creating the intended future would be shifting from the Afterlife to the souls on Earth, to the newly forming groups, to *us*!

At this point, *we* have to carry the intent. And that's why it now fell to us to resolve the polarization and to help shift the particular individuals, right here in this valley, who were still caught in the Fear and who felt justified in manipulating the economy for their own purposes, justified in seizing control of the future.

At exactly the same time, all four of us glanced at each other in the darkness, the hologram still surrounding us, the soul groups still merged in the background, glowing brightly. Then I noticed a huge hawk fly onto a limb ten feet above the group and gaze down at us. Beneath it, less than five feet away, a rabbit hopped to within three feet of my right elbow and stopped, followed seconds later by a bobcat, who sat directly beside it. What was happening?

Abruptly a silent vibration tingled my solar plexus; the experiment had been reactivated!

"Look over there!" Curtis yelled.

Fifty yards away, barely distinguishable in the moonlight, was a narrow fissure, shaking the bushes and small trees, extending slowly in our direction.

I looked at the others.

"It's up to us now," Maya shouted. "We have enough of the Vision now; we can stop them."

Before we could act, the earth under us shook violently and the fissure accelerated toward us. Simultaneously several vehicles pulled to a stop in the underbrush, their lights shining through fuzzy silhouettes made by the trees and dust. Unafraid, I maintained my energy and focused again on the hologram.

"The Vision will stop them," Maya yelled again. "Don't let the Vision go! Hold it!"

Embracing the image of the future before us, I again felt the group marshal energy toward Feyman, as if holding our intention like a giant wall against his intrusion, imaging his group being pushed back by the energy, fleeing in terror.

I glanced at the crevice still racing toward us, confident it would soon stop. It accelerated instead. Another tree fell. Then another. As it sped into the group, I lost my concentration and rolled backward, choking on the dust.

"It's still not working!" I heard Curtis yell.

I felt as if it was all happening again. "Up this way," I shouted, struggling to see in the sudden darkness. As I ran, I could barely make out the dim outlines of the others; they were veering away from me to the east.

I climbed up the stony ridge that formed the left wall of the canyon and didn't stop until I was a hundred yards away. Kneeling in the rocks, I looked out into the night. Nothing moved, but I could hear Feyman's men talking at the canyon entrance. Quietly I made my way farther up the slope, angling northwest, still watching carefully for any sign of the others. Finally I found a way to climb down to the canyon floor again. Still no movement anywhere.

Then, as I began to walk north again, someone suddenly grabbed me from behind.

"What—" I yelled.

"Shsssssssss," a voice whispered. "Be quiet. It's David."

# HOLDING
# THE
# VISION

I turned and looked at him in the moonlight, observing the long hair, the scarred face.

"Where are the others?" he whispered.

"We were separated," I replied. "Did you see what happened?"

He moved his face closer. "Yes, I was watching from the hill. Where do you think they'll go?"

I thought for a moment. "They'll head toward the falls."

He motioned for me to follow and we started in that direction. After several minutes had passed, he glanced back as he walked and said, "When you were sitting together at the entrance back there, your energy pooled, and then swelled far out into the valley. What were you doing?"

In an attempt to explain, I summarized the whole story: finding Wil and entering the other dimension; seeing Williams and running into Joel and Maya; and especially meeting Curtis and trying to bring in the World Vision to defeat Feyman.

"Curtis was back there with you at the mouth of the canyon?" David asked.

"Yes, and Maya and Charlene, although I think there are supposed to be seven of us . . ."

He gave me another quick glance, almost chuckling. All of the tense, pent-up anger he had displayed in town seemed to have completely disappeared. "So you found the ancestors too, didn't you?"

I hurried up to walk beside him. "You reached the other dimension?"

"Yes, I saw my soul group and witnessed my Birth Vision, and just as you, I remembered what happened before, that we've all come back to bring in the World Vision. And then—I don't know how—when I was watching all of you back there in the moonlight, it was as if I was with you, was part of your group. I saw the World Vision around me." He had stopped in the shadow of a large tree that blocked the moon, his face rigid and cast back.

I turned to face him. "David, when the group of us were together back there, and we brought in the World Vision, why didn't it stop Feyman?"

He moved forward into the light and immediately I recognized him as the angry chief who had rebuked Maya. Then his rock-hard expression shifted and he burst out laughing.

"The key aspect of this Vision," he said, "is not the mere experience of it, although that's hard enough. It's how we *project* this Vision of the future, how we *hold it* for the rest of humanity. That's what the Tenth Insight is really all about. You didn't hold the Vision for Feyman and the others in a way that would help them wake up." He looked at me a moment longer, then said, "Come on, we have to hurry."

After we had traveled perhaps half a mile, a bird of some kind cried out toward our right, and David stopped abruptly.

"What was that?" I asked.

He cocked his head as the cry again filled the night. "That's a screech owl, signaling the others that we are here."

I gave him a blank expression, remembering how strange the animals had been acting ever since I arrived in the valley.

"Does anyone in that group know the animal signs?" he asked.

"I don't know; maybe Curtis?"

"No, he's too scientific."

I then remembered that Maya had mentioned following the sounds of birds when she had found us in the cave. "Perhaps Maya!"

He looked at me questioningly. "The physician you mentioned, who uses visualization in her work?"

"Yes."

"Good. That's perfect. Let's do what she does and pray."

I turned and looked at him as the owl cried out again. "What?"

"Let's . . . visualize . . . that she remembers the gift of the animals."

"What is the gift of the animals?"

A trace of anger flashed across his face, and he paused for a moment, closing his eyes, obviously trying to shake off the emotion. "Haven't you understood that when an animal shows up in our lives, it is a coincidence of the highest order?"

I told him about the rabbit and the flock of crows and the hawk, which had shown up as I had first entered the valley, and then about the bobcat cub, the eagle, and the young wolf that had appeared later. "Some of them even showed up when we saw the World Vision."

He nodded expectantly.

"I knew something significant was happening," I said, "but I didn't know exactly what to do except to follow some of them. Are you saying that all these animals had a message for me?"

"Yes, that's exactly what I'm saying."

"How do I know what the message is?"

"It's easy. You know because of the particular *kind* of animal you are attracting at any one time. Each species that crosses our paths tells us something about our situation, what part of ourselves we must call upon to handle the circumstances we face."

"Even after everything that's happened," I said, "that's hard to believe. A biologist would say animals are primarily robots, operating on dumb instinct."

"Only because animals reflect our own level of consciousness and expectation. If our level of vibration is low, the animals will merely be there with us, performing their usual ecological functions. When a skeptical biologist reduces animal behavior to mindless instinct, he sees the restriction that he himself has put upon the animal. But as our vibration shifts, the actions of the animals that come to us become ever more synchronistic, mysterious, and instructional."

I just stared.

Squinting, he said, "The hare that you saw was pointing out a direction for you both physically and emotionally. When I talked to you in town, you seemed depressed and fearful, as though you were losing faith in the Insights. If you watch a wild rabbit for a long time, you can perceive that it models how to really face our fear, so that we can later move past it into creativity and abundance. A rabbit lives in close proximity to animals that feed on it, but it handles the fear and stays there and is still very fertile and productive and upbeat. When a rabbit appears in our lives, it is a signal to find the same attitude within ourselves. This was the message to you; its presence meant you had the opportunity to remember the medicine of rabbit and to fully look at your own fear and move beyond. And because it occurred during the beginning of your trip, it set the tone of your whole adventure. Hasn't your trip been both fearful and abundant?"

I nodded.

He added, "Sometimes it means that the abundance can be of a romantic nature too. Have you met anyone?"

I shrugged, remembering the new energy I had felt with Charlene. "Maybe, in a way. What about the crows I saw and the hawk that I followed when I found Wil?"

"Crows are the holders of the laws of spirit. Spend time with crows and they will do amazing things that always increase our perception of spiritual reality. Their message was to open up, to remember the spiritual laws that were presenting themselves to you in this valley. Seeing them should have prepared you for what was to come."

"And the hawk?"

"Hawks are alert, and observant, ever vigilant for the next bit of information, the next message. Their presence means that it is important at that time to increase our alertness. Often they signal that a messenger is close." He cocked his head.

"You mean, it was foretelling the presence of Wil?"

"Yes."

David went on to explain why the other animals I had seen had been drawn my way. Cats, he told me, implore us to remember our ability to intuit and to self-heal. The bobcat cub's message, arriving as it did, just before meeting Maya, was to signal that an opportunity to heal was near. Similarly an eagle soars to great heights, and represents an opportunity to actually *venture* into the higher realms of the spirit world. When I saw the eagle on the ridge, David said, I should have prepared for seeing my soul group and for understanding more of my own destiny. Lastly, he told me, the young wolf was there to energize and awaken my latent instinct for courage and my ability to teach, so that I might find the words to help bring together the other members of the group.

"So the animals represent," I said, "parts of ourselves we need to get in touch with."

"Yes, aspects of ourselves that we developed when we were those animals during the course of evolution, but have lost."

I thought of the vision of evolution I had witnessed at the canyon entrance with the group. "You're speaking of the way life progressed forward, species by species?"

"We were there," David continued. "Our consciousness moved through each animal as it represented the end point of life's development and then leaped to the next. We experienced the way each species views the world, which is an important aspect of the complete spiritual consciousness. When a particular animal comes around, that means we're ready to integrate its consciousness into our waking awareness again. And I'll tell you something: there are some species that we aren't even close to catching up with. That's why it's so important to preserve every life-form on this Earth. We want them to endure not just because they are a part of the balanced ecosphere, but because they represent aspects of ourselves that we're still trying to remember."

He paused for a moment, looking out into the night.

"This is also true of the rich diversity of human thought, represented by the various cultures around the planet. None of us knows exactly where the current truth of human evolution resides. Each culture around the world has a slightly different worldview, a particular mode of awareness, and it takes the best of all cultures, integrated together, to make a more ideal whole."

An expression of sadness crossed his face. "It's too bad that four hundred years had to pass before the real integration of the European and Native cultures could begin. Think of what has happened. The Western mind lost touch with the mystery and reduced the magic of the deep woods to lumber and the mystery of wildlife to pretty animals. Urbanization has isolated the great majority of people, so we now think a journey into nature is a stroll on the golf course. Do you realize how few of us have experienced the mysteries of the wilderness?

"Our National Parks represent all that is left of the great cathedral forests and rich plains and high deserts that once characterized this continent. There are too many of us now for the wild areas that still exist. In many parks there are waiting lists over a year long. And still, the politicians seem bent on selling off more and more of the public lands. Most of us are forced to draw from decks of animal cards to see what animal signs are coming into our lives, instead of being able to take quests into the truly wild areas of the world to experience the real thing."

Suddenly the screech owl's cry erupted so close that the sound made me jump involuntarily.

David was squinting impatiently. "Can we pray now?"

"Listen," I said, "I don't know what you mean. Do you want to pray or visualize?"

He tried to calm his voice. "Yes, I'm sorry. Impatience seems to be a residual emotion I have with you." He took a breath. "The Tenth Insight—learning to have faith in our intuitions, remembering our birth intention, holding the World Vision—all of it is about understanding the essence of real *prayer*.

"Why does every religious tradition assume a form of prayer? If God is the one, all-knowing, all-powerful God, then why would we have to beseech his help or impel him to do something? Why wouldn't he just set up commandments and covenants and judge us accordingly, taking direct action when *he* wanted to, not us? Why would we have to ask for his special intervention? The answer is that when we pray in the correct fashion, we are not asking God to do something. God is inspiring us to act in his place to enact his will on the Earth. We are the emissaries of the divine on this planet. True prayer is the method, the visualization, that God expects us to use in discerning his will and implementing it in the physical dimension. His kingdom come, his will be done, on Earth, as it is in heaven.

"In this sense, every thought, every expectation—all of what we visualize happening in the future—is a prayer, and tends to create that very future. But no thought or desire or fear is as strong as a vision that is in alignment with the divine. That's why bringing in the World Vision, and holding it, is important: so we will know what to pray for, what future to visualize."

"I understand," I said. "How do we help Maya become aware of the owl?"

"What did she say to do when she talked to you about healing?"

"She said we should visualize patients remembering what they intended to do with their lives but still hadn't done. She said that real healing springs from a renewed sense of what one wants to do once health is regained. When they remember, then we can also join them in holding this more specific plan."

"Let's do the same now," David said. "Hopefully, her original intention was to follow the sound of this bird."

David closed his eyes, and I followed his lead, trying to visualize an image of Maya awakening to what she was supposed to do. After a few minutes I opened my eyes and David was staring at me. The owl screamed again right above our heads.

"Let's go," he said.

Twenty minutes later we were standing on the hill above the falls. The owl had followed, calling out periodically, and had stationed itself fifty feet to our right. In front of us, the pool glistened in the moonlight, muted only by wisps of fog that drifted along its surface. We waited for ten or fifteen minutes without speaking.

"Look! There!" David said, pointing.

Among the rocks to the right of the pool I could make out several figures. One of them looked up and saw us; it was Charlene. I waved and she recognized me. Then David and I made our way down the rocky slope to where they were standing.

Curtis was ecstatic at seeing David, grabbing his arm. "We'll stop these people now." For a moment they looked at each other in silence, then Curtis introduced Maya and Charlene.

I met eyes with Maya. "Did you have any trouble finding your way here?"

"At first, we were confused and lost in the darkness, but then I heard the owl and I knew."

"The presence of an owl," David said, "means that we have the opportunity to see through any possible deception by others, and if we avoid the tendency to harm or lash out, we can, like the owl, cut through the darkness to hold a higher truth."

Maya was watching David closely. "You look familiar," Maya said. "Who are you?"

He looked at her questioningly. "You were told my name. It's David."

She grabbed his hand gently. "No, I mean who are you to me, to us?"

"I was there," he said, "during the wars, but I was so full of hatred for the whites that I didn't support you; I didn't even listen to you."

"We're doing it differently now," I said.

David glared at me reflexively, then caught himself and softened, as he had before. "Back in that war, I had even less respect for you than the others. You wouldn't take a stand. You ran away."

"It was fear," I replied.

"I know."

For several more minutes everyone talked with David about the emotions we were feeling, discussing everything we could remember about the tragedy of the war on the Native Americans. David went on to explain that his soul group was made up of mediators and that he had come this time to work through his anger at the European mentality, and then to work for the spiritual recognition of all indigenous cultures and the inclusion of all people.

Charlene glanced at me, then turned to David. "You're the fifth member of this group, aren't you?"

Before he could answer, we felt a vibration racing through the ground under our feet; it sent irregular ripples across the surface of the pool. Accompanying the tremor was another eerie melodious whine that filled the forest. Out of the corner of my eye I saw flashlights moving on the hill fifty feet above us.

"They're here!" Curtis whispered.

I turned to see Feyman at the edge of an overhang directly above our heads; he was adjusting a small dish antenna on what looked like a portable computer.

"They're going to focus on us and try to fine-tune the generator that way," Curtis said. "We've got to get out of here."

Maya reached over and touched his arm. "No, please, Curtis, maybe it will work this time."

David moved closer to Curtis, then said lowly, "It can work."

Curtis stared at him for a moment, then finally nodded his agreement, and we began to raise our energy again. As in the two previous attempts, I began to see higher-self expressions on every face, and then our soul groups appeared and merged into a circle around us, including for the first time the members of David's group. As the memory of the World Vision returned, we were again pulled into the overall intent to transfer energy and knowledge and awareness into the physical dimension.

Also, as before, we saw the fearful polarization occurring in our time, and the panoramic vision of the positive future that would succeed it once the special groups formed and learned how to intercede, how to *hold the Vision*.

Suddenly another tremor shook the ground violently.

"Stay with the Vision," Maya shouted. "Hold the image of how the future can be."

I heard a fissure tear through the ground to my right, but I kept my concentration. In my mind I again saw the World Vision as a force of energy that was emanating outward from our group in all directions and pushing Feyman back away from us, defeating the energy of his Fear vision. To my left, a huge tree ripped from its roots and crashed to the ground.

"It's still not working," Curtis shouted, jumping to his feet.

"No, wait," David said. He had been deep in thought, and now he reached out and grabbed Curtis, pulling him down beside him. "Don't you see what's wrong?! We're treating Feyman and the others as if they are enemies, trying to push them back. Doing that actually strengthens them, because they have something to fight against. Rather than fighting them with the Vision, we have to include Feyman and the operatives in what we're visualizing. In reality, there are no enemies; we're all souls in growth, waking up. We have to project the World Vision toward them as though they are just like us."

I suddenly recalled seeing Feyman's Birth Vision. Now it all made perfect sense: the view of Hell, understanding the obsessive trance states that humans use to ward off fear, seeing the ring of souls as they tried to intervene. And then observing Feyman's original intention.

"He *is* one of us!" I shouted. "I know what he intended to do! In actuality, he came to break through his need for power; he wanted to prevent the destruction that could be caused by the generators and the other new technology. He saw himself meeting with us in the darkness. He's the sixth member of this group."

Maya leaned forward. "This works just like in the process of healing. We have to image him remembering what he is really here to do." She glanced at me. "That helps break the fear block, the trance, at every level."

As we began to concentrate on including Feyman and his men, our energy leaped forward. The night became illuminated and we could clearly see Feyman and two men on the hill. The soul groups seemed to move more closely into focus, appearing more humanlike, while at the same time we became more luminescent, like them. From the left, more soul groups seemed to be joining.

"It's Feyman's soul group!" Charlene said. "And the soul groups of the two men with him!"

As the energy increased, the massive hologram of the World Vision again encircled us.

"Focus on Feyman and the others the way we focused on each other," Maya shouted. "Visualize that they remember."

I turned slightly and faced the three men. Feyman was still working furiously at his computer, the other two men looking on. The hologram encircled them as well, especially the image of each person awakening at this historical moment to his or her true purpose. As we watched, the forest was cast in a perceptible field of swirling, amber energy, which seemed to pass through Feyman and his associates. Simultaneously I saw the same wisps of white light that had protected Curtis and Maya and me hovering over the men, and afterward the white streaks of light grew in size and began to emanate outward in all directions, disappearing finally into the distance. After a few minutes the ground tremors and strange sounds stopped. A breeze blew the last of the dust toward the south.

One of the men stopped watching Feyman and eased away from us into the trees. For several seconds Feyman continued to work on his keyboard, then gave up in frustration. He looked down at us and picked up the computer, cradling it gently with his left arm. With the other hand, he pulled out a handgun and began to walk our way. The other man, armed with an automatic weapon, followed.

"Don't let go of the image," Maya cautioned.

When they were twenty feet away, Feyman set the computer down and punched at the keyboard again, keeping the pistol ready. Several large rocks, loosened earlier, broke free and crashed into the pool.

"You didn't come here to do this," Charlene said softly. The rest of us focused on his face.

The operative, keeping his weapon aimed at us, walked closer to Feyman and said, "We can't do anything else here. Let's go."

Feyman waved him off, then began to type angrily again.

"Nothing is working," Feyman yelled at us. "What are you doing?" He looked at the operative. "Shoot them!" he screamed. "Shoot them!"

For an instant the man looked at us coldly. Then, shaking his head, he backed away and disappeared into the rocks.

"You were born to prevent this destruction from happening," I said.

He dropped the gun to his side and stared at me. For an instant his face lightened, appearing exactly as I had seen it during his Birth Vision. I could tell he was remembering something. Seconds later a look of fright swept across his face, turning quickly into anger. He grimaced and held his stomach, then turned and retched onto the rocks beside him.

Wiping his mouth, he raised the gun again. "I don't know what you're trying to do to me, but it won't work." He took several steps forward, then seemed to lose energy. The gun fell to the ground. "It doesn't matter, you know? There are other forests. You people can't be at all of them. I'm going to make this generator work. Do you understand? You're not taking this away from me!"

He stumbled backward a few feet, then turned and ran into the darkness.


When we reached the hill above the bunker, a great wave of relief swept through the group. After Feyman had left, we had cautiously made our way back to the site of the experiment, not knowing what we would find. Now, as we looked, the bunker area was aglow with dozens of truck lights. Most of the vehicles bore the insignia of the Forest Service, although the FBI was represented, along with the local Sheriff's Department.

I crawled forward several more feet on the crest of the hill and looked closely to see if anyone was being interrogated or held in any of the cars. They all looked empty. The door of the bunker was open and officers seemed to be going in and out as if investigating a crime scene.

"They've all left," Curtis said, leaning forward on his knees and gazing past the trunk of a large tree. "We stopped them."

Maya turned and sat down. "Well, at least we stopped them here. They won't try the experiment again in this valley."

"But Feyman was right," David said, looking at the rest of us. "They can go to some other place, and no one will know." He stood up. "I've got to go in there. I'll tell them the whole story."

"Are you crazy?" Curtis said, walking up to him. "What if the government is part of this?"

"The government is just people," David replied. "Not all of them are involved."

Curtis stepped up closer. "There has to be another way. I'm not letting you go in there."

"There will be someone in one of those agencies who will listen to us," David said. "I'm sure of it."

Curtis was silent.

Charlene was leaning on a rock several feet away, and said, "He's right. Someone could be in just the right position to help."

Curtis shook his head, grappling with his thoughts. "That might be true, but you'll need someone with you who can accurately describe the technology . . ."

"That means you'll have to go too," David said.

Curtis managed to return a smile. "Okay, I'll go with you but only because we have an ace in the hole."

"What?" David asked.

"A guy that we left tied up back in a cave."

David put a hand on his shoulder. "Come on, you can tell me about it on the way. Let's see what happens."

After anxious good-byes to the rest of us, they moved away to the right to approach the bunker site from another direction.

Suddenly Maya whispered loudly for them to wait.

"I'm going too," she said. "I'm a physician; people know me in the area. You might need a third witness."

The three of them looked at Charlene and me, obviously wondering if we might join them as well.

"Not me," Charlene said. "I think I'm needed elsewhere."

I also declined and asked them not to mention us. They agreed and then walked away toward the lights.

Left alone, Charlene and I met eyes. I recalled the deep feeling I had experienced toward her in the other dimension. She was taking a step toward me, about to speak, when both of us detected a flashlight fifty yards to our right.

Carefully we moved deeper into the trees. The light changed position and headed right toward us. We kept still and low to the ground. As the light approached, I began to hear a lone voice, someone apparently talking to himself. I knew this person; it was Joel.

I caught Charlene's eye. "I know who it is," I whispered. "I think we should talk to him."

She nodded.

When he was twenty feet away, I called out his name.

He stopped and shined his light toward us. Recognizing me immediately, he walked over and crouched down where we were.

"What are you doing out here?" I asked.

"There's not much left back there," he replied, pointing toward the bunker. "There's an underground laboratory over there that has been completely cleaned out. I thought I would try to go to the falls; but when I got out there in the dark I changed my mind."

"I thought you were leaving the area," I said. "You were so skeptical."

"I know. I was going to leave, but I . . . well, I had a dream that disturbed me. I thought I'd better stay and try to help. The Forest Service people thought I was crazy, but then I ran into a deputy from the county Sheriff's Department. Someone had sent him a message, so we came out here together. That's when we found this laboratory."

Charlene and I looked at each other, then I briefly told Joel about the confrontation with Feyman and the eventual outcome.

"They were creating that much damage?" Joel asked. "Was anyone hurt?"

"I don't think so," I replied. "We were lucky."

"And how long ago did your friends go down there?"

"Just a few minutes ago."

He looked at both of us. "You're not going in yourselves?"

I shook my head. "I thought it would be better if we watched how the authorities handle all this, without their knowing."

Charlene's expression confirmed that she felt the same way.

"Good thinking," Joel said, looking back toward the bunker site. "I think I had better get back down there, though, just so they'll know the press is aware of those three witnesses. How can I get in touch with you?"

"We'll call *you*," Charlene said.

He handed me a card, nodded to Charlene, and headed toward the bunker.

Charlene caught my eye. "He was the seventh person in the group, wasn't he?"

"Yeah, I think so."

We were silent with our thoughts for a moment, then Charlene said, "Come on, let's try to get back to town."

We had walked for almost an hour when suddenly we heard the sound of songbirds, dozens of them, somewhere to our right. Dawn was just breaking and a cool mist rose from the forest floor.

"Now what?" Charlene asked.

"Look over there," I said. Through a break in the trees to the north was a huge, old poplar, perhaps eight feet in diameter. In the half-light of daybreak, the area around the tree appeared brighter somehow, as if the sun, still below the horizon, had been in position to burst through to radiate downward on that one spot.

I experienced the sense of warmth that had grown so familiar.

"What is it?" Charlene asked.

"It's Wil!" I said. "Let's go over there."

When we were within ten feet, Wil peeked around the tree, smiling broadly. He had changed; what was it? As I continued to study his body, I realized that his luminosity was the same, but he was now more clearly in focus.

He hugged us both.

"Were you able to see what happened?" I asked.

"Yes," he said. "I was there with the soul groups; I saw everything."

"You're in sharper focus. What did you do?"

"It wasn't what I did," he replied. "It was what you and the group did, especially Charlene."

"What do you mean?" Charlene asked.

"When the five of you increased your energy, and consciously remembered most of the World Vision, you lifted this whole valley into a higher vibratory pattern. It rose closer to the vibratory level of the Afterlife, which means that I now appear clearer to you, as you appear clearer to me. Even the soul groups will become more readily visible in this valley now."

I looked hard at Wil. "Everything we've seen in this valley, everything that has happened. It's all the Tenth Insight, isn't it?"

He nodded. "These same experiences are occurring to people all over the planet. After we grasp the first nine Insights, each of us is left at the same place—trying to live this reality day-to-day, in the face of what seems to be a growing pessimism and divisiveness all around us. But at the same time, we are continuing to gain a greater perspective and clarity about our spiritual situation, about who we really are. We know we are awakening to a much larger plan for planet Earth.

"The Tenth is about maintaining our optimism and staying awake. We're learning to better identify and believe in our own intuitions, knowing that these mental images are fleeting recollections of our original intention, of how we wanted our lives to evolve. We wanted to follow a certain path in life, so that we could finally remember the truth that our life experiences are preparing us to tell, and bring this knowledge into the world.

"We are now seeing our lives from the higher perspective of the Afterlife. We know that our individual adventures are occurring within the context of the long history of human awakening. With this memory, our lives are grounded, put into context; we can see the long process through which we have been spiritualizing the physical dimension, and what we have left to do."

Wil paused momentarily and moved closer to us. "Now we will see if enough groups like this one come together and remember, if enough people around the world grasp the Tenth. As we have seen, it is now our responsibility to keep the intention, to ensure the future.

"The polarization of Fear is still rising, and if we are to resolve it and move on, each of us must participate personally. We must watch our thoughts and expectations very carefully, and catch ourselves every time we treat another human being as an enemy. We can defend ourselves, and restrain certain people, but if we dehumanize them, we add to the Fear.

"We all are souls in growth, we all have an original intention that is positive; and we can all remember. Our responsibility is to hold that idea for everyone we meet. That's the true Interpersonal Ethic; that's how we uplift, that's the contagion of the new awareness that is encircling the planet. We either fear that human culture is falling apart, or we can *hold the Vision* that we are *awakening*. Either way, our expectation is a prayer that goes out as a force that tends to bring about the end we envision. Each of us must consciously choose between these two futures."

Wil seemed to drift into thought, and in the background, against the far ridge toward the south, I caught sight again of the streaks of white light.

"With all that was happening," I said, "I never asked you about these movements of white light. Do you know what they are?"

Wil smiled, and reached out and gently touched both of our shoulders. "They're the angels," he said. "They respond to our faith and vision and make miracles. They seem to be a mystery even to those in the Afterlife."

At that moment I was seized by a mental image of a community, somewhere in a valley much like this one. Charlene was there, and others, including many children.

"I think we are supposed to understand the angels next," Wil continued, gazing out toward the north as if seeing an image of his own. "Yes, I'm sure of it. Are you two coming?"

I gazed at Charlene, whose look confirmed that she had seen the same vision as I.

"I don't think so," she said.

"Not right now," I added.

Without speaking Wil pulled us into a brief embrace, then turned and walked away. At first, I was reluctant to let him go, but I remained silent. A part of me realized this journey was far from over. Soon, I knew, we would see him again.

# Advanced
# DRAWING SKILLS
## A COURSE IN ARTISTIC EXCELLENCE

Barrington Barber

**BARNES**
**& NOBLE**
**BOOKS**

NEW YORK

This edition published by Barnes & Noble, Inc.
by arrangement with
Arcturus Publishing Limited

2005 Barnes & Noble Books

M 10 9 8 7 6 5 4 3 2 1

ISBN 0-7607-7086-7

Jacket design by Alex Ingr

Printed in China

# Contents

# *Introduction*

To get the most out of this book, you will need to be familiar with the basic drawing practices I introduced in *The Fundamentals of Drawing*. If you have used that book, or feel you know enough without referring to it, welcome to the next interesting stage of drawing. Although we use the term 'advanced' in the title, the book is aimed not at professionals but at still-aspiring artists who have done a lot of work and want to develop their skills further.

If you are still using the exercises in the last book as practice tools, that's very commendable. In this book, I aim to encourage you to look more deeply into the art of drawing and to bring a more investigative approach to what you do. Such an approach teaches us not to be put off by difficulties, because they can be overcome with a little persistence and a lot of practice. If you are now drawing quite well and have proved your ability to yourself, it is quite easy to improve, even if the further steps you must take appear to be difficult at first.

So, the first lesson of this book echoes recurring themes of the last: practise regularly, and don't mind making mistakes in the process. Mistakes are not bad so long as you correct them as soon as you see them. You will find that assessing your ability will help to make you more objective about your work. However, this new knowledge won't happen overnight, so be patient. And remember: the time you spend altering your drawings to improve them is never lost – that is how you will improve your skills.

Making contact with other people who are also trying to become better artists will help your progress, too. Drawing is not a private exercise but a public one, so do show your work to other people. It may not be to everybody's liking and you may have to swallow criticisms that dent your pride. If this happens, look at your own work again with a more objective eye and see if those criticisms are justified. Of course, not all criticism is correct. But usually we know when it is, and when it is we should act on it. Your best critics will be other students of art because they speak from their own experience. If you know any professional artists, talk to them about their work. You will find their advice useful. Go to art shows and galleries as often as you can and see what the competition is up to. The experience will help to push your work further in the right direction. Notice your own weaknesses, try to correct them, but don't ignore your strengths. And while you build on success, try to eliminate the gaps in your knowledge and expertise. Above all, don't give up. Steady hard work often accomplishes more than talent.

WHAT YOU WILL DISCOVER

In the following sections we will be looking at all sorts of drawing; some you will be familiar with, and some will be new to you. Many of my examples are close copies of the work of first-rate artists, who provide a wealth of ideas and methods that can be learnt from. Some of the drawings are my own and hopefully they will also teach you something. In considering the drawings of master artists and how they were done, I have tried to relate them to our experience of drawing and suggest ways of improving your abilities.

Topics such as anatomy and perspective are looked at in some detail, as is the difficulty of drawing movement. Detailed on the facing page are the major themes running through the book and how they can help you develop your drawing skills. Included in this Introduction also, just as a taster, are examples of drawings that exemplify the major topics we shall explore.

*Line and style: The loose and yet taut line evident in the copy of Matisse's odalisque (below) can take years to perfect, but there is no reason why you should not try to produce something similar now – it will enormously improve your drawing skills.*

*A vivid sense of style can make even a line drawing stand out. The simple, refined but original design of this cut out bronze figure from the Hellenic period (right) is first class. Once we have seen drawing of this calibre we can begin to emulate it.*

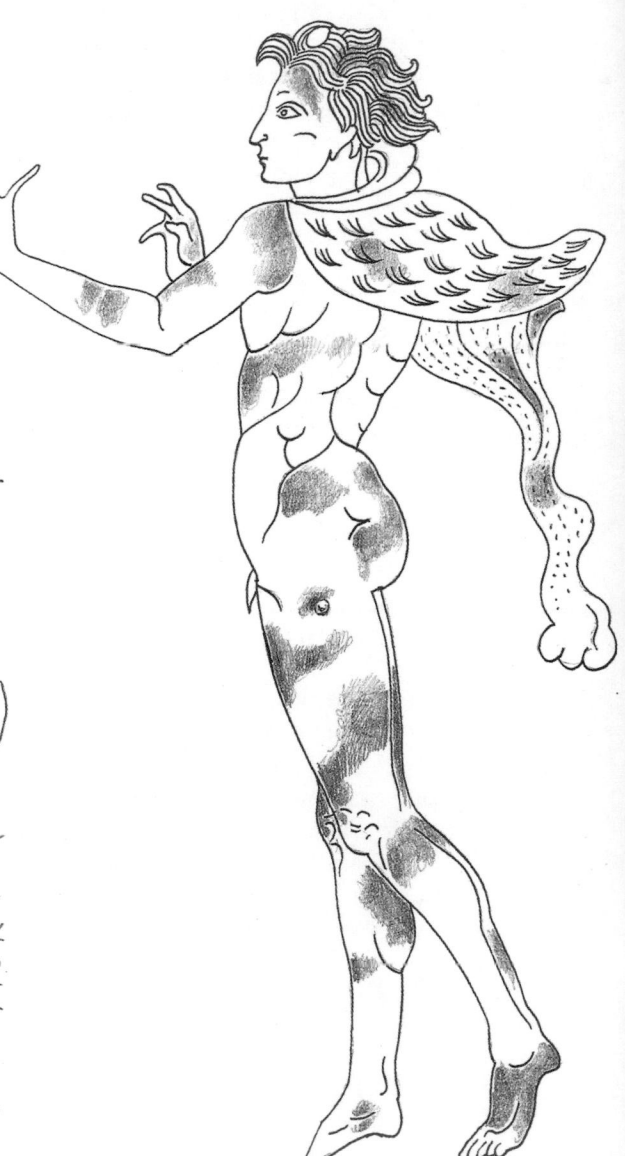

 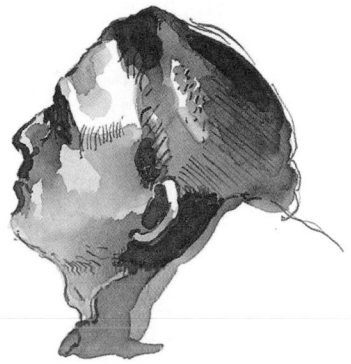

*Different approaches: Careful refined pencil drawing (left), a copy of a Michelangelo; and an immediate and unpremeditated drawing in pen, line and wash, original by Guercino.*

**Major Themes:**

- Form and how to produce an effect of dimension, with shapes conditioned by light and shade and other dimensional devices – see pages 79–109.

- Devices and approaches that may help us to improve the accuracy of our drawing (see pages 48–77). We'll also consider how to analyse the mass of information thrown at our retina.

- Ways of portraying an emotional state or mood in a picture – see pages 111–125. This is done by the design, the choice of subject matter, or by the techniques and drawing medium. All work and all are valid.

- Studying from nature – see pages 127–163. In this and other sections you will find exercises in drawing and analysis, to understand how to see a subject more clearly and how to represent what you see.

- Caricature – see pages 165–75. Although this is not a major part of art it does encapsulate the sharp vision that an artist needs in order to see past the obvious. There is a lot beyond our daily perception.

- The work of artists who found ways of seeing the world anew – see pages 15–45. In their hands what might seem an ordinary situation suddenly becomes full of promise and life.

- The importance of drawing what you *can* see. Not to draw what can't be seen might seem obvious, but it is a very precise discipline for the artist with lots of ideas in his head who sometimes attempts to invent without substance. It's easier – and the end result more convincing – to train yourself to see more, perceive more clearly and draw exactly what is seen. Anyway, try it out. You might be surprised.

HOW YOU WILL LEARN

It is hoped you will have a great time with the suggestions in this book. Having taught art now for a long time – and practised it even longer – I can say with confidence that if you want to learn to draw well there is nothing to stop you.

Some of the styles and techniques will suit you instantly whereas with others you may find yourself having to work hard. Don't worry if you don't instantly get on with some of them. See them as a challenge to your obvious intelligence; if you want to draw, you must be very intelligent, no matter what your academic record. You will discover that just trying a new technique will bring improvement in the other methods you use. Seemingly difficult exercises firm up our talent. When you succeed at them, give yourself a pat on the back, because it means you are really getting interested. That, ultimately, is what counts, and what improves levels of skill.

Above all, remember that your own will and desire to draw and the normal use of your senses are all that are required to start the deeper investigation into the visual world that this book hopes to encourage. Art is a marvellous part of life, and drawing is the real basis for painting and sculpture. The more deeply you engage in the arts, the more you are adding to the cultural value of our society.

*Different effects with chalk: Both of these drawings are in the classical manner, but notice how different they look. In the copy of the Vouet (left) the carefully modulated toning makes us very aware of the aesthetic value.*

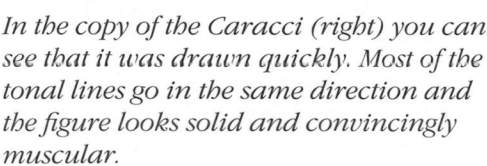

*In the copy of the Caracci (right) you can see that it was drawn quickly. Most of the tonal lines go in the same direction and the figure looks solid and convincingly muscular.*

*Different effects with brush and ink: These two landscapes give very different effects although a very similar technique was used for both.*

DRAWING YOUR WORLD

Before we begin, I would like you to bear in mind a few points that I hope will stay with you beyond the period it takes you to absorb the contents of this book. It concerns methods of practice and good habits.

One invaluable practice is to draw regularly from life. That is, drawing the objects, people, landscapes and details around you. These have an energy and atmosphere that only personal engagement with them can capture. Photographs or other representations are inadequate substitutes and should only be used as a last resort as reference (see top caption on opposite page).

Always have a sketch-book or two and use them as often as possible. Constant sketching will sharpen your drawing skills and keep them honed. Collect plenty of materials and tools – pencils, pens, rubbers, sharpeners, ink, paper of all sorts – and invest in a portfolio to keep all your drawings in.

*Keep a sketch-pad with you always – you never know when you'll stumble across a scene that you want to put down on paper.*

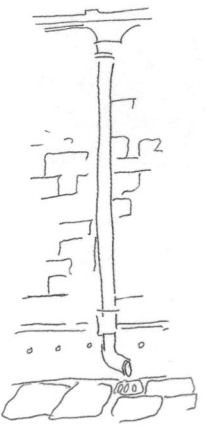

*These quick sketches of different parts of buildings are the result of drawing often and at any time. There is always the possibility of making a sketch of something seen out of a window. It's very good practice, too.*

Don't throw away your drawings for at least a year after you've finished them. At that distance you can be more objective about their merits or failings, and have a clear idea of which ones work and which ones don't. In the white-hot creative moment you don't actually know whether what you've done is any good or not. You are too attached to your end result. Later on you'll be more detached and be clearer in your judgement.

Build a portfolio of work and sometimes mount your drawings. Then, if anyone wants to see your work, you will have something to show them. Don't be afraid of letting people see what you have done. In my experience, people always find drawings interesting. Have fun with what you are doing, and enjoy your investigations of the visual world.

*When drawing from life is not possible, use your own photographs of objects or scenes of interest. This is better than relying on other people's shots, because invariably your visual record will remind you of what it was about that image you wanted to capture.*

*One of the most important lessons I hope you will take from this book is the value of simplicity. Successful drawing does not demand a sophisticated or complex approach. Look at this sketch. Its quality derives from a simple approach to shapes and the assimilation of their graphic effects into one picture. I had to make an effort to keep those shapes basic and simple. Always try to do the same in your drawings.*

# *Drawing from the Masters*

The point of this section is not to encourage you to blindly copy the methods of Raphael or Leonardo or any of the other great masters whose works we'll be looking at. The most important aspect of drawing of this quality is the acute observation that it requires. Great artists observe the world around them with great accuracy. I have deliberately not provided captions for the images reproduced here, because I want you to regard this section as an exercise in looking.

From these examples I want you to begin to understand how to put technique at the service of your observations by varying the length and pressure of your strokes. Eventually, after a lot of practice, you will find that you can judge exactly how heavy, light, long or short your strokes should be to achieve a specific effect. Hopefully, you'll also find that you can get quite fast at it.

One of the great bonuses of studying drawing and painting is that our vision refines and we begin to drop the prejudices and preconceptions that normally accompany our view of the world – attributes that are abundantly in evidence in the work of the artists whose methods we look at in this section.

ANCIENT GREEK ART

These Greek vase drawings, some of the earliest known (dating from c. 510 BC), are so sophisticated and elegant they might have been drawn by a modern-day Picasso or Matisse, except that Matisse would not have been as exact and Picasso would probably not have been as anatomically correct. The simple incised line appears to have been done easily and quickly and yet must have been the result of years of practice. Yet more remarkable is that these drawings were not done on flat paper but on the curving surface of a vase or crater. The economy of line is a lesson to all aspiring artists.

LEONARDO DA VINCI (1459–1519)

When we look at a Leonardo drawing we see the immense talent of an artist who could not only see more clearly than most of us, but also had the technical ability to express it on paper. We see the ease of the strokes of silverpoint or chalk outlining the various parts of the design, some sharply defined and others soft and in multiple marks that give the impression of the surface moving around the shape and disappearing from view.

Leonardo regulates light and shade by means of his famous *sfumato* method (Italian for 'evaporated'), a technique by which an effect of depth and volume is achieved by the use of dark, misty tones. The careful grading of the dark, smudgy marks helps us to see how the graduations of tone give the appearance of three dimensions.

The effect of dimension is also shown with very closely drawn lines that appear as a surface, and are so smoothly, evenly drawn that our eyes are convinced. There is elegance in the way he puts in enough tone but never too much. To arrive at this level of expertise requires endless practice. However it is worth persevering with practising techniques because they enable you to produce what you want with greater ease. Techniques need to be mastered and then forgotten. All this will take time.

RAPHAEL (RAFFAELO SANZIO) (1483–1520)

The perfection of Raphael's drawings must have seemed quite extraordinary to his contemporaries, even though they had already seen the works of Filippo Lippi, Botticelli, Michelangelo and Leonardo. His exquisitely flowing lines show his mastery as a draughtsman; notice the apparent ease with which he outlines the forms of his Madonna and Child, and how few lines he needs to show form, movement and even the emotional quality of the figures he draws. His loosely drawn lines describe a lot more than we notice at first glance. It is well worth trying to copy his simplicity, even though your attempts may fall far short of the original. The originals are unrepeatable, and it is only by studying them at first hand you will begin to understand exactly how his handling of line and tone is achieved.

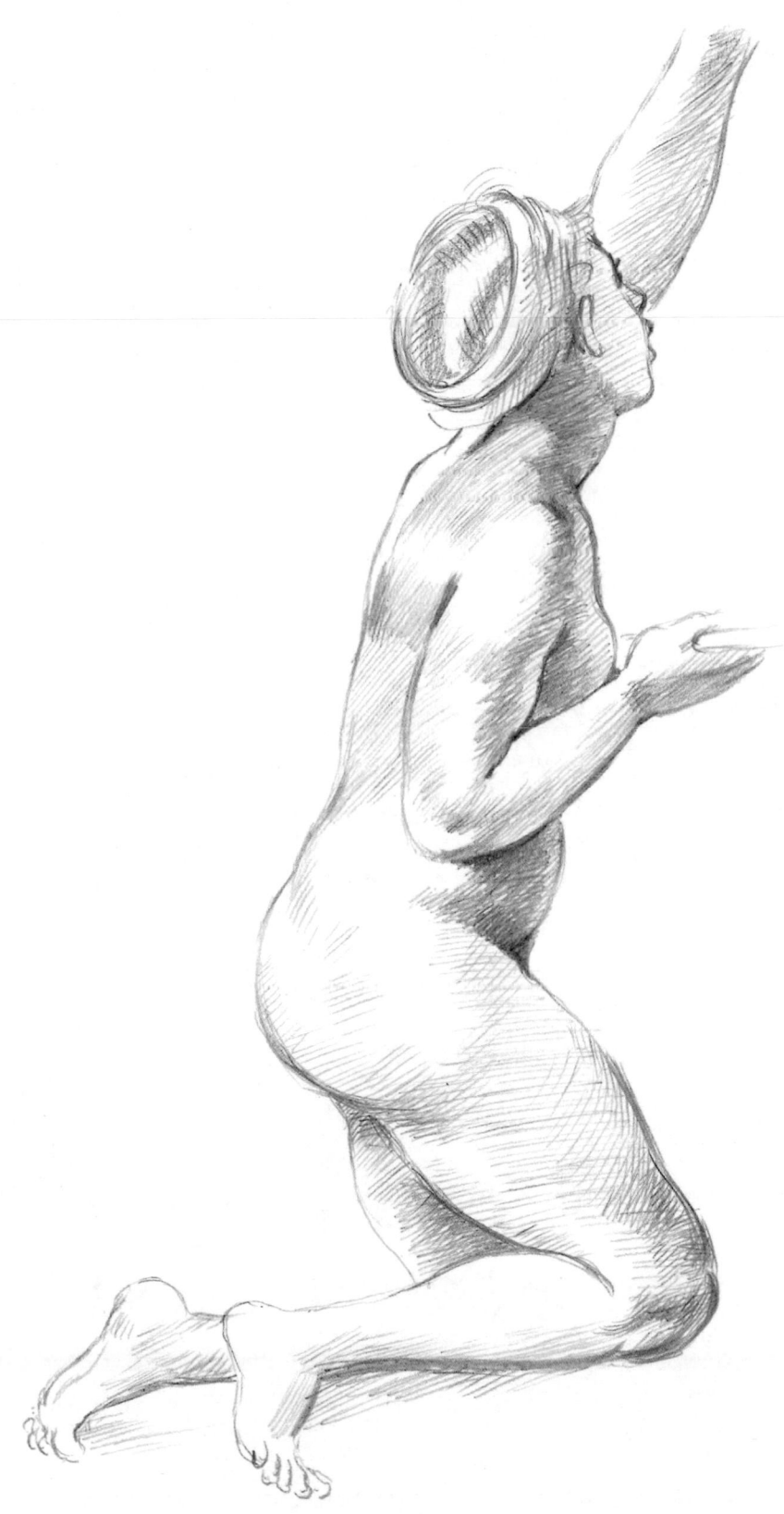

## MICHELANGELO BUONARROTI (1475–1564)

Michelangelo is arguably the most influential figure in the history of art. Study his drawings and then look at the work of his contemporaries and the artists who followed him and you will see how great was his influence. The copies shown here incorporate the original techniques he introduced. In the pen and ink drawing the style is very free and the shapes very basic, suggesting figures in motion; the ink drawing with traces of chalk is still pretty sketchy but more considered, allowing the viewer to discern character and type of costume. The final example is a very exact drawing, the careful *sfumato* in black chalk giving a clear definition of the arrangement of the flexing muscles under the skin. Michelangelo's deep knowledge of anatomy enabled him to produce an almost tactile effect in his life drawing. He shows clearly that there are no real hollows in the human form, merely dips between the mounds of muscles. This is worth noting by any student drawing from life and will give more conviction to your drawing.

PETER PAUL RUBENS (1577–1640)
Now let us look at the beautiful delicately drawn chalk drawings of Rubens who, like Titian, was referred to as a prince of painters. Before he produced his rich, flowing paintings, full of bravura and baroque asymmetry, he would make many informative sketches to clarify his composition. These sketches are soft and realistic, with the faintest of marks in some areas and precise modelling in others.

The rather gentle touch of the chalk belies the powerful composition of the figures. When completed the paintings were full and rich in form. His understanding of when to add emphasis and when to allow the slightest marks to do the work is masterly.

Rubens was one of the first landscape painters, although he did this type of work only for his own satisfaction. His drawings of landscapes and plants are as carefully worked out and detailed as those of any Victorian topographical artist.

## HANS HOLBEIN THE YOUNGER (1497/8–1543)

Holbein left behind some extraordinarily subtle portrait drawings of various courtiers whom he painted during his time as court painter to Henry VIII. These works are now in the Queen's Collection (most of them at Windsor, but some are in the Queen's Gallery at Buckingham Palace), and are worth studying for their brilliant subtle modelling. These subjects have no wrinkles to hang their character on, and their portraits are like those of children, with very little to show other than the shape of the head, the eyes, nostrils, mouth and hair. Holbein has achieved this quality by drastically reducing the modelling of the form and putting in just enough information to make the eye accept his untouched areas as the surfaces of the face. We tend to see what we expect to see. A good artist uses this to his advantage. So, less is more.

REMBRANDT (HARMENSZ VAN RIJN) (1606–69)
The drawings of Rembrandt probably embody all the qualities that any modern artist would wish to possess. His quick sketches are dashing, evocative and capture a fleeting action or emotion with enormous skill. His more careful drawings are like architecture, with every part of the structure clear and working one hundred per cent. Notice how his line varies with intention, sometimes putting in the least possible and at other times leaving nothing to chance. What tremendous skill!

To emulate Rembrandt we have to carefully consider how he has constructed his drawings. In some of his drawings the loose trailing line, with apparently vague markings to build up the form, are in fact the result of very clear and accurate observation. The dashing marks in some of his other, quicker sketches show exactly what is most necessary to get across the form and movement of the subject. Lots of practice is needed to achieve this level of draughtsmanship.

## GIOVANNI BATTISTA TIEPOLO (1692–1770)

Tiepolo is noted for his painted walls and, particularly, ceilings. Although difficult to emulate, his methods of drawing are worth studying. Loose, scrawling lines are accompanied by splashes of wash to give them solidity. What appear to be little more than scribbles add up to wonderful examples of a master draughtsman's first thoughts on a painting. Compare his drawings closely with his elegant paintings and you will see premonitions of the latter in the former.

## JEAN-ANTOINE WATTEAU (1684–1721)

One of the most superb draughtsmen among the French artists of the 18th century, Watteau painted remarkable scenes of bourgeois and aristocratic life. His expertise is evident in the elegant and apparently easily drawn figures he drew from life. When we look at them, it seems that somehow we can already draw like this or perhaps that we never shall.

Like all great artists he learnt his craft well. We too can learn to imitate his brilliantly simple, flowing lines and the loose but accurate handling of tonal areas. Notice how he gives just enough information to infer a lot more than is actually drawn. His understanding of natural, relaxed movement is beautifully seen. You get the feeling that these are real people. He manages to catch them at just the right point, where the movement is balanced but dynamic. He must have had models posing for him, yet somehow he infers the next movement, as though the figures were sketched quickly, caught in transition. Many of his drawings were used to produce paintings from.

JEAN-AUGUSTE-DOMINIQUE INGRES (1780–1867)

Ingres was, like Raphael, noted for his draughtsmanship. His drawings are perfect even when unfinished, having a precision about them which is unusual. He is thought to have made extensive use of the *camera lucida* (see page 51), which is probably correct, but nevertheless the final result is exceptional by any standards.

The incisive elegance of his line and the beautifully modulated tonal shading produce drawings that are as convincing as photographs. Unlike Watteau's, his figures never appear to be moving, but are held still and poised in an endless moment.

The student who would like to emulate this type of drawing could very well draw from photographs to start with, and when this practice has begun to produce a consistently convincing effect, then try using a live model. The model would have to be prepared to sit for a lengthy period, however, because this type of drawing can't be hurried. The elegance of Ingres was achieved by slow, careful drawing of outlines and shapes and subtle shading.

EUGENE DELACROIX (1798–1863)

The great Romantic French painter Delacroix could draw brilliantly. He believed that his work should show the essential characteristics of the subject matter he was portraying. This meant that the elemental power and vigour of the scene, people or objects should be transmitted to the viewer in the most immediate way possible. His vigorous, lively drawings are more concerned with capturing life than including minuscule details for the sake of it. He would only include as much detail as was necessary to convince the viewer of the verisimilitude of his subject. As you can see from these examples, his loose powerful lines pulsate with life.

JOSEPH MALLORD WILLIAM TURNER (1775–1851)

Turner started his career as a topographical painter and draughtsman and made his living producing precise and recognizable drawings of places of interest. He learnt to draw everything in the landscape, including all the information that gives the onlooker back the memory of the place he has seen. This ability stayed with him, even after he began to paint looser and more imaginative and elemental landscapes. Although the detail is not so evident in these canvases, which the Impressionists considered the source of their investigations into the breaking up of the surface of the picture, the underlying knowledge of place and appearance remains and contributes to their great power.

The outline drawing of the abbey (shown left) is an early piece, and amply illustrates the topographic exactitude for which the artist was famous in his early years. The second example is much more a painter's sketch, offering large areas of tone and flowing lines to suggest the effect of a coastal landscape.

## EDGAR DEGAS (1834–1917)

Degas was taught by a pupil of Ingres, and studied drawing in Italy and France until he was the most expert draughtsman of all the Impressionists. His loose flowing lines, often repeated several times to get the exact feel, look simple but are inordinately difficult to master. The skill evident in his paintings and drawings came out of continuous practice. He declared that his epitaph should be: 'He greatly loved drawing'. He would often trace and retrace his own drawings in order to get the movement and grace he was after. Hard work and constant efforts to improve his methods honed his natural talent.

## PIERRE AUGUSTE RENOIR (1841–1919)

Renoir could be called the man who loved women. His pictures of young women, dressed or undressed, are some of the sweetest drawings of the female form ever produced. He always has the painter's eye and sacrifices any detail to the main effect of the picture. When he does produce a detail, it is extremely telling and sets the tone for the rest of the picture. His drawings and paintings of late 19th century Paris are imbued with an extremely happy atmosphere which has captured the imagination of artists ever since.

## GEORGES SEURAT (1859–91)

Seurat's style of drawing is very different from what we have seen so far; mainly because he was so interested in producing a mass or area of shape that he reduced many of his drawings to tone alone. In these pictures there are no real lines but large areas of graduated tone rendered in charcoal, conté or thick pencil on faintly grainy textured paper. Their beauty is that they convey both substance and atmosphere while leaving a lot to the viewer's imagination. The careful grading of tone is instructive, as is how one mass can be made to work against a lighter area.

PAUL CEZANNE (1839–1906)
Cézanne attempted to produce drawings and paintings that were true to the reality of form as he saw it. He is the structural master-draughtsman without parallel in this section. All artists since his time owe him a debt of gratitude. His great contribution to art was to produce a body of work that saw the world from more than one viewpoint. The Cubists were inspired by his example to try to draw the objective world from many angles – whether or not they succeeded is arguable.

HENRI MATISSE (1869–1954)
Even without the aid of bright, rich colours Matisse could invest his work with great sensuality. His drawings are marvellously understated yet graphic thanks to the fluidity of line. Awkwardness is evident in some of them, but even with these you never doubt that they express exactly what he wanted. There are no extraneous marks to diffuse the image and confuse the eye. As he got older and suffered from arthritis in his hands, Matisse resorted to drawing with charcoal on the end of a long stick. Despite this handicap, the large, simple images he produced by this method possess great power.

*Matisse*

PABLO PICASSO (1881–1973)

Picasso dominated the art world for the greater part of the 20th century. He took every type of artistic tradition and reinvented it, demonstrating that a master-artist can break all the rules and still produce work that strikes a chord with the casual observer. The image below, for example, is an interesting hybrid among the other examples shown here: two pieces of toned paper cut out for the neck and face with the features and hair drawn in with pencil.

Although he distorted conventional shapes almost out of recognition, the final result was imbued with the essence of the subject he was illustrating. He experimented in all mediums, but in his drawings we can see the amazing dexterity with which he confounded our preconceptions and gave us a new way of seeing art. His sketchbooks reveal his wide range of abilities and are an inspiration to all artists.

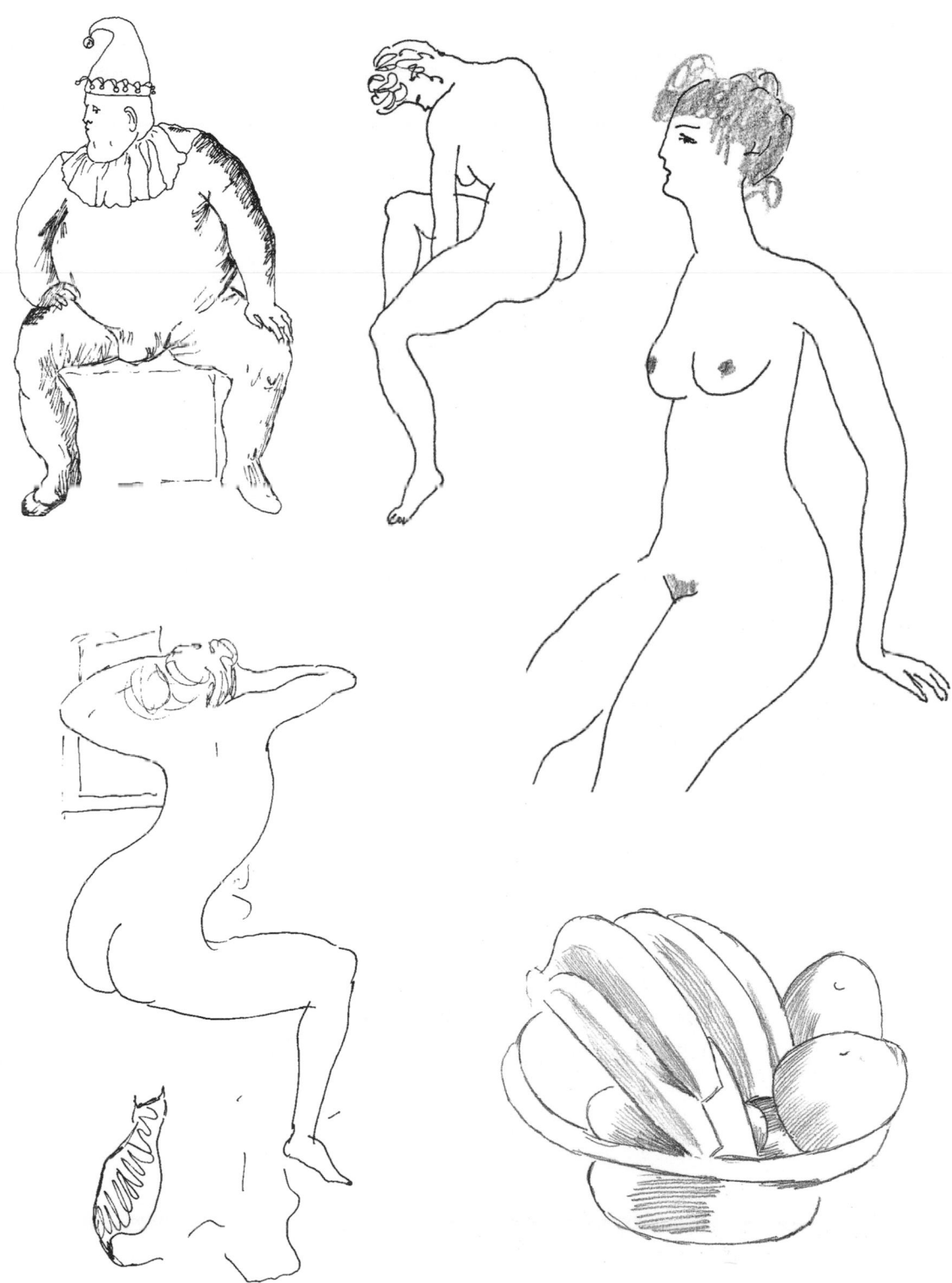

HENRY CARR (1894–1970)
The English illustrator and painter Henry Carr was an excellent draughtsman, as these portraits show. He produced some of the most attractive portraits of his time because of his ability to adapt his medium and style to the qualities of the person he was drawing. The subtlety of the marks he makes to arrive at his final drawing varies, but the result is always sensitive and expressive. A noted teacher, his book on portraiture is well worth studying.

# The Experience of Drawing

As you have learnt from the previous section, there is no substitute for observation in drawing. When you look long and hard at anything that you wish to draw, ask yourself the question, 'What am I seeing?' Don't just give yourself answers like 'a landscape', 'a teapot', 'a human being', etc, because such answers close down your observation. Look instead at colour, shape, form, texture, outline and movement. These apply to everything visual and help you to analyse your impressions, which can assist your seeing. However, keep looking, even when you think you know what you're looking at. Nothing stays the same for more than a few seconds; the light changes, for example, giving you a new version of what you're looking at, even if it's only a still form. The exciting thing about all this is that you never get bored. There is infinite variety, even in familiar scenes that we see every day.

When you start to draw from life it is always difficult to see how to make the three-dimensional image in front of you fit onto the paper without it looking awkward, stiff, inaccurate or flat. There is no avoiding this exercise, however, if you want to find out whether you have real drawing ability.

In this section we'll be looking at a range of subjects as they really are: agglomerations of shapes. As well as the shapes of the things themselves, you will notice the shapes between things. There are no spaces in drawing or painting, just other areas of tone. You will find with the subjects you choose that the shapes butt up tightly to one another. Look at the whole image with interest and without preconception. Try to notice everything and don't regard one part of the whole as superior to the rest. It is not.

ANALYZING SHAPES

Ordinarily when you look at a scene, object or person, your eyes will first register the shapes in an objective way and then your mind will supply information that enables you to recognize what you are seeing. The names, concepts or labels the mind supplies are not helpful to you as an artist, however, and you need to ignore them if you are to see objectively the shapes that are actually there.

One way of getting a more objective view is to analyse the shapes you are looking at in terms of their geometry. For example, a circular object seen at any angle forms an ellipse, and if you know how to draw an ellipse correctly you will get a good image of the object. Anything spherical is just a circle with toning to fool the eye into believing in the object's sphericality.

The spaces between objects are often triangles or rectangles. Objects within a group can be seen as being at different angles to each other: a leg may be propped up at an angle of 45 degrees from the upright torso, and the lower leg may be at right-angles to the thigh.

This sort of visual analysis is very useful for you, the observer, to undertake and will help the accuracy of your drawing. Once you recognize the angles you are drawing, you will find it difficult to draw them badly.

*Observing a subject in almost geometric terms helps to simplify our approach to drawing. Look at this very simple picture. Both figures can be contained in a triangle. To the right of the little girl the space can be cut off along her right side so that she and her father's legs fit into a parallelogram. The space under her left arm, extending to her father's foot, makes another triangle.*

**Measuring Proportions**

Another useful form of analysis is to employ some common unit of measurement to get the proportions of different objects in your drawing right. For example, the shape and size of a door or window can give you a basic unit of measurement with which to measure the other units in a composition. In figure drawing, the head is a useful unit for measuring the human body. If you use a form of analysis, just remember that the unit has to remain constant throughout the composition, otherwise the proportion will not be right.

Rule of thumb is one of the most common units of measurement (see opposite page). The logic of this method is that your arm will not grow any longer during the time it takes to complete your drawing, so no matter how many measurements you take, your measuring device will remain at the same distance from your eye. Remember, though, that if you move your position you will have to start again because every proportion may alter.

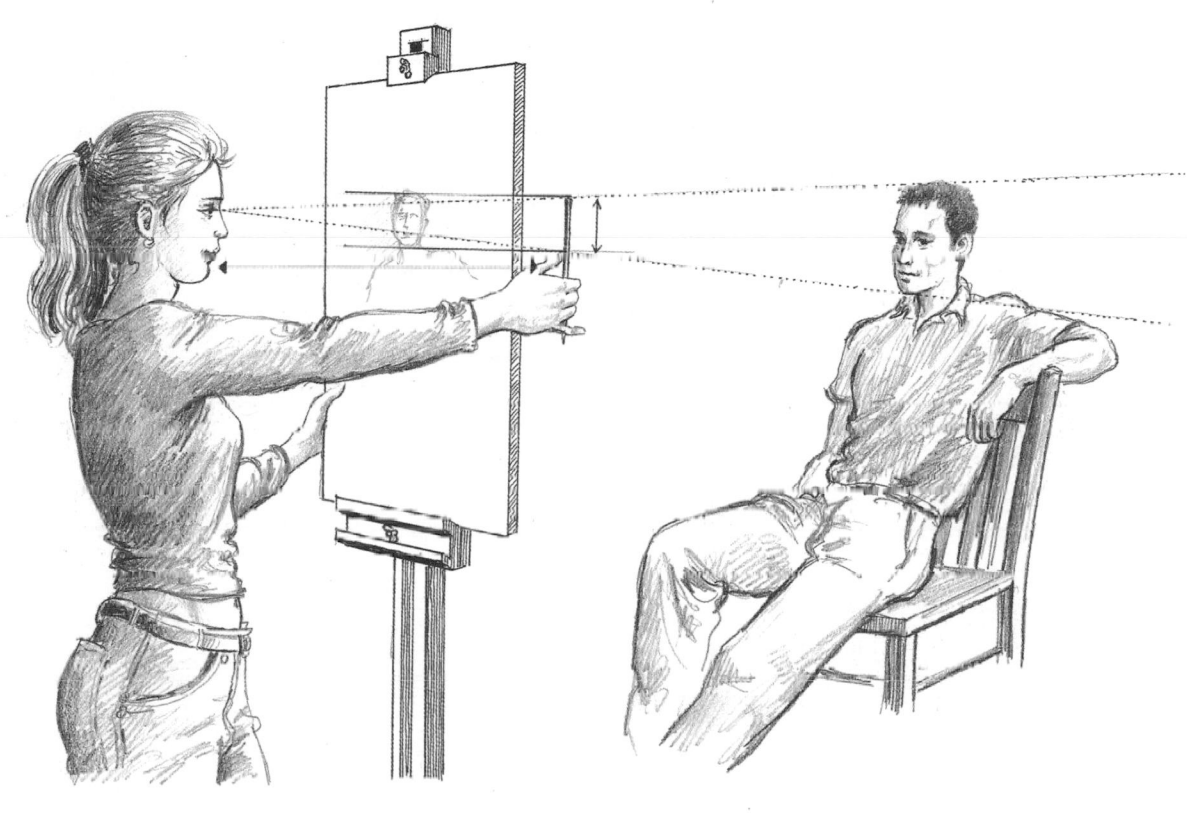

## Using rule of thumb

*Here the rule of thumb measurement is used to gauge the proportions of a figure. The arm is outstretched and the pencil held upright in line with the drawing board. The measurement taken (of the head, in this instance) is called 'sight-size'.*

*Once the measurement is taken it can be transferred to the paper. As long as you measure everything in your scene in this way, staying the same distance from the model and*

*keeping the pencil at arm's length when measuring, the method will give you a fairly accurate range of proportions.*

*This method is of limited value to beginners, however: the drawing will not be large and beginners really need to draw large in order to correct their mistakes more easily. Experienced artists will be able to translate the proportions into larger measurements when drawing larger than sight-size.*

## TECHNICAL AIDS

Photographs and slides can be used by artists to render a scene accurately. What they can not give is a personal and thus richer view of a subject. This can only be achieved if the artist takes the time to go to the actual scene and look for himself.

The old masters used tools such as the *camera obscura* and *camera lucida* – literally, 'dark room' and 'light room' – to ensure the accuracy of their perspective and proportion. Another device used by artists of old to help this sort of technical analysis was a draughtsman's net or grid. This was a screen with crossed strings or wires creating a net or grid of exactly measured squares through which the artist could look at a scene. As long as the artist ensured that his eye was always in the same position each time he looked through the screen, and as long as a similar grid was drawn on his sheet of paper, the main composition could be laid out and each part related correctly.

These methods are not ends in themselves, however, and although they provide the main outlines of a composition, they cannot give the subtle distinctions that make a work of art attractive. To capture these, the artist has to use his own eye and judgement.

*The draughtsman's net or grid is a construct for use in the Renaissance manner. Usually artists make them themselves or have them made by a framemaker. The squares can be either marked directly onto the glass or indicated by stretching thin cords or wires across a frame. The glass is then set in a stand through which the object is viewed.*

*Patience is required to transfer the image of a subject viewed in this way onto paper: it is very easy to keep moving your head and thus changing your view in relation to both the frame and the subject. The trick is to make sure that the mark on the object and the mark on the grid where two lines meet are correctly aligned each time you look.*

Canaletto and Vermeer are just two of the artists who used the *camera obscura* in their work. It has the same effect as the *camera lucida*, although achieving it by different means. Used by painters for landscapes, cityscapes and interior scenes, the device was a tent or small room with a pin-hole or lens in one side which cast an image of the object onto a glass screen or sheet of paper, which could then be traced. It was an excellent device for architectural forms as long as one ignored the outer limits of the image, which tended to be distorted.

*In a camera lucida or lucidograph a prism is used to transfer the image of a scene onto paper or board. This enables the artist to draw around the basic shape to get the proportions correct before he looks normally at the object.*

*The technique was well adapted for use in small areas of drawing and was probably favoured by illustrators and painters for portraits or still lifes. The lucidograph was used extensively by Ingres and possibly Chardin and Fantin Latour; David Hockney was encouraged to try it in his work after he detected the method in the drawings of Ingres.*

*A slide-projector can give a similar effect to a lucidograph, although of course it allows you to use a much larger format and any kind of scene that can be photographed. It has been used extensively by artists who want to reproduce master paintings or enlarge their own work. Its only drawback is the difficulty of keeping your shadow out of the way.*

PROPORTIONS IN DETAIL

It is easy enough after some practice to remember the basic proportions of the human face seen from the front and the human body seen standing erect in full view. You will find other subjects much more variable, however. For them you will need to use a system to help you ensure that the different parts of your composition are in proportion to each other. This is particularly true when there is a lot of perspective depth in a scene, requiring you to show the relationship between the objects closer to you and the objects further away. Even in landscapes, where a certain amount of cheating (politely called 'artistic licence') is allowable because of the tremendous variation in proportions depending on your viewpoint, it is necessary to have some method of organizing the proportions of trees to houses to people and to far-away objects on the horizon. Even more important than ordering these variables is an accurate assessment of the angle of objects to your eye-level.

When the eye-level is low, smaller, closer objects dominate the view much more than when the eye-level is high. Trees on the skyline can look bigger or nearer when they are silhouetted against the light, because they have more definition. If there is a large object in the centre of your composition, it will tend to grab the eye. There is even a proportional effect in colour and tone. A very bright or very dark object standing in sharp contrast to the background grabs the attention, and even if this object is quite small it will appear larger than it is. The effect is that quite small objects of strong tone or colour will give an appearance of being larger than they are.

*A well-defined dark silhouette on the skyline set against a light sky will dominate a scene and appear closer than it really is.*

*A bright, light object standing out against a dark-toned background will dominate a scene despite its small size.*

## FORESHORTENING

When drawing objects or people seen from one end and looking along the length of the object or figure, the parts of the object nearer to your eye will appear much larger when compared to those at the further end. Many beginners find this truth quite difficult to grasp. The belief that the head cannot possibly be as large as the legs tends to influence them into disregarding the evidence of their own eyes and amending their drawing to fit their misconception. However, it is easy enough to make a simple measurement to help convince the mind of what the eye actually sees. Try it for yourself after you have studied the next drawing.

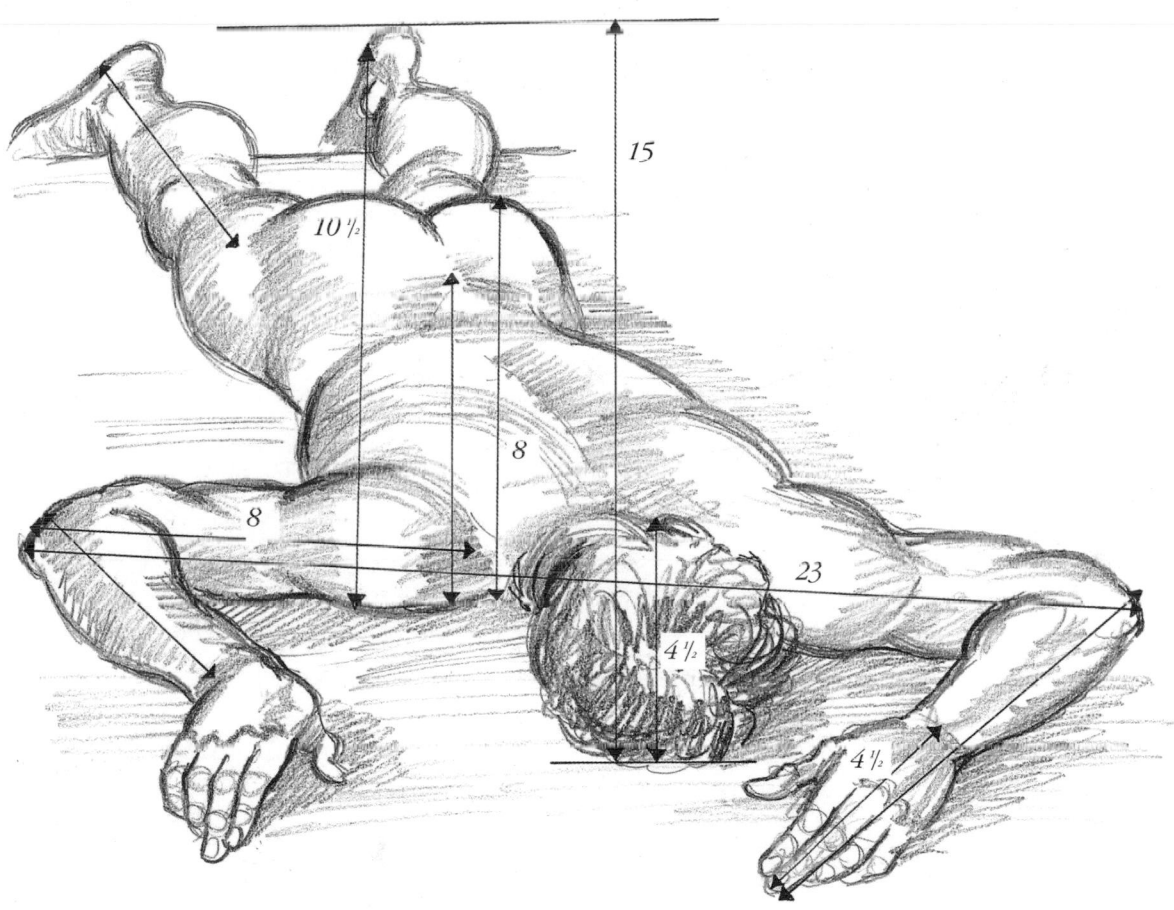

### The strange proportions of foreshortening

*Note the depth of the head (4½ units), which is the same as the open hand, and the foreshortened forearm and foreshortened leg. At 8 units the torso is only just less than twice the size of the head. The full length of the body from shoulder to ankle (10½ units) is just over twice the head. The upper arm is the same length as the torso (8 units). The distance from elbow to elbow (23) is longer than the distance from head to heel (15).*

THE EFFECT OF DIFFERENT EYE-LEVELS

These three drawings show how the effect of a picture is altered by the relationship of figures to the horizon or eye-line. In the first two pictures the viewer is standing and in the last picture the viewer is seated. This change in the relationship of the figures to the horizon-line has had quite an effect on the composition, and has indeed changed its dynamic.

You can see in galleries of paintings how artists have used this dynamic, particularly the Impressionists – look at examples of the work of Degas and Monet.

*In the first picture the eye-level is considerably higher than the people reclining on the beach. The viewer has a sense of looking down on the figures, which appear to be part of the overall scene and are not at all dominant.*

The eye-level of these two standing figures is the same as ours, making them appear more active. We are standing, as are they. (Note that the line of the horizon is at the same level as their eyes.)

Here the eye-level is much lower than that of the two figures; even the girl bending down is still head and shoulders above our eye-level. The figures now appear much more important and powerful in the composition.

ODD PROPORTIONS

The importance of relating proportions within the human figure correctly becomes very apparent when you have a figure in which some parts are foreshortened and others are not. In this example you'll notice that the right leg and arm are pointing towards the viewer, whereas the left leg and arm are not. As a result, the area taken up by the respective legs and arms is quite different in both proportion and shape. The right arm is practically all hand and shoulder and doesn't have the length evident with the left arm. The right leg is almost a square shape and strikingly different from the long rectangles of the left leg. The rectangles about the head and torso are also interestingly compared with the different arms and legs.

Once you begin to see such proportional differences within a subject, you will find your drawing of the whole becomes easier.

## VIVE LA DIFFERENCE

People are not alike in form, and few conform to the classical ideal. The examples shown here are of the same height and vertical proportion but vastly different in width. If presented to the inexperienced artist in a life class, both would be problematical, because beginners tend to draw what they think people should look like, and will even out oddities to fit their preconceptions. Often they will slim down a fat model or fatten up a thin one. If they themselves are slim, they will draw the model slimmer than they are. Conversely, if they are on the solid side, they will add flesh to the model. In effect they are drawing what they know, not what they see. This doesn't result in accurate draughtsmanship and has to be eliminated if progress is to be made. Remember: horizontal proportions are measured in exactly the same way as vertical proportions.

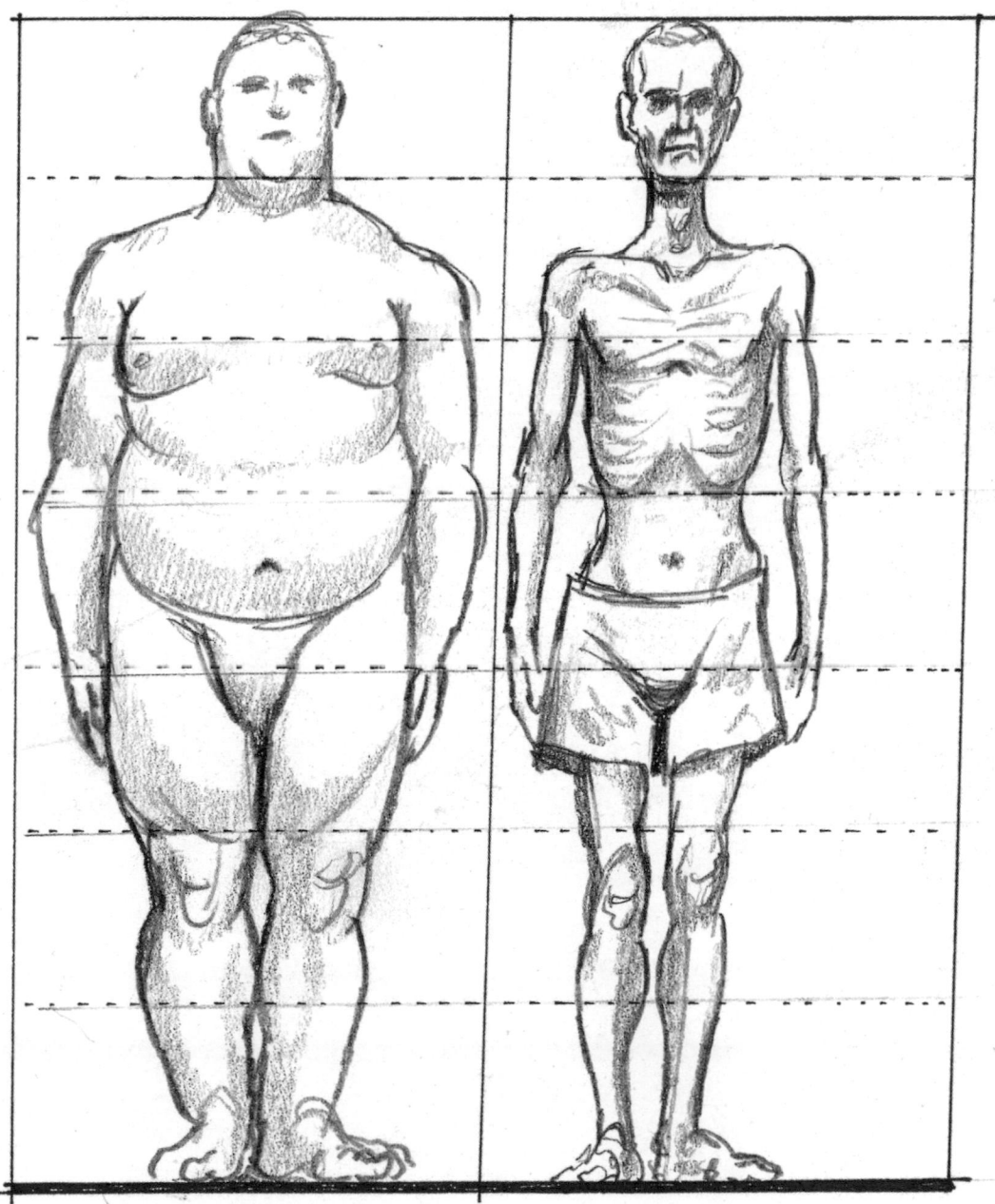

## AREAS OF DARK AND LIGHT

In all three drawings shown here notice how the light areas outline the dark shapes and dark areas outline the light shapes. You will find that some shapes run into each other to make a large shape and this is often easier to draw than a multitude of smaller shapes.

*Very large geometric shapes, such as walls, doors and windows, (left and opposite page) can provide a natural grid for a picture, making it easier to place other shapes, such as figures or, in an outdoor scene, trees.*

*In this drawing, based on a Vermeer, the simplified forms of the figures show clearly against the large expanse of the wall and floor. The framed picture helps to place the figures, as does the table and chair. The window, the source of light, is very dominant against the dark wall.*

ANGLES

Look at the angles in the figure shown below. As long as you can visualize a right-angle (90 degrees) and half a right-angle (45 degrees), and possibly a third (30 degrees) or two-thirds (60 degrees) of a right-angle, you should have no difficulty making sense of them. Let's break them down:

The wall in relation to the horizontal base on which the figure is resting is a right-angle (90 degrees) (A). But what about the rest of the angles shown?

(B) – the angle of the torso to the horizontal base.
(C) – the angle between the thigh and the horizontal base.
(D) – the angle between the thigh and the lower leg.
(E) – the angle between the lower leg and the horizontal base.
(F) – the angle of the head to the torso.
(G) – the angle of the head to the wall.

All these questions need to be answered. Just ask yourself – is it a full right-angle, or just less, or just more? Is it nearer a third or nearer a half right-angle? Accurate answers to these questions will help you to envisage the structure of the drawing on the page correctly.

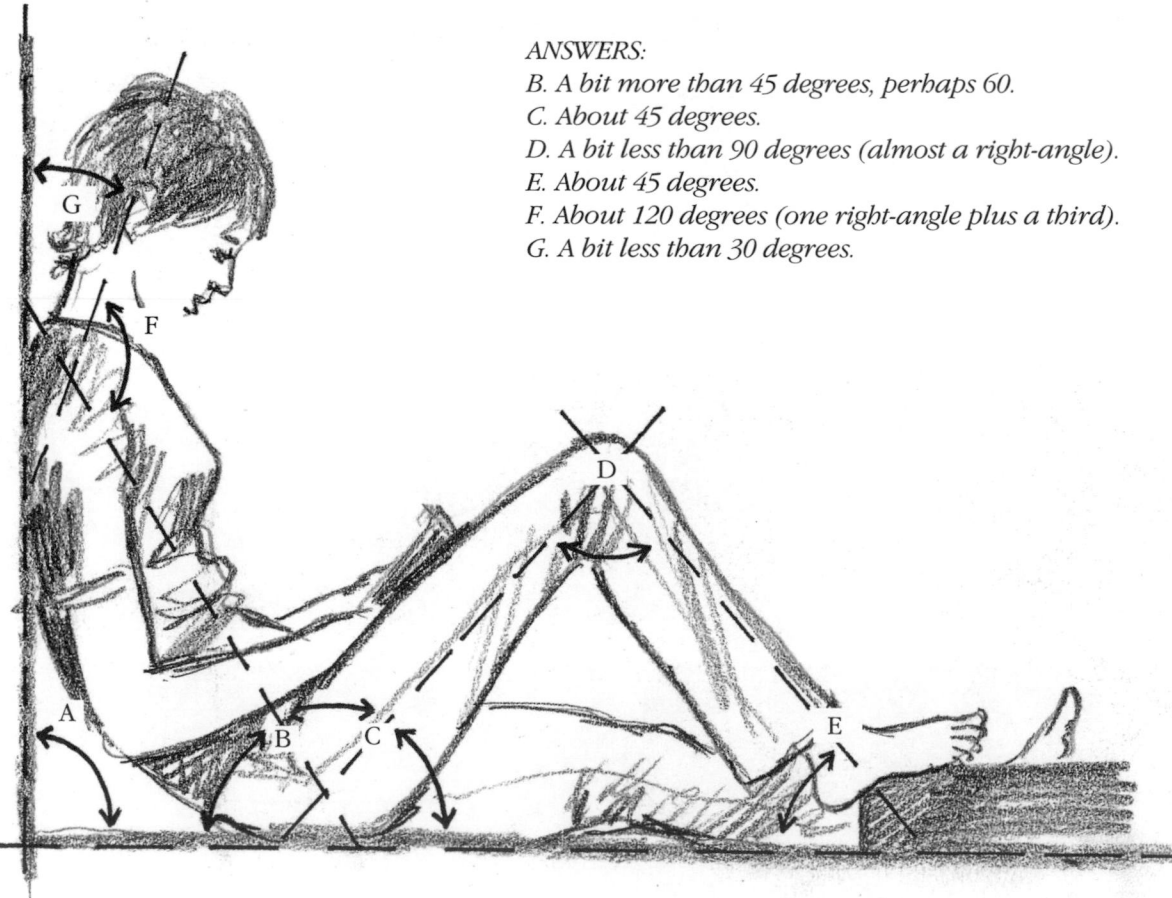

*ANSWERS:*
*B. A bit more than 45 degrees, perhaps 60.*
*C. About 45 degrees.*
*D. A bit less than 90 degrees (almost a right-angle).*
*E. About 45 degrees.*
*F. About 120 degrees (one right-angle plus a third).*
*G. A bit less than 30 degrees.*

## RELATING TRIANGLES AND RECTANGLES

The lines in the next drawing may look complex but they are in fact a way of simplifying a grouping by pinpointing the extremities of the figures. Adopting this method will also help you to hold the composition in your mind while you are drawing.

*Let's identify the triangular relationships in this fairly natural composition: the father's head to his lower foot and to the mother's lower foot; also his head to his hands; the boy's head with his feet; the father's knees and feet; the mother's skirt shape and the relationship of head to elbow to knee. The table and lamp form a ready-made triangle.*

---

### Triangles and Angles Simplified

You don't have to be a great geometrician to understand systems based on angles and triangles. When it comes to triangles, just note the relative sizes of their sides: in an equilateral triangle all three sides are equal (and all angles are equal); in an isoceles triangle one side is shorter than the other two; and in a parallelogram the opposite sides are equal in length and parallel.

Angles are even simpler. An angle of 90 degrees looks like the corner of a square. Half a right-angle is 45 degrees, and a third is 30 degrees. These are the only angles you'll need to be able to recognize. All the others can be related to them, and thought of in terms of more or less than 30, 45 or 90 degrees.

## HUMAN ARCHITECTURE

Learning to relate the skeleton and muscular structure of the body to the outer appearance becomes more important as you progress with figure drawing. You will need to study the structure of the body in detail if you really want your drawings to look convincing. The drawing below gives you some idea of the complexity of detail involved.

The Renaissance artists, of course, learnt about anatomy from dissected human and animal bodies. However, for most of us books on anatomy are quite good enough to give the main shapes, although a real skeleton (which quite a few artists and doctors have) will give more detailed information.

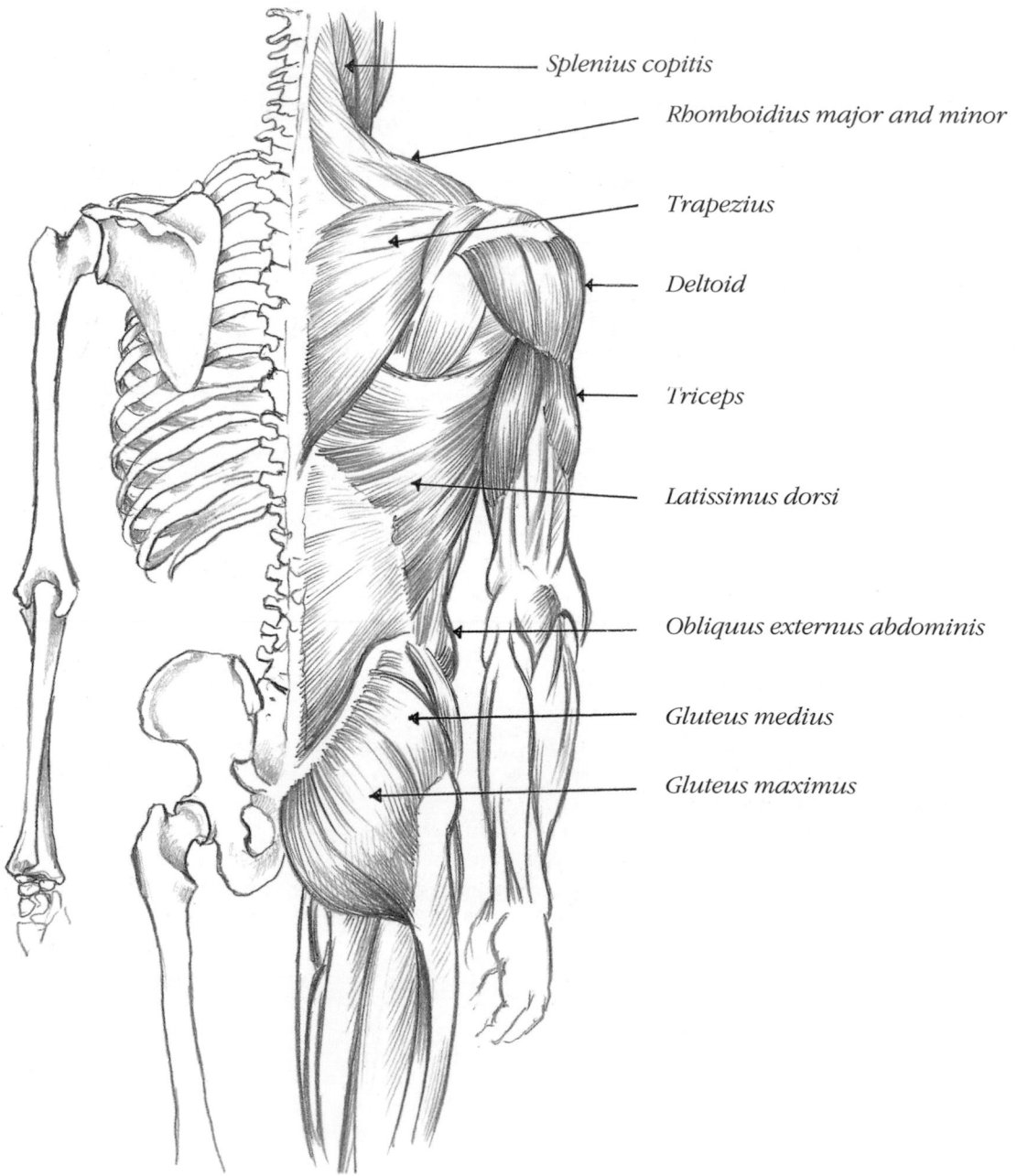

*Splenius copitis*

*Rhomboidius major and minor*

*Trapezius*

*Deltoid*

*Triceps*

*Latissimus dorsi*

*Obliquus externus abdominis*

*Gluteus medius*

*Gluteus maximus*

## THE HEAD

The head is defined mostly by the shape of the skull underneath its thin layer of muscle, and to a lesser extent by the eye-balls. The rather flat groups of muscles on the skull produce all our facial expressions, so it is very useful to have some idea of their arrangement and function, especially if you want to draw portraits.

### Muscles of the Head

A. *Corrugator (pulls eyebrows together)*
B. *Frontalis (moves forehead and eyebrows)*
C. *Temporalis (helps move jaw upwards)*
D. *Orbicularis oculis (closes eye)*
E. *Compressor nasi (narrows nostrils, pushes nose down)*
F. *Quadratus labii superioris (raises upper lip)*
G. *Zygomaticus major (upward traction of mouth)*
H. *Levator anguli oris (raises angle of mouth)*
I. *Orbicularis oris (closes mouth, purses lips)*
J. *Masseter (upward traction of lower jaw)*
K. *Buccinator (lateral action of mouth, expels fluid or air from cheeks)*
L. *Risorius (lateral pulling on angle of mouth)*
M. *Depressor anguli oris (downward traction of angle of mouth)*
N. *Depressor labii inferioris (downward pulling of lower lip)*
O. *Mentalis (moves skin on chin)*

**Bones of the Skull**

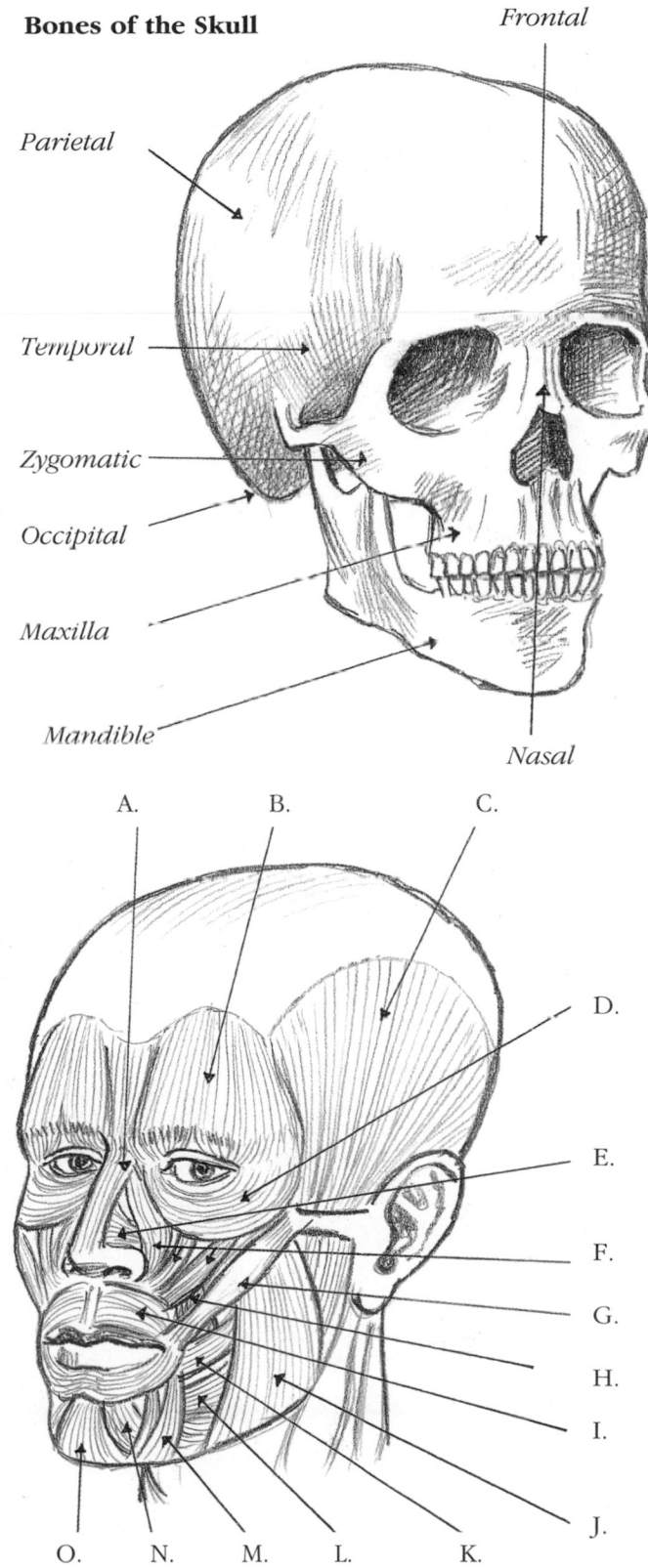

63

ELLIPSES

An ellipse is a circle seen from an oblique angle. Ellipses on the same level above or below the eye level will be similar in proportion. Several circular objects on a circular base will have the same proportions, as you will see if you look at the drawing below.

*The lampshade, base of the lamp-stand, table-top, and top and bottom of the glass are all ellipses related to the same eye-level. The lower ellipses are related to the same eye level and as they are all about the same level they will be very similar in proportions of width to height although of different sizes.*

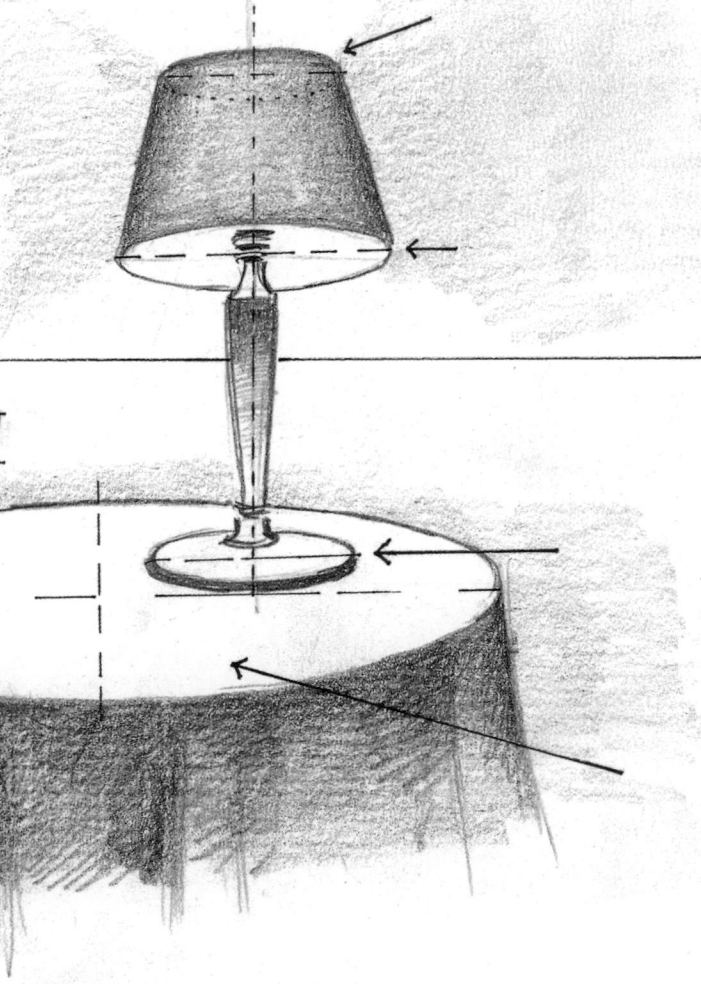

## USING A COMMON UNIT OF MEASUREMENT

A large subject such as a street scene, in which proportions and perspective have to be taken into account, can be difficult to draw accurately unless you use some system of measurement.

For the urban scene shown below, I chose an element within the scene as my unit of measurement (the lower shuttered window facing out of the drawing) and used it to check the proportions of each area in the composition. As you can see, the tall part of the building facing us is about six times the height of the shuttered window. The width of the whole building is twice the height of the shuttered window in its taller part and additionally six times the height of the shuttered window in its lower, one-storey part near the edge of the picture.

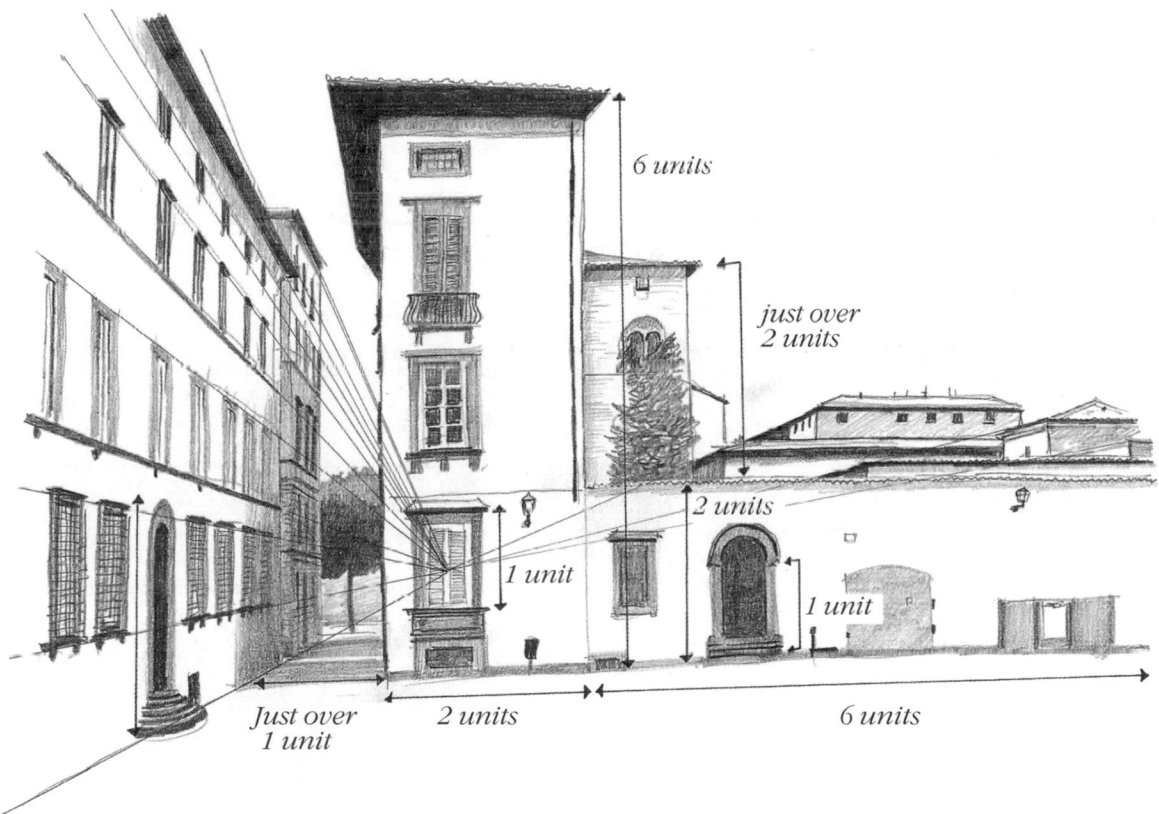

## Keeping Measurement in Perspective

A unit of measurement enables us to maintain the accuracy of our drawing, but it is only meant to provide a rough guide. Once you are used to drawing you will find the eye an extraordinarily accurate instrument for judging proportion and size. Sometimes we just need to check to make sure we've got them right, and at such times units and the like come into their own.

PERSPECTIVE

There are many things to be borne in mind with perspective. The main point is that it is impossible to put down exactly what we see in the two dimensions of drawing and painting. A certain amount of adjustment and artistic licence has to be allowed. A flat map can't replicate the world's surface, which is curved, and so will have to sacrifice either area shape or area proportion. When we look at something ordinarily, our eyes scan the scene. However, when we look at a picture, our vision is drawn as though from one point. This means that the outside edges of the cone of vision (as it's called) will not be easily drawn with any accurate relationship to the centre of vision. The artist, therefore, has to limit his area of vision to one that can be taken in at one glance. The artist must also be aware of his own eye-level or where the horizon really is, however much it is obscured by hills, trees or buildings. The actual cone or field of vision is about 60 degrees, but the artist will limit his picture to much less unless he is going to show distortion.

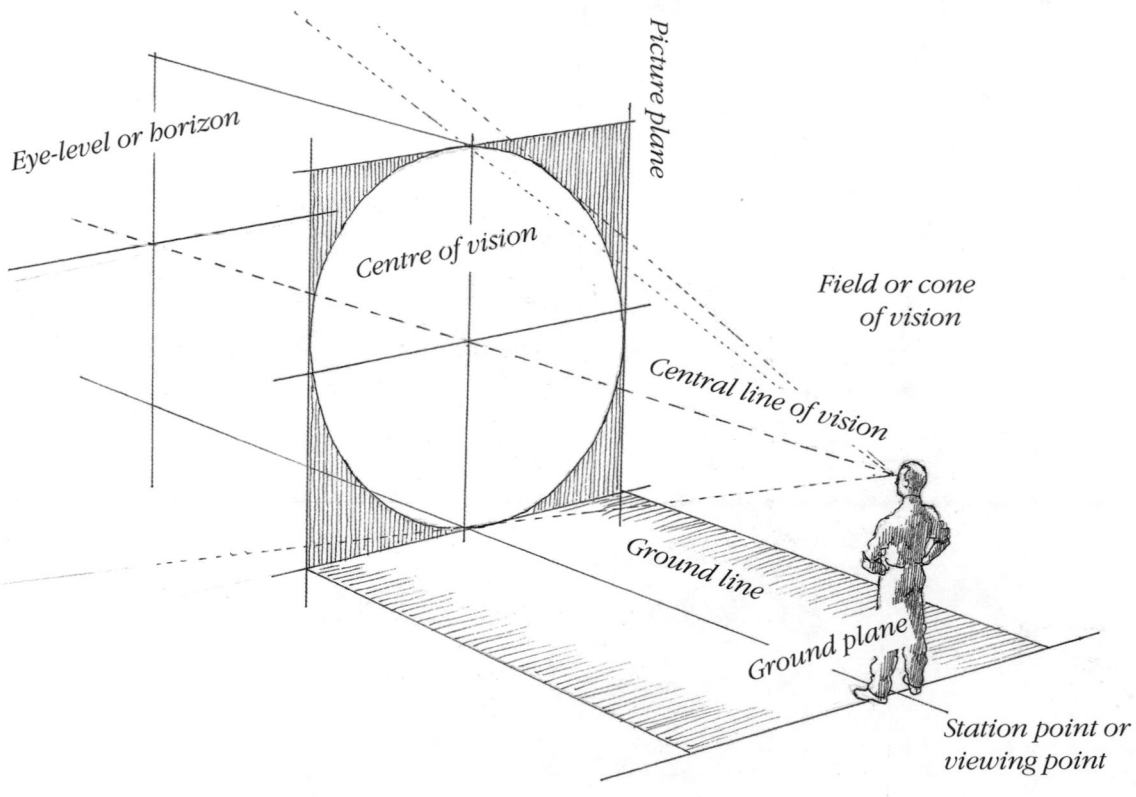

## RELATIONSHIPS IN THE PICTURE PLANE

In the example shown here we look at the relationships between the tree, post and flowers and the horizon line. As you can see, the height of the tree in the picture appears not as high as the post, although in reality the post is smaller than the tree. This is due to the effect of perspective, the tree being further away than the post. There is also an area of ground between the bottom of the tree and the flower. The horizon line is the same as the eye-level of the viewer.

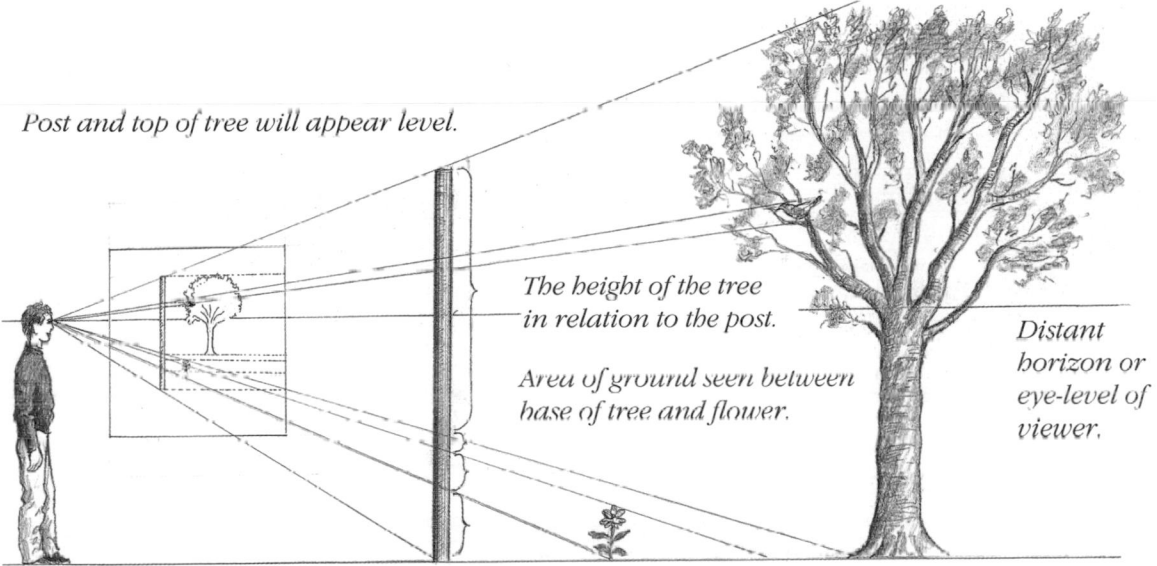

*Post and top of tree will appear level.*

*The height of the tree in relation to the post.*

*Area of ground seen between base of tree and flower.*

*Distant horizon or eye-level of viewer.*

*Distance between bottom of tree and bottom of post.*

## AERIAL PERSPECTIVE

When you are drawing scenes that include a distant landscape as well as close up elements, you must give the eye an idea of how much air or space there is between the foreground, middle ground and background. In this drawing these areas are clearly delineated. The buildings and lamp-posts close to the viewer are sharply defined and have texture and many tonal qualities. The buildings further away are less defined, with fewer tonal variations. The cliffs behind this built-up area are very faint, with no detail or texture and without much variation in tone.

## PERSPECTIVE: ALBERTI'S SYSTEM

The Renaissance architect and scholar Leon Battista Alberti (1404–72) put together a system of producing perspective methods for artists based on Filippo Brunelleschi's (1377–1446) discoveries in the science of optics. His system enabled a new generation of painters, sculptors and architects to visualize the three dimensions of space and use them in their work.

With Alberti's system the artist has to produce a ground plan of rectangles in perspective and then build structures onto this base. In order to do this he has to work out a way of drawing up the plan relating to the rays of vision and the eye-level or horizon so that measured divisions on the plan can be transferred into an apparent open window onto the scene being depicted. The viewpoint of artist and viewer is central and on the eye-level line, and this gives the picture conviction in depth and dimension.

*Picture plane (edge on).*

*Horizon line or eye-level.*

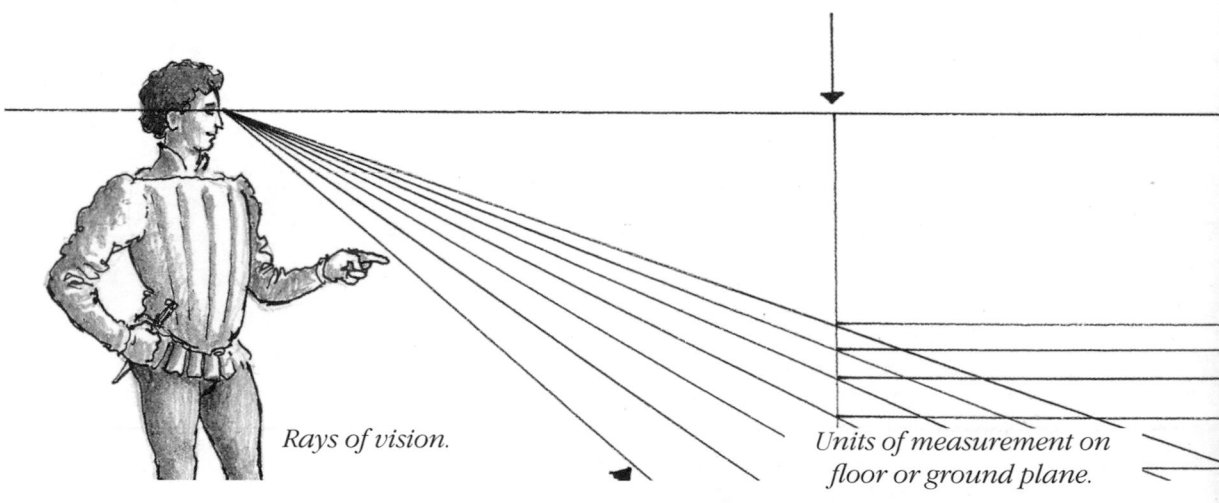

*Rays of vision.*

*Units of measurement on floor or ground plane.*

### Using Alberti's ground plan

*Once you have produced the ground plan grid, with the eye-level and vanishing point, you can then decide the height of your object or building – in the example shown right, it is 5 units of the floor grid. Using a compass, describe two arcs to connect verticals drawn from the four corners of the proposed building to the edges of the top of the*

*structure; draw horizontal lines for the near and far edges, and lines connected to the vanishing point for the two side edges.*

*The projections of front and side elevations shown here give a very simple structure. Alberti's system can be used to determine the look of far more complex structures than the one illustrated.*

## Producing Alberti's ground plan

*The ground line is measured in units that are related to a vanishing point on the horizon and can be seen as related to the picture plane. A simple diagonal drawn across the resulting chequered pavement can be used to check the accuracy of the device.*

*Once the pavement effect has been produced, any other constructions can be placed in the space, convincing the viewer*

*that he is looking into a three-dimensional space. This only works because of the assumptions we make about size and distance. If the lines of perspective are disguised to look like real things, such as pavements and walls, the eye accepts the convention and 'sees' an image understood as depth in the picture. Of course, all details have to conform in order to convince.*

*Vanishing point.*

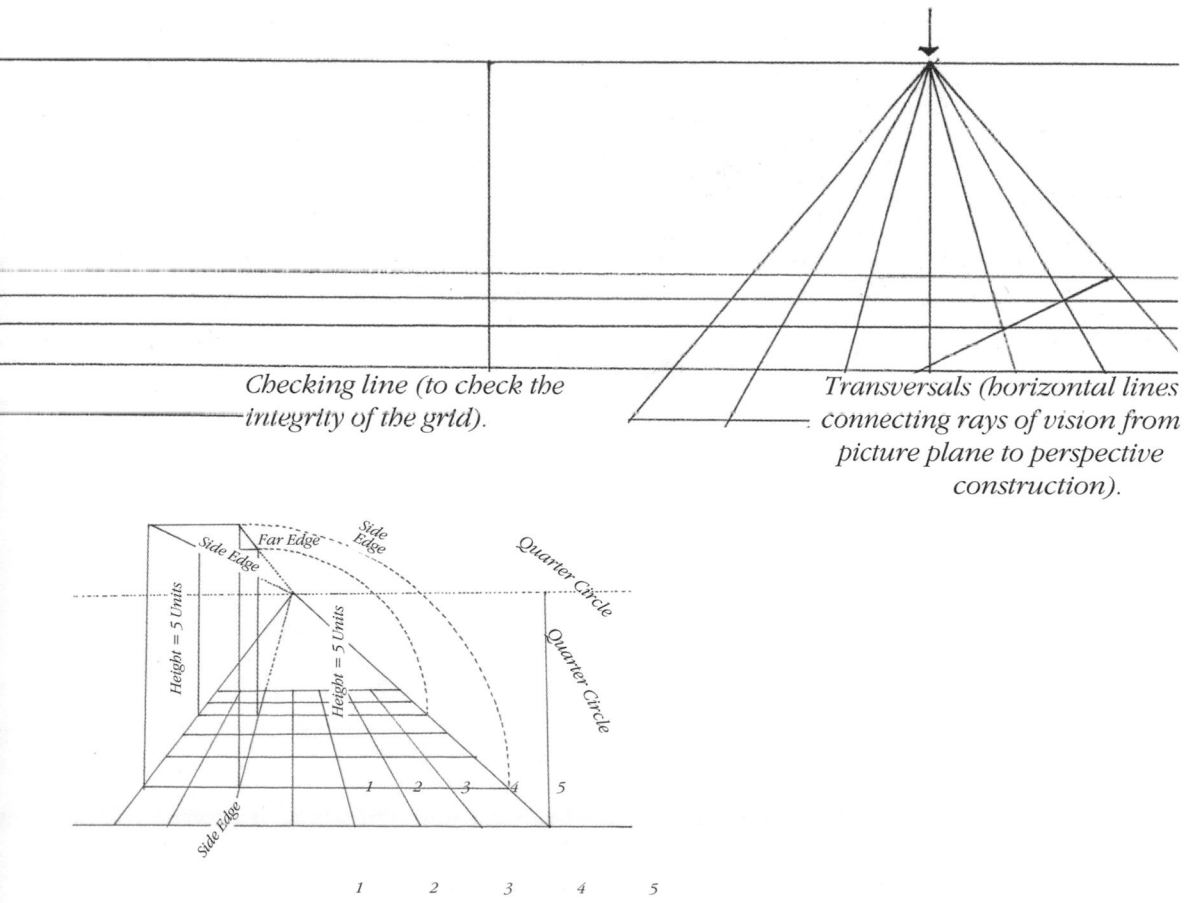

*Checking line (to check the integrity of the grid).*

*Transversals (horizontal lines connecting rays of vision from picture plane to perspective construction).*

Side Edge

Far Edge

Side Edge

Quarter Circle

Quarter Circle

Height = 5 Units

Height = 5 Units

Side Edge

Side Edge

1  2  3  4  5

| 1 | 2 | 3 | 4 | 5 |
|---|---|---|---|---|
| Unit | Unit | Unit | Unit | Unit |

PERSPECTIVE: FIELD OF VISION

The system we look at next is quite easy to construct. You don't require training in mathematics to get it right, just the ability to use a ruler, set square and compass precisely. Although the picture does not have depth in actuality, the eye is satisfied that it does, because it sees an area of squares which reduces geometrically as it recedes into the background.

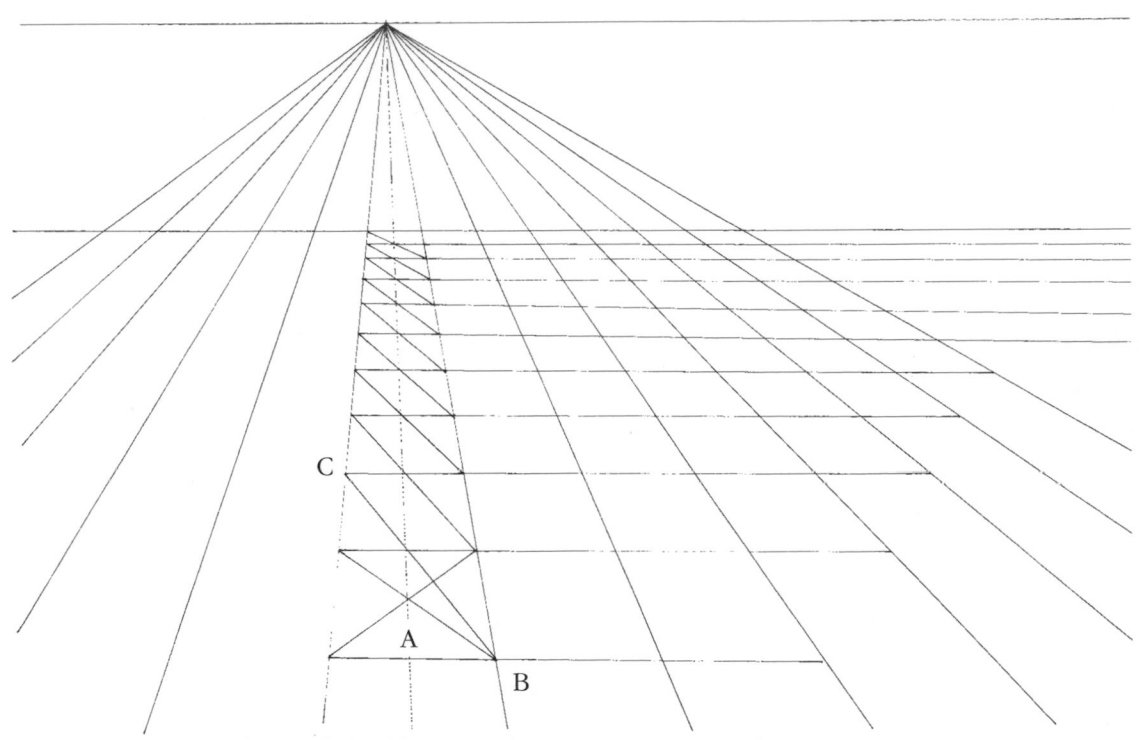

### Constructing an area of squares

*Any square portions, such as paving slabs, tiles or even a chequer-board of fields, can be used to prove the illusion of depth in a picture.*

*Take one slab or square size (A), draw in diagonal lines and from the crossing point of these diagonals mark a construction line to the vanishing point. In order to get the next rows of paving slabs related to the first correctly and in perspective, draw a line from the near corner (B) to the point where the construction line to the vanishing point*

*cuts the far edge of the square. Continue it until it cuts the next line to the vanishing point (C) and then construct your next horizontal edge to the next paving slab. Repeat in each square until you reach the point where the slabs should stop in the distance. Having produced a row of diminishing slabs, you can continue the horizontal edges of the slabs in either direction to produce the chequer-board of the floor. Notice the impressive effect you get when you fill in alternate squares.*

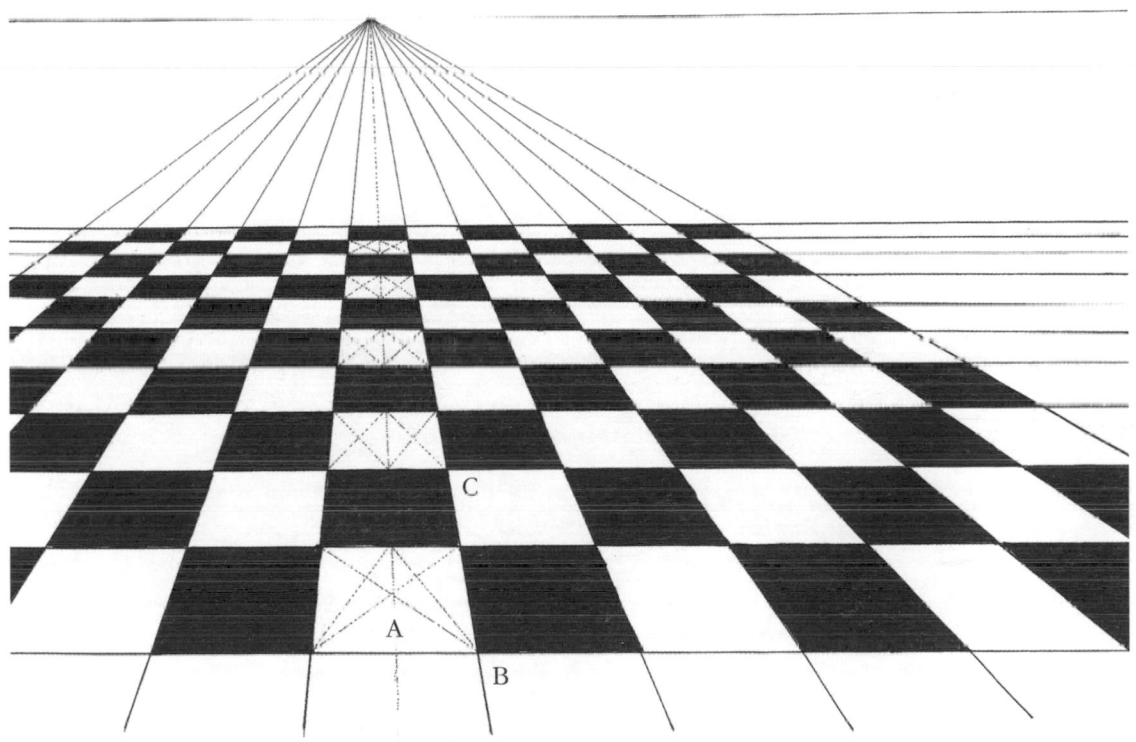

### More About Chequer-Board

The sort of chequer-board floor or pavement you have been learning about has often been used in paintings to help the illusion of depth. In early Renaissance pictures it was thought to be amazingly realistic. These days we are a bit more used to seeing such devices and so other effects have been brought into play to help us accept the illusion of dimensionality. However, do experiment with the chequer-board ground – it's very simple and very effective. And don't forget to incorporate the lessons you've learnt about the relationship of figure to the horizon or eye-line: if you place figures or objects on it, make sure that as they recede into the picture – standing on squares that are further back – they diminish in size consistent with your eye level (see pages 54–55).

MOVEMENT

Drawing movement is not as difficult as it might seem at first, although it does need quite a lot of practice. You'll find it helpful if you can feel the movement you are portraying in your own body, because this will inform the movement you are trying to draw. The more you know about movement the better. It's a good idea to observe people's movements to check out how each part of the anatomy behaves in a range of poses and attitudes.

Photographs of bodies in action are very useful, but limited in the range they offer. It is noticeable that action shots tend to capture moments of impact or of greatest force. Rarely do you find an action shot of the movements in-between. With a bit of careful observation, watching and analyzing, you should be able to see how to fill in the positions between the extremes.

*Here we see a man in the various stages of throwing a javelin. The point at which he is poised to throw and the moment when the javelin is launched are the two extremes of* *this process. However, you may find that drawing the man in a position between these extremes gives you a composition with more drama and tension.*

*Similarly here, the point between the head completing its turn from one side to the other offers a different quality and perhaps a more revealing perspective on the subject.*

*In these examples the only really obvious movement is the hand lifting the cup to drink. The first drawing sets the scene; the second shows the intent; and the third completes the action. The loose multiple line used in the second and third drawings helps to give the effect of movement.*

## MOVEMENT: CONTROLLED AND UNCONTROLLED

*The most effective drawings of people falling accidentally capture the sheer unpredictability of the situation. In this example the arms and legs are at all sorts of odd angles and the expression is a mixture of tension, fear and surprise. He is wondering where and how he's going to land. Deliberately I made the line rather uncertain to enhance the effect of the uncertainty in the situation.*

*In this example, the odd angle of the viewer's vision provides a contrast with the lines of the water and side of the pool, creating tension although it's obvious what is happening. This is not drama in the making but a moment frozen in time. The slight strobe effect of the diving-board also helps to give the impression that we are witnessing something first-hand.*

*I used a clip from a newspaper as my model for this rugby player kicking a ball. My version is slightly amended from the original to accentuate the 'fuzz' of the out-of-focus kicking foot. The speed of this movement* *contrasts with the rest of the figure, which is much more clearly defined. The balance of the position is very important, to accentuate the force of the kick and the concentration of the kicker on those distant goal-posts.*

ADDING TO YOUR VOCABULARY

A practising artist must be ready to draw at any time. If you want to excel at drawing, sketching has to become a discipline. Get into the habit of seeing things with a view to drawing them. This means, of course, that you'll have to carry a sketch-pad around with you, or something that you can jot your impressions in. You'll find yourself making sketches of unrepeatable one-offs that can't be posed, as I did with some of the sketches shown here.

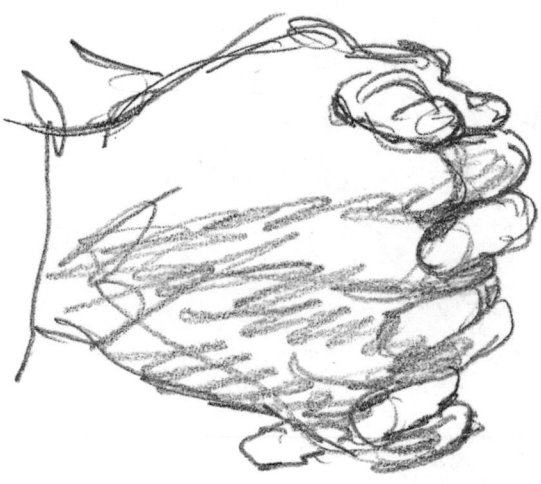

A quick note, even if not very accurate, is all you need to make a worthwhile addition to your vocabulary of drawing. Often it is impossible to finish the sketch, but this doesn't matter. Some of the most evocative drawings any artist produces are quick, spontaneous sketches that capture the fleeting movement, attitude, angle of vision or view of a movement. They are often the drawings you return to again and again to use in compositions or to remind yourself of an atmosphere or place.

When drawing scenes with large areas of building it is useful to simplify the areas of light and shade to make it more obvious how the light defines the solidity of the buildings. In both these examples a large area of shadow anchors the whole composition and gives it depth and strength.

In the first drawing we are aware that the open area with buildings around it is a square; in the second we are in no doubt that the very dark area is an arch through a solid building. In both examples the light and shade help to convince.

### Don't Forget Your Sketch-Book

A pocket-sized book with hard covers and thinnish paper is generally the best for most quick sketches, being simple to use and forcing you to be economic with your lines, tones or colours. A clutch pencil or lightweight plastic propelling pencil with a fine lead is ideal; preferably carry more than one. A fine line pigment liner is also very useful and teaches you to draw with confidence no matter how clumsy the drawing.

Continual practice makes an enormous difference to your drawing skill and helps you to experiment in ways to get effects down fast and effectively. If you're really serious you should have half a dozen sketch-books of varying sizes and papers, but hard-backed ones are usually easier to use because they incorporate their own built-in drawing board. A large A2 or A3 sketch-book can be easily supported on the knees when sitting and give plenty of space to draw. Cover the pages with many drawings, rather than having one on each page, unless your drawing is so big that it leaves no room for others.

# Form and Shape

What the eye sees is shape, colour, light and shade, and not much else. However, the mind goes to work on the experience, relates it to other experiences and translates the shape and form into something we can recognize, such as a man, woman, horse, dog, tree, house or whatever.

Shape is the outline visual impression we have of an object. However, because we get used to seeing certain objects in certain positions our minds develop visual templates and we tend to see what we expect to see rather than what is actually there. Shape changes constantly, depending on our position in relation to it, and this can cause us endless problems as viewers and artists.

Form is the three-dimensional appearance of an object or body; in other words, the spatial area it inhabits. Form is more difficult to draw than shape because of the problems of representing three dimensions on a flat surface. To make our representations realistic, we have to find ways of expressing shapes coming towards the viewer or receding from the viewpoint.

The artist has to experiment both in seeing and drawing in order to come to an understanding of the language of shape and form and how to manipulate it. This section is intended to help you use your eyes more experimentally, to look beyond your expectations and your normal process of recognition.

ARCHITECTURAL FORMS

The brain has two sides; right and left. Science tells us that if we could activate the right side of the brain when we draw, our drawings would be more accurate, because it is this side which processes all our visual impressions. If this side was fully engaged when we drew, we would look at shapes as shapes and not draw what we expect the shape to be.

One way of tricking the brain is to hold an image upside down and then try to draw it. You will find your brain connecting with the image on a purely visual level: the left, or verbal, side of the brain connects with normal recognition but once this is broken the right side takes over.

I have tried this exercise with both adults and children and found it to be most effective. Children are particularly good at it and find it much easier to switch back and forth between the two sides. Adults always want to 'know', and so are constantly engaging the verbal side.

The series of exercises over the next few pages is designed to help you try to switch off that left side.

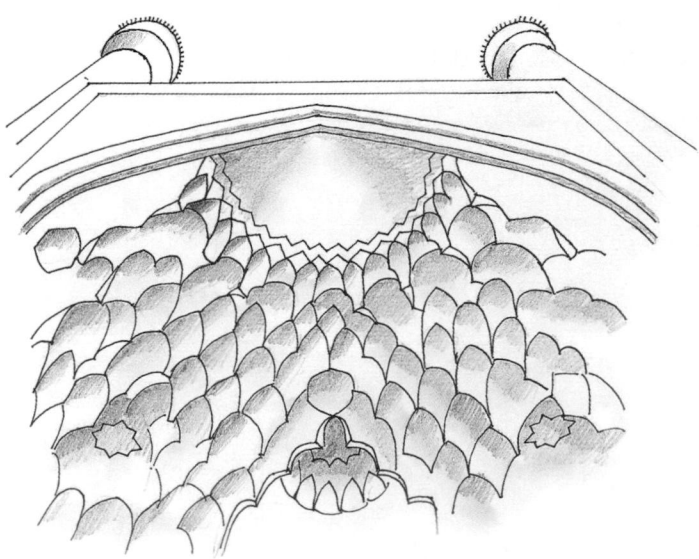

*Gothic (above) and Islamic (left) vaulting share some similarities in terms of the shapes used in their creation, but you could not mistake one type for the other. Look at these two examples, noting their similarities and differences.*

Although form tends to follow function, this does not mean it is strait-jacketed by the relationship. Many variations are possible, and this is where choice comes into play. We compare images by being aware of the implications of a form. Our decision to use a form in a picture is based on an assessment of suitability.

*Aesthetic and social requirements for living change over time and these can bring about great differences in 'look'. The medieval home (above) was functional for its time, but does not share the sharp, clean-cut lines of its modern counterpart*

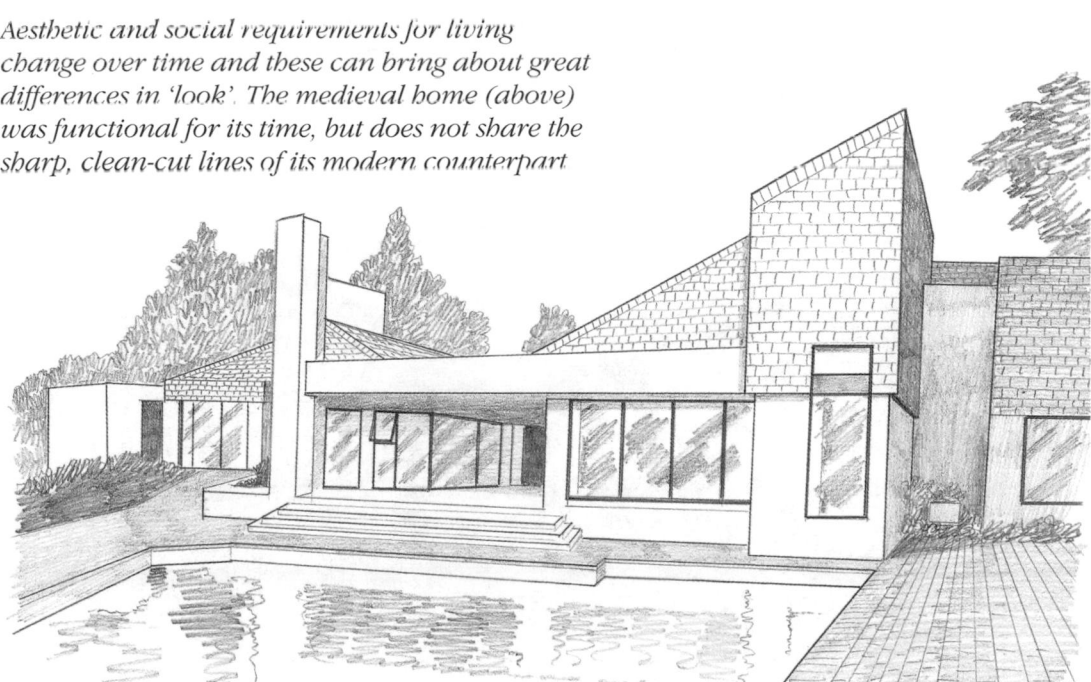

SHAPE RECOGNITION

Let's look at a few shapes in silhouette. What clues to identity are carried in these simple outlines? The American Mustang, the British Spitfire and the German Stuka are all World War Two low-wing monoplane fighter aircraft. They are easy to tell apart and to identify because of the particular details evident in their main frames. Similarly, the Harrier jump-jet and Sea King helicopter shown on the facing page are not difficult to differentiate from other types of aircraft.

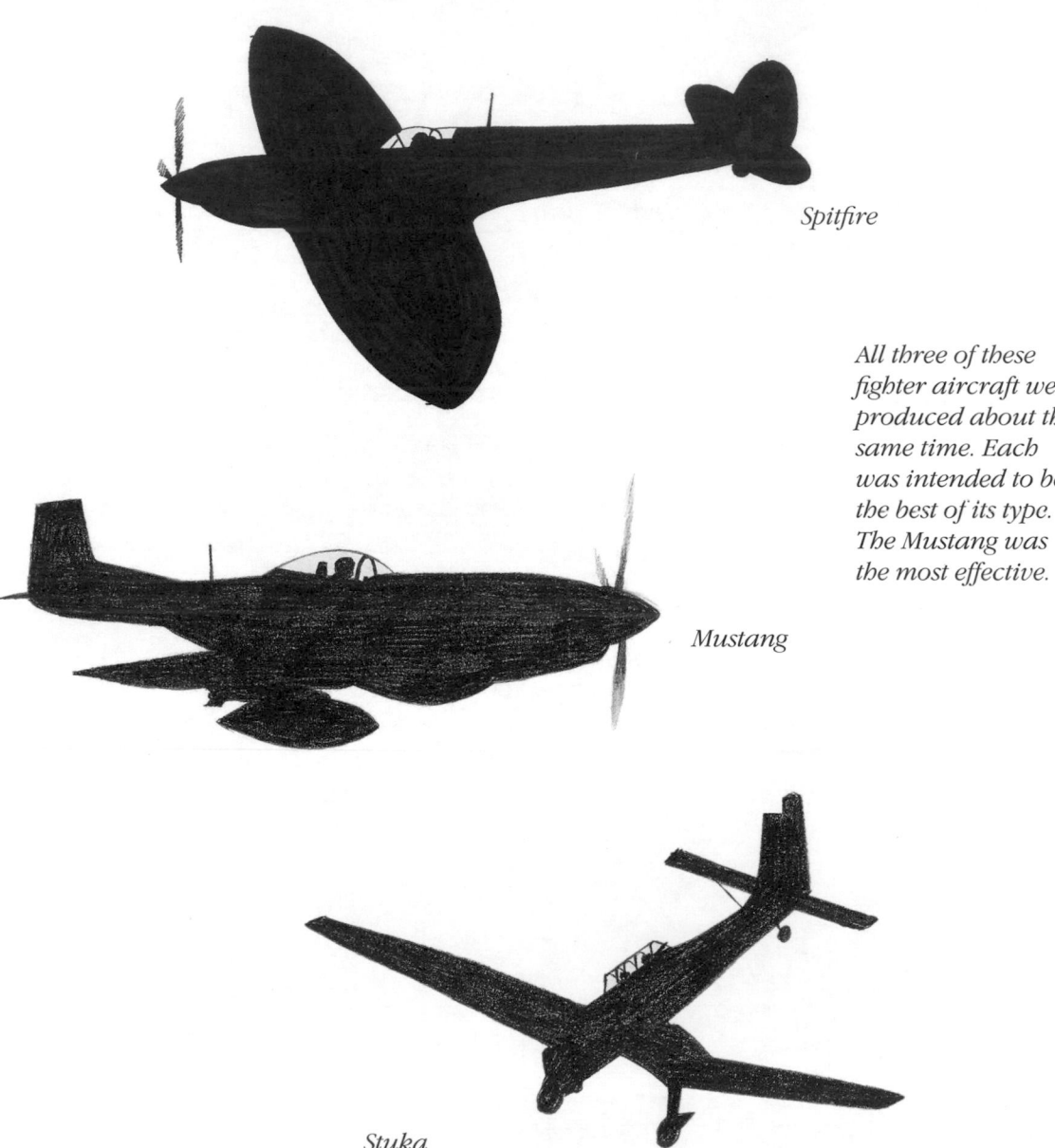

*Spitfire*

*All three of these fighter aircraft were produced about the same time. Each was intended to be the best of its type. The Mustang was the most effective.*

*Mustang*

*Stuka*

*Harrier*

*Both of these types of aircaft take off vertically but possess different means of achieving it.*

*Sea King*

Our ability to recognize shapes is learned in childhood as we become aware of the wider world. Our visual vocabulary grows according to the means at our disposal. All the silhouettes on this spread arouse memories of my childhood, and the hours I spent poring over them in my picture books.

If we are to draw well, we must have the ability to connect shapes and yet differentiate between them. If we are unable to do this, we will end up producing drawings that have as much character as the images on street signs.

*The continent of Africa as seen from a spacecraft. This is so familiar to us from maps that one is surprised by the accuracy of those early map-makers, who did not have the benefit of cameras or spacecraft and yet gave us the correct shape.*

*A World War Two German Army helmet.*

*The characteristic shape of a 16th-century Spanish Morion helmet.*

*Both types of helmet provided protection for the head in battle but had rather different weaponry to contend with.*

*These two ships have similar functions but evolved in different places with slightly different technologies. The shape of each is characteristic, and you would be unlikely to mistake one for the other.*

*The Santa María, Columbus's craft.*

*A Chinese junk.*

## SYMBOLS AND ASSOCIATIONS

Some buildings become the signatures of places or legends, because of the association made for them. If we see a picture of the Eiffel Tower, we immediately think 'Paris'. When we see an image of the Taj Mahal, even a sketchy drawing such as the one shown, associations of India or the East come into our minds. Similarly, Cervantes' creation Don Quixote will forever be associated with Spanish windmills.

There are many other examples of images which are indelibly associated with places, things or ideas. How many can you think of?

Instinctive recognition is an odd effect of partly seeing and partly expecting. When you are trying to draw the shape of something, it becomes clear that it has characteristics that help to define its role. Its shape enables it to do what it does.

The shape of the most aggressive predator in the ocean is very well-known to us from our experience of films and photographs. There is no mistaking its formidable shape, even in silhouette. How is it that the outline of a white swan on a dark background is so peaceful, while that black, shark shape is so full of sinister power? Because we know how these shapes affect the viewer and the associations they attach to them.

As artists we can use this knowledge to convey messages in our pictures. This isn't as easy as it sounds if we wish to make our picture work properly. It demands an awareness of shapes and their associations for viewers across broad and disparate areas of life.

*Archetypal images of opposites: danger and serenity.*

CREATING FORM

Our fairly sophisticated recognition system has to be persuaded to interpret shapes as three-dimensional form. One way of doing this is to produce an effect that will be read as form, although in reality this may only comprise an arrangement of lines and marks. Let's look at some examples.

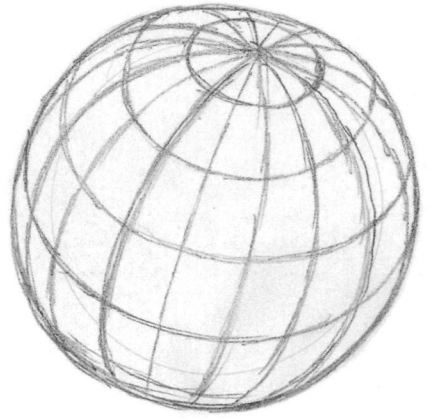

*A diagrammatic form is often given in atlases to represent the world. Why is it that this particular arrangement of lines inside a circle makes a fairly convincing version of a sphere with its latitude and longitude lines? We don't really think it is a sphere, but nevertheless it carries conviction as a diagram.*

*Let's go a stage further. In this drawing of a bleached out photograph of an onion the reduced striations or lines make the same point. We recognize this kind of pattern and realize that what we are looking at is intended to portray a spherical object which sprouts. We can 'see' an onion.*

*So is this a round fruit? No, of course not. But the drawn effect of light and shade is so familiar from our study of photographs and film that we recognize the rotund shape as a piece of fruit.*

---

### Visual Conditioning

We have been educated to accept the representation of three-dimensional objects on a flat surface. This is not the case in all parts of the world. In some remote areas, for example, people cannot recognize three-dimensional objects they are familiar with from photographs.

---

*When we look at this hexagonal divided into parallelograms of light, dark and medium tones, we want to interpret it as a cube or block shape.*

*These rather scribbled lines and marks can be seen as a leaping cat-like creature and a human form engaged in sporting activity. Of course they are not really those things, but there are enough clues to prompt our ever-ready memory to remind us of forms we have seen. The mind quickly fills in the details even when a form is rudimentary.*

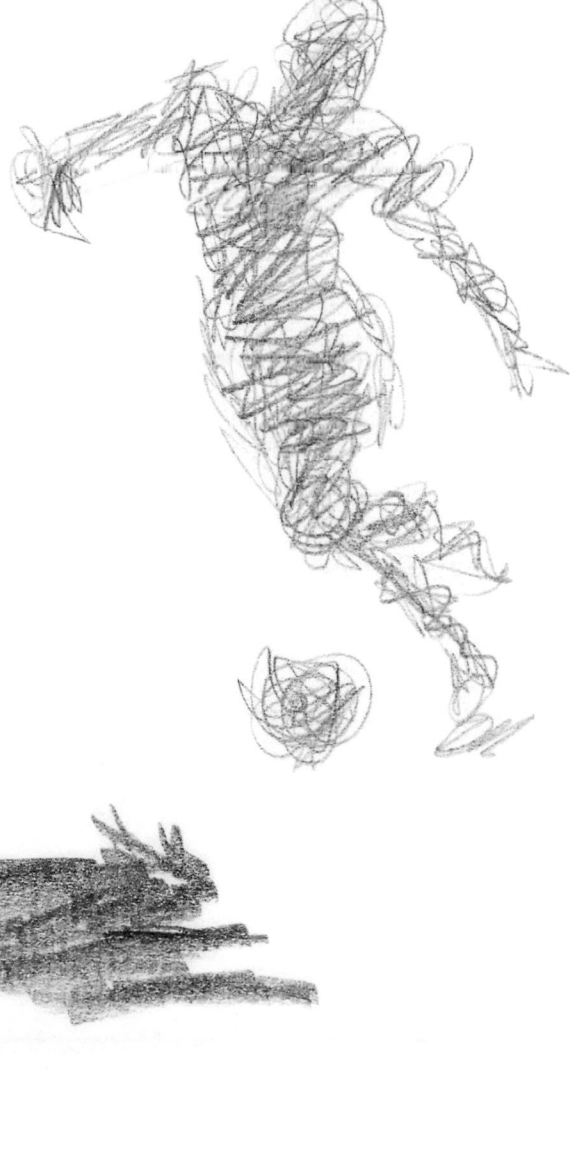

APPROACHES TO FORM

So what methods can we use to portray form convincingly so that the onlooker sees a solidity that is in fact merely inferred? Well, on these pages we have the human figure – probably the most subtle, difficult but most satisfying subject for drawing – and some details of the eye. These show different ways of analyzing form. Every artist has to undertake his own investigations of form. They involve methods of looking as well as methods of drawing, and through practising them you educate the eye, hand and mind.

*We can draw lines around the sections of a form to give us a sort of computerized vision of the dimensions of the shape – as in this recumbent figure.*

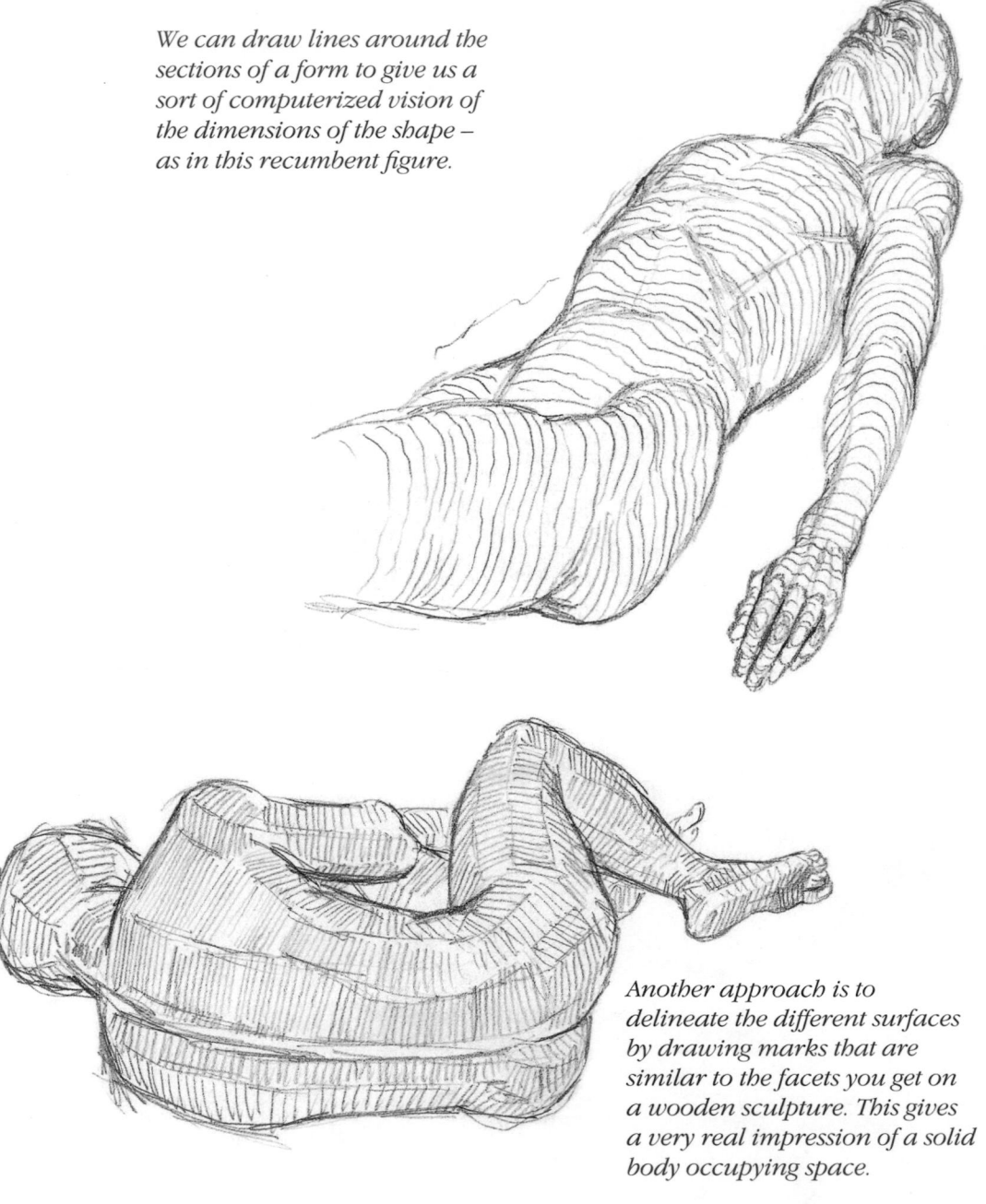

*Another approach is to delineate the different surfaces by drawing marks that are similar to the facets you get on a wooden sculpture. This gives a very real impression of a solid body occupying space.*

In a close-up like this, every detail of the form of the eye is shown. It is a very good exercise to take something as obvious as one of our own features, and view it closely in a mirror. Try this yourself: study the form of your eye and then try to draw its every wrinkle or hair or reflection. Note how the lids appear to curve around the smooth ball of the eye itself and how the eyelashes stick out across the lines of the eyelid and the eye.

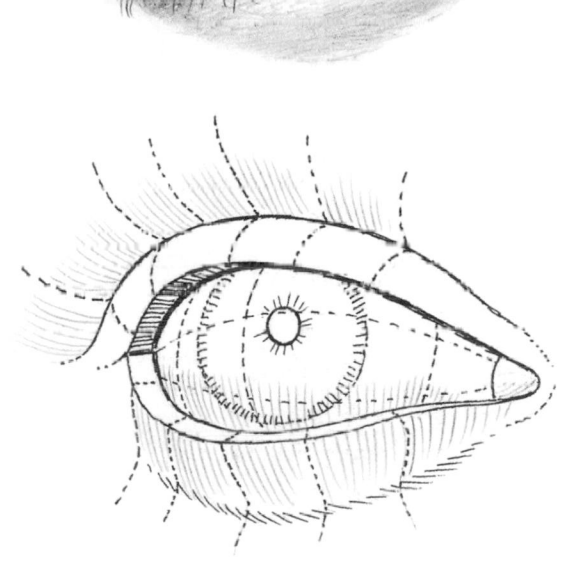

This could be the under-drawing of the first picture: the diagrammatic form of the main part of the eye with indications of its curves and edges.

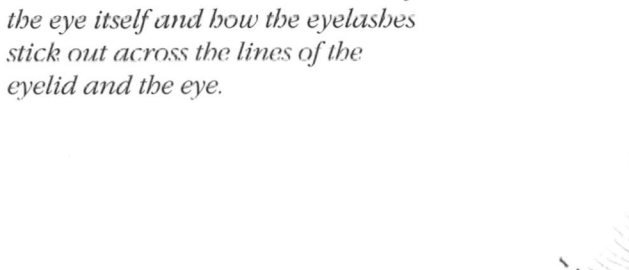

The Italian painter Giorgio Morandi had a particular vision of form that is like no other. His etchings of still-life subjects have a dark solidity about them, as in this example. He achieved this effect by piling on fine lines of cross-hatching which, taken in combination, create very substantial, dramatic darks and lights.

91

As we have already seen with the diagram of the globe on page 88, lines that are built into a diagram can give us all the visual clues we need to an object's shape. In the natural world these lines are often provided for us. Where they do not occur naturally, artists have invented them to help their exploration of form.

In the self-portrait and the view of the village of Estaque shown on this page, Cézanne has somehow managed to show form in space; that is, give an effect of solidity or depth by his rather sparse shading and markings of the shape. He has not shown the classical shade and light relationship, but he hasn't entirely left them out either.

*The economy evident in the drawing below is even more pronounced in this landscape. Large areas of blank space are limited by faint markings showing the main blocks of buildings. A few heavier markings here and there emphasize the shadows or intensity of colour in the scene. This rather minimal way of denoting solid masses in space gives a very strong sense of the space between the* *buildings in the foreground and those further away. If you decide to show form in this way, be careful not to put in too many lines or heavier marks. Fewer marks seem to produce greater awareness of form in the viewer.*

*In this self-portrait the area of darkest tone helps to give the impression of the important areas of form, especially around the eyes and nose. The large tonal areas down one side of the forehead and beard help to connect the main protuberances of the face with the generally rounded shape of the head. With great economy of drawing, Cézanne is able to convince us that we are seeing a three-dimensional head.*

*These shells are structured in such a way as to provide their own contour lines, the striations or growth lines indications of their natural evolution. Even without light and shade, the clearly seen lines proceeding around the form of the shell give us a good idea of how the shell is shaped. They offer a useful exercise in understanding shapes.*

*Cézanne tried to discover the form of objects by drawing multiple lines around their edges. He was trying to give multiple views of his objects, such as you get when you view something from many slightly different angles. In this example his lines suggest that you can actually see round the edges of the objects.*

### Cubism

The Cubists (artists such as Braque, Picasso, Léger and Ozenfant) took Cézanne's analysis one stage further by attempting to draw objects from contrasting viewpoints – from the side, front, above, below, and so on. In the process they had to fragment their images to be able to show these various approaches in one picture. This led to the typical cuboid sets of images for which they were named. These artists were successful in changing how we look at the world, although their methods are rarely employed now.

The most formidable task confronting any artist is how to draw the three-dimensional human form convincingly in one way or another. There are many ways of doing this. Over the next couple of pages we consider three fairly obvious ones.

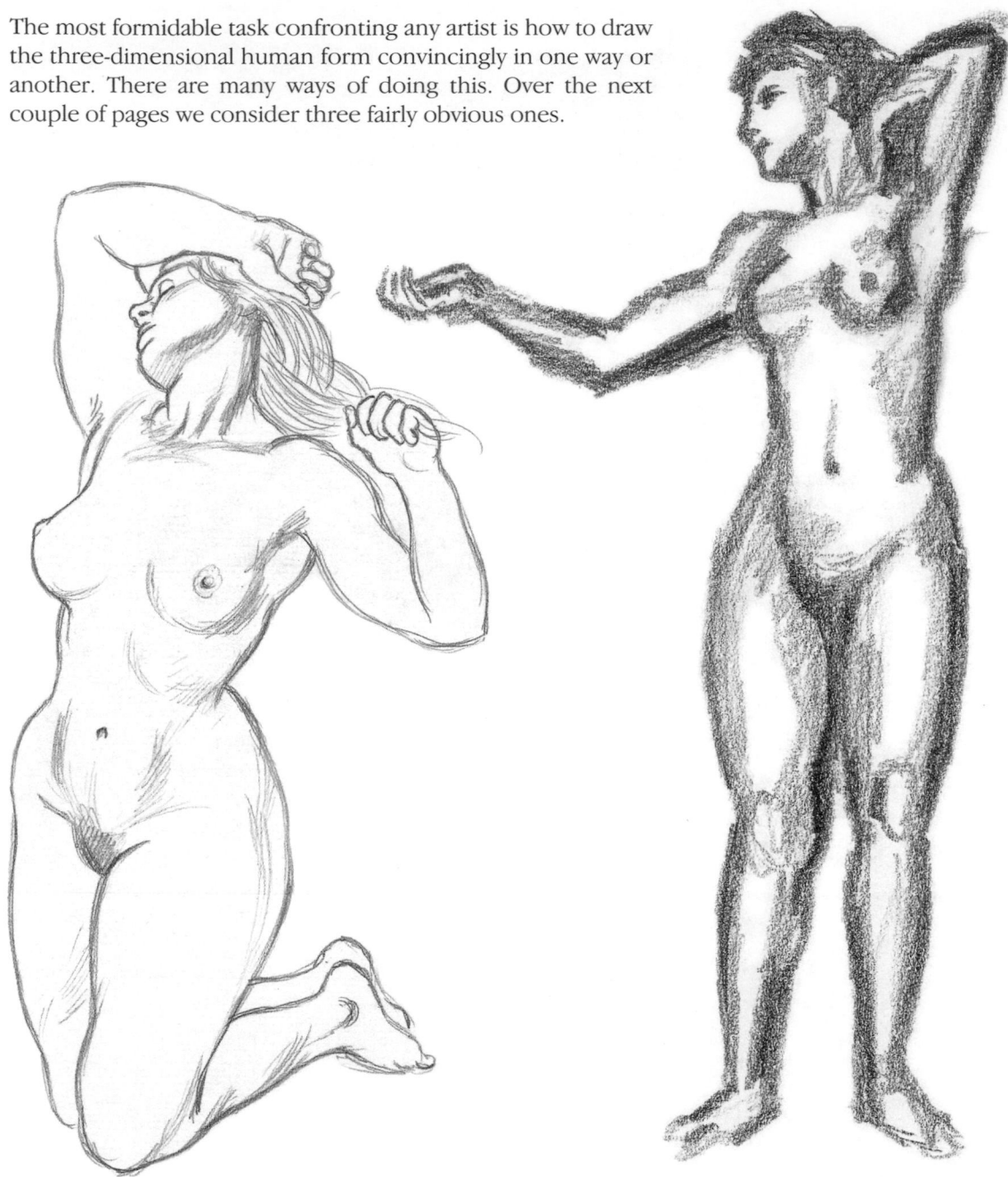

*The work of Franz Stück is linear in style; the bulk of the form is realized with very few lines, allowing our mind to fill in the empty spaces with the fullness of the flesh.*

*This example, also a copy of a Stück, is more dramatically drawn. Although the edges are soft there is a powerful fullness of form, with chalky looking tonal marks indicating the roundness of the body.*

*Otto Greiner's approach to form is essentially that of the classical artist, as this copy shows, with the light and shade carefully and sensitively handled. It's an effective if slow and painstaking method, but well worth mastering.*

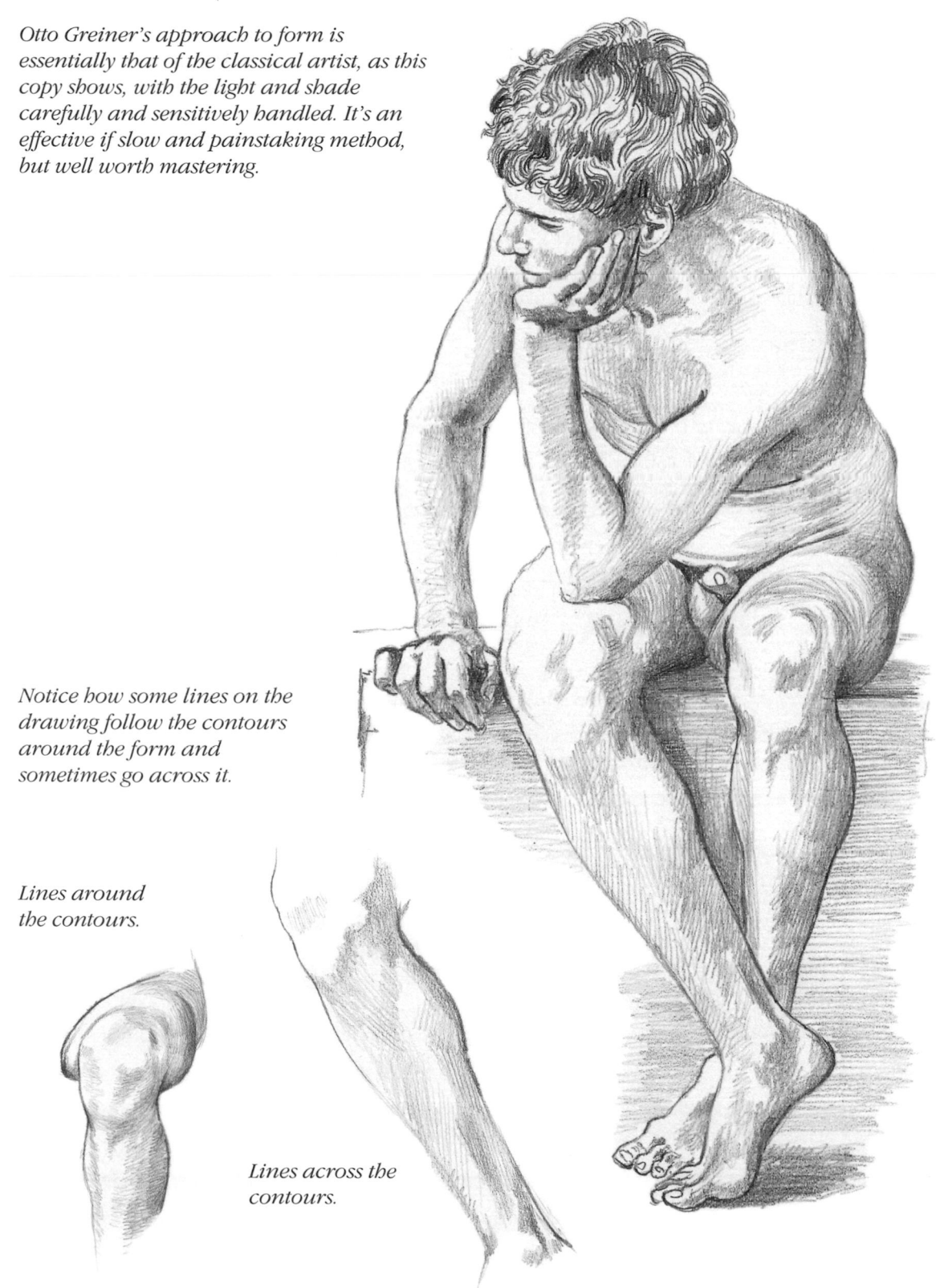

*Notice how some lines on the drawing follow the contours around the form and sometimes go across it.*

*Lines around the contours.*

*Lines across the contours.*

These copies of two heads by David Hockney show different methods of using tone to show form. As a consequence of the different treatment, the effect he has achieved in each drawing is very marked.

*The handling here is comparatively sensitive, elegant and very economical, with just enough form showing to enable the viewer to make sense of the shape.*

*This self-portrait is a much more rugged affair. The dominant tonal area gives us a very generalized feel of the shape of the head, thereby sacrificing individual characteristics to achieve a more dimensional effect.*

Whereas on a face all the surfaces move smoothly into each other, even on the craggiest visage, on a building each surface is distinct from the next. Most buildings are rectilinear, cuboid or cylindical and do not have ambiguous curves. The challenge of making a structure that remains upright and lasts in time means that the edges of its surfaces are more sharply defined and the shapes much simpler than those found in natural form. As a consequence it is much easier to show mass.

Here we have two examples of drawings of buildings in which the aim is to communicate something of the materiality and form of these buildings. The first, of a tower by Christopher Wren, follows the shapes almost as if the artist is constructing the building anew as his pencil describes it.

The approach taken for a famous London landmark, Battersea Power Station, is very different, as befits a great monument to an industrial age.

*A very powerful three-dimensional effect has been achieved here by vividly portraying the massive simplicity of the building's design with sharply drawn shadows and large light areas.*

*This drawing captures the elegant balancing forms of classical architecture as practised by Christopher Wren, with spaces through the form and much articulation of the surfaces to create a lightness in the stone structure as well as visual interest.*

## UNIVERSALS IN FORM

Both Ewan Uglow and Geoffrey Elliott produce figures that represent universals in form. Neither is trying to produce portraits in the accepted way. Uglow's figures cannot be said to represent unique, identifiable persons, and Elliott is obviously more interested in the general forms inhabiting the landscape than trying to reproduce individuals on paper. Both approaches teach us that to draw well you don't have to produce an intimate portrait of the person you are drawing. Good drawing can be purely an expression of aesthetics and an experience of form.

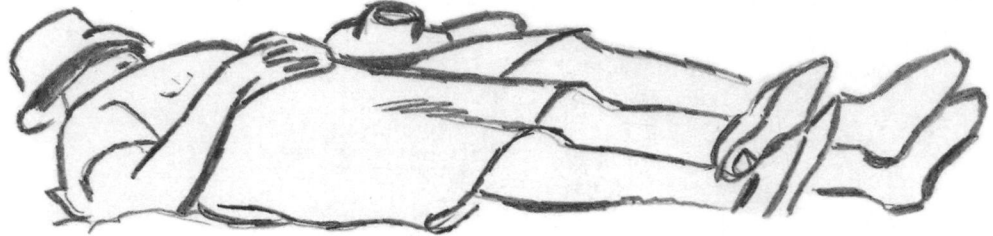

*These reclining figures are from Geoffrey Elliott's sketch-book of drawings of people on a beach in Sussex. Like Uglow's figures, they are universal in form, but personal qualities emerge despite the absence of obvious emotional expression or movement.*

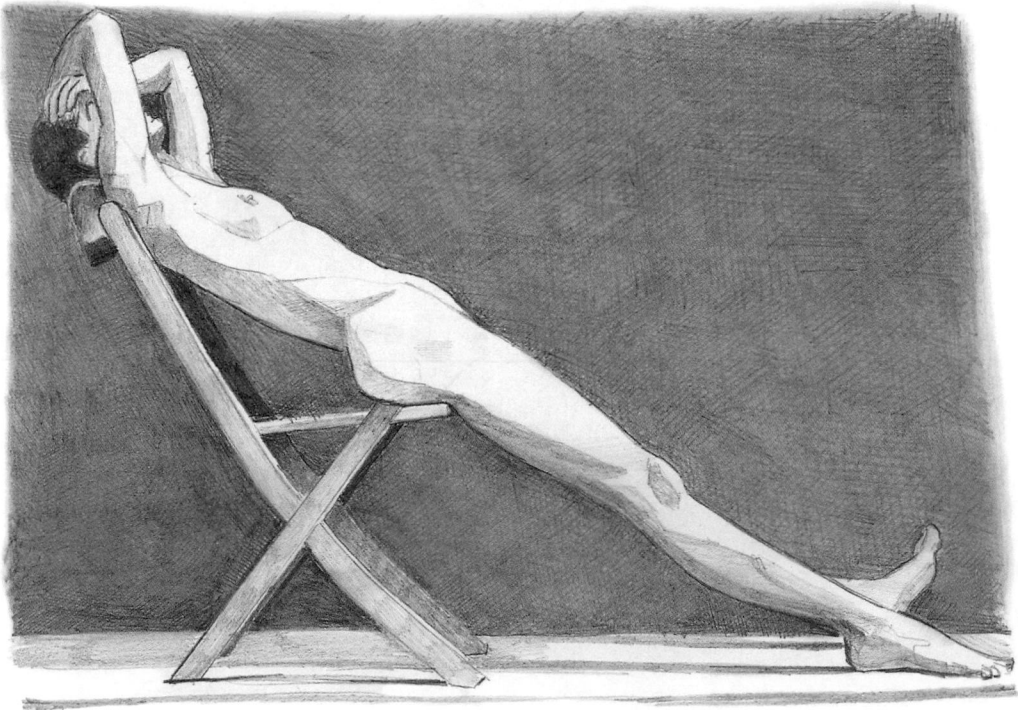

*Euan Uglow's masterly way of producing a figure is extremely accurate but time-consuming; he has been known to spend years on just one painting. Uglow built-up this nude figure from hundreds of painstakingly measured marks on canvas or paper to produce an effect of monumentality. This geometric vigour is also reflected in the carefully placed surfaces of tone and colour, which build to a structured and powerful view of the human form. Inevitably this approach necessitates the sacrifice of some elements of individuality.*

EXERCISES IN SIMPLIFYING FORM

An object's real shape can be investigated by drawing it from many different angles. For this exercise, we look at a boot, but it could be any object of your choosing. A model can be used for the same exercise. Try drawing him or her from different viewpoints, sometimes standing, sometimes sitting, etc. You will find this detailed investigation into shape very worthwhile.

Simplification is essential if we are to produce accurate drawings. This goes for anything we choose to represent on paper. Lastly on this page, I have chosen a figure for you to practise.

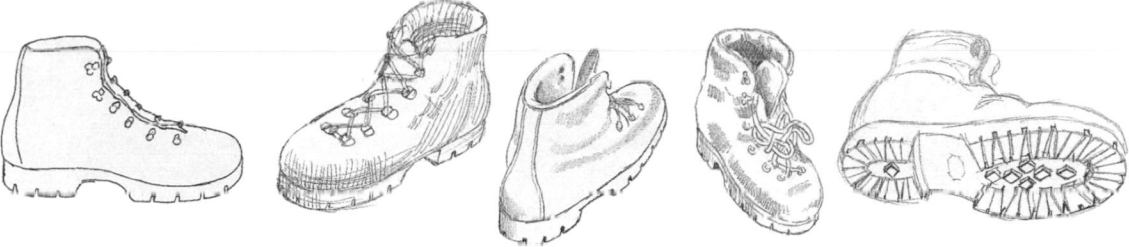

*To begin, select an angle from which the object is clearly identifiable. When you have done this, change its position, and continue changing it until you have seen and drawn the object from many different angles – from above, below, on its side, from the front, the back. Continue until you feel that you know how the shape works.*

*With a still figure it is a good idea to reduce it to its simplest geometric shapes. For example, if the figure is seated on a chair the arrangement could be seen as a rectangular block with a tall tower-like part projecting above.*
*Alternatively, a person sitting with knees up to their chin and arms around their legs produces a wedge-like shape.*

*Such simplification can greatly assist the business of getting the proportions and the position of the figure correct. Once you have drawn the simple solid geometrical shape, you can draw into it knowing that this is your ground plan.*

ELEMENTAL SHAPES

Elemental shapes are as expressive as they are defining, and offer many difficulties when it comes to drawing them. Whatever you do, don't retreat from the problems thrown up by your attempts. All are resolvable if you put in a bit of effort.

A good way to start is by selecting various symbols of the elements and studying them closely. Let's take them in order of difficulty, starting with earth and water.

*Earth can be shown by grains of soil or even a turf. Easier still is to choose a tree as your symbol, one whose branches can easily be seen. Winter is, of course, the best time to get a clear view of the architecture of deciduous varieties, which offer the most interesting shapes.*

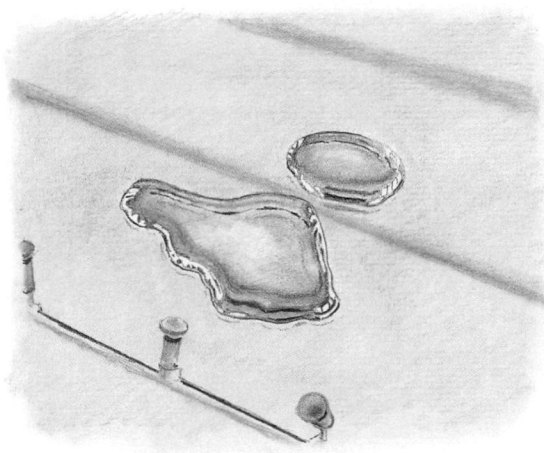

*Water is an even harder form to understand than earth. First, try drawing some still water spilt onto a reflective surface, such as a mirror. Careful, detailed study will be necessary to really reveal its properties. Draw the outline edge of the shape first, look at the tonal qualities and then at the reflection in the water. This is not difficult as long as you draw everything you can see.*

*Moving water provides an even harder challenge. You will need to spend some time watching it and some time simplifying what you see. Eventually, though, you will begin to see the shapes it makes. Sometimes photographs can help in this respect. Don't be too subtle in your initial attempts.*

How do you draw what can't be seen? With air, the most obvious way is through the medium of clouds. Beautiful groups of water vapour hanging in the air, forming loose shapes, can describe air very effectively, especially when you see a whole procession of clouds stretching back to the horizon, as here. Try to draw a similar skyscape.

*Fire is a really tricky subject. Start with a candle flame before you tackle the flickering flames of a big blaze. You can use photographs for reference, but unless you look closely at a real fire you won't get the feeling of movement or be aware of the variety of shapes.*

*The early Japanese and Chinese artists had very good ways of drawing flames.*

INDIVIDUAL EXPRESSION: PICASSO

It's not just the physical forms in a drawing that can be emphasized by careful manipulation of mark making. Pablo Picasso was a master at communicating the qualities that are not so obvious.

In these drawings copied from his sketchbooks, we see three different ways that marks drawn can both correspond to form and put across more emotional messages than just the form's existence in space. They show how an innovative artist can bend the rules of form to recreate form in a new way.

*This formal head with an enigmatic expression has the appearance of an African carved wooden mask. The drawing derives its power from the way Picasso has handled the simple surface shapes. There is no attempt to produce the subtler gradations of form. Both flat and curved surfaces have simple modulations.*

*Here the outline form is an amazing example of a line doing a lot of work to show movement, emotion and spatial dimension. The particular distortions of the forms convey a feeling of substance in a vivid almost rubbery way. The outline is not formal but wiry and energetic and gives a strong impression of drama and emotion.*

*In this drawing the extreme emotional power is brought out by the clever distortion of the physical shapes of the head without totally losing the effect of human grief. The face seems to be almost dissolving in tears while the hands and teeth create immense tension or anguish.*

Multiple lines of varying length seem to describe the contours of this powerful self-portrait in ink. The technique used is very interesting. Instead of being built up with successive layers of smooth, controlled hatching, the features are drawn with hook-like wiry lines. It's almost as though the artist has drawn directly onto his own face.

Each mark helps to describe the curve of the surface of the facial features. The method is effective because he has not tried to be economical with his lines. The scribbly looking marks used to carefully build up the face give a sort of coarse texture, the effect of which is to increase the feeling of substantiality.

*Here Picasso's style is fairly formal but the scratchy, blotty ink technique seems the result of quick drawing of a rather poised subject with little movement in the head itself. The form is realized extremely economically by the splatter of marks, which give a generalized feeling of solidity without any detail. The artist's approach produces a rather statuesque effect.*

*This head is distorted by its emotional intensity but reads very well as a convincing, solid face and head. Picasso sacrificed accuracy of shape for intensity of feeling and expression. Despite this the head doesn't look unreal and is convincing as a portrayal of powerful emotions in a human face.*

105

### EXERCISES: REALIZING FORM

We now look at the sort of exercises that will help you to begin to see how to realize form with some power. They are all difficult but extremely useful and very satisfying when you begin to make them work. It will require repeated practice, of course, but if you want to be an effective artist there is no avoiding hard work.

*A geometric pattern on a three-dimensional shape is a marvellous exercise for the draughtsman, and shows how a linear device on a surface can describe the form of that surface.*

*This tartan-patterned biscuit tin presents various problems. First is drawing the outline with its elliptical top and cylindrical sides. Secondly is the pattern, which proceeds round the curved edge of the tin, but is shown flat on the lid with some perspective.*

*Draw your outline with the basic pattern inscribed, as shown. Even without the addition of tone or detail, this gives some idea of the roundness of the sides and the flatness of the top.*

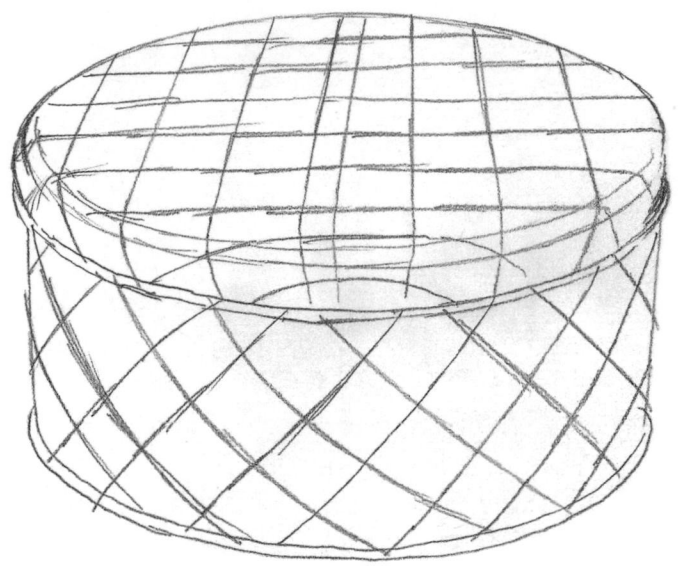

*With this cup and saucer the printed landscape is tricky but interesting. You have to get the details of the printing exactly marked around the curve of the cup, otherwise the cup will look flat. One thing that makes it a bit easier is the fact that some of the details in the pattern are not clear, and so a few mistakes won't necessarily make much difference. The main point to observe is the way the picture reduces in width as it curves around the cup.*

*The general outline gives the basic shape and some indication of the scene around the curved surfaces of both cup and saucer. But it is not until more detail is added with variations in tone that the roundness of the cup becomes evident.*

Another testing exercise is to draw an elderly human face in detail, with all the lines, textures and marks produced by old age. If this is too difficult with a human model (it does take rather a long time and your model may get restless), try drawing from a detailed close-up photograph.

*My drawing of the famous pioneer of photography Alfred Stieglitz was done from a photograph taken by one of his pupils. The detail in that original is brilliant and it is quite a tour-de-force to produce it in pencil or ink. When you try it, you'll find that you have to discipline yourself to produce every mark, every little ripple of flesh and tuft of hair with many small careful marks. Allow yourself plenty of time for this exercise.*

Human anatomy is perhaps the ultimate test for the draughtsman. If you want to excel at portrait drawing it's worth trying to acquire a skull or the use of one from a medical person or another older artist who might probably have access to one. Carefully draw it from different angles in great detail. Don't hurry, be precise, rub out any mistakes, re-draw ruthlessly and don't be satisfied until the drawing is almost photographic in detail.

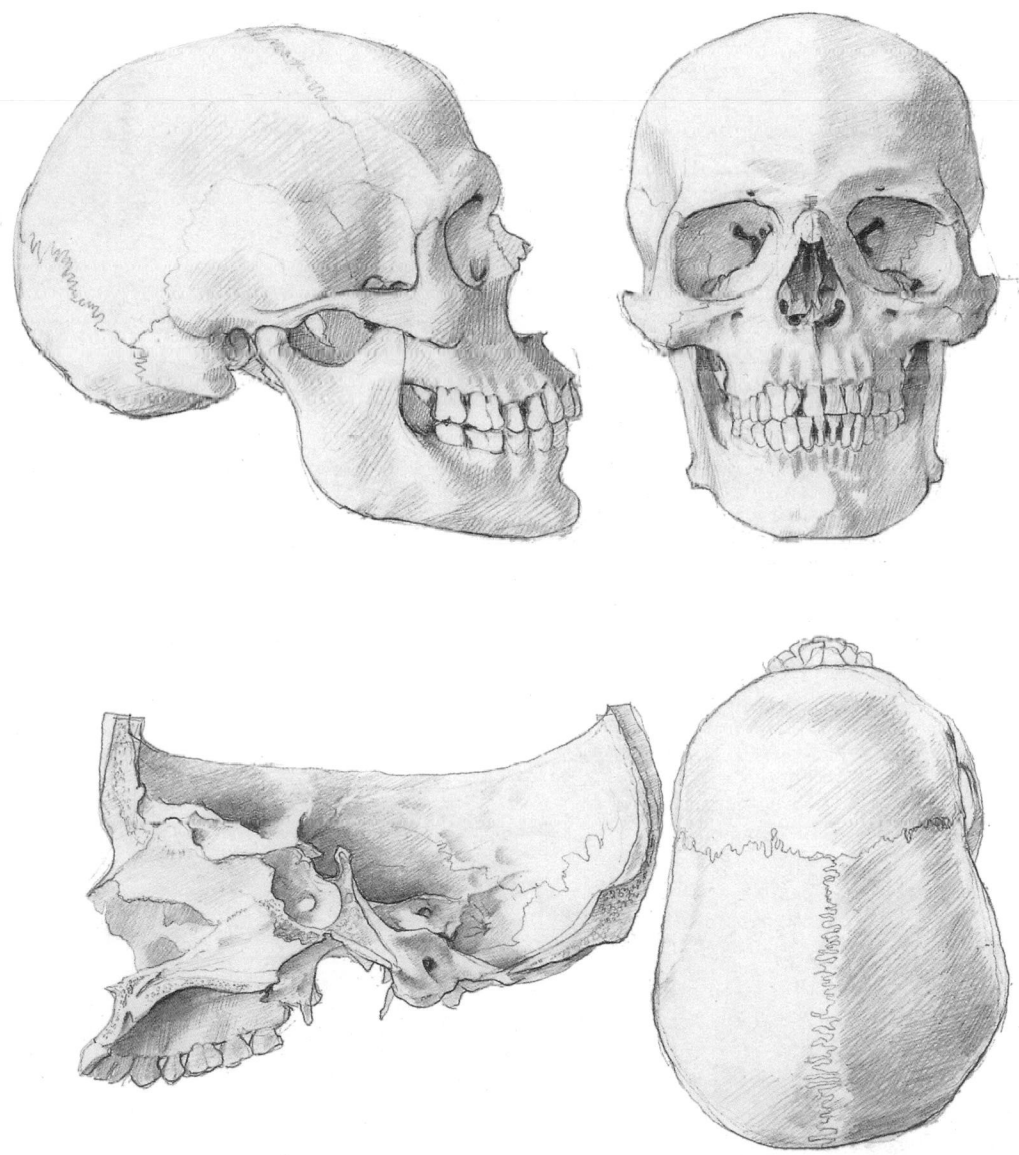

*The example shown is a skull that can be taken apart, although in the complete view the lines of division and the hooks that hold the parts together have been left out. The interior of the skull is a particularly tough challenge because it is unfamiliar to most of us. Keep the drawing precise and clean looking, so that you have no difficulty in seeing where you go wrong. This will make your mistakes easier to correct.*

# Assessing What Works

When we embark on designing and drawing a composition, we instinctively look for the best way to express our experience. If we are drawing directly from nature, we may arrange our subject or our own viewpoint in order to get the best possible view.

We may have to alter the lighting with artificial means or move to a position where the light is more conducive to the effect we wish to produce. The object we choose initially for a still life may not be quite right and we may take some time selecting exactly the right one, polishing it, putting it in different positions and generally organizing the shapes to get the best possible arrangement.

A landscape obviously can't be moved around in fact but most artists adjust parts of it to suit their composition. If a tree is in the 'wrong' place it can be left out of the picture or moved around on the canvas without too much difficulty.

When it comes to portraits, apart from getting the best light, background and profile, you can also look at clothes, hairstyle and accessories to make a difference to your composition. The decision to draw just the head, or head and shoulders, half length or full length can also greatly affect the final result.

Every picture needs careful consideration to bring out its full potential. Sometimes you'll find yourself changing your approach at least once to get a drawing right.

EMPHASIS AND LOCATION

Over the next six pages we look at compositional methods over a range of genres from landscape to still life. The examples included are in different styles and in time extend from the Renaissance to the 20th century. All of them contain devices designed to draw you in and ensure you understand the point of the drawing. The diagrams are included to indicate the narrative flow and show you how the visual attention is attracted from one part of a picture to another.

*In this straightforward narrative (a copy of Taddeo Gaddi's mural of the Annunciation to the shepherds, in Santa Croce, Florence), we see the shepherds reacting to a bright light in the middle of the picture, on a steeply sloping hill with some trees at the top. In the top right-hand corner there's an area of dark sky and an angel floating out of a brightly-lit cloud, indicating to the shepherds. Down at the bottom, there's a small flock of sheep with a dog looking on. The position of the angel swooping downwards and the shepherds angled across the centre of the picture give an unambiguous, almost strip-cartoon version of the story. The brightness of the angel tells us of his importance, and the position and actions of the shepherds mark them out as central characters. Everything else in the picture is just a frame to convince you that this is outdoors and a fitting context for the shepherds.*

This is a copy of a landscape by the 19th-century American painter John Kensett. Rocky wooded banks curve into the picture at about centre-stage. To help the viewer, Kensett has included a group of wildfowl just about to take off from the water. The viewer's attention is immediately grabbed by this movement, and by the detail of the foreground rocks. The inward curve of the water pulls your eyes to the distant mountain peak, rearing up above the surrounding hills. Even the cloudscape helps to frame the rather distinctive mountain, which is on the centre-line. Kensett uses these very precise devices to get us to look at the whole landscape and appreciate the singularity of its features.

The view taken by Degas here is quite extraordinary. We see the upper part of the girl, upside-down as she bends to pick up a sponge. The tub acts as a large, stable base shape and the towel and chair on the floor lead us to the window indicated in the background. Just over half the picture is taken up with this unusual view of quite a simple action and gives an interesting dynamic to the composition. It looks almost as if we have caught sight of this intimate act through an open door. We are close, but somehow detached from the activity, which helps to give the picture a statuesque quality.

Degas has found a very effective way of creating interest just by the arrangement on the canvas. Ordinary, but extra-ordinary.

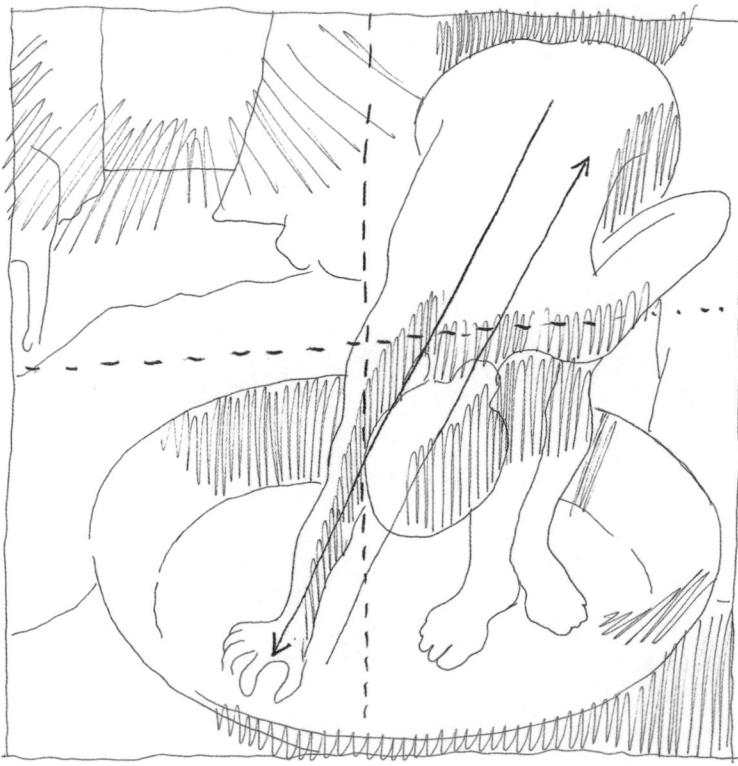

*Like Degas, the American painter Edward Hopper was keen to depict everyday life as he saw it. In this picture, there is no dramatic situation, and not one figure, although the open door suggests that someone may be nearby. The composition is very still, despite the waves on the near surface of the sea glimpsed through the door.*

*It seems we are looking at a depiction of a timeless summer's day, as experienced in a house by the sea, bright, still, and balanced by the shadow and the light. Despite the simplicity, there is a touch of expectancy, as though someone will soon step into the space. The composition is attention grabbing and oddly peaceful at one and the same time.*

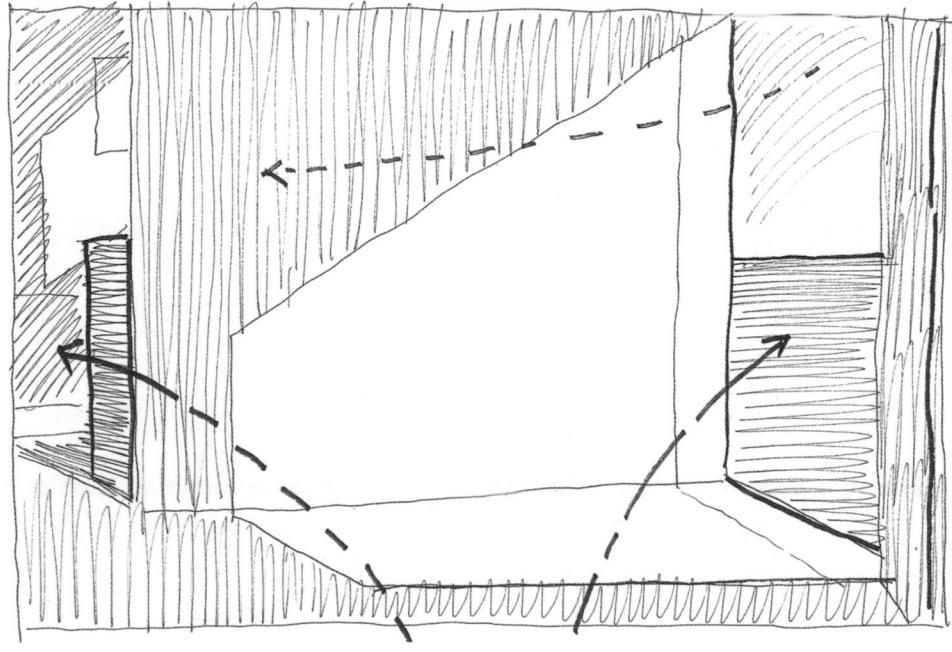

The Spaniard Juan Sánchez Cotán found an effective, dramatic way to arrange and light quite ordinary objects in this still life. The dark background, the dangling fruit and cabbage, the cut melon and aubergine on the edge of the ledge produce an almost musical sweep of shapes, all highlighted dramatically.

Would Cotán have seen fruit and vegetables arranged like this in late 16th/early 17th century Spain, or did he create this design himself specifically for his painting? Either way, the arrangement is very effective and a brilliant way of injecting drama into quite ordinary subject matter.

We return to Degas to finish this section. We are in a 19th-century dance studio, with a master continuing to instruct his pupils as they rest. All the attention is on the master with his stick, which he uses to beat out the rhythm. The perspective takes you towards him. The way the girls are arranged further underlines his importance. The beautiful casual grouping of the frothy dancers, starting with the nearest and swinging around the edge of the room to the other side, neatly frames the master's figure. He holds the stage.

SYMBOLS AND ASSOCIATIONS

The face is the most obvious barometer of human feeling. However, it is possible to show moods or emotions in other ways – the position or movement of a body can be powerful indicators, for example – and not just rely on the obvious. An even more interesting approach is to let nature be a mirror, and transfer human emotions onto natural features. Consider the examples you will see over the following pages.

*The head of Michelangelo's 'David' in Florence symbolizes the defiance of that city towards the hostile autocracies by which it was surrounded. A small but rich and inventive state, Florence was a free republic whose citizens and guilds had a voice in government. Michelangelo's statue of the shepherd boy who kills the giant warrior Goliath is a powerful symbol of the independence of that city and its determination to protect its status.*

*A breaking wave used as a metaphor for exhilaration is not new. In this example the impact might have been greater and the feeling of exhilaration emphasized if there was a figure of a surfer under the wave.*

*A beautiful still lake with reflections and calm skies seen in morning or evening light gives the feeling of serenity, especially with the small native boat being propelled smoothly, without haste, across the surface of the water.*

*This image symbolizes serenity partly by situation and partly by technique. The artist has made efforts to excise any disturbances from the picture.*

119

EXTREMES OF EXPRESSIVITY

Here we look at three very different ways of being expressive. The face as a measure of emotional expression is an obvious way to show the mood of a picture by association, but as you will see from these drawings, there are faces and faces. The galloping horse and jockey is a more abstract example of how to produce a visceral response.

 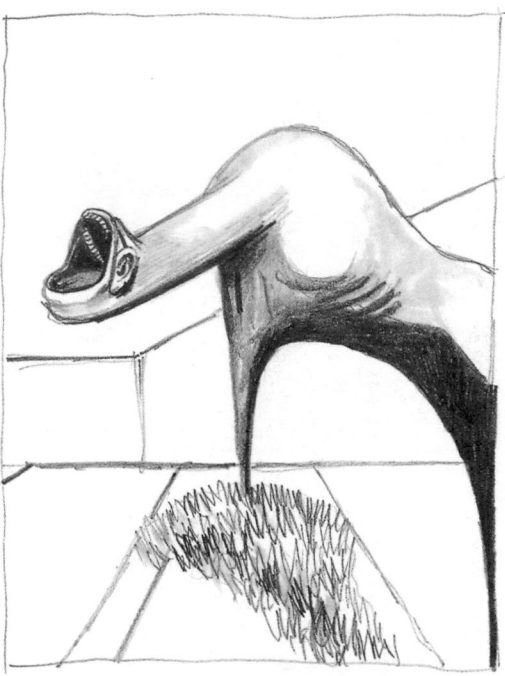

*Francis Bacon's figures at the base of his 'Three Studies for a Crucifixion' seem to represent a raw, blind fury or perhaps even revenge. Bacon himself identified the figures as representations of the Furies who, in classical myth, torment evil-doers before and after death. Although not classical studies, they seem to apply to classical myth.*

*Happiness*　　　　　　　*Intensity*

This image is an attempt to convey the idea of speed. The racehorse and jockey are glimpsed pounding down a course, dirt flying up behind. The idea is reinforced by how the image is drawn: the rider with stirrups short, behind raised out of the saddle, the horse's neck stretched, tail streaming, powerful legs bunched up to take the next stride. The economical use of lines also suggests that the image is moving past us at speed.

*Satisfaction*

*Despair*

The gentle lyricism in Marc Chagall's drawings could not be further from the feeling of unease, almost revulsion, that we met in Francis Bacon's work. Chagall used a charming, playful way of drawing in much of his work. Most of his paintings have either lyrical or joyful associations in their design, colour or the technique he employed. He chose to portray the magical quality of life and touch our emotions in subtle ways.

*Chagall's picture of the circus (opposite) has an almost childlike sense of fun and enjoyment, emphasized by the rather naive handling of the drawing. Everybody seems to be having a good time, even the clowns and acrobats, but without becoming disorderly or too exuberant.*

*The picture of a poet reclining (above), produces an air of gentle melancholy. This is partly due to the rather odd position of the figure, which is lying along the base of the picture, and partly due to the dark trees and almost ghostly toy-like animal shapes grazing in the background.*

Edvard Munch's 'The Scream' is an expressive and subjective picture that is now read as a general statement about ourselves, particularly the angst and despair experienced by modern man.

The area depicted in the painting was favoured by suicides, and was close to slaughter-houses and a lunatic asylum where Munch's sister was incarcerated.

The artist wrote of the setting: 'the clouds were turning blood red. I sensed a scream passing through nature.'

The original painting has a blood-red sunset in steaks of red and yellow, with dark blues and greens and blacks in the large dark areas to the right. The swirling lines and skull-like head with its unseeing eyes and open mouth produce a very strong effect.

*'The Kiss', by Viennese artist Gustav Klimt, shows the power of desire in a very graphic manner. The heavily ornamented clothing, while revealing very little of the flesh of the lovers, increases the tactile quality in the work. The firm grasp of the man's hands on the girl's face and head, her hands clinging to his neck and wrist, and her ecstatic expression tell us of the force and intensity of their sexual desire.*

### Expressing Yourself

All of the images we have looked at in this section try to convey to the viewer a feeling or idea that is not being expressed in words. Indeed, in many of the examples, it would be very difficult to express precisely or concisely the effect they have. One picture can be worth a thousand words. It is not easy to get across a concept by visual means, but with a bit of practice it is possible. Try to produce such an image yourself. You can use or adapt the approaches or methods we've been looking at. When you've produced something, show it to your friends and listen to their reactions. If your attempt is suggestive of the idea you wanted to convey, they will quickly be able to confirm it.

# *Studying Life from Nature*

Throughout history artists have acquired their basic vocabulary through detailed observation of the natural world. Even if the final result in a work is abstracted or manipulated extensively, it is informed by a study of nature.

If you want to make your work convincing, look at the created world around you. Don't view it exclusively through the mediums of photography, television or video. Personal experience will lend a power and knowledge to your work that not only informs you as the artist but also the reviewers of your work. This is very apparent when you look at the work of an artist who has actually experienced at first hand the things he draws. It is also pretty clear to the observant viewer when an artist is only working from second-hand sources, because their drawings tend to lack power.

To achieve realism in your drawings, start by observing plants in detail; even if you live in an urban environment you should be able to find a wide variety to study. You can then move on to animals and human beings. Don't worry about posing them to begin with; just observing them will pay off if you are reasonably systematic about recording what you see so that it remains in your memory.

Observe, too, the effects of light falling on people and objects and how the effects of distance and weather create interesting changes in subject matter. Everything you see and note can be used to advantage in your work. All you need is the time and opportunity to take it all in.

PLANTS AND FLOWERS

The essential structure of a plant is not difficult to see if you study it for a time. Take a group of leaved plants: you soon notice how one type will have leaves in clusters that spring up at the points of the leaves, whereas in another the leaves will hang down around a central point. Some plants have stalks coming off the branches evenly at the same point, others have the stalks staggered alternately down the length of the stem. Once you are familiar with a plant's characteristic shape and appearance, you will begin to notice it or similar properties in other plants. Observation will lend verisimilitude to even your most casual sketches. Look at the examples of plants on this spread, noting their similarities and differences.

*The appearance of the Tulip is very formal and upright, with its closed cup-like flower and long stiff stalk and leaves.*

*The Sedum has a beautiful spiralling arrangement of leaves that curves up into a dish-like form. Rain must fill up the hollow of the leaf and run down the stalk to water the plant's roots.*

*The leaves of the Hydrangea come off the stem at opposite sides to each other in a symmetrical arrangment. Notice how they curve upwards and then how the curve is reversed, with the upper surface bulging out towards the tip.*

The easiest way to study plants is by sketching them as often as you can. Before you begin to draw, look at the plant closely: at the bloom (if there is one), and note how the leaves grow off the stalk. Look at it from above, to see the leaves radiating out from the centre; and from the side to see the different appearance of the leaf shapes as they project towards you, away from you and to each side as they spiral round the stem. Note the texture of the leaves, and how it compares with that of other plants.

When your subject is a flower-head, draw it from an angle, where you can see the pattern of the petals around the centre of the blossom or a profile view of them. Notice the texture of the petals and how the centre of the flower contrasts with the main part of the bloom. When you draw the flower, include a leaf or two to show the contrast in tone or texture between the leaf and the petals.

*The blossom of the Camellia looks so fragile and contrasts beautifully with the solid, perfect shape of the leaves.*

The more you draw plants, the more details you will notice and the broader your vocabulary will become. After you have been drawing plants for a while, try drawing one from memory. This type of exercise helps to sustain the image that your senses have recorded and will help you to memorize shapes and textures. You will find drawing from memory gives a simpler result than drawing from life, because you tend to leave out unnecessary details. The ability to produce a conventional shape easily without reference is a great asset. Once you have this ability, you will be able to bring a greater sense of realism to your drawings.

*Here we have two blooms from the same plant (a Clematis) at different stages of its growth. The difference is quite dramatic.*

*The Clematis captured as it is just opening, with its smooth looking petals hanging down.*

*The fully open bloom, centre showing to the sun. By this stage the edges of the petals are quite crinkly.*

## PLANTS: GROWTH PATTERNS

Nature offers so much variety, as you will discover once you start studying it in earnest. In the examples shown on this spread you will find three very different effects in as many examples.

Compare them, and note the differences you observe. You will find these patterns of growth fascinating as you investigate them more fully and extend your experience.

*The blossom of the Cherry clings closely to the dark stiff, almost spiky branches.*

*The habit of the Stewartia is to gracefully hold its leaves and small blossoms away from the main branch.*

*The acorns and leaves of the Oak jut out from their stalk.*

**Exercising Eye and Hand**

It cannot be over-emphasized that, in order to become a proficient artist, you need to get into the habit of drawing every day. If you do, very soon you will become adept at handling almost any shape. Keep trying different objects, and be adventurous, trying more difficult subjects once you've got somewhere with easier ones.

TREES: GROWTH PATTERNS

Drawing trees has always been a favourite pastime of artists even when a commission is not involved. Trees are such splendid plants and often very beautiful but they are not that easy to draw well.

Before you begin, consider the sketches on this page.

*Have a look at the bigger trees in your local park or, if you're lucky enough to live out of town, in your local woods and hedgerows. Notice the strength of the root structure when it is evident above ground, like great gnarled hands clutching at the earth. Next, look closely at the bark on the main trunk and branches, then at its texture. Make sketches of what you see.*

*Oak*

*Beech*

*Horse Chestnut*

## SHAPES

Getting a feel for the whole shape of the tree you want to draw is important. Often the best way to approach this is to draw in a vague outline of the main shape first. Then you need to divide this up into the various clumps of leaves and give some indication of how the main branches come off the trunk and stretch out to the final limit of the shape.

Of course, if your subject is a deciduous tree in winter the network of branches will provide the real challenge. The branches are a maze of shapes and success can only be achieved if you manage to analyse the main thrust of their growth and observe how the smaller branches and twigs hive off from the main structure. Luckily, trees don't move about too much, and so are excellent 'sitters'.

*These three types of deciduous tree present very different shapes and textures. Discover for yourself how different they are by finding an example of each, observing each one closely and then spending time drawing the various shapes. Note the overall shapes and the branch patterns – see accompanying drawings.*

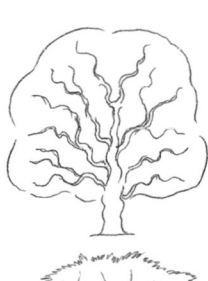
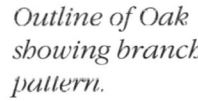

*Outline of Oak showing branch pattern.*

*Outline of Beech showing branch pattern.*

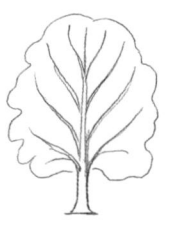

*Outline of Horse Chestnut showing branch pattern.*

133

## TREES: PATTERNS

Drawing branches can prove problematical for even experienced artists. The exercise below is designed to get you used to drawing them. Don't worry about rendering the foliage precisely, just suggest it.

*I drew this large tree in spring when its leaves were not completely out. It was an ideal subject for demonstrating the intricate tracery of branches because of its position on a wooded slope, which meant that its foliage was largely restricted to the tops of the branches.*

*When you first look at a tree like this it is not at all easy to see how to pick out each branch. One useful approach is to draw the main stems without initially worrying whether they cross in front of or behind another branch. Only when you draw a branch that crosses the first one need you make a note of whether it crosses behind or in front.*

*As you add more branches, the depth and space within the tree will become apparent. Ignore any leaves except as vague rounded shapes; you can add them afterwards, if you want.*

When seen in silhouette every tree produces a distinctive web pattern. The point of this next exercise is to try to put in as much detail as you can, including leaves (if there are any) and twigs. To achieve this you have to draw the silhouette at a reasonable size; i.e. as large as possible on an A4 sheet of paper.

One of the best varieties to choose for this exercise is a Hawthorn, or May, tree. Its twisting, prickly branches and twigs make a really dense mesh, which can be very dramatic. Try drawing it in ink, which will force you to take chances on seeing the shapes accurately immediately; you are committing yourself by not being able to rub out. It won't matter too much if you are slightly inaccurate in detail as long as the main pattern is clear to you.

Winter is the best time to do this exercise, although the worst time to be drawing outdoors. You could, at a pinch, carefully copy a good photograph of such a tree in silhouette, but this would not be such a good test or teach you as much.

*This silhouette is rather as you would see it against the sunlight and makes an extraordinary, intricate pattern. There is no problem with the branches being behind or in front of other branches, as there was in the example on the previous page.*

LOOKING AT THE HEAD
When a person is presented as a subject, the obvious approach is to sit them down in a good light, look at them straight on and begin to draw. However, the obvious does not always produce the best or most accurate result. If you concentrate solely on getting a likeness of a subject, you miss out on the most important and most interesting aspects of portrait drawing.

The aim of this next exercise is to encourage you to look at the head as a whole. There's much more to the head than mere features, as you will discover if you look at it from many different angles, excluding the obvious one. Take a look at the two drawings shown below.

*The head leaning back. This angle gives a clear view of underneath the chin and the nose, both areas we rarely notice ordinarily. Seen from this angle the person is no longer instantly recognizable, because the forehead has disappeared and the hair is mostly behind the head.*

*Notice the large area of neck and chin, and the nostrils, which are coming towards the viewer. See how the nose sticks up out of the main shape of the head. When seen at this angle the ears seem to be in a very odd position, and their placement can be quite tricky. Notice that the eyes no longer dominate the head.*

*The head looking downwards. This allows a good view of the top of the head, which tends to dominate the area in view. Notice how the eyes disappear partly under the brow; how the eyelashes stick out more noticeably; how the nose tends to hide the mouth and the chin almost disappears.*

Once you have looked at various heads of different people you will begin to classify them as whole shapes or structures and not just as faces. This approach teaches that although there are many different faces, many heads share a similar structure. The individual differences won't seem half so important once you realize that there are only a few types of heads and each of us has a type that conforms to one of these.

If you want to fully investigate this phenomenon, get your models to pose with their heads at as many different angles as possible, and explore the structure of what you see. You can use the poses I have provided or create your own.

*Mostly when we look at people our attention is too easily captured by the appearance of their eyes and mouth, because these are the principal determiners of facial expression. Once you ignore the facial expression, you*

*will begin to notice in more detail the shapes of the features. When drawing the head, focus your attention on the forehead, jaw, cheekbones and nose. They give the face its structure and thereby its character.*

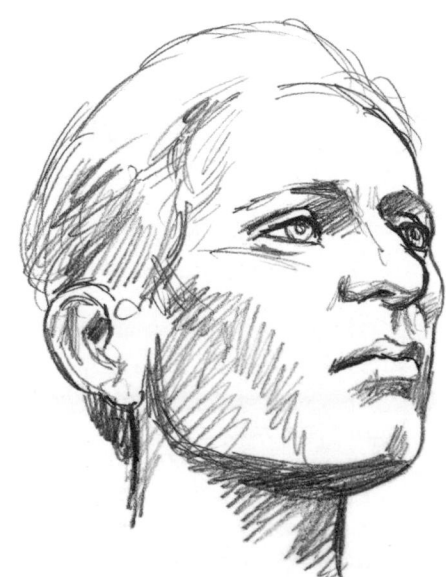

FIGURE DRAWING: FACIAL FEATURES

The features are worth sketching many times from more than one angle until you begin to understand exactly what happens with every part. You can do this quite easily by just moving your point of view while the model remains still. However, sometimes the head needs to be tilted, the eyes moved and the lips flexed to get a better idea of the way these features change. Time spent working on this now means that your drawing will take on a new conviction in the future and you will begin to notice subtleties that were perhaps less obvious to you before.

### Eyes

 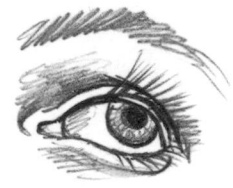

*You will quickly notice that the eye looking up and the eye looking down are vastly different in expression.*

*The eye seen from below looking up, and seen from above looking up, add extra permutations to the variety of shapes.*

*See how the eye seen from the side gives a much clearer view of the ball shape and how the lens seems to sit on the surface of the eyeball, the pupil appearing to recede into the shape of the lens.*

*When the eyes look down the upper eye-lid takes on the shape of the eyeball it is covering and the open part of the eye forms a sort of crescent shape. The upper lid increases and the lower one creases rather.*

### Ears

*Not many people can move their ears, so they are less of a problem than any other feature. Their convolutions are unfamiliar because rarely do we look at them. Seen from the front or back most ears are inconspicuous. The shapes of ears do vary, but have several main shapes in common. Look at these examples.*

## Nose

The nose doesn't have a great deal of expression although it can be wrinkled and the nostrils flared. However, its shape often presents great difficulty to beginning students. Drawing the nose from in front gives the artist a lot of work to describe the contours without making it look monstrous.

*A clear dark shadow on one side helps a lot when drawing the nose from the front.*

*If you want to reduce the projection of the nose, a full facing light will tend to flatten it in terms of visible contours.*

*However, from the side it is clear how it is shaped. The nostrils are a well defined part of the nose and from the front are the best part to concentrate on to infer the shape of the rest of the features.*

## Mouth

The mobility of the mouth ensures that next to the eyes it is the most expressive part of the face. Although there are many different types of mouth, these can be reduced to a few types once you begin to investigate them.

*First of all, draw from the front, followed by three-quarter views from left and right, and then from the side.*

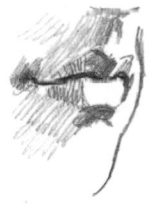

*Next draw from slightly above and slightly below; this gives you the basic shape of the mouth. Note the edge of the lips; some parts project and give a definite edge to the lip. On other parts the colour of the lip is in the same plane as the surface of the face.*

*When you have a fairly clear idea of the basic form of the mouth, see what happens when it opens. First, try drawing it slightly open from at least two views (front and side) and then wider, and then wide open. Notice what happens to the lips when the mouth is open, how they stretch, and how creases appear in the cheeks either side and below.*

*Next, look at the mouth smiling; first with the mouth shut, and then more open.*

## PERSPECTIVE VIEWS: LEGS

One of the most difficult problems with drawing the human figure (or any other figure for that matter) arises when the body or the limbs of the figure being drawn are foreshortened by perspective; an example might be when a leg or arm is projecting towards your viewpoint. Instead of the expected shape of the limb you get an oddly distorted proportion that the mind often wants to correct. However, if you are going to draw accurately, you have to discount what the mind is telling you and observe directly, measuring if necessary to make sure that these rather odd proportions are adhered to. In this way, a limb seen from the end on (see illustrations) will carry real conviction.

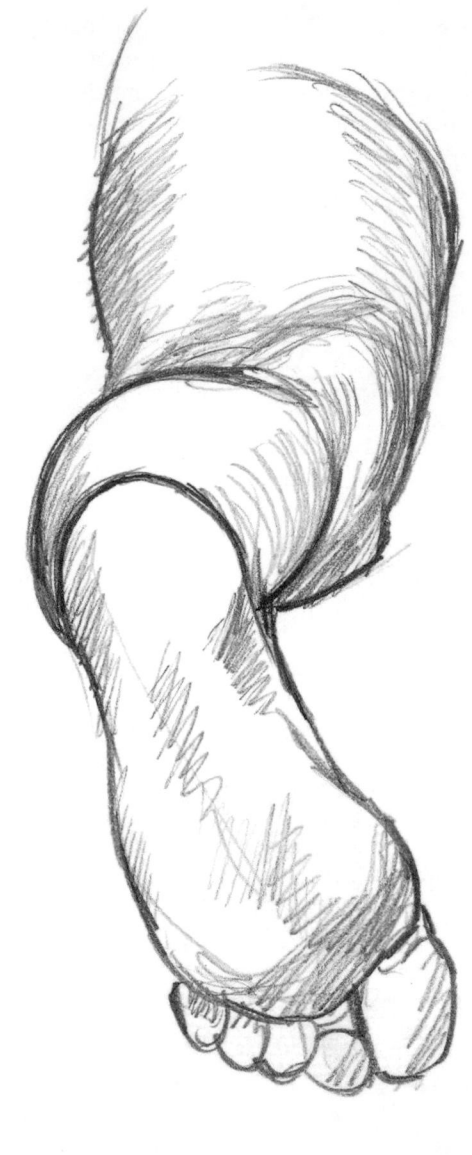

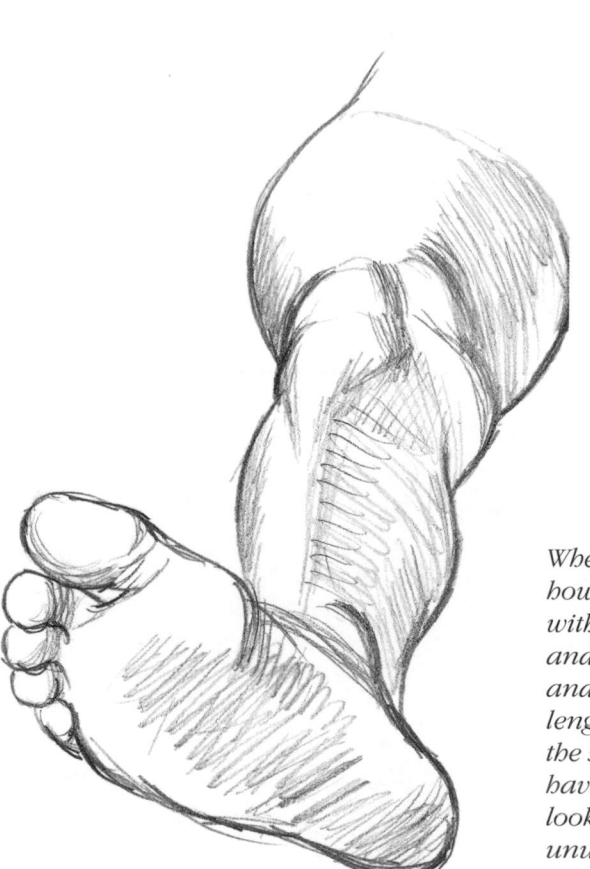

*When viewing the leg from the foot end, notice how large the sole of foot looks in comparison with the apparent length of the leg. The muscles and the knee project outwards, their roundness and angularity very pronounced, while their length is reduced to almost nil. If you observe the shapes produced by this view, you shouldn't have any problem. Don't tell yourself that it looks wrong, because it's not; it's just an unusual point of view.*

PERSPECTIVE VIEWS: ARMS

The same situation is evident with the arm as with the leg. In this case the size of the hand will often appear outrageously large, practically obscuring the rest of the arm. Seen from this end-on perspective, the bulge of any muscle or bone structure becomes a much more important feature describing the shape of the arm. Instead of a long, slender shape which we recognize as 'arm', we see a series of bumps, rounded shapes, closely stacked up against each other, so that the length of the arm is minimal and the round section of the arm shape becomes what you see and draw.

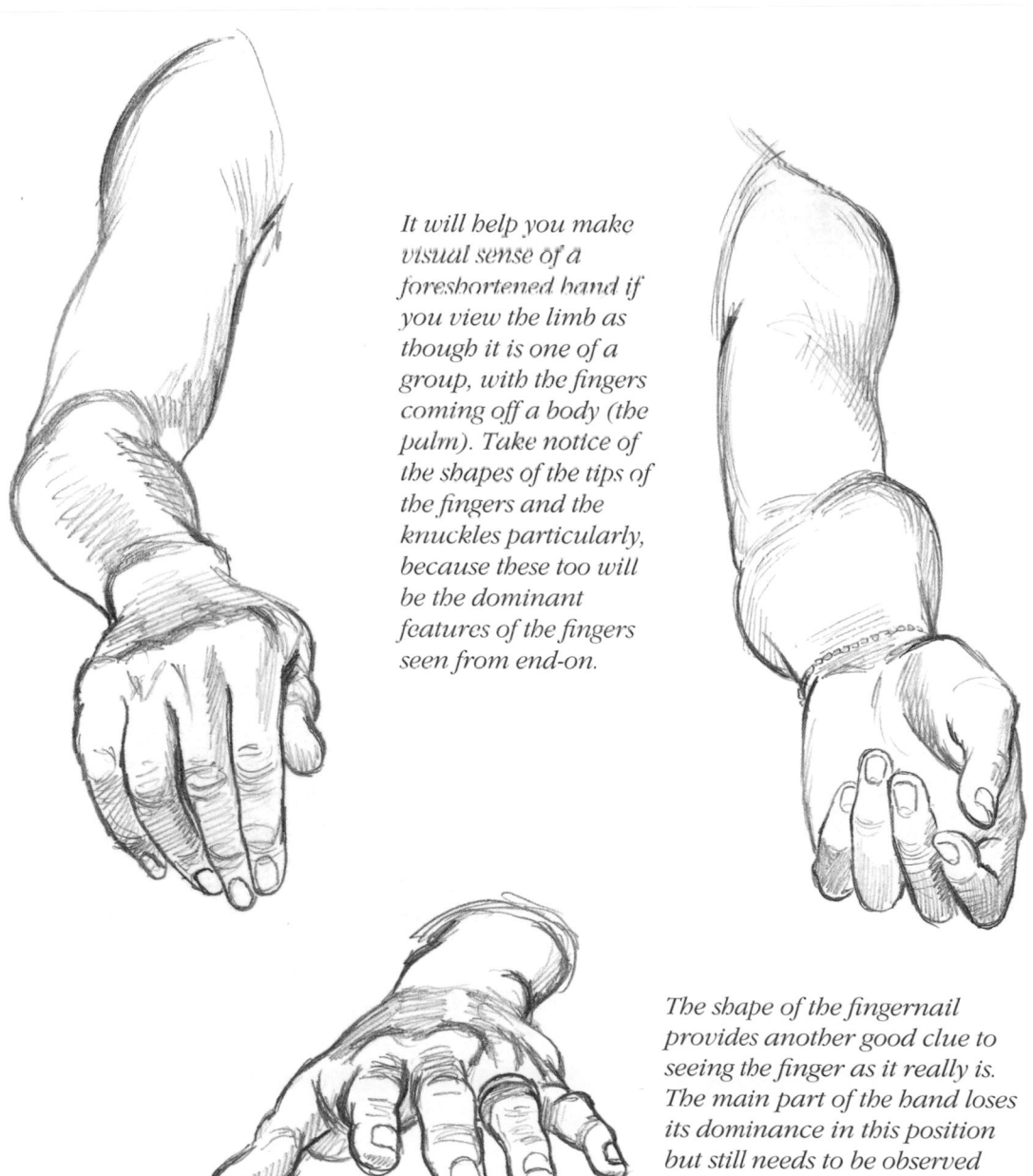

*It will help you make visual sense of a foreshortened hand if you view the limb as though it is one of a group, with the fingers coming off a body (the palm). Take notice of the shapes of the tips of the fingers and the knuckles particularly, because these too will be the dominant features of the fingers seen from end-on.*

*The shape of the fingernail provides another good clue to seeing the finger as it really is. The main part of the hand loses its dominance in this position but still needs to be observed accurately.*

HANDS

Hands are relatively easy to study, especially if you use your own as models. If you equip yourself with a mirror you should be able to look at them from almost any angle. Of course, it will also be necessary to look at the hands of an older or younger person and also one of the opposite sex. You will find there are significant differences in shape depending on age and sex.

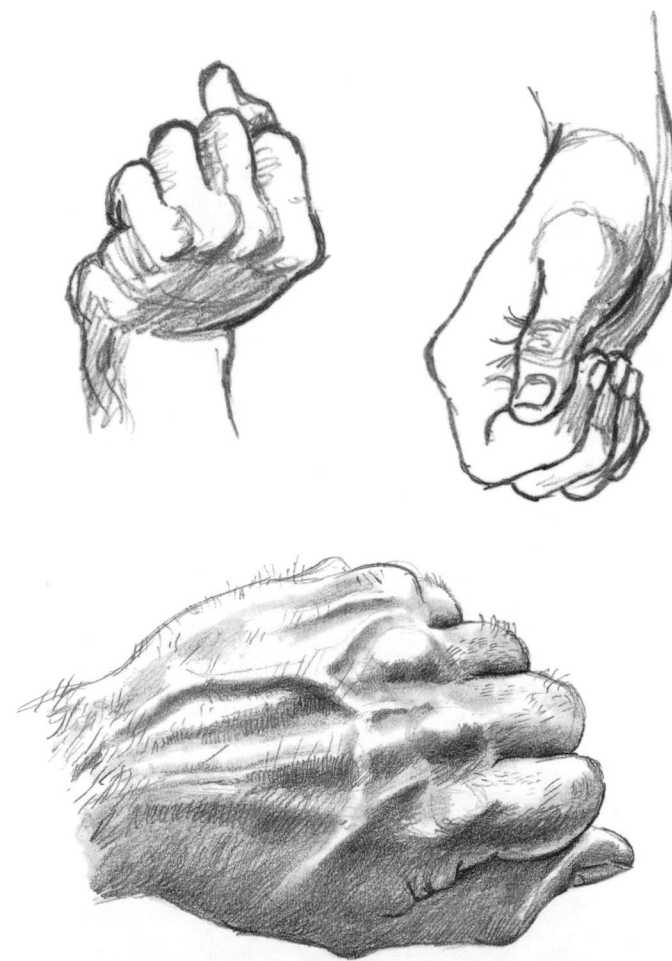

*Always start off by observing the main structure of the hand, based on the bones underneath, and then carefully observe the hardness or softness of the flesh and skin.*

*The back of the hand gives the clearest indication of the age of your model. Older hands have more protuberant veins and looser, more wrinkled skin around the knuckles. The hands of small children seem smooth all over.*

## DIFFERENCES IN MUSCULATURE

All human bodies have a tendency towards either a harder or softer muscularity, and both characteristics can make quite a difference to the effect of your finished picture. Look at the examples shown here.

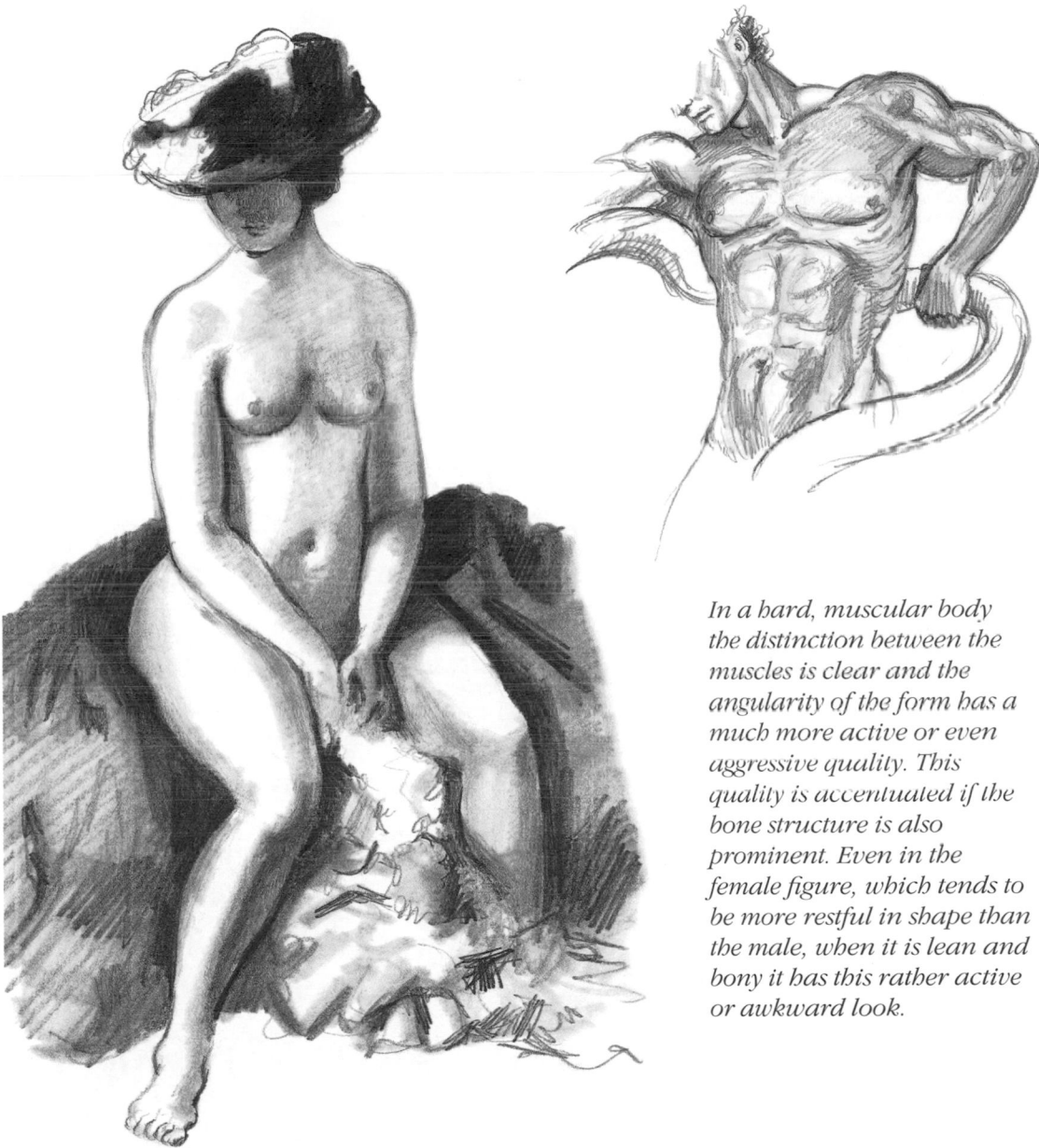

*In a hard, muscular body the distinction between the muscles is clear and the angularity of the form has a much more active or even aggressive quality. This quality is accentuated if the bone structure is also prominent. Even in the female figure, which tends to be more restful in shape than the male, when it is lean and bony it has this rather active or awkward look.*

*A soft, undulating figure, where the differences between the jointing parts of the muscles are not very obvious, gives a very smooth, rounded appearance to the form, and this has an effect of calmness or weightiness. When the flesh is too heavy the weight tends to look more awkward and so is less indicative of calm. Generally, though, softer bodies look more restful than harder ones.*

## FIGURES: COMPOSITION

When it comes to producing drawings of several figures in a composition, the biggest problem, assuming you have had enough experience of drawing live figures, is the way that parts of one figure disappear behind parts of another. Sometimes it is easy to get the composition wrong and end up with an awkward-looking arrangement.

*In this simple group of two lovers embracing, compositional success has been achieved by ensuring that the figures combine in such a way that they appear to melt together, with the limbs entwining in a natural way.*

*When you are posing a picture it is important to be alert to the position of a hand or leg looking awkward. If this happens, try to find the position that is most likely to show the warmth of feeling or the beauty of the pose. In the example shown, notice how the heads relate in such a way that they almost obliterate us, the viewers, from the view.*

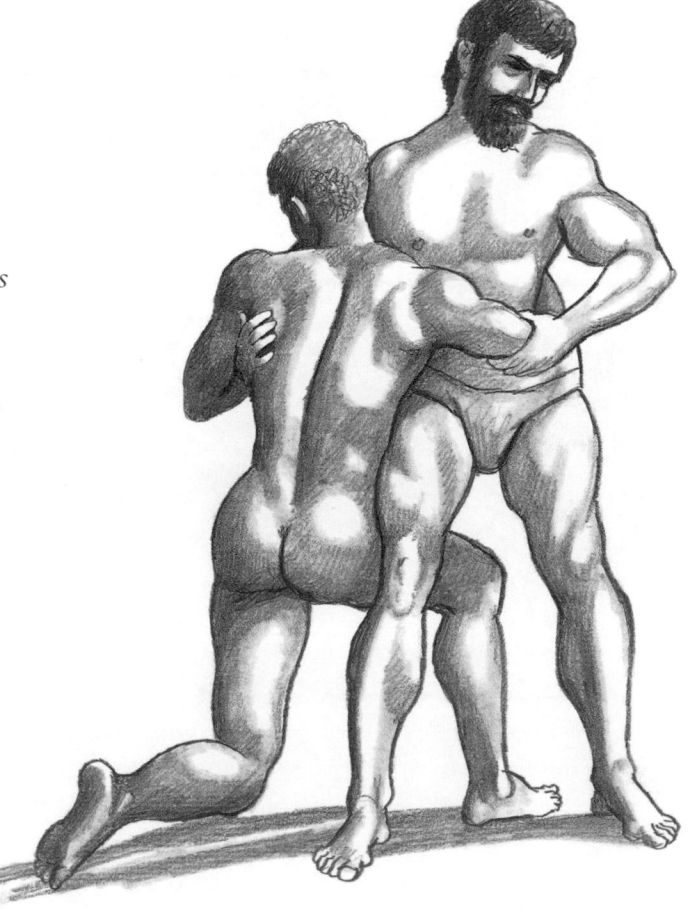

*This drawing of two Victorian wrestlers is based on a painting by William Etty. One figure is being forced down, but the standing figure looks as though it might be levered across from the lower figure's knee. The main point of this picture is the forcefulness of the action and whether the two figures seem to be struggling against each other. Perhaps Leonardo or Michelangelo would give us more expression of the struggle, but nevertheless this composition does evoke the effort that these two strong men are making. The link between the two figures is central to the success of the work.*

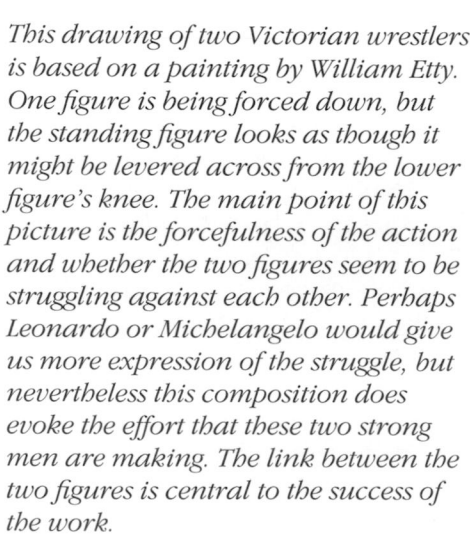

Two hands clasped give a similar problem to entwined figures in a larger composition. You'll find them easier to tackle if you try to see them as if you were looking at a whole figure.

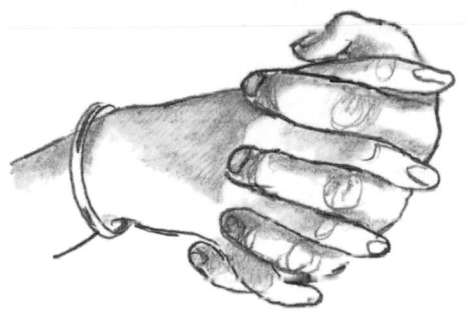

In this copy of a Caravaggio, the body of Christ is being lifted into its tomb. This event is made interesting and dramatic by the arrangement of the figures and their relationship. The movement of the figure carrying the dead body contrasts starkly with the inert corpse. The limpness of the legs of the dead man contrasts with the gnarled knotty legs of the carrier. The shape made by the man's encircling arms and the bent over figure with his arm under the shoulders and back of Christ are quite complex. Even the strands of grave cloth and the cloak of the younger carrier help to define the activity.

I have omitted from my copy the group of three mourning women which is in the original, because they are not actively engaged in carrying the body.

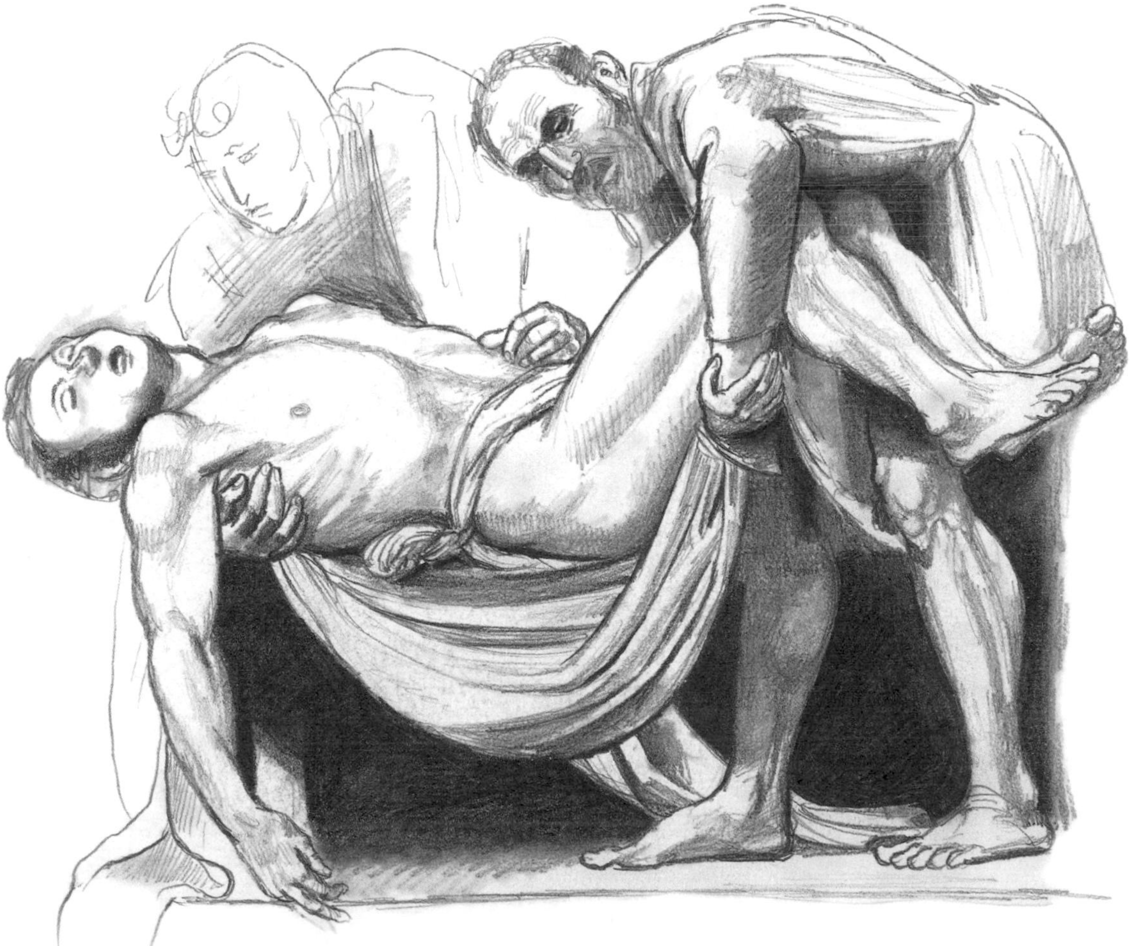

## CLOSE UPS OF JOINTS

When studying the human skeleton or its bones and musculature, it is a good idea at some stage to home in on one joint and draw it in exact detail. Concentrate on making it as anatomically correct as you can, as though you were a draughtsman preparing a specimen for the medical profession.

This sort of detailed study is very effective in making us see more when we come to draw the human figure from life, and it can inform our drawing enormously. There is no substitute for this approach if you want your drawings to carry conviction. The knowledge gained by it seems to go through the hand into the mind, and when we draw it seems to come out again to inform the viewer, even if he has never seen it himself in real life. This is why the works of the old master-draughtsmen still carry so much power.

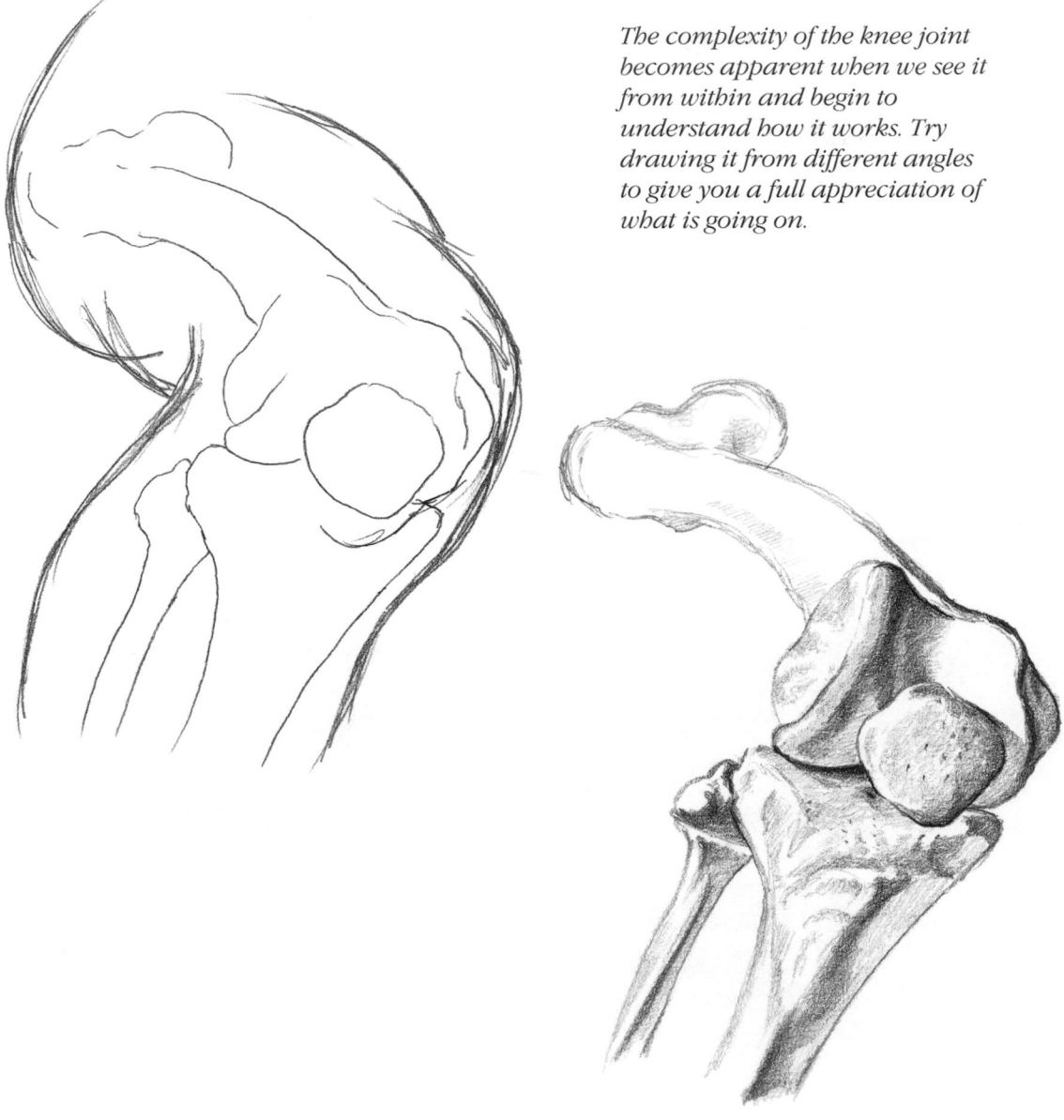

*The complexity of the knee joint becomes apparent when we see it from within and begin to understand how it works. Try drawing it from different angles to give you a full appreciation of what is going on.*

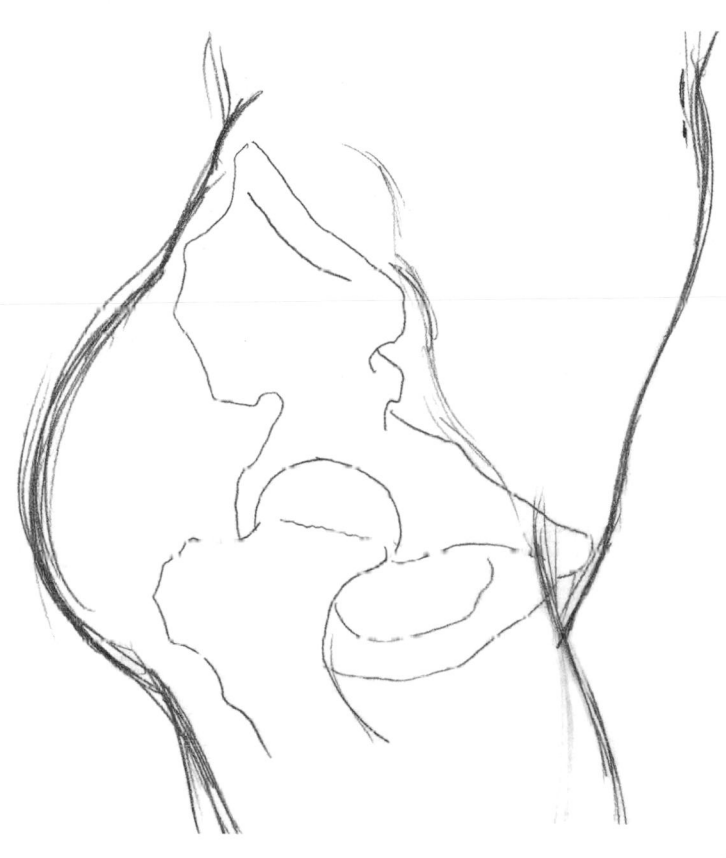

*The hip-joint, where the pelvis and thigh bone rotate, ball in cup, so to speak, has extraordinary flexibility, as detailed study will reveal.*

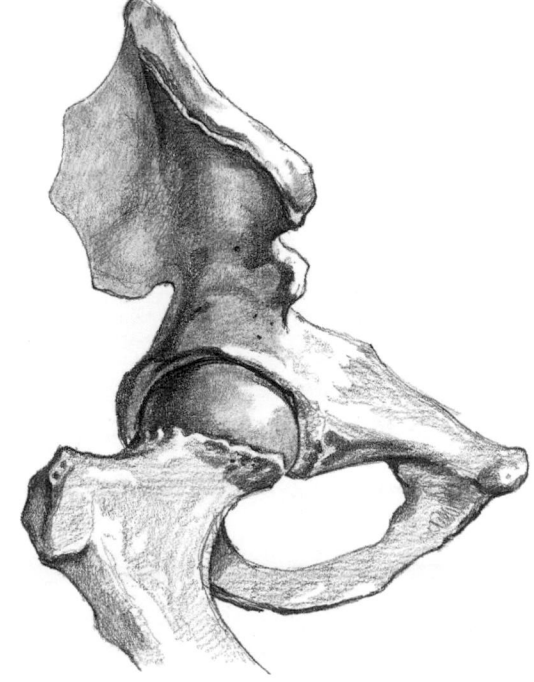

CLOTHING AND MOVEMENT

Next we look at clothing and how the movement and actions of the wearer affect it. Of course, how an item of clothing behaves will depend on the type of material of which it is made, so you need to be aware of different properties and characteristics and how to render them realistically in various situations.

*A very simple movement of a girl pulling on her jacket produces all sorts of wrinkles and creases in a rather stiff material. The creases at the bend of the arm are relatively soft, however, which generally indicates an expensive material. As the American Realist painter Ben Shahn, remarked, 'There is a big difference between the wrinkles in a $200 suit and a $1,000 suit.' (This was said in the 1950s, so the prices are relative.) What he was remarking on was the fact that more expensive materials fold and crease less markedly and the creases often fall out afterwards, whereas a suit made of cheaper materials has papery looking creases that remain after the cloth was straightened.*

*The clothing worn by this figure (right) hangs softly in folds and suggests a lightweight material such as cotton. The shape of the upper body is easily seen but the trousers are thick enough to disguise the shape of the leg.*

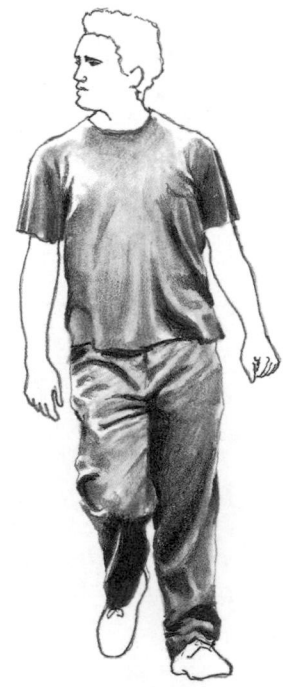

*This drawing (left) was made from a picture of a dancer playing a part. The baggy cotton-like material has a slightly bobbly texture and its looseness in the sleeves and legs serves to exaggerate his movements. Both the action and costume reinforce the effect of floppy helplessness.*

*A bit of clever posing by a fashion photographer was responsible for the original from which the drawing below was made. The model was actually photographed lying on the floor with the dress spread out to make it look as though she was moving in a smooth-flowing dance. The photograph was taken in the 1930s, before the benefits of high-speed cameras and film, and represents an imaginative way round a technical problem. It proves that you can cheat the eye.*

*The sturdy girl dancer above is swirling a length of thin, light silken material. The movement of the hair and garment tell you quite a bit about her movements and the materiality of the hair and cloth.*

Here are three drawings of different types of clothing showing vastly different effects of folds and creases, mainly due to the nature of the material used in each case.

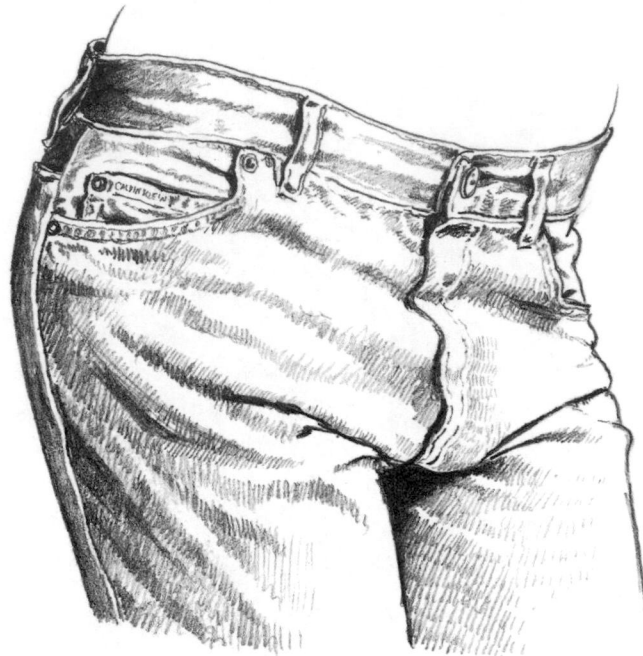

*These jeans, made of tough hard-wearing cotton, crease easily and characteristically, and the creases remain even when the cloth is moved.*

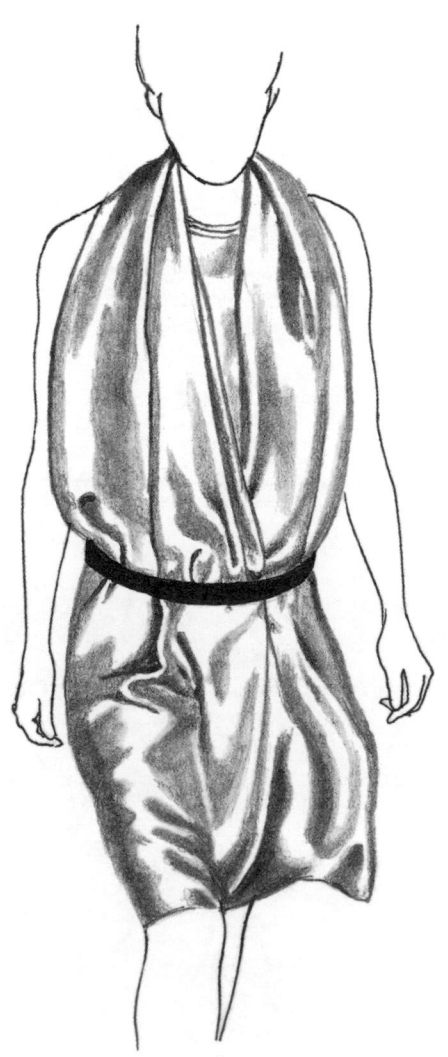

*A couture garment made of heavy satin and tailored to keep the folds loose and mainly vertical. The movement is not extreme and so the weight and smoothness of the material ensure an elegant effect.*

*When you come to draw this type of material be sure to get a strong contrast between dark and light to capture the bright reflective quality of the garment.*

*The raincoat sleeve shown below is similar in character to our first example: a stiffish material but one made to repel water and so has a very smooth sheen. The folds are large, the sleeve being loose enough to allow ease of movement. Even in this drawing, they look as though they would totally disappear when the arm was straightened.*

HAIR

Here is another material associated with the body – hair. We look at two examples and the technical problems involved when trying to draw them. This particular material comes in thin strands that can either curl, tangle or smoothly lay against each other, and these characteristics allow very different qualities to be shown in a drawing. You will find all of these challenging but fascinating to attempt.

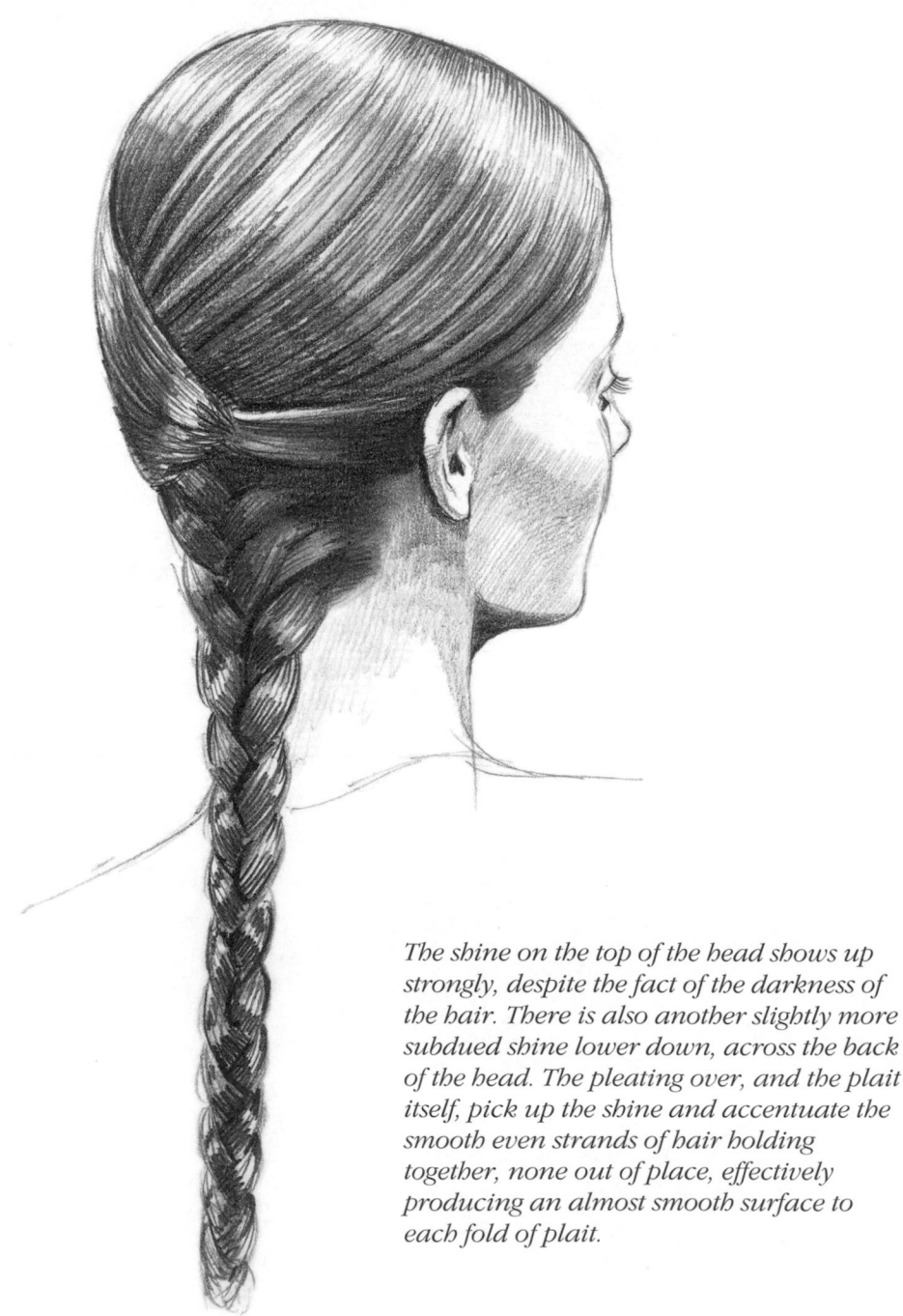

*The shine on the top of the head shows up strongly, despite the fact of the darkness of the hair. There is also another slightly more subdued shine lower down, across the back of the head. The pleating over, and the plait itself, pick up the shine and accentuate the smooth even strands of hair holding together, none out of place, effectively producing an almost smooth surface to each fold of plait.*

A lot of effort has gone into this hairstyle, with every seemingly wayward strand beautifully arranged. Contrived it may be, but it does show to good effect how hair can wave and corkscrew in ringlets. Notice the many highlights on the bends of the curls and the darker richer tones underneath. It's not easy to make this style look natural in a drawing, but this is a good attempt.

## EARTH

When drawing the solid rocks that make up the surface of the world, it can be instructive to think small and build up. Pick up a handful or soil or gravel and take it home with you for close scrutiny, then try to draw it in some detail. You will find that those tiny pieces of irregular material are essentially rocks in miniature. You can get a very clear idea of how to draw the earth in all its guises by recognizing the essential similarities between earth materials and being prepared to take a jump from almost zero to infinity.

*If we attempt to draw a rocky outcrop or the rocks by the sea or along the shore of a river, it is really no different from drawing small pieces of gravel, only with an enormous change of scale. It is as though those pieces of* *gravel have been super-enlarged. You will find a similar random mixture of shapes, though made more attractive to our eyes because of the increase in size.*

*One more step is to visit a mountainous area and look at the earth in its grandest, most monumental form. This example has the added quality of being above the snow-line and showing marvellously simplified icy structures against contrasting dark rocks.*

*Now look at a large cliff-face, with its cleavages and striations of geological layering, some of it, no doubt, partially hidden by plants, but nevertheless showing the structure very clearly.*

## WATER

The character and mood of water changes depending on how it is affected by movement and light. Over the next few pages we look at water in various forms, which present very different problems for artists and very different effects on viewers. To understand how you can capture the effect of each of the forms shown here requires close first-hand study, supported by photographic evidence of what is happening, followed by persistent efforts to draw what you think you know.

*A waterfall is an immensely powerful form of water. Most of us don't see such grand works of nature as this magnificent example. Of course, you would need to study one as large as this from a distance to make some sense of it. This drawing is successful largely because the watery area is not overworked, but has been left almost blank within the enclosing rocks, trees and other vegetation. The dark tones of the vegetation throw forward the negative shapes of the water, making them look foaming and fast moving.*

*Unless you were looking at a photograph, it would be almost impossible to draw with any detail the effect of an enormous wave breaking towards you as you stood on a shore. Leonardo made some very good attempts at describing the movement of waves in drawings, but they were more diagrammatic in form.*

This is water as most of us who live in an urban environment see it, still and reflective. Although the surface of a stretch of water may look smooth, usually there is a breeze or currents causing small shallow ripples. Seen from an oblique angle these minute ripples give a slightly broken effect along the edges of any objects reflected in the water. When you draw such a scene you need to gently blur or break the edges of each large reflected tone to simulate the rippling effect of the water.

In this very detailed drawing of a stretch of water rippling gently, there appear to be three different tones for the smooth elliptical shapes breaking the surface. This is not an easy exercise but it will teach you something about what you actually see when looking at the surface of water.

## WATER: CONTRASTING MOODS

The contrast in moods between the choppy sea depicted in the first drawing and the glassy looking water in the second couldn't be more extreme. Pay particular attention to the absence of any reflecting light in the first example, and the fact that the second drawing comes across as all-reflection.

*In this view of a choppy inky sea, with breaking crests of foam, the skyline is dark and there is no bright reflection from the sky. The shapes of the foaming crests of the wind-blown waves are very important. They must also be placed carefully so that you get an effect of distance, with large shapes in the foreground graduated to smaller and smaller layers as you work your up the page towards the horizon.*

*Observe how foam breaks; take photographs and then invent your own shapes, once you've seen the typical shapes they make. No two crests of foam are alike, so you can't really go wrong. But, if you are depicting a stormy sea, it is important to make the water between the crests dark, otherwise the effect might be of a bright, albeit breezy, day.*

This whole drawing is made up of the sky and its reflection in the river below. The lone boat in the lower foreground helps to give a sense of scale. Although the trees are obviously quite tall in this view, everything is subordinated to the space of the sky, defined by the clouds, and the reflected space in the water. The boat and a few ripples are there to tell the viewer that it is water and not just air. The effect of this vast space and mirror is to generate awe in the viewer.

## Practice with Water

Water is one of the most interesting of subjects for an artist to study and certainly adds a lot to any composition. As you will have noticed, the different shapes it can make and the myriad effects of its reflective and translucent qualities are quite amazing. Over the last few pages we've looked at various ways of portraying water but by no means all of them. The subject is limitless, and you will always manage to find some aspect of it that is a little bit different. Go out and find as many examples as you can to draw.

THE SKY: CONTRASTS

Air is invisible, of course, so cannot really be drawn, but it can be inferred by looking at and drawing clouds and skyscapes. Whether fluffy, ragged, streaky or layered, clouds give a shape to the movements of the elements in the sky and are the only visible evidence of air as a subject to draw.

*Here we see dark, stormy clouds with little bits of light breaking through in areas around the dark grey. The difficulty is with the subtle graduations of tone between the very heavy dark clouds and the parts where the cloud cover is thinner or partly broken and allows a gleam of light into the scene. Look carefully at the edges of the clouds, how sometimes they are very rounded and fluffy and sometimes*

*torn and ragged in shape. If you get the perspective correct, they should be shown as layers across the sky, flatter and thinner further off and as fuller more rolling masses closer to. You can create a very interesting effect of depth and space across the lower surfaces of the cloudscape with bumps and layers of cloud that reduce in depth as they approach the horizon.*

*When the clouds allow more sun to shine through, they look much less heavy and threatening and often assume quite friendly looking shapes. Essentially, though, it is the same vapour as in the stormy sky but with more light,*

*enabling us to see its ephemeral nature.*

*The effect of beams of sunlight striking through clouds has a remarkable effect in a picture, and can give a feeling of life and beauty to even a quite banal landscape.*

*A lot has been achieved here with very simple means. The clouds are not complicated and it is the sun's rays (marked in with an eraser) and the aircraft that do much of the work, giving the illusion of height and also*

*limitless space above our view. The broken light, the light and dark clouds and sunlight glinting against the wings and fuselage of the aircraft give the drawing atmosphere.*

THE SKY: USING SPACE

The spaces between clouds as well as the shapes of clouds themselves can alter the overall sense we get of the subject matter in a drawing. The element of air gives us so many possibilities, we can find many different ways of suggesting space and open views. Compare these examples.

*This open flat landscape with pleasant soft-looking clouds gives some indication of how space in a landscape can be inferred. The fluffy cumulus clouds floating gently across the sky gather together before receding into the vast horizon of the open prairie. The sharp perspective of the long, straight road and the car in the middle distance tell us how to read the space. This is the great outdoors.*

*Another vision of air and space is illustrated here: a sky of ragged grey and white clouds, and the sun catching distant buildings on the horizon of the flat, suburban heathland below. Note particularly the low horizon, clouds with dark, heavy bottoms and lighter areas higher in the sky.*

*Despite the presence of dark, dramatic clouds in this scene at sunset the atmosphere is not overtly gloomy or brooding. The bright sun, half-hidden by the long flat cloud, radiates its light across the edges of the clouds, which tell us that they are lying between us and the sun. The deep space between the dark layers of cloud gives a slightly melancholic edge to the peacefulness.*

163

# *Extremes of Expression*

Artists in all ages have been interested in extremes of expression and experimenting with the handling of grotesque or humorous depictions of faces and bodies. In the medieval period, they were almost exclusively to be found in sculpture within and without chapels and cathedrals. Look at the misericords, or brackets, on the underside of any seat in choir stalls of this period and you will often find grotesque and fantastic carvings. Similarly the stone gargoyles or spouts which carry water clear of the sides of buildings were often sculpted to resemble the heads of beasts or monsters.

When we get to the Renaissance period, celebrated artists such as Leonardo were drawing grotesque faces and heads, and in some instances taking them to fantastic extremes. The development of printing techniques enabled artists with a social or political message to take caricature beyond the realms of pure fun. William Hogarth, who trained as an engraver before he studied painting, campaigned vigorously against a number of social ills through his work. Later social caricaturists, such as Thomas Rowlandson and James Gillray, went even further in their efforts to change opinion. Their lampoons were reproduced extensively and sold in the streets. Both men were very accomplished artists.

In the 19th century, with the quick delivery of newspapers all over the country, caricature took off in a big way. The satirical weekly newspaper *Punch*, which first appeared in 1841, was packed full of unflattering depictions of leading politicians and other visual comments on scandals, political manoeuvrings and social injustice. In our own time the production of cartoons on film has led to the extension of the art to television.

Inexperienced artists try so hard to be technically correct that often they turn out drawings that look wooden and lack expression. Caricature is a great antidote, helping to free us from an over-reliance on accuracy and to find a genuine means of expression in our work.

## GROTESQUES TO FANTASY

Leonardo da Vinci has left us many extraordinary examples of caricature which are undoubtedly not true to life but still recognizable. No one knows why the great man was so fascinated by this type of drawing but perhaps it is not surprising he wanted to see how far he could go with it.

In the second half of the 16th century the Milanese painter Giuseppe Arcimbaldo took caricature in a different direction, producing fantasy portrait heads in which the features were composed of clusters of fruit and vegetables. Some later commentators considered him to be an ancestor of the Surrealists.

Examples from both artists are seen here.

*The features of this man (original by Leonardo) are greatly exaggerated and can in no way be taken as realistic – nose protuding, mouth pushed up at the centre and down at the sides. The great lump of a chin completes the ludicrous effect, which glazed eyes and rather lumpy ears don't diffuse.*

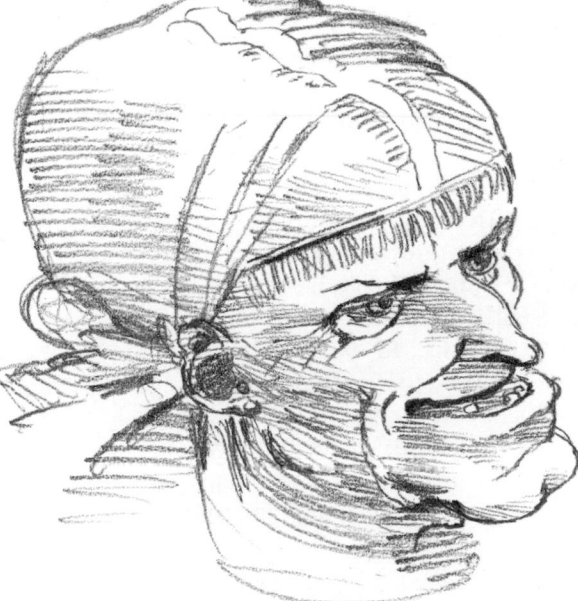

*This second copy of a Leonardo is more realistic apart from the protruding jaw which is taken to unnatural lengths. The first face looked rather stupid; this one looks more intelligent and even kindly.*

*This extraordinary face by Arcimbaldo is reputed to be of the Hapsburg Emperor Rudolph II. Although made up of fruit and vegetables it is easily readable as a particular human face. The drawing is an amusing conceit but one doesn't know whether it was meant to make fun of its subject or was just a curious exercise in ingenuity.*

## CARICATURE AS SATIRE

The work of the great caricaturists was born out of social and political turmoil. Hogarth, Rowlandson and Gillray, three of Britain's greatest exponents of caricature, came to the fore at a time of unprecedented change. All three were valued more for their caricaturing skills than their serious gifts, an oversight that was particularly hard on Hogarth, who was undoubtedly a major artist.

In Spain, Francisco Goya was also railing against the injustices and follies he saw around him. He chronicled the horrors of the occupation by Napoleon's armies in both paint and ink. In his smaller studies we get snapshots of the human condition in extremes of expression that ring true.

*Hogarth's view of the journalist and political agitator John Wilkes.*

*A money-lender as seen through the sharp eye of Rowlandson.*

*In his series of drawings known as 'Los Caprichos', Goya castigated a host of iniquities. Here it is the Catholic Church, represented by two rather disreputable looking monks.*

*At the end of the 18th century Napoleon became a target for English caricaturists, who, like their countrymen, feared what might happen once he had overrun mainland Europe. Initially portrayed by them as a tiny monkey-like character with a big hat, he evolved into a portly villain with a scowl and a big chin.*

*No one was safe from the caricaturists' pen, even the Duke of Wellington, a great hero of the popular press thanks to his victories in the Napoleonic Wars. The treatment of him in these two contemporary examples, after he had swapped his uniform for a frock coat and entered Parliament, is fairly good natured.*

*Political leaders at home came in for just as much attack from the caricaturists as their foreign counterparts.*

*In these two examples (above) it is a weasely-looking William Pitt the Younger by Gillray. Fresh-faced in the first illustration (he was after all only 24 when he became British Prime Minister for the first time), he seems to have matured a little in the second, with clusters of freckles on the nose and cheek and the makings of a moustache and beard.*

*Pitt's great political rival, Charles James Fox, by Rowlandson.*

169

## CARICATURE AS ART

In 19th-century France political comment was often mixed with an illustrative kind of art which combined to make a rather strange brew. The result was certainly caricature but of a type that was more finished and obviously polished. The Salon culture of the French art world would have been horrified by less. The influence of the Impressionists would soon be felt, however, even in caricature.

*Honoré Daumier made many drawings which hovered at the edges of caricature. The first of the two examples of his work shown here is from a French treatise on suffrage. The second, taken from a journal, is of 19th century France's leading literary figure, Victor Hugo, hence the immense brow.*

*Jean-Louis Forain was a regular contributor to journals as a caricaturist and graphic artist. This example of his work shows a departure in style from the satirical drawing usually seen in France up to this time. Very few lines have been used to depict the sleek, moustachioed bourgeois gentleman in evening dress.*

*An early caricature by Impressionist Claude Monet of his art teacher.*

*A contemporary of Forain, Arthur Rackham became popular for his book illustrations, especially of children's stories. Rackham's imaginative approach went down well not only with children, who were sometimes almost frightened by them, but by their parents who particularly admired his finely drawn grotesquerie.*

## STEREOTYPING

All the well-known public figures of the last fifty years or so are mostly remembered by us because we are familiar with caricature images of them we have seen in newspapers and magazines and on films and television.

As well as emphasizing perceived personal weaknesses or humorous aspects of public figures, caricature can also be used creatively to suggest solid virtues, such as those of perhaps the two most famous national stereotypes of all time, Uncle Sam and John Bull.

*A century separates the creation of Uncle Sam (c. 1812) and John Bull (c.1712), the one epitomizing the US government and the other the average British citizen.*

*The great dictators of the 20th century are rather better known by their cartoon image than their real faces.*

*Hitler*

*Mussolini*

*Stalin*

*Mao*

MODERN TRENDS

The modern trend in caricature is to fix on one or two obvious physical characteristics and subordinate everything else to the effect these create. Presenting an absolute minimum likeness can only work, of course, if an audience is very familiar with the figures depicted. In the following examples, aimed at a British market, note that the caricatures of the two lesser known figures, Murdoch and Le Pen, are more carefully drawn than the others.

*British Prime Minister Tony Blair and his wife, Cherie.*

*Former US President Bill Clinton.*

*Australian media tycoon Rupert Murdoch.*

*French right-wing politician Jean-Marie Le Pen (after Gerald Scarfe).*

BUILDING A CARICATURE

The process of turning a perfectly normal looking person into a cartoon figure to accentuate their traits is the same whether the subject is familiar to millions of households or just one. It can be a fun exercise. The subject I have chosen here is my eldest son. His features are perfectly normal, but as I know quite a lot about him I can accentuate certain areas to bring out his personality to the casual observer. Let's begin the process.

*1. It is a good idea first to draw the person you wish to caricature several times, to get to know the shapes of their features and how these relate to each other.*

*2. I have slightly exaggerated his way of staring intensely, his bony physiognomy, strong jaw. I've also tried to suggest his height (6ft 4in).*

*3. Here I begin to produce something like a caricature. Notice how I have made him grin, although he wasn't doing this when I drew him. People who know him are familiar with his broad, up-turning grin, intense stare, large bony forehead, nose, cheekbones and jaw, and these are the characteristics I have tried to bring out.*

1.

2.

3.

## EXPERIMENTING

I could have taken that final illustration further and gone on until all superfluous lines had been deleted. You can do this more effectively if you know your subject well. You need knowledge to be able to build into your caricature attitudes, movements and favourite expressions in order to inject a bit of humour as well as get across a likeness with a minimum of detail.

Here are two examples for you to experiment with and see how far you can take the exaggeration before the subject becomes unrecognizable. Try to capture the obvious features first and then the general effect of the head or face.

Don't try caricaturing your friends, unless you don't mind losing them or they agree. If you can't get the subject you want to pose for you, try to obtain good photographs of them. These won't provide quite such good reference, but as long as you draw on your knowledge of the person as well, they should be adequate.

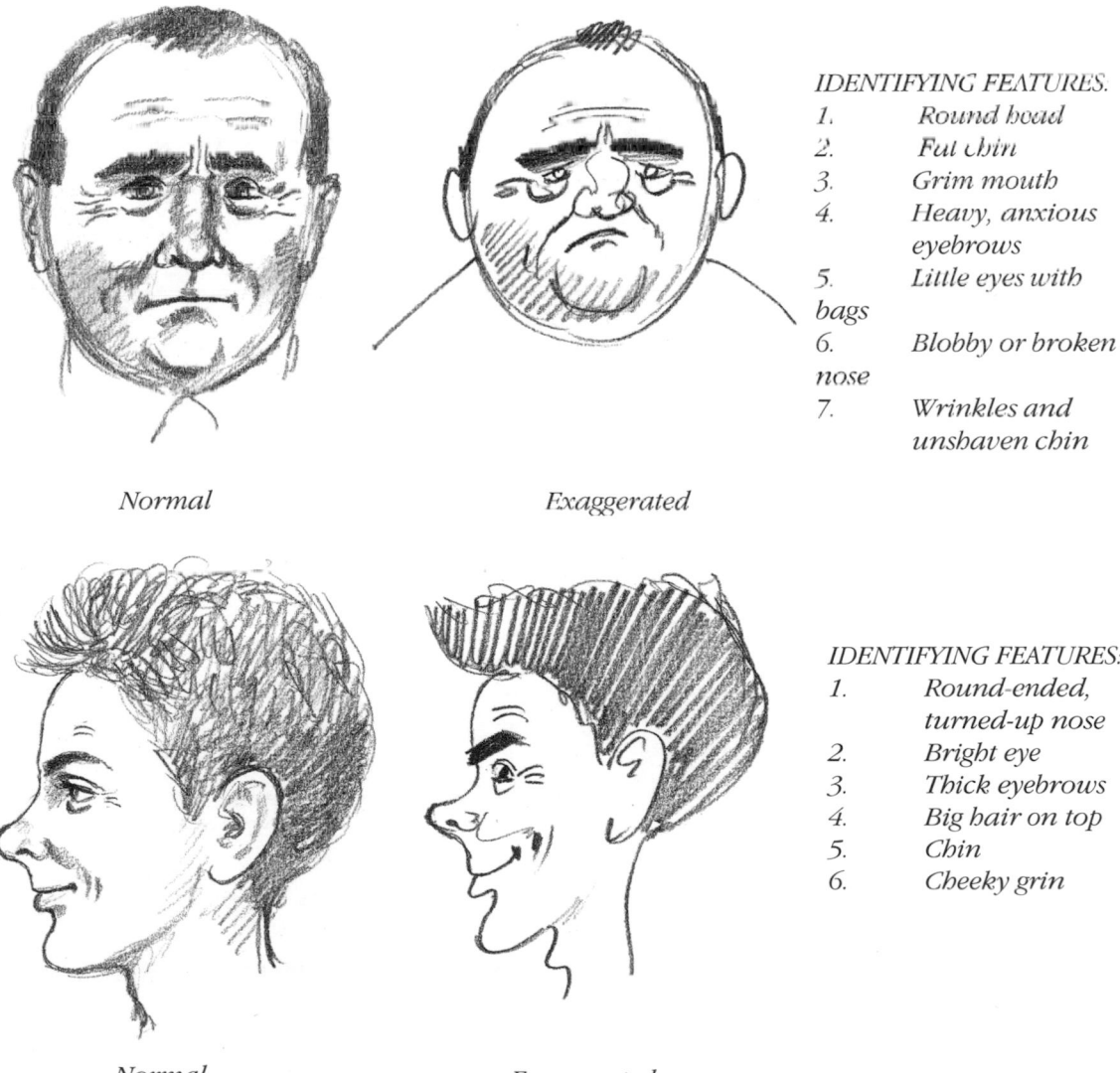

*Normal*          *Exaggerated*

*IDENTIFYING FEATURES.*
1.   *Round head*
2.   *Fat chin*
3.   *Grim mouth*
4.   *Heavy, anxious eyebrows*
5.   *Little eyes with bags*
6.   *Blobby or broken nose*
7.   *Wrinkles and unshaven chin*

*Normal*          *Exaggerated*

*IDENTIFYING FEATURES:*
1.   *Round-ended, turned-up nose*
2.   *Bright eye*
3.   *Thick eyebrows*
4.   *Big hair on top*
5.   *Chin*
6.   *Cheeky grin*

# *Styles and Techniques*

To develop an individual style and method of working, you have to experiment. This is quite easy, given the wide range of materials and implements available. Next, we consider different implements and papers and the effects that can be achieved with them – for example, various types of pencil, as well as pen and ink, line and wash, chalk, pastel and charcoal. We also look at scraper-board, a technique not used very much these days, and some rather interesting if labour-intensive ways of making marks on paper.

In addition we look at some of the approaches to the art of drawing taken by different artists at different times. Some of these may seem alien or too different from the way of working you are used to. Don't be concerned if this is the case. Experimentation gives us the opportunity to discover new techniques and approaches, and to incorporate them in our work. Do try your hand at all of them, and see if you can invent a new style. The main point is to have some fun.

## IMPLEMENTS AND MATERIALS

The implements we draw with are important, as is the material we draw on. A keen artist will draw with anything and make it work to his advantage. Artists have to draw, no matter the situation they are in. If nothing else is available, they'll use sticks in sand, coal on whitewashed walls, coloured mud on flat rocks – anything to be able to draw. If you don't have a wide range of equipment at your disposal, don't let that stop you. Use whatever is to hand. However, if at all possible, supply yourself with the best materials you can afford. If you try as many new tools and materials as you can, you will discover what suits you best. Here are some obvious basic implements.

### Pencil

The simplest and most universal tool of the artist is the humble pencil, which is very versatile. It ranges from very hard to very soft and black (H, HB, B, 2B, etc.) and there are differing thickness. Depending on the type you choose, pencil can be used very precisely and also very loosely.

You should have at least three degrees of blackness, such as an HB (average hardness and blackness), 2B (soft and black) and 4B (very soft and black).

For working on a toned surface, you might like to try white carbon pencil.

### Graphite

Graphite pencils are thicker than ordinary pencils and come in an ordinary wooden casing or as solid graphite sticks with a thin plastic covering. The graphite in the plastic coating is thicker, more solid and lasts longer, but the wooden casing probably feels better. The solid stick is very versatile because of the actual breadth of the drawing edge, enabling you to draw a line a quarter of an inch thick, or even thicker, and also very fine lines. Graphite also comes in various grades, from hard to very soft and black.

### Charcoal

Charcoal pencils in black and grey and white are excellent when you need to produce dimensional images on toned paper and are less messy to use than sticks of charcoal and chalk. However, the sticks are more versatile because you can use the long edge as well as the point. Drawings in this type of media need 'fixing' to stop them getting rubbed off, but if interleaved with pieces of paper they can be kept without smudging. Work you wish to show for any length of time should be fixed with spray-can fixative.

### Chalk

This is a cheaper and longer-lasting alternative to white conté or white pastel.

### Pen

Push-pens or dip-pens come with a fine pointed nib, either stiff or flexible, depending on what you wish to achieve. Modern fine-pointed graphic pens are easier to use and less messy but not so versatile, producing a line of unvarying thickness. Try both types.

The ink for dip-pens is black 'Indian ink' or drawing ink; this can be permanent or water-soluble.

### Brush

A number 0 or number 2 nylon brush is satisfactory for drawing. For applying washes of tone, a number 6 or number 10 brush either in sablette or sable or any other material capable of producing a good point is recommended.

### Paper and board

Any decent smooth cartridge paper is suitable for drawing. A rougher surface gives a more broken line and greater texture. Try out as many different papers as you can. For brushwork, use a modestly priced watercolour paper to start with. Most line illustrators use a smooth board but you may find this too smooth and your pen sliding across it so easily that your line is difficult to control.

Scraper-board has a layer of china-clay which is thick enough to allow dry paint to be scraped off but thin enough not to crack off. It comes in black and white. White scraper-board is the more versatile of the two, and allows the ink to be scraped with a sharp point or edge when it is dry to produce interesting textures or lines. The black version has a thin layer of black ink printed evenly over the whole surface which can be scraped away to produce a reverse drawing resembling a woodcut or engraving. Try them out. Cut your first piece of board into smaller pieces so that you can experiment with a range of different approaches. (The more unusual techniques involving scraper-board are dealt with later in this section.)

The tools you need to work effectively with scraper-board can be obtained at any good art or craft shop.

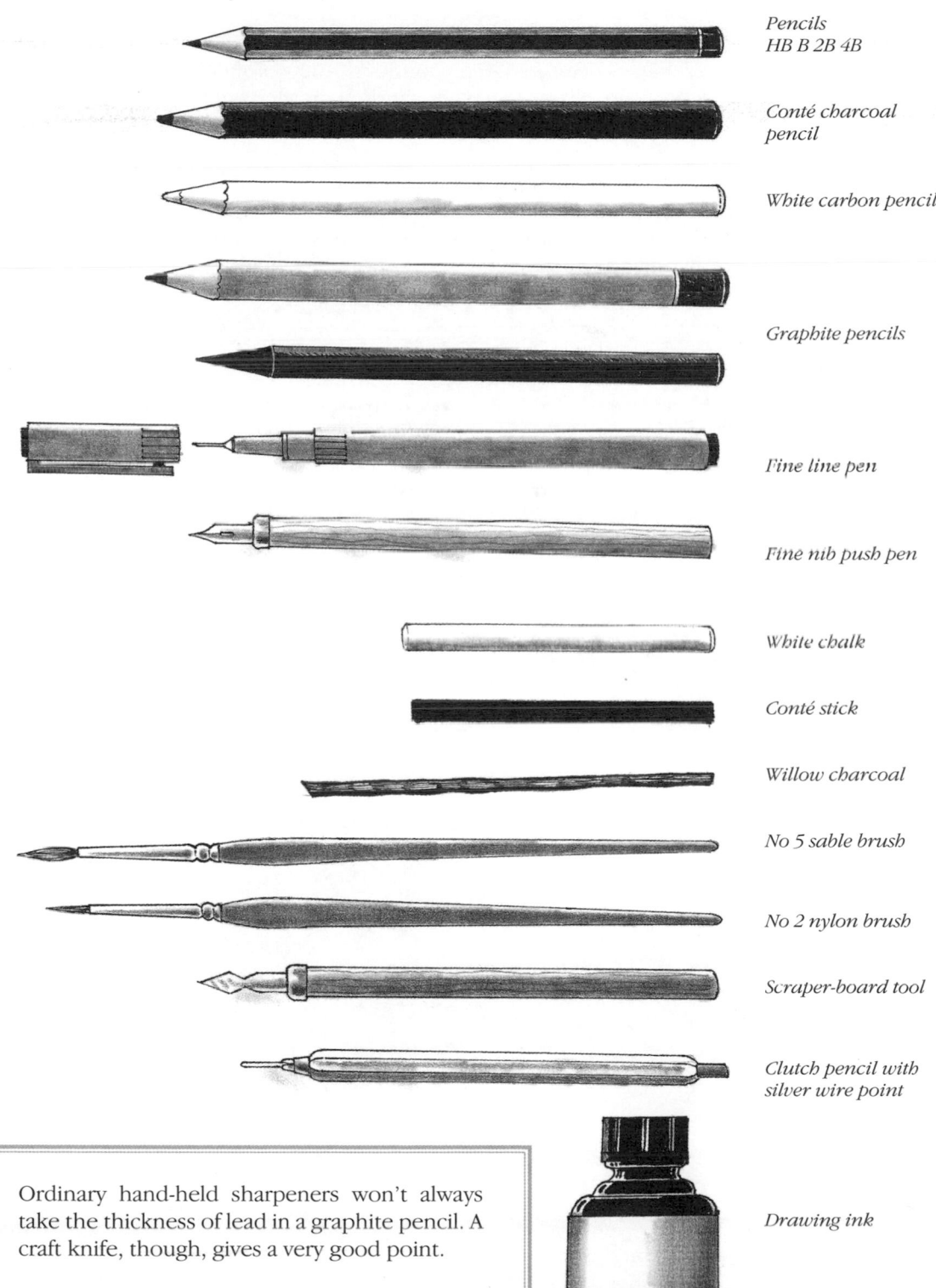

Pencils
HB B 2B 4B

Conté charcoal pencil

White carbon pencil

Graphite pencils

Fine line pen

Fine nib push pen

White chalk

Conté stick

Willow charcoal

No 5 sable brush

No 2 nylon brush

Scraper-board tool

Clutch pencil with silver wire point

Drawing ink

Ordinary hand-held sharpeners won't always take the thickness of lead in a graphite pencil. A craft knife, though, gives a very good point.

## PENCIL DRAWING

Pencil can be used in many ways. When it was invented – sometime in the 17th century – it revolutionized artists' techniques because of the enormous variety of skilful effects that could be produced with it, and soon came to replace well established drawing implements such as silverpoint.

The production of pencils in different grades of hardness and blackness greatly enhanced the medium's versatility. Now it became easy to draw in a variety of ways: delicately or vigorously, precisely or vaguely, with linear effect or with strong or soft tonal effects.

Here we have several types of pencil drawing, from the carefully precise to the impulsively messy, from powerful, vigorous mark making to soft, sensitive shades of tone.

*Michelangelo is a good starting point for ways of using pencil. His work was extremely skilful and, as you can see from this drawing, his anatomical knowledge was second to none. The careful shading of each of the muscle groups in the body gives an almost sculptural effect, which is not so surprising when you consider that sculpture was his first love. To draw like this takes time and patience and careful analysis of the figure you are drawing.*

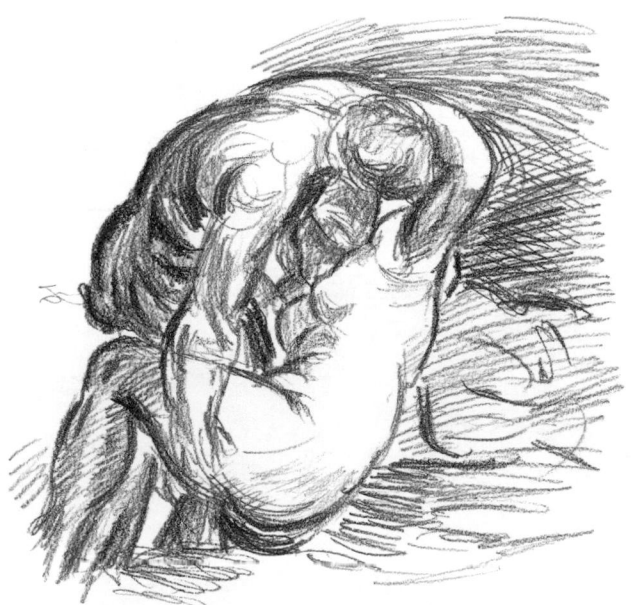

*Titian's drawing, however, is quite different. This artist's knowledge of colour was so good that even his drawings look as though they were painted. He is obviously feeling for texture and depth and movement in the space and is not worried about defining anything too tightly. The lines merge and cluster together to make a very powerful tactile group.*

*Now look at this vigorous drawing by Delacroix, the great French Romantic artist. The powerful flowing lines show the activity and forcefulness of the figure. Where shading has been applied it is very strongly blocked in areas of dark shadows.*

*Handling pencil in this way requires confidence. When you are learning it is useful sometimes just to let go and have a shot at producing a strong image. You have nothing to lose – you can always have another go if your drawing goes wrong.*

PRECISION

In these examples the pencil is used almost scientifically with the line taking pre-eminence. Sometimes it is used to produce an exact effect of form, sometimes to show the flow and simplicity of a movement.

*This meticulous pencil drawing, by the German Julius Schnorr von Carolsfeld, is one of the most perfect drawings in this style I've ever seen. The result is quite stupendous, even though this is just a copy and probably doesn't have the precision of the original. Every line is visible. The tonal shading which follows the contours of the limbs is exquisitely observed. This is not at all easy to do and getting the repeated marks to line up correctly requires great discipline. It is worth practising this kind of drawing because it will increase your skill at manipulating the pencil and test your ability to concentrate.*

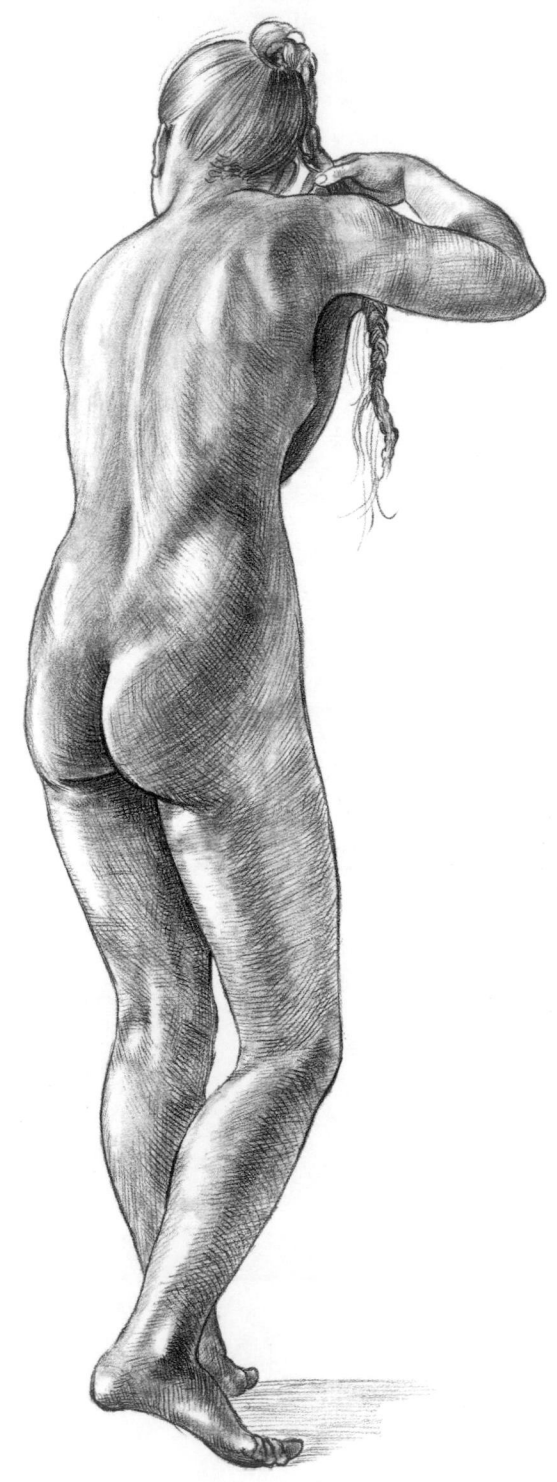

## THE SIMPLE OUTLINE

In different ways all the drawings on this page use a simple outline. Such simplicity serves to 'fix' the main shape of the drawing, ensuring the effect of the additional detailed shading.

A much more economical method of drawing has been used for two of the drawings here, but note that this has not been at the expense of the information offered about the subjects depicted.

*Both Matisse (copy of a self-portrait, above) and Victor Ambrus (left) appear to have used several different grades of pencil for these drawings; some lines are very soft and black, others much less so. Knowing how far to go is an art in itself. Ambrus has achieved balance by outlining the main shape of the dog with a soft grey line and then adding details of the curly hair and dark ears, head and nose with darker, crisper lines.*

*Only one of the objects in this still-life group has been drawn in great detail. The rest of them are in a bare outline drawing. This is an unfinished drawing but does show how to achieve a convincing solidity by first drawing clearly defined outline shapes before leaping in at the deep end with detailed drawing.*

183

## PEN AND INK

Pen and ink is special in that once you've put the line down it is indelible and can't be erased. This really puts the artist on his mettle because, unless he can use a mass of fine lines to build a form, he has to get the lines 'right' first time. Either way can work.

Once you get a taste for using ink, it can be very addictive. The tension of knowing that you can't change what you have done in a drawing is challenging. When it goes well, it can be exhilarating.

*Leonardo probably did the original of this as a study for a painting. Drawn fairly sketchily in simple line, it shows a young woman with a unicorn, a popular courtly device of the time. The lines are sensitive and loose but the whole hangs together very beautifully with the minimal of drawing. The curving lines suggest the shape and materiality of the parts of the picture, the dress softly creased and folded, the face and hand rounded but firm, the tree slightly feathery looking. The use of minimal shading in a few oblique lines to suggest areas of tone is just enough to convey the artist's intentions.*

*This copy of a Raphael is more heavily shaded in a variety of cross-hatching, giving much more solidity to the figures despite the slightly fairy-tale imagery. The movement is conveyed nicely, and the body of the rider looks very substantial as he cuts down the dragon. The odd bits of background lightly put in give even more strength to the figures of knight, horse and dragon.*

*This next copy, of a Michelangelo drawing, is much more heavily worked over, with hefty cross-hatching capturing the muscularity of the figure. The texture is rich and gives a very good impression of a powerful, youthful figure. The left arm and the legs are unfinished but even so the drawing has great impact.*

*Rarely have I seen such brilliant line drawing in ink of the human figure as those of the painter Guercino. In this example the line is extremely economical and looks as though it has been drawn from life very rapidly. The flowing lines seem to produce the effect of a solid body in space, but they also have a marvellous lyrical quality of their own. Try drawing like this, quickly without worrying about anything except the most significant details, but getting the feel of the subject in as few lines as possible. You will have to draw something directly from life in order to get an understanding of how this technique works.*

*In his masterly original of this drawing in line (and ink), Tintoretto was careful to get the whole outline of the figure. The curvy interior lines suggest the muscularity of the form. There is not too much detail but just enough to convince the eye of the powerful body; every muscle here appears to ripple under the skin. The barest of shading suggests the form.*

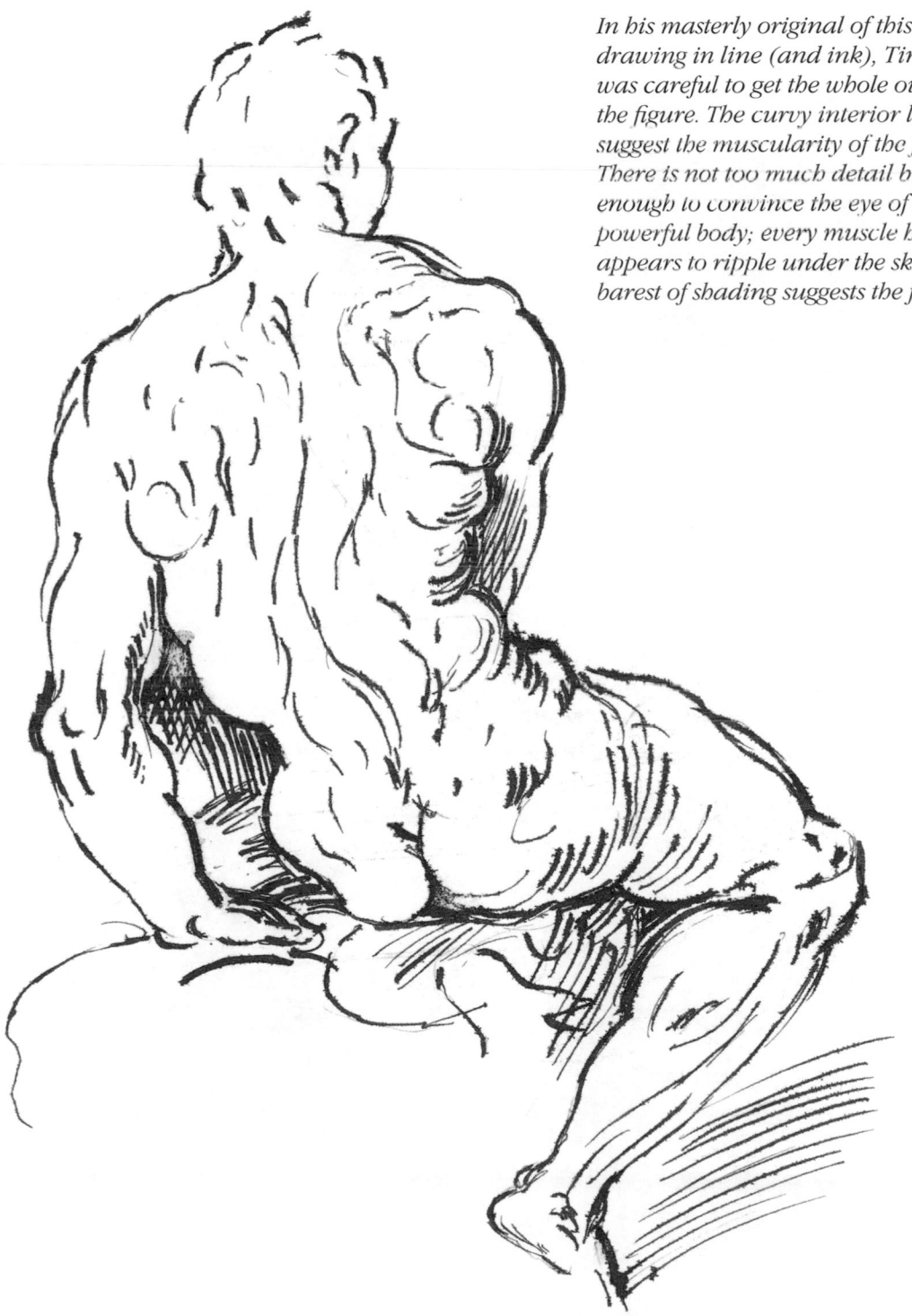

PRACTISING WITH PEN AND INK

The drawings on this page show what can be achieved with pens of different nib thickness. The series of heads shows the effect that can be achieved with a fine nib. The mass of lines going in many directions give a definite impression of solidity as well as depth of shadows and light.

The figure of the boy is drawn with a felt tip pen. This is not the most sensitive of tools but, as long as you don't expect too much from it as a medium, it does enable you to draw quickly and reasonably effectively.

*The heads of the boy and girl show the importance of background when attempting to describe the way form builds around a rounded object. Some areas have been left clear to suggest light catching the hair, ears, nose, etc., and these stand out against the cross-hatched background tone.*

*To practise this technique, try it on small*

*areas initially. The aim is to learn to control your pen strokes so that you can lay them closely together without them becoming jumbled. You will need several attempts to make the lines only go over the areas you want them to. Try drawing in the main shape with pencil first and then ink over it so that you have pencil lines to draw up to.*

*The thickness of felt tip pen limits your options so far as size is concerned. As you can see here, you have to draw bigger or reduce areas of tone to their simplest.*

*This copy of a head by Matisse is remarkably freely drawn and yet the multiple lines build up into a dense texture of materiality that looks very convincing.*

PRACTICE

This set of women's heads gives you a chance to try different methods of using line in pen and ink. All methods are possible and can be used to good effect. Think about your lines first, before laying them down in pencil. Look at my notes first before you begin to attempt to draw them.

*1. With its fairly solid black lines and simplification of form, this drawing resembles a woodcut. Just a fine line suggests roundness of form.*

*2. Curved, loosely drawn lines without any tone are used here, to give maximum effect for minimal drawing. A flexible pen nib is necessary to get slightly broader and also finer lines alternating. Note the simplicity of the facial features.*

*3. Even the outlined frame adds to the decorative effect of this drawing. The intensely layered curls on the head make a pattern rather than a realistic effect, as does the pleated collar around the shoulders. The face is sharply drawn but without much attempt at form. The large areas of white shoulders and neck and blank background help to emphasize the decorative quality of the drawn parts.*

*4. The face here is again economically drawn: just two black eyes, and mere touches for the nose and mouth. The hair outlining the face and neck, though, has been rendered as a jungle-like mass of black lines overlaying each other. Slightly more formal lines in the background allow the hair to fade into the paper and emphasize the paleness of the face.*

*5. This drawing is also mostly concerned with the decorative effect of the precisely waved lines of hair, crossed by the carefully delineated pearl head-dress, all flatly drawn with the clear sharp lines reminiscent of an engraving. The dots that make up the background are carefully spaced to ensure that one area is not darker than another. Against this darker background the sharply drawn profile and eyes appear almost in silhouette. No attempt has been made to produce depth of form.*

1.            2.

3.            4.

5.            6.

*The joy of drawing like this comes in making patterns of the lines and dots, and because this can't be hurried, it is very therapeutic.*

*6. This head is similar to the third one in that the hair and collar of the dress are carefully built up patterns to suggest an ornate hair-do and an elegant negligée. The difference between the two drawings is mainly in the background. In this drawing there is no obvious perspective. The squares within squares suggest there must be depth behind the head.*

## LINE AND WASH

Now we move on to look at the effects that can be obtained by using a mixture of pen and brush with ink. The lines are usually drawn first to get the main shape of the subject in, then a brush loaded with ink and water is used to float across certain areas to suggest shadow and fill in most of the background to give depth.

A good-quality solid paper is necessary for this type of drawing; try either a watercolour paper or a very heavy cartridge paper. The wateriness of the tones needs to be calculated to the area to be covered. In other words, don't make it so wet that the paper takes ages to dry.

*This copy of a Rembrandt is very dramatic in its use of light and shade.*

When using line and wash in landscape drawing, the handling of the wash is particularly important, because its different tonal values suggest space receding into the picture plane. Here we look at three drawings by Claude Lorrain.

*This sensitive pen line drawing of part of an old Roman ruin has a light wash of watery ink to suggest the sun shining from behind the stones. The wash has been kept uniform. The outlines of the stone blocks give you lines to draw up to.*

*These two deer are fairly loosely drawn in black chalk. A variety of tones of wash has been freely splashed across the animals to suggest form and substance.*

*This purely wash drawing of the Tiber at Rome has a few small speckles of pen work near the horizon. The tones vary from very pale in the distance to gradually darkening as we approach the foreground, which is darkest of all. The dark tone is relieved by the white patch of the river, reflecting the light sky with a suggestion of reflection in a softer tone. A brilliant sketch.*

*Master landscape painter Claude Lorrain gives a real lesson in how to draw nature in this study of a tree. Executed with much feeling but great economy, the whole drawing is done in brushwork.*

*To try this you need three different sizes of brush (try Nos. 0 or 1, and 6 and 10), all of them with good points. Put in the lightest areas first (very dilute ink), then the medium tones (more ink less water), and then the very darkest (not quite solid ink).*

*Notice how Lorrain doesn't try to draw each leaf, but makes interesting blobs and scrawls with the tip of the brush to suggest a leafy canopy. With the heavier tones he allows the brush to cover larger areas and in less detail.*

*He blocks in some very dark areas with the darkest tone and returns to the point of the brush to describe branches and some clumps of leaf.*

## CHALK ON TONED PAPER

The use of toned paper can bring an extra dimension to a drawing and is very effective at producing a three-dimensional effect of light and shade. Whether you are drawing with chalk, pastel or charcoal it is very important to remember that the paper itself is in effect an implement, providing all the tones between the extremes of light and dark. You must resist the temptation to completely obliterate the toned paper in your enthusiasm to cover the whole area with chalk marks. Study the following examples.

*This head is drawn simply in a medium toned chalk on a light paper. Here the challenge is not to overdo the details. The tones of the chalk marks are used to suggest areas of the head, and definite marks have been kept to a minimum.*

*The mid-tone of the paper has been used to great effect in this copy of Carpaccio's drawing of a Venetian merchant. Small marks of white chalk pick out the parts of garments, face and hair that catch the light. No attempt has been made to join up these marks. The dark chalk has been used similarly: as little as the artist felt he could get away with. The medium tone of the paper becomes the solid body that registers the bright lights falling on the figure. The darkest tones give the weight and the outline of the head, ensuring that it doesn't just disappear in a host of small marks.*

As we have seen in the examples on the previous spread, the use of toned paper reduces the area that has to be covered with chalk and heightens the effect of the chalk marks, especially if these have been made in white. The three illustrations shown here exemplify the range of effects that can be achieved with toned paper.

In Watteau's picture of a goddess (left) the dark outline emphasizes the figure and limbs, as do the patches of bright light on the upper facing surfaces.

The two drawings shown on this page were executed in white and dark chalk on medium toned paper. The approach taken with the first is about as economical as you can get. The form of the surface of the girl's face and figure is barely hinted at down one side, with just the slightest amount of chalk. A similar effect is achieved on the other side, this time in dark chalk. The uncovered paper does much of the rest of the work.

The second drawing takes the use of dark and light much further, creating a substantial picture. In places the white chalk is piled on and elsewhere is barely visible. The dark chalk is handled in the same way. More of the toned paper is covered, but its contribution to the overall effect of the drawing is not diminished for that.

195

The French neo-classicist master Pierre Paul Prud'hon was a brilliant worker in the medium of chalk on toned paper. In these copies of examples of his work, he shows us two very effective ways of using light and dark tones to suggest form.

*In this drawing of Psyche, marks have been made with dark and light chalk, creating a texture of light which is rather Impressionistic in flavour. The lines, which are mostly quite short, go in all directions.*

*The impression created is of a figure in the dark. This is helped by the medium tone of the paper, which almost disappears under the pattern of the mark making.*

The chalk marks in this close up are very disciplined. A whole range of tones is built from the carefully controlled marks, which show up the form as though lit from above. Here, too, the middle tone is mostly covered over with gradations of black and white.

## SCRAPER-BOARD TECHNIQUE

Scraper-board drawing evolved during the early days of photographic reproduction in newspapers as a response to the needs of advertisers, who wanted to show their wares and products to best advantage but were limited by the poor quality of the printing processes then available. The technique gave very clear, precise definition to photographs, and so became the means of rendering advertisements for newsprint. Over time, of course, the screen printing of photographs improved so much that it has become just another art technique. Scraper-board does have some qualities of its own, however. It is similar in some respects to wood engraving, wood cuts or engraving on metal, although because of the ease of drawing it is more flexible and less time-consuming.

*In this drawing the boatman appearing across a misty lake or river was first sketched in pencil, then blocked out in large areas of ink. The figure of the man, the oars and the atmospherics were done in diluted ink to make a paler tone. The boat was drawn in black ink. Using a scraper-board tool, lines were carefully scratched across the tonal areas, reducing their tonal qualities further. Some areas have few or no scratched lines, giving a darker tone and an effect of dimensionality.*

You can see in the two examples below how scraper-board technique lends itself to a certain formalized way of drawing. The scratch marks can be made to look very decorative. The Christmas card drawing and lettering is in a very similar technique and has been produced using both scraper-board and pen and ink. The main effort is taken up with making the shapes decorative and giving the main lines a textural quality; this is achieved by using either a brush or the side of a flexible nib.

*The top illustration was first drawn in black ink. The areas of ink were then gone over using the scraper tool to reduce the heaviness of the shaded areas and clean up the edges to achieve the shape required.*

*The Christmas card drawing is mainly thick line in brush with a few lines in pen added afterwards to provide details. The scraper tool was then used to sharpen up the outline and the spaces between the areas of black.*

### Using the Technique
Scraper-board technique is similar to cross-hatching with a pencil, although with the former you are drawing white on black, of course. The surface of the board can be scratched over several times, as long as the marks have not cut too deeply into the china clay. Any areas that need to be strengthened or corrected can be filled in with ink. Correcting lines using this technique is very easy: you just scratch out the wrong bits and redraw them.

**MERRY CHRISTMAS**

## BLOTTING TECHNIQUE

First used by illustrators in the 1950s, this technique was made famous by Andy Warhol in his fashion illustrations. The idea is to take a piece of ordinary cartridge paper, or blotting paper – either will achieve the same effect – and fold it in half. After drawing each line in ink you blot it into the opposite side of the page (see illustrations below). You have to take a painstaking approach, blotting as you build up the drawing, because otherwise the ink dries too quickly. A dip-pen is the best tool, because modern graphic pens don't produce ink that is wet enough.

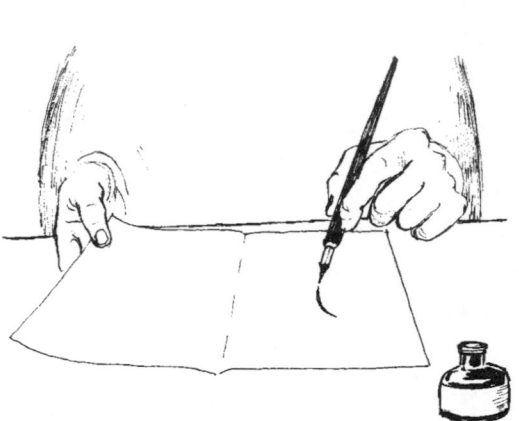

*1. Draw a line.*

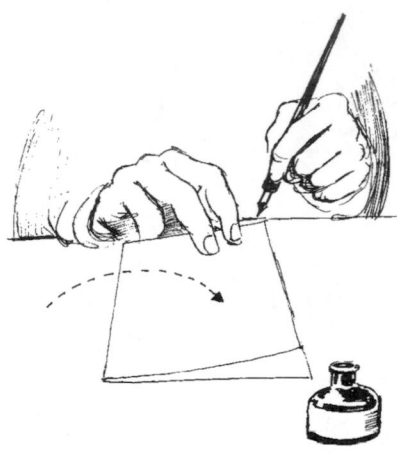

*2. Fold paper over to blot the ink on the opposite side.*

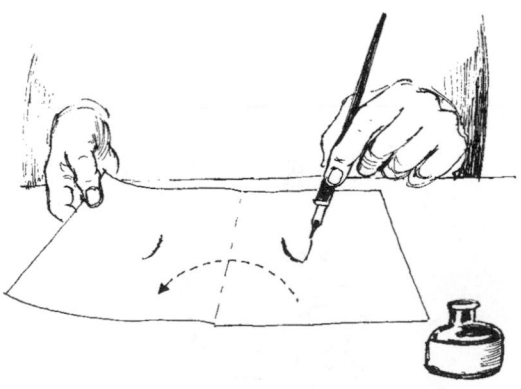

*3. Draw your next line and repeat the procedure, folding your paper over to blot the ink on the opposite side.*

### Producing an Effect

Generally it is best to draw only a few lines at a time and then blot them immediately. If you draw too many lines before blotting them the ink will dry and the point of using this technique will be lost. However, you have to experiment with timings and weight of line, because sometimes a pleasing effect can result from an unpromising start. In the last drawing on the opposite page, for example, the multiple lines on the face dried so quickly that the blotted version looked much less tonal than the original. I liked the effect, though, and didn't try to change it. How you want your finished drawing to look is up to you.

*Original drawing*

*Blotted version*

*Original drawing*

*Blotted version*

*Original drawing*

*Blotted version*

CARD-EDGE TECHNIQUE

This technique was invented at about the same time as the blotting technique we've just looked at. The first step is to cut out small pieces of card. The edges of these are then dipped into soft wet paint (gouache designer colours are best) and used to draw lines onto a blank sheet. The effect is initially very strong, becoming fainter and fainter as the paint gets used up or dries.

Like blotting technique, it is a slow process and you cannot produce much in the way of curved shapes, but the end result can be very powerful. In terms of how it is used and the effects that can be achieved with it, it is rather similar to painting with a palette knife.

*In this example the gouache on the edge of the card was almost dry when it was used to paint the clouds and front surface of the house. For the roof and dark trees in the background the card was very wet and full of paint.*

### New Horizons

The use of gouache paint to make a drawing is not an attempt to introduce you to painting, although I would be surprised if you were not interested in doing that as well as drawing. Merely it illustrates a point I have already made, that you should feel free to draw with whatever takes your fancy. An artist cannot be limited by notions of what is proper for him or her to use as a medium. Ultimately the choice is yours. When exercising this choice, try to be inquisitive and adventurous. Any use of a new medium will help your drawing, because it makes you re-assess how you actually produce the finished article. Never use only one medium, even if you prefer it over all others. Your life as an artist is an ever-expanding view of the universe, and if you stick with only one or a select few you will find your artistic horizons narrowing and your work becoming predictable and repetitive. Don't be afraid of what you don't know. Once you start working with a new medium you will be surprised how quickly you appreciate its qualities and find ways of adapting them to your purpose.

## SILVER-POINT TECHNIQUE

The last and probably for most people the least likely technique to be attempted is silver-point drawing, the classic method used in the times before pencils were invented. Many drawings by Renaissance artists were made in this way. Anybody interested in producing very precise drawings should try this most refined and effective technique.

First you have to buy a piece of silver wire (try a jeweller or someone who deals in precious metals) about a millimetre thick and about three inches long. This is either held in a wooden handle taped to it or – the better option – within a clutch-action propelling pencil that takes wire of this thickness. Then you cover a piece of cartridge paper (use fairly thick paper because it is less likely to buckle) with a wash of permanent white gouache designer paint; the coat must cover the whole surface and mustn't be either too thick or too watery. When the white paint has dried, you draw onto it with the silver wire; ensure that the end of the wire is smooth and rounded to prevent it tearing the paper. Don't press too hard. The silver deposits a very fine silky line, like a pencil, but lasts much longer. Silver point is a very nice material to draw with. I thoroughly recommend that you make the effort to try it. It's very rewarding as well as instructive.

Joanna B.        Barrington Barber

*To use silver point you need to prepare a background to draw onto. I drew this example onto white paint with a bit of reddish-brown mixed in.*

# *Art Appreciation*

There are other ways to improve your drawing abilities apart from practising. One approach that is rather pleasurable as well as instructive is to go to as many exhibitions of drawings and paintings as you can. Even if it means travelling a fair distance, this is very worthwhile. Not only does it widen your education in art by making you familiar with first-rate artists, but you will also begin to refine your own perceptions, finding higher levels to aim for in your own work. I myself visit Italy every year to show people around the great works of art in places such as Florence, Venice, Rome and Naples and always find the stimulation very useful for my own work. But don't only look at work by historic masters. Also make the attempt to visit galleries that show the work of current artists, because it is always very instructive to see what your contemporaries are doing and often fuels your own ideas for new directions in your own work.

By your practice of drawing and this appreciation of the art around you, you will experience a measurable upgrading of your own perceptions and understanding of the possibilities at your disposal. This can be great fun as well as uplifting. In any country there are large urban centres where the nation's art is gathered for the public to view, but also you find small colonies of artists tucked away in all sorts of small towns and villages, and their work is worth looking out. Finally, of course, prints and books are very good sources of art appreciation. If you can't afford to buy them, there are vast libraries full of them where they can be studied for free.

## WHAT DO YOU SEE?

When viewing the work of other artists, try to analyze what makes it so attractive to you. Ask yourself questions. Don't be ashamed or coy if some of your answers suggest that your response is of a religious or spiritual nature. These are often the truest reasons why we like a work and should be acknowledged. Whatever the chord that is struck when you perceive a work, recognition of it will lead you towards understanding your own work and the direction it might take.

There is room for all sorts of artists in this world and one of the great freedoms of modern art practitioners is that they have completely redefined the reasons behind art. They may not be right, or you may not agree with them, but the freedom to find your own way towards art appreciation is of tremendous value.

*When looking at art, question your own perceptions. Is it the subject matter? Is it the technical brilliance of the artist? Is it the colour? Is it the form? Is it the medium used to produce the work? Is it the subtler ideas behind the form? Is it because it reminds you of someone? All these questions are valid. Many more will undoubtedly occur to you. The main point is to discover your true response to a picture that attracts you. Sometimes the answer is very simple, but sometimes the appreciation lies much deeper within yourself and will take some unearthing. Persevere and your reward will be considerable.*

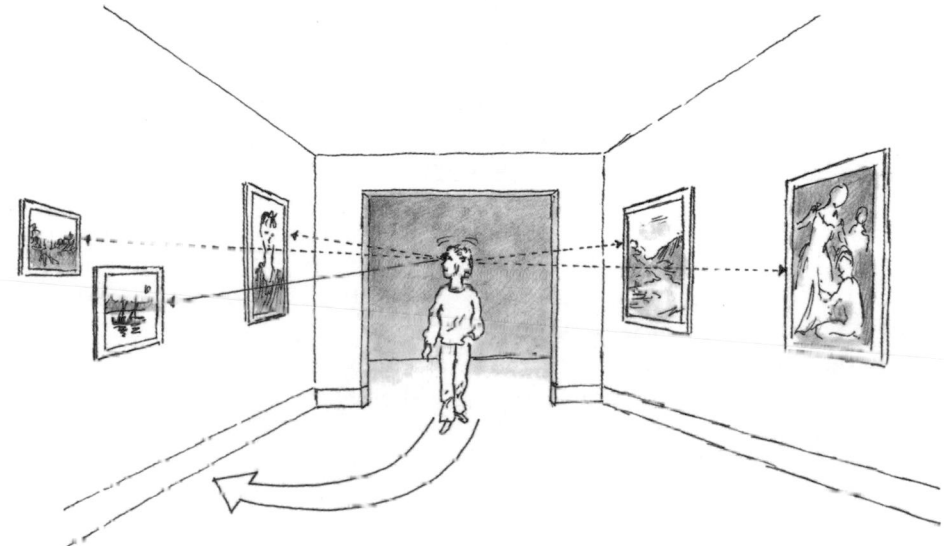

*Don't try to look at everything. Wait until something really arouses your attention, and then give it your full attention. Spend at least three minutes just looking in detail at everything in the picture, without commenting. Then your questioning of what is in front of you will be very useful in clarifying your understanding.*

*When looking at reproductions of famous works, notice where these works are held. If it is somewhere near enough for you to visit, do so. No matter how good the quality of a reproduction, the original possesses an extra dimension, and this will leap out at you as soon as you set eyes on the actual work. It is rather like discovering an old friend and seeing them totally afresh. First-hand knowledge of an original also helps to inform you of what is missing when you try to draw from a print of it. Without that knowledge you could not begin to make up for the lack.*

ENGAGING WITH LIFE

We have now come full circle. Good art contains an essential ingredient that has to be experienced directly from the work. For this ingredient to be present the artist himself almost certainly must have direct experience of what he is communicating. Drawing from life is therefore of paramount importance. When faced with real people, animals, objects, landscapes, townscapes, whatever, the artist has to assess and then render shape, proportion, tonal variation, perspective and anatomy without losing the verisimilitude of the experience. Obviously, there is some simplification and selection of what is exactly seen. Even so, this is a pretty tall order, and it is because talented artists try to do this all the time that their work is so good. Never forget: drawing from life will increase your ability to draw well. Drawing from drawings or photographs, or making up out of your head are valid, but if you don't return often to the natural visible world your drawings will never be convincing. Quite apart from the benefits it confers, it is the most interesting way to draw, and interest is what keeps art fresh and alive, both for the artist and the viewer.